# RIZZOLI & ISLES:
# LAST TO DIE

A NOVEL

# TESS GERRITSEN

BALLANTINE BOOKS • NEW YORK

2013 Ballantine Books Premium Mass Market Edition

Copyright © 2012 by Tess Gerritsen
Short story "John Doe" copyright © 2012 by Tess Gerritsen
Excerpt from *Girl Missing* by Tess Gerritsen copyright © 1994 by Tess Gerritsen

Published in the United States by Ballantine Books, an imprint of The Random House Publishing Group, a division of Random House, Inc., New York.

BALLANTINE and colophon are registered trademarks of Random House, Inc.

Originally published in hardcover in the United States by Ballantine Books, an imprint of The Random House Publishing Group, a division of Random House, Inc., in 2012.

This book contains an excerpt from the forthcoming book *Girl Missing* by Tess Gerritsen (originally published in the United States as *Peggy Sue Got Murdered* and in the United Kingdom as *Girl Missing*). This excerpt has been set for this edition only and may not reflect the final content of the forthcoming edition.

ISBN 978-0-345-51552-0
eBook ISBN 978-0-345-53595-5

Cover design: Jae Song
Cover image: © Wessel/Wessells/Arcangel Images

Printed in the United States of America

www.ballantinebooks.com

9 8 7 6 5 4 3 2 1

Ballantine mass market edition: July 2013

# PRAISE FOR TESS GERRITSEN
# AND HER RIZZOLI & ISLES NOVELS

"Gerritsen has a knack for creating great characters and mysterious plots that seem straightforward but also dazzle with complexity and twists."
—*The Washington Post*

"Rizzoli is one of the best-written detectives, male or female, around today."
—Fresh Fiction

"[Gerritsen's] books should be mandatory reading for all mystery lovers."
—*Miami Examiner*

"One of the most versatile voices in thriller fiction today."
—*Providence Journal*

"Gerritsen is at her absolute best here. . . . *Last to Die* proves one thing above all else: that Tess Gerritsen is a damn fine storyteller."
—*Hartford Books Examiner*

"Gerritsen delivers yet another of her byzantine and mind-blowing thrillers!"
—*RT Book Reviews* on *Last to Die*

"Pulse-pounding."
—*Publishers Weekly* on *Last to Die*

"Suspenseful and nail-biting . . . There's a reason Jane Rizzoli and Maura Isles are such a hit with readers."
—*Bangor Daily News* on *Last to Die*

"Gerritsen never repeats herself and is not afraid to take chances with new plot directions and twists. . . . This is a key book in a series that keeps getting better and better."
—Bookreporter on *Last to Die*

"Suspense doesn't get smarter than this. Not just recommended but mandatory."
—LEE CHILD on *The Silent Girl*

## BY TESS GERRITSEN

*Harvest*
*Life Support*
*Bloodstream*
*Gravity*
*The Surgeon*
*The Apprentice*
*The Sinner*
*Body Double*
*Vanish*
*The Mephisto Club*
*The Bone Garden*
*The Keepsake*
*The Silent Girl*
*Rizzoli & Isles: Last to Die*

# RIZZOLI & ISLES:
# LAST TO DIE

*We called him Icarus.*

*It was not his real name, of course. My child-hood on the farm taught me that you must never give a name to an animal marked for slaughter. Instead you referred to it as Pig Number One or Pig Number Two, and you always avoided looking it in the eye, to shield yourself from any glimpse of self-awareness or personality or affection. When a beast trusts you, it takes far more resolve to slit its throat.*

*We had no such issue with Icarus, who neither trusted us nor had any inkling of who we were. But we knew a great deal about him. We knew that he lived behind high walls in a hilltop villa on the outskirts of Rome. That he and his wife, Lucia, had two sons, ages eight and ten. That despite his immense wealth, he had simple tastes in food, and a favorite local restaurant, La Nonna, at which he dined almost every Thursday.*

*And that he was a monster. Which was the reason we came to be in Italy that summer.*

*The hunting of monsters is not for the faint of heart. Nor is it for those who feel bound by such trivial doctrines as law or national borders. Monsters, after all, do not play by the rules, so neither can we. Not if we hope to defeat them.*

*But when you abandon civilized standards of conduct, you run the risk of becoming a monster yourself. And that is what happened that summer in Rome. I did not recognize it at the time; none of us did.*

*Until it was too late.*

# ONE

**O**N THE NIGHT THAT THIRTEEN-YEAR-OLD Claire Ward should have died, she stood on the window ledge of her third-floor Ithaca bedroom, trying to decide whether to jump. Twenty feet below were scraggly forsythia bushes, long past their spring bloom. They would cushion her fall, but most likely there'd be broken bones involved. She glanced across at the maple tree, eyeing the sturdy branch that arched only a few feet away. She'd never attempted this leap before, because she'd never been forced to. Until tonight she'd managed to sneak out the front door without being noticed. But those nights of easy escapes were over, because Boring Bob was on to her. *From now on young lady, you are staying home! No more running around town after dark like a wildcat.*

If I break my neck on this jump, she thought, it's all Bob's fault.

Yes, that maple branch was definitely within reach. She had places to go, people to see, and she couldn't hang around here forever, weighing her chances.

She crouched, tensing for the leap, but suddenly froze as an approaching car's headlights angled around the corner. The SUV glided like a black shark beneath her window and continued slowly up the quiet street, as if searching for a particular house. Not ours, she thought; no one interesting ever turned up at the residence of her foster parents Boring Bob and Equally Boring Barbara Buckley. Even their names were boring, not to mention their dinner conversations. *How was your day, dear? And yours? The weather's turning nice, isn't it? Can you pass me the potatoes?*

In their tweedy, bookish world, Claire was the alien, the wild child they'd never understand, although they tried. They really did. She should be living instead with artists or actors or musicians, people who stayed up all night and knew how to have fun. *Her* kind of people.

The black SUV had vanished. It was now or never.

She took a breath and sprang. Felt the night air whoosh in her long hair as she soared through the darkness. She landed, graceful as a cat, and the branch shuddered under her weight. Piece of cake. She scrambled down to a lower branch and was about to jump off when that black SUV returned. Again it glided past, engine purring. She watched it until it vanished around the corner; then she dropped onto the wet grass.

Glancing back at the house, she expected Bob to come storming out the front door, yelling at her: *Get back inside now, young lady!* But the porch remained dark.

Now the night could begin.

She zipped up her hoodie and headed toward the town common, where the action was—if you could call it that. At this late hour, the street was quiet, most of the windows dark. It was a neighborhood of picture-perfect houses with gingerbread trim, a street populated by college professors and gluten-free vegan moms who all belonged to book groups. *Ten square miles surrounded by reality* was how Bob affectionately described the town, but he and Barbara belonged here.

Claire did not know where she belonged.

She strode across the street, scattering dead leaves with her scuffed boots. A block ahead, a trio of teens, two boys and a girl, stood smoking cigarettes beneath the pool of light cast by a streetlamp.

"Hey," she called out to them.

The taller boy waved. "Hey, Claire Bear. I heard you were grounded again."

"For about thirty seconds." She took the lit cigarette he offered her, drew in a lungful of smoke, and exhaled with a happy sigh. "So what's our plan tonight? What're we doing?"

"I hear there's a party over at the falls. But we need to find a ride."

"What about your sister? She could take us."

"Naw, Dad took her car keys. Let's just hang

around here and see who else shows up." The boy paused, frowning past Claire's shoulder. "Uh-oh. Look who just did."

She turned and groaned as a dark blue Saab pulled up at the curb beside her. The passenger window rolled down and Barbara Buckley said, "Claire, get in the car."

"I'm just hanging out with my friends."

"It's nearly midnight and tomorrow's a school day."

"It's not like I'm doing anything illegal."

From the driver's seat, Bob Buckley ordered, "Get in the car *now,* young lady!"

"You're not my parents!"

"But we *are* responsible for you. It's our job to raise you right, and that's what we're trying to do. If you don't come home with us now, there'll be— there'll be, well, consequences!"

*Yeah, I'm so scared I'm shaking in my boots.* She started to laugh, but suddenly noticed that Barbara was wearing a bathrobe and Bob's hair was standing up on one side of his head. They'd been in such a hurry to chase after her that they hadn't even gotten dressed. They both looked older and wearier, a rumpled, middle-aged couple who'd been roused from bed and, because of her, would wake up exhausted tomorrow.

Barbara gave a tired sigh. "I know we're not your parents, Claire. I know you hate living with us, but we're trying to do our best. So please, get in the car. It's not safe for you out here."

Claire shot an exasperated glance at her friends, then climbed into the Saab's backseat and swung the door shut. "Okay?" she said. "Satisfied?"

Bob turned to look at her. "This isn't about us. It's about you. We swore to your parents that you'd always be looked after. If Isabel were alive, it would break her heart to see you now. Out of control, angry all the time. Claire, you were given a second chance, and that's a gift. Please, don't throw it away. Now buckle up, okay?"

If he'd been angry, if he'd yelled at her, she could have dealt with it. But the look he gave her was so mournful that she felt guilty. Guilty for being a jerk, for repaying their kindness with rebellion. It was not the Buckleys' fault that her parents were dead. That her life was screwed up.

As they drove away, she sat hugging herself in the backseat, remorseful but too proud to apologize. Tomorrow, I'll be nicer to them, she thought. I'll help Barbara set the table, maybe even wash Bob's car. Because damn, this car sure does need it.

"Bob," said Barbara. "What's that car doing over there?"

An engine roared. Headlights hurtled toward them.

Barbara screamed: *"Bob!"*

The impact threw Claire against her seat belt as the night exploded with terrible sounds. Shattering glass. Crumpling steel.

And someone crying, whimpering. Opening her eyes, she saw that the world had turned upside down, and she realized that the whimpers were her own. "Barbara?" she whispered.

She heard a muted *pop,* then another. Smelled gasoline. She was suspended by the seat belt, and the strap cut so deeply into her ribs that she could scarcely breathe. She fumbled for the release. It clicked open and her head thumped down, sending pain shooting up her neck. Somehow she managed to twist around so she was lying flat, the shattered window in view. The smell of gasoline was stronger. She squirmed toward the window, thinking about flames, about searing heat and flesh cooking on her bones. *Get out, get out. While there's still time to save Bob and Barbara!* She punched through the last pebbly fragments of glass, sent them clattering onto the pavement.

Two feet moved into view and halted in front of her. She stared up at the man who blocked her escape. She could not see a face, only his silhouette. And his gun.

Tires shrieked as another car roared toward them.

Claire jerked back into the Saab like a tortoise withdrawing into the safety of her shell. Shrinking from the window, she covered her head with her arms and wondered if this time the bullet would hurt. If she would feel it explode in her skull. She was curled so tightly into a ball that all she heard was the sound of her own breathing, the whoosh of her own pulse.

She almost missed the voice calling her name.

"Claire Ward?" It was a woman.

*I must be dead. And that's an angel, speaking to me.*

"He's gone. It's safe to come out now," the angel said. "But you must hurry."

Claire opened her eyes and peered through her fingers at the face staring sideways through the broken window. A slender arm reached toward her, and Claire cowered from it.

"He'll be back," the woman said. "So hurry."

Claire grasped the offered hand, and the woman hauled her out. Broken glass tinkled like hard rain as Claire rolled onto the pavement. Too quickly she sat up, and the night wobbled around her. She caught one dizzying glimpse of the overturned Saab and had to drop her head again.

"Can you stand?"

Slowly, Claire looked up. The woman was dressed all in black. Her hair was tied back in a ponytail, the blond strands bright enough to reflect a faint glimmer from the streetlamp. "Who are you?" Claire whispered.

"My name doesn't matter."

"Bob—Barbara—" Claire looked at the overturned Saab. "We have to get them out of the car! Help me." Claire crawled to the driver's side and yanked open the door.

Bob Buckley tumbled out onto the pavement, his eyes open and sightless. Claire stared at the bullet hole punched into his temple. "Bob," she moaned. *"Bob!"*

"You can't help him now."

"Barbara—what about Barbara?"

"It's too late." The woman grabbed her by the shoulders and gave her a hard shake. "They're dead, do you understand? They're both dead."

Claire shook her head, her gaze still on Bob. On the pool of blood now spreading like a dark halo around his head. "This can't be happening," she whispered. "Not again."

"Come, Claire." The woman grabbed her hand and pulled her to her feet. "Come with me. If you want to live."

# TWO

O N THE NIGHT FOURTEEN-YEAR-OLD WILL Yablonski should have died, he stood in a dark New Hampshire field, searching for aliens.

He had assembled all the necessary equipment for the hunt. There was his ten-inch Dobsonian mirror, which he'd ground by hand three years ago, when he was only eleven years old. It had taken him two months, starting with coarse eighty-grit sandpaper and progressing to finer and finer grits to shape and smooth and polish the glass. With his dad's help, he'd built his own alt-azimuth mount. The twenty-five-millimeter Plössl eyepiece was a gift from his uncle Brian, who helped Will haul all this equipment out into the field after dinner whenever the sky was clear. But Uncle Brian was a lark, not an owl, and by ten P.M. he always called it a night and went to bed.

So Will stood alone in the field behind his aunt and uncle's farmhouse, as he did most nights when the sky was clear and the moon wasn't shining, and searched the sky for alien fuzzyballs, otherwise known as comets. If he ever discovered a new comet, he knew exactly what he would name it: *Comet Neil Yablonski,* in honor of his dead father. New comets were spotted all the time by amateur astronomers; why couldn't a fourteen-year-old kid be the next to find one? His dad once told him that all it took was dedication, a trained eye, and a lot of luck. *It's a treasure hunt, Will. The universe is like a beach, and the stars are grains of sand, hiding what you're looking for.*

For Will, the treasure hunt never got old. He still felt the same excitement whenever he and Uncle Brian hauled the equipment out of the house and set it up under the darkening sky, the same sense of anticipation that *this* could be the night he discovered Comet Neil Yablonski. And then the effort would be worth it, worth the countless nocturnal vigils fueled by hot chocolate and candy bars. Even worth the insults flung at him by his former classmates in Maryland: *Fat boy. Stay-Puft Marshmallow.*

Comet hunting was not a hobby that made you tan and trim.

Tonight, as usual, he'd begun his search soon after dusk, because comets were most visible just after sunset or before sunrise. But the sun had set hours ago, and he still hadn't spotted any fuzzyballs. He'd seen a few passing satellites and a briefly flaring meteor, but nothing else that he hadn't seen before in this sector of the sky. He turned the telescope to a different sector, and the bottom star of Canes Venatici came into view. The hunting dogs. He remembered the night his father had told him the name of that constellation. A cold night when they'd both stayed up till dawn, sipping from a thermos and snacking on . . .

He suddenly jerked straight and turned to look behind him. What was that noise? An animal, or merely the wind in the trees? He stood still, listening for any sounds, but the night had turned unnaturally silent, so silent that it magnified his own breathing. Uncle Brian had assured him there was nothing dangerous in those woods, but alone here in the dark, Will could imagine all sorts of things with teeth. Black bears. Wolves. Cougars.

Uneasy, he turned back to his telescope and shifted the field of vision. A fuzzyball suddenly appeared smack in the eyepiece. *I found it! Comet Neil Yablonski!*

*No. No, stupid, that wasn't a comet.* He sighed in disappointment as he realized he was looking at M3, a globular cluster. Something that any decent astronomer would recognize. Thank God he hadn't woken up Uncle Brian to see it; that would have been embarrassing.

The snap of a twig made him spin around again. Something was moving in the woods. Something was definitely there.

The explosion threw him forward. He slammed facedown onto the turf-cushioned ground, where he lay stunned by the impact. A light flickered, brightening, and he lifted his head and saw that the stand of trees was shimmering with an orange glow. He felt heat against his neck, like a monster's breath. He turned.

The farmhouse was ablaze, flames shooting up like fingers clawing at the sky.

"Uncle Brian!" Will screamed. "Aunt Lynn!"

He ran toward the house, but a wall of fire barred the way, and the heat drove him back, a heat so intense that it seared his throat. He stumbled backward, choking, and smelled the stench of his own singed hair.

*Find help! The neighbors!* He turned to the road and ran two steps before he halted.

A woman was walking toward him. A woman dressed all in black, and lean as a panther. Her blond hair was pulled back in a ponytail, and the flickering firelight cast her face in sharp angles.

"Help me!" he screamed. "My aunt and uncle—they're in the house!"

She looked at the farmhouse, now fully consumed by flames. "I'm sorry. But it's too late for them."

"It's *not* too late. We have to save them!"

She shook her head sadly. "I can't help them, Will. But you, I can save *you*." She held out her hand. "Come with me. If you want to live."

# THREE

SOME GIRLS LOOKED PRETTY IN PINK. SOME GIRLS could don bows and lace, could swish around in silk taffeta and look charming and feminine.

Jane Rizzoli was not one of those girls.

She stood in her mother's bedroom, staring at her reflection in the full-length mirror, and thought: Just shoot me. Shoot me now.

The bell-shaped dress was bubblegum pink with a neckline ruffle as wide as a clown's collar. The skirt was puffy with row upon grotesque row of more ruffles. Wrapped around the waist was a sash tied in a huge pink bow. Even Scarlett O'Hara would be horrified.

"Oh, Janie, look at you!" said Angela Rizzoli, clapping her hands in delight. "You are so beautiful, you'll steal the show from me. Don't you just love it?"

Jane blinked, too stunned to say a word.

"Of course, you'll have to wear high heels to pull it all together. Satin stilettos, I'm thinking. And a bouquet with pink roses and baby's breath. Or is that old-fashioned? Do you think I should go more modern with calla lilies or something?"

"Mom . . ."

"I'll have to take this in for you at the waist. How come you've lost weight? Aren't you eating enough?"

"Seriously? *This* is what you want me to wear?"

"What's the matter?"

"It's . . . *pink.*"

"And you look beautiful in it."

"Have you *ever* seen me wear pink?"

"I'm sewing a little dress just like it for Regina. You'll look so cute together! Mom and daughter in matching dresses!"

"Regina's cute. I'm definitely not."

Angela's lip began to quiver. It was a sign as subtly ominous as the first twitch of a nuclear reactor's warning dial. "I worked all weekend making that dress. Sewed every stitch, every ruffle, with my own hands. And you don't want to wear it, even for my wedding?"

Jane swallowed. "I didn't say that. Not exactly."

"I can see it in your face. You hate it."

"No, Mom, it's a *great* dress." *For a frigging Barbie, maybe.*

Angela sank onto the bed, and her sigh was worthy of a dying heroine. "You know, maybe Vince and I should just elope. That would make everyone happier, wouldn't it? Then I won't have to deal with Frankie. I won't have to worry about who's included on the guest list and who isn't. And you won't have to wear a dress you hate."

Jane sat on the bed beside her, and the taffeta puffed up on her lap like a big ball of cotton candy. She punched it down. "Mom, your divorce isn't even final yet. You can take all the time you want to plan this. That's the fun of a wedding, don't you think? You don't have to rush into anything." She glanced up at the sound of the doorbell.

"Vince is impatient. Do you know what he told me? He says he wants to claim his bride, isn't that sweet? I feel like that Madonna song. Like a virgin again."

Jane jumped up. "I'll answer the door."

"We should just get married in Miami!" Angela yelled as Jane walked from the bedroom. "It'd be a whole lot easier. Cheaper, too, 'cause I wouldn't have to feed all the relatives!"

Jane opened the front door. Standing on the porch were the two men she least wanted to see on this Sunday morning.

Her brother Frankie laughed as he entered the house. "What's with the ugly dress?"

Her father, Frank Senior, followed, announcing: "I'm here to speak to your mother."

"Dad, this isn't a good time," said Jane.

"I'm here. It's a good time. Where is she?" he asked, looking around the living room.

"I don't think she wants to talk to you."

"She has to talk to me. We need to put a stop to this insanity."

"Insanity?" said Angela, emerging from the bedroom. "Look who's talking about insanity."

"Frankie says you're going through with this," said Jane's father. "You're actually going to marry that man?"

"Vince asked me. I said yes."

"What about the fact that *we're* still married?"

"It's only a matter of paperwork."

"I'm not going to sign them."

"What?"

"I said I'm not gonna sign the papers. And you're not gonna marry that guy."

Angela gave a disbelieving laugh. "*You're* the one who walked out."

"I didn't know you'd turn around and get married!"

"What am I supposed to do, sit around pining after you left me for *her*? I'm still a young woman, Frank! Men want me. They want to sleep with me!"

Frankie groaned. "Jesus, Ma."

"And you know what?" added Angela. "Sex has never been better!"

Jane heard her cell phone ringing in the bedroom. She ignored it and grabbed her father's arm. "I think you'd better leave, Dad. Come on, I'll walk you out."

"I'm *glad* you left me, Frank," said Angela. "Now I've got my life back and I know what it's like to be appreciated."

"You're my wife. You still belong to me."

Jane's cell phone, which had gone briefly silent,

was ringing again, insistent and now impossible to ignore. "Frankie," she pleaded, "for God's sake, help me here! Get him out of the house."

"Come on, Dad," Frankie said, and clapped his father on the back. "Let's go get a beer."

"I'm not finished here."

"Yes, you are," said Angela.

Jane sprinted back to the bedroom and dug the ringing cell phone out of her purse. Tried to ignore the arguing voices in the hallway as she answered: "Rizzoli."

Detective Darren Crowe said, "We need you on this one. How soon can you get here?" No polite preamble, no *please* or *would you mind*, just Crowe being his usual charming self.

She responded with an equally brusque: "I'm not on call."

"Marquette's bringing in three teams. I'm lead on this. Frost just got here, but we could use a woman."

"Did I just hear you right? Did you say you actually *need* a woman's help?"

"Look, our witness is too shell-shocked to tell us much of anything. Moore's already tried talking to the kid, but he thinks you'll have better luck with him."

*Kid.* That word made Jane go still. "Your witness is a child?"

"Looks about thirteen, fourteen. He's the only survivor."

"What happened?"

Over the phone she heard other voices in the

background, the staccato dialogue of crime scene personnel and the echo of multiple footsteps moving around a room with hard floors. She could picture Crowe swaggering at the center of it with his puffed-out chest and bulked-up shoulders and Hollywood haircut. "It's a fucking bloodbath here," he said. "Five victims, including three children. The youngest one can't be more than eight years old."

I don't want to see this, she thought. Not today. Not any day. But she managed to say: "Where are you?"

"The residence is on Louisburg Square. Goddamn news vans are packed in tight here, so you'll probably need to park a block or two away."

She blinked in surprise. "This happened on Beacon Hill?"

"Yeah. Even the rich get whacked."

"Who are the victims?"

"Bernard and Cecilia Ackerman, ages fifty and forty-eight. And their three adopted daughters."

"And the survivor? Is he one of their kids?"

"No. His name's Teddy Clock. He's been living with the Ackermans for a couple of years."

"Living with them? Is he a relative?"

"No," said Crowe. "He's their foster child."

# FOUR

A S JANE WALKED INTO LOUISBURG SQUARE, SHE spotted the familiar black Lexus parked among the knot of Boston PD vehicles and she knew that ME Maura Isles was already on the scene. Judging by all the news vans, every TV station in Boston was also here, and no wonder: Of all the desirable neighborhoods in the city, few could match this square with its jewel-like park and leafy trees. The Greek Revival mansions overlooking the park were home to both old wealth and new, to corporate moguls and Boston Brahmins and a former US senator. Even in this neighborhood, violence was no stranger. *The rich get whacked, too,* Detective Crowe had said, but when it happened to them, everyone paid attention. Beyond the perimeter of police tape, a crowd jostled for better views. Beacon Hill was a popular stop for tour groups, and today those tourists were certainly getting their money's worth.

"Hey, look! It's Detective Rizzoli."

Jane spotted the female TV reporter and camera-man moving toward her, and she put up her hand to hold off any questions. Of course they ignored her and pursued her across the square.

"Detective, we hear there's a witness!"

Jane pushed through the crowd, muttering: "Police. Let me through."

"Is it true the security system was turned off? And nothing was stolen?"

The damn reporters knew more than she did. She ducked under the crime scene tape and gave her name and unit number to the patrolman on guard. It was merely a matter of protocol; he knew exactly who she was and had already ticked off her name on his clipboard.

"Shoulda seen that gal chase Detective Frost," the patrolman said with a laugh. "He looked like a scared rabbit."

"Is Frost inside?"

"So is Lieutenant Marquette. The commissioner's on his way in, and I half expect His Honor will be showing up, too."

She looked up at the stunning four-story redbrick residence and murmured: "Wow."

"I figure it's worth fifteen, twenty million."

But that was before the ghosts moved in, she thought, staring at the handsome bow windows and the elaborately carved pediment above the massive front door. Beyond that front door were horrors she had no stomach to confront. Three dead children. This was the curse of parenthood; every dead child wears the face of your own. As she pulled on gloves and shoe covers, she was donning emotional protection as well. Like the construction worker who puts on his hard hat, she donned her own armor and stepped inside.

She looked up at a stairwell that soared four stories to a glass-domed roof, through which sunlight streamed in a shower of gold. Many voices, most of them male, echoed down that stairwell from the upper floors. Although she craned her neck, she could not spot anyone from the foyer, could just hear those voices, like the rumblings of ghosts in a house that, over a century, would have sheltered many souls.

"A glimpse of how the other half lives," said a male voice.

She turned to see Detective Crowe standing in a doorway. "And dies," she said.

"We've parked the boy next door. The neighbor lady was kind enough to let him wait in her house. The kid knows her, and we thought he'd feel more comfortable being interviewed there."

"First I need to know what happened in *this* house."

"We're still trying to figure that out."

"What's with all the brass showing up? I heard the commissioner's on his way."

"Just take a look at the place. Money talks, even when you're dead."

"Where did this family's money come from?"

"Bernard Ackerman's a retired investment banker.

His family's owned this house for two generations. Big-time philanthropists. You name the charity, they probably gave to it."

"How did this go down?"

"Why don't you just take the tour?" He waved her into the room from which he'd just emerged. "You tell me what *you* think."

Not that her opinion mattered much to Darren Crowe. When she'd first joined the homicide unit, their clashes had been bitter, and his disdain all too apparent. She still detected hints of it in his laugh, his tone of voice. Whatever respect she'd earned in his eyes would always be probationary, and here was yet another opportunity to lose it.

She followed him through a parlor where the twenty-foot ceiling was ornately painted with cherubs and grapevines and gold-leaf rosettes. There was scarcely any chance to admire that ceiling or the oil paintings, because Crowe walked straight through into the library, where Jane saw Lieutenant Marquette and Dr. Maura Isles. On this warm June day, Maura was wearing a peach-colored blouse, an uncharacteristically cheerful color for someone who usually favored wintry blacks and grays. With her stylishly geometric haircut and her elegant features, Maura looked like a woman who might actually live in a mansion like this, surrounded by oil paintings and Persian carpets.

They stood surrounded by books, displayed in floor-to-ceiling mahogany shelves. Some of those volumes had tumbled onto the floor, where a silver-haired man lay facedown, one arm propped up-right against the bookcase, as though reaching for a volume even in death. He was dressed in pajamas and slippers. The bullet had penetrated both his hand and his forehead, and on the shelf above the body a starburst of blood had splattered the leather-bound spines. The victim put up his hand to block the bullet, thought Jane. He saw it coming. He knew he was going to die.

"My time-of-death estimate is consistent with what the witness told you," Maura said to Marquette.

"Early morning, then. Sometime after midnight."

"Yes."

Jane crouched down over the body and studied the entrance wound. "Nine millimeter?"

"Or possibly a three fifty-seven," said Maura.

"You don't know? We don't have casings?"

"Not a single one in the whole house."

Jane looked up in surprise. "Wow, he's a tidy killer. Picks up after himself."

"Tidy in a number of ways," said Maura, thoughtfully regarding the deceased Bernard Ackerman. "This was a quick and efficient kill. A minimum of disorder. Just like upstairs."

Upstairs, thought Jane. The children.

"The rest of the family," said Jane, sounding more matter-of-fact than she felt, "did they die around the same time as Mr. Ackerman? Was there any delay?"

"My estimate is only approximate. To be more

precise, we'll need better information from the witness."

"Which Detective Rizzoli here is going to get for us," said Crowe.

"How do you know I'll do any better with the boy?" said Jane. "I can't work magic."

"We're counting on you, because we don't have much to work with. Just a few fingerprints on the kitchen doorknob. No sign of forced entry. And the security system was switched off."

"Off?" Jane looked down at the body. "It sounds like Mr. Ackerman admitted his own killer."

"Or maybe he just forgot to turn it on. Then he heard a noise and came downstairs to check."

"Robbery? Is anything missing?"

"Mrs. Ackerman's jewelry box upstairs looks untouched," said Crowe. "His wallet and her purse are still on the bedroom dresser."

"Did the killer even go into their bedroom?"

"Oh yeah. He went into the bedroom. He went into all the bedrooms." She heard the ominous note in Crowe's voice. Knew that what waited upstairs was far worse than this blood-splattered library.

Maura said, quietly: "I can take you upstairs, Jane."

Jane followed her back into the foyer, neither one of them speaking, as if this was an ordeal best borne in silence. As they ascended the grand staircase, Jane glimpsed treasures everywhere she looked. An antique clock. A painting of a woman in red.

These details she automatically registered even as she braced herself for what waited on the upper floors. In the bedrooms.

At the top of the stairs, Maura turned right and walked to the room at the end of the hall. Through the open doorway, Jane glimpsed her partner Detective Barry Frost, his hands gloved in lurid purple latex. He stood with elbows hugging his sides, the position every cop instinctively assumes at a crime scene to avoid cross-contamination. He saw Jane and gave a sad shake of his head, a look that said: *This is not where I want to be on this beautiful day, either.*

Jane stepped into the room and was momentarily dazzled by the sunlight streaming in through floor-to-ceiling windows. This bedroom needed no curtains for privacy, as the windows looked out over a walled courtyard where a Japanese maple tree was leafed in brilliant burgundy, where blooming roses were in their full flush. But it was the woman's body that demanded Jane's attention. Cecilia Ackerman, clothed in a beige nightgown, lay on her back in bed, the covers pulled up to her shoulders. She appeared to be younger than her age of forty-eight, her hair artfully streaked with blond highlights. Her eyes were closed, and her face was eerily serene. The bullet had entered just above her left eyebrow, and the powder ring on her skin showed that it was a contact wound, the barrel pressed to her forehead at the time the trigger was pulled. You were asleep when the killer pulled the trigger, thought

Jane. You did not scream or resist, you posed no threat. Yet the invader walked into this room, crossed to the bed, and fired a bullet into your head.

"It gets worse," said Frost.

She looked at her partner, who appeared haggard in the harsh morning light. This was more than mere fatigue she saw in his eyes; whatever he'd seen had left him shaken.

"The children's bedrooms are on the third floor," Maura said, a statement so matter-of-fact that she might have been a Realtor describing the features of this grand house. Jane heard creaking overhead, the footsteps of other team members moving in the rooms above them, and she suddenly thought of the year she'd helped plan her high school's Halloween house of horrors. They'd splashed around fake blood and staged garishly gruesome scenes, far more gruesome than what she saw in this bedroom with its serenely reposing victim. Real life required little gore to horrify.

Maura headed out of the room, indicating that they'd seen what was significant here and it was time to move on. Jane followed her back to the staircase. Golden light shone down through the skylight, as if they were climbing a stairway to heaven, but these steps led to quite a different destination. To a place Jane did not want to go. Maura's uncharacteristically summery blouse seemed as glaringly incongruous as wearing hot pink to a funeral. It was a minor detail, yet it bothered Jane, even annoyed her, that of all the days that Maura would choose to wear such a cheerful color, it would be on a morning when three children had died.

They reached the third floor and Maura made a graceful sidestep, maneuvering one paper-covered shoe over some obstacle on the landing. Only when Jane cleared the top step did she see the heart-breakingly small form, covered with a plastic sheet. Crouching down, Maura lifted a corner of the shroud.

The girl was lying on her side, curled up into a fetal position, as though trying to retreat to the dimly remembered safety of the womb. Her skin was coffee-colored, her black hair woven into cornrows decorated with bright beads. Unlike the Caucasian victims downstairs, this child appeared to be African American.

"Victim number three is Kimmie Ackerman, age eight," said Maura, speaking in a flatly clinical voice, a voice that Jane found more and more grating as she stared down at the child on the landing. Just a baby. A baby who wore pink pajamas with little dancing ponies. On the floor near the body was the imprint of a slender bare foot. Someone had stepped in this child's blood, had left that footprint while fleeing the house. It was too small to be a man's footprint. *Teddy's.*

"The bullet penetrated the girl's occipital bone, but didn't exit. The angle is consistent with a shooter who was taller and firing from behind the victim."

"She was moving," said Jane softly. "Trying to run away."

"Judging by her position here, it appears she was fleeing toward one of these bedrooms on the third floor when she was shot."

"In the back of the head."

"Yes."

"Who the fuck does something like that? Kills a baby?"

Maura replaced the sheet and stood up. "She may have witnessed something downstairs. Seen the killer's face. That would be a motive."

"Don't go all logical on me. Whoever did this walked into the house *prepared* to kill a kid. To wipe out a whole family."

"I can't speak to motive."

"Just the manner of death."

"Which would be homicide."

"You *think*?"

Maura frowned at her. "Why are you angry with me?"

"Why doesn't this seem to bother you?"

"You think this doesn't bother me? You think I can look at this child and not feel what you're feeling?"

They stared at each other for a moment, the child's body lying between them. It was yet another reminder of the gulf that had split their friendship since Maura's recent damaging testimony against a Boston cop, testimony that had sent that cop to prison. Although betrayals of the thin blue line are not quickly forgotten, Jane had had every intention of healing the rift between them. But apologies were not easy, and too many weeks had passed, during which their rift had hardened to concrete.

"It's just . . ." Jane sighed. "I hate it when it's kids. It makes me want to strangle someone."

"That makes two of us." Though the words were said quietly, Jane saw the glint of steel in Maura's eyes. Yes, the rage was there, but better masked and under tight control, the way Maura strove to control almost everything else in her life.

"Rizzoli," called out Detective Thomas Moore from a doorway. Like Frost, he looked beaten down, as if this day's toll had aged him a decade. "Have you talked to the boy yet?"

"Not yet. I wanted to see what we're dealing with first."

"I spent an hour with him. He hardly said a word to me. Mrs. Lyman, the next-door neighbor, said that when he showed up at her house around eight this morning, he was almost catatonic."

"It sounds like what he really needs is a shrink."

"We have a call in to Dr. Zucker, and the social worker's on her way. But I thought maybe Teddy might talk to you. Someone who's a mother."

"What did the boy see? Do you know?"

Moore shook his head. "I just hope he didn't see what's in this room."

That warning was enough to make Jane's fingers feel chilled inside the latex gloves. Moore was a tall man, and his shoulders blocked her view into the bedroom, as if he was trying to protect her from the sight that awaited her. In silence, he stepped aside to let her pass.

Two crime scene techs were crouched in a corner, and they looked up as Jane walked in. Both were young women, part of the new wave of female criminalists who now dominated the field. Neither one looked old enough to have children, to know what it was like to press worried kisses to a feverish cheek or to panic at the sight of an open window, an empty crib. With motherhood came a whole host of nightmares. In this room, one of those nightmares had come true.

"We believe these victims are the Ackermans' daughters Cassandra, age ten, and Sarah, age nine. Both adopted," said Maura. "Since they're out of their beds, something must have awakened them."

"Gunshots?" said Jane softly.

"There were no reports of gunfire heard in the neighborhood," said Moore. "A suppressor must have been used."

"But something alarmed these girls," said Maura. "Something that made them climb out of bed."

Jane had not moved from her spot near the door. For a moment no one spoke, and she realized that they were all waiting for her to approach the bodies, to do her cop thing. Exactly what she had no wish to do. She forced herself to move toward the huddled bodies and knelt down. *They died holding each other.*

"Judging by their positions," said Maura, "it appears that Cassandra tried to shield her younger sister. Two of the bullets passed through Cassandra's body first, before they penetrated Sarah's. Single coup de grâce shots were fired into the heads of each girl. Their clothing doesn't appear disturbed, so I see no obvious evidence of sexual assault, but I'll need to confirm that at autopsy. That will be later this afternoon, if you'd like to observe, Jane."

"No. I would *not* like to observe. I'm not even supposed to be here today." Abruptly she turned and walked out of the room, paper shoes crackling as she fled the sight of the two girls coiled together in death. But as she moved toward the stairwell, she again saw the body of the youngest child. Kimmie, eight years old. Everywhere I look in this house, she thought, there's heartbreak.

"Jane, are you all right?" said Maura.

"Aside from wanting to rip this bastard limb from limb?"

"I feel exactly the same way."

*Then you do a better job of hiding it.* Jane stared down at the draped body. "I look at this kid," she said softly, "and I can't help seeing my own."

"You're a mom, so it's only natural. Look, Crowe and Moore will attend the autopsy. There's no need for you to be there." She glanced at her watch. "It's going to be a long day. And I haven't even packed yet."

"Is this the week you're visiting Julian's school?"

"Come hell or high water, tomorrow I leave for

Maine. Two weeks with a teenage boy and his dog. I have no idea what to expect."

Maura had no children of her own, so how could she possibly know? She and sixteen-year-old Julian Perkins had nothing in common beyond their shared ordeal last winter, fighting to survive in the Wyoming wilderness. She owed her life to the boy, and now she was determined to be the mother he had lost.

"Let's see, what can I tell you about teenage boys?" said Jane, trying to be helpful. "My brothers had stinky shoes. They slept till noon. And they ate about twelve times a day."

"Male pubertal metabolism. They can't help it."

"Wow. You've *really* turned into a mom."

Maura smiled. "It's a good feeling, actually."

But motherhood comes with nightmares, Jane reminded herself as she turned away from Kimmie's body. She was glad to retreat down the staircase, glad to escape this house of horrors. When at last she stepped outside again, she breathed in deeply, as though to wash the scent of death from her lungs. The media horde had grown even thicker, TV cameras lined up like battering rams around the crime scene perimeter. Crowe stood front and center, Detective Hollywood playing to his audience. No one noticed Jane as she slipped past and walked to the house next door.

A patrolman stood guard on the front porch, grinning as he watched Crowe perform for the cameras. "So who do you think's gonna play him in the movie?" he asked. "Is Brad Pitt pretty enough?"

"No one's pretty enough to play Crowe." She snorted. "I need to talk to the boy. He's inside?"

"With Officer Vasquez."

"We're waiting for the shrink, too. So if Dr. Zucker shows up, send him in."

"Yes, ma'am."

Jane suddenly realized she was still wearing gloves and shoe covers from the crime scene. She peeled them off, stuffed them into her pocket, and rang the bell. A moment later a handsome silver-haired woman appeared at the door.

"Mrs. Lyman?" said Jane. "I'm Detective Rizzoli."

The woman nodded and waved her inside. "Hurry. I don't want those awful TV cameras to see us. It's such an invasion of privacy."

Jane stepped into the house, and the woman quickly closed the door.

"They told me to expect you. Although I'm not sure how you'll be able to do much better with Teddy. That nice Detective Moore was so patient with him."

"Where is Teddy?"

"He's in the garden conservatory. Poor boy's hardly said a word to me. Just showed up at my front door this morning still wearing his PJs. I took one look at him and knew something awful had happened." She turned. "It's this way."

Jane followed Mrs. Lyman into the entrance hall

and looked up at a staircase that was the mirror image of the Ackermans' residence. And like the Ackermans', this house featured exquisite—and expensive-looking—artwork.

"What did he say to you?" asked Jane.

"He said, 'They're dead. They're all dead.' And that was about all he could get out. I saw blood on his bare feet, and I immediately called the police." She stopped outside the door to the conservatory. "They were *good* people, Cecilia and Bernard. And she was so happy because she finally had what she wanted, a house full of children. They were already in the process of adopting Teddy. Now he's all alone again." She paused. "You know, I don't mind keeping him here. He's familiar with me, and he knows this house. It's what Cecilia would have wanted."

"That's a generous offer, Mrs. Lyman. But Social Services has foster families who are specially trained to deal with traumatized children."

"Oh. Well, it was just a thought. Since I already know him."

"Then you can tell me more about him. Is there anything that might help me connect with Teddy? What are his interests?"

"He's very quiet. Loves his books. Whenever I visited next door, Teddy was always in Bernard's library, surrounded by books about Roman history. You might try breaking the ice by talking about that subject."

*Roman history. Yeah, my specialty.* "What else is he interested in?"

"Horticulture. He loves the exotic plants in my conservatory."

"What about sports? Could we talk about the Bruins? The Patriots?"

"Oh, he has no interest in that. He's too refined." *Which would make me a troglodyte.*

Mrs. Lyman was about to open the conservatory door when Jane said, "What about his birth family? How did he end up with the Ackermans?"

Mrs. Lyman turned back to Jane. "You don't know about that?"

"I'm told he's an orphan, with no living relatives."

"That's why this is such a shock, especially for Teddy. Cecilia wanted so badly to give him a fresh start, with a real chance at happiness. I don't think there'll ever be a chance. Now that it's happened again."

"Again?"

"Two years ago, Teddy and his family were anchored aboard their sailboat, off Saint Thomas. In the night, while the family was sleeping, someone came aboard. Teddy's parents and his sisters were murdered. Shot to death."

In the pause that followed, Jane suddenly realized how quiet the house was. So quiet that she asked her next question in a hushed voice. "And Teddy? How did he survive?"

"Cecilia told me he was found in the water, floating in his life jacket. And he didn't remember how he got there." Mrs. Lyman looked at the closed door to the conservatory. "Now you understand why this is so devastating for him. It's awful enough to lose your family once. But to have it happen again?" She shook her head. "It's more than any child should have to endure."

# FIVE

**T**HEY COULD NOT HAVE CHOSEN A MORE SOOTH-ing place for a traumatized child than Mrs. Lyman's garden conservatory. Enclosed in glass, the room's windows faced a private walled garden. Morning sunlight streamed in through the windows, nourishing a humid jungle of vines and ferns and potted trees. In that lush overgrowth Jane did not spot the boy, but saw only the female police officer who quickly rose from a rattan garden chair.

"Detective Rizzoli? I'm Officer Vasquez," the woman said.

"How's Teddy?" said Jane.

Vasquez glanced at a corner, where the vines had grown over to form a thick canopy, and whispered: "He hasn't said a word to me. Just kind of hides away and whimpers."

Only then did Jane locate the spindly figure crouched beneath the bower of vines. He was folded into himself, arms hugging his legs to his chest. Although they'd told her he was fourteen, he looked much younger, clothed in powder-blue pajamas, a forelock of light brown hair hiding his face.

Jane dropped down to her knees and crawled toward him, ducking beneath vines as she moved deeper into the leafy shadows. The boy didn't move as she settled down beside him in his jungle hiding place.

"Teddy," she said. "My name is Jane. I'm here to help you."

He didn't look up, didn't respond.

"You've been sitting here awhile, haven't you? You must be hungry."

Was that a shake of the head she saw? Or was it a shudder, a seismic quake from all the pain bottled up inside that fragile body?

"What do you think about some chocolate milk? Maybe ice cream? I bet Mrs. Lyman has some in her refrigerator."

The boy seemed to recede even more deeply into himself, curling into such a tight knot that Jane feared they would never be able to pry open those limbs. She peered up through the tangle of vines at Officer Vasquez, who stood watching intently. "Can you leave us?" she said. "I think it's a little too much right now, having both of us in the room."

Vasquez left the conservatory, closing the door behind her. For ten minutes, fifteen, Jane didn't say a word, nor did she look at the boy. They sat side by side, companions in silence, and the only sound was the gentle splash of water in a marble fountain. Leaning back in the bower, she gazed up at the arching branches overhead. In this Garden of Eden, sheltered from the cold, even banana and orange trees thrived, and she imagined walking into this room on a winter's day, when the snow was falling outside, and breathing in the scent of warm earth and green plants. This is what money buys you, she thought. Eternal springtime. While she kept her gaze fixed on the sunlight above, she was aware of the boy's breathing beside her. It was slower, calmer than it had been moments ago. She heard leaves rustle as he settled against the vines, but she resisted the temptation to look at him. She thought about the earsplitting tantrums that her two-year-old daughter had thrown last week, when little Regina had screamed again and again, *Stop looking at me! Stop looking!* Jane and her husband, Gabriel, had laughed, which only enraged Regina more. Even two-year-olds did not like being stared at, and resented having their privacy invaded. So she tried not to invade Teddy Clock's, but merely shared his leafy cave. Even when she heard him move, her attention stayed focused instead on the dappled sunshine shining through the branches above.

"Who are you?" The words were barely a whisper. She forced herself to remain still, to let a pause settle between them.

"I'm Jane," she said, just as softly.

"But who are you?"

"I'm a friend."

"No, you're not. I don't even know you."

She considered his words and had to admit they were true. She was not his friend. She was a cop who needed something from him, and once she'd gotten it she would hand him over to a social worker.

"You're right, Teddy," she admitted. "I'm not really a friend. I'm a detective. But I do want to help you."

"No one can help me."

"I can. I will."

"Then you'll die, too."

That statement, said so flatly, sent a cold whisper up Jane's back. *You'll die, too.* She turned to stare at the boy. He wasn't looking at her, just stared bleakly ahead as if seeing a hopeless future. His eyes were such a pale blue, they seemed unearthly. His light brown hair looked as wispy as corn silk, one drooping forelock curled over a pale, prominent forehead. His feet were bare, and as he rocked back and forth she glimpsed smudges of dried blood under his right toes; she remembered the footprints leading away from the landing, leading away from eight-year-old Kimmie's body. Teddy had been forced to step in her blood to flee the house.

"Will you really help me?" he said.

"Yes. I promise."

"I can't see anything. I lost them, and now I'm afraid to go back and find them."

"Find what, Teddy?"

"My glasses. I think they're in my room. I must have left them in my room, but I can't remember . . ."

"I'll find them for you."

"That's why I can't tell you what he looked like. Because I couldn't see him."

Jane went still, afraid to interrupt him. Afraid that anything she said, any move she made, would make him pull back into his shell. She waited, but heard only the sound of the splattering water in the fountain.

"Who are you talking about?" she finally asked.

He looked at her, and his eyes seemed lit like blue fire from within. "The man who killed them." His voice broke, his throat choking down the words to a high keen. "I wish I could help you, but I can't. I can't, I can't . . ."

It was a mother's instinct that made her suddenly open her arms, and he tumbled against her, face pressed to her shoulder. She held him as he quaked with shudders so powerful that she felt his body might shatter apart, that she was the only force holding together this shaking basket of bones. He might not be her child, but at that moment, as he clung to her, his tears soaking into her blouse, she felt every bit his mother, ready to defend him against all the world's monsters.

"He never stops." The boy's words were so muffled against her blouse that she almost missed them. "Next time, he'll find me."

"No, he won't." She grasped him by the shoulders and gently pushed him away so she could look at his face. Long lashes cast shadows on his powder-white cheeks. "He won't find you."

"He'll come back." Teddy hugged himself, turning inward to some distant, safe place where no one could reach him. "He always does."

"Teddy, the only way we can catch him, stop him, is if you help us. If you tell me what happened last night."

She saw his thin chest expand, and the sigh that followed sounded far too weary and defeated for someone so young. "I was in my room," he whispered. "I was reading one of Bernard's books."

"And then what happened?" Jane prompted.

Teddy focused his haunted eyes on her. "And then it started."

BY THE TIME JANE returned to the Ackerman residence, the last of the bodies was being wheeled out—one of the children. Jane paused in the foyer as the stretcher rolled past her, wheels squeaking across the gleaming parquet floor, and she could not block out the sudden image of her own daughter, Regina, lying beneath the shroud. With a shudder she turned, and saw Moore coming down the stairs.

"Did the boy talk to you?"

"Enough to tell me he didn't see anything that will help us."

"Then you got a lot further with him than I did. I had a feeling you'd be able to reach him."

"It's not as if I'm all that warm and fuzzy."

"But he did talk to you. Crowe wants you to be the boy's primary contact."

"I'm now the official kid wrangler?"

He gave an apologetic shrug. "Crowe's the lead."

She looked up the stairs toward the upper floors, which now seemed strangely quiet. "What's going on here? Where is everyone?"

"They're following up on a tip about the house-keeper, Maria Salazar. She has the keys and the password to the security system."

"You'd expect a housekeeper to have those."

"It turns out she also has a boyfriend with a few issues."

"Who is he?"

"Undocumented alien named Andres Zapata. He has a rap sheet in Colombia. Burglary. Drug smuggling."

"History of violence?"

"Not that we're aware of. But still."

Jane focused on the antique clock hanging on the wall, an item that no self-respecting burglar would have passed up. And she remembered what she'd heard earlier, that Cecilia's purse and Bernard's wallet were both found in the bedroom, and the jewelry box had been untouched.

"If this was a burglary," she said, "what did he take?"

"A house this size, with so many valuables to

choose from?" Moore shook his head. "The only person who might be able to tell us what's missing is the housekeeper."

Who now sounded like a suspect.

"I'm going up to see Teddy's room," she said and started up the stairs.

Moore did not follow her. When she reached the third floor, she found herself alone; even the CSU team had already departed. Earlier she had merely glanced at the doorway; now she stepped inside and slowly surveyed Teddy's neatly kept room. On the desk facing the window was a stack of books, many of them old and clearly well loved. She scanned the titles: *Ancient Techniques of Warfare. An Introduction to Ethnobotany. The Cryptozoology Handbook. Alexander in Egypt.* Not the sort of reading she'd expect of a fourteen-year-old, but Teddy Clock was unlike any boy she'd ever come across. She saw no TV, but a laptop computer sat open beside the books. She tapped on a key and the screen came alive, to the last website Teddy had viewed. It was a Google search page, and he had typed in: *Was Alexander the Great murdered?*

Judging by the orderly desk, the squared-off stack of books, the boy was addicted to neatness. The pencils in his drawer were all sharpened like spears ready for battle, the paper clips and stapler each in their own slots. Only fourteen and already hopelessly obsessive-compulsive. Here is where he'd been sitting at midnight last night, he'd told her, when he'd heard the faint pops, then Kimmie's screams as she'd run up the stairs. His penchant for neatness compelled him to close the book, *Alexander in Egypt,* even though he was terrified. He knew what those pops, those cries, signified.

*It's what happened before. The same sounds I heard on the boat. I knew it was gunfire.*

There was no window to crawl out of, no easy escape from this third-floor bedroom.

So he'd turned off his light. He heard the girls' cries, heard more pops, and hid in the first place a scared child would retreat to: under the bed.

Jane turned to look at the perfectly smooth duvet, at sheets tucked in as tightly as a soldier's bunk. Had Teddy's obsessive-compulsive neatness resulted in these perfectly made-up linens? If so, it may well have saved his life. As Teddy cowered under the bed, the killer had turned on the lights and walked in.

*Black shoes. That's all I saw. He had black shoes, and he was standing right by my bed.*

A bed that, at midnight, had not been slept in. To an intruder, it would appear that the child who lived in this room was away that night.

The killer with the black shoes walked out. Hours passed, but Teddy stayed under that bed, cowering at every creak. He thought he heard footsteps return, quieter, stealthier, and imagined the killer was still there in the house, waiting.

He did not know what time it was when he fell asleep. He only knew that when he woke up, the sun was shining. Only then did he finally crawl from his hiding place, stiff and sore from lying half the night on the floor. Through the window, he saw Mrs. Lyman working in her garden. Next door was safety; next door was someone he could run to.

And so he did.

Jane knelt down and looked under the bed. There was so little clearance beneath the box spring that she would never be able to fit under it. But a scared boy had squeezed into that space, smaller than a coffin. She glimpsed something deep in those shadows and had to lie facedown on the floor before she could reach under far enough to grasp the object.

It was Teddy's missing glasses.

She rose back to her feet and took one last look around the room. Although the sun shone brightly through the window, and outside it was a summery seventy-five degrees, within these four walls she felt a chill and shivered. It was odd that she had not felt that cold sensation in the rooms where members of the Ackerman family had died. No, it was only here that the horror of what happened last night still seemed to linger.

Here, in the room of the boy who had lived.

# SIX

"TEDDY CLOCK," SAID DETECTIVE THOMAS Moore, "must be the unluckiest boy on the planet. When you consider all that's happened to him, no wonder he's displaying serious emotional problems."

"Not like he was normal to begin with," Darren Crowe said. "The kid's just plain strange."

"Strange in what way?"

"He's fourteen years old and he doesn't do sports? Doesn't watch TV? He spends every night and weekend hunched over his computer and a bunch of dusty old books."

"Some people wouldn't consider that strange."

Crowe turned to Jane. "You've spent the most time with him, Rizzoli. You've gotta admit the kid's not right."

"By *your* standards," said Jane. "Teddy's a lot smarter than that."

A chorus of *whoa*s went around the table as the

other four detectives watched for Crowe's reaction to that not-so-subtle insult.

"There's knowledge that's useless," Crowe retorted. "And then there's street smarts."

"He's only fourteen and he's survived two massacres," she said. "Don't tell me this boy doesn't have street smarts."

As the team lead in the Ackerman investigation, Crowe was acting more abrasive than usual. Their morning team meeting had been going for almost an hour now, and they were all on edge. In the thirty-some hours since the slaughter of the Ackerman family, the media frenzy had intensified, and this morning Jane had awakened to the tabloid headline HORROR ON BEACON HILL, accompanied by a photo of their prime suspect, Andres Zapata, the missing boyfriend of the Ackermans' housekeeper. It was an old mug shot from a drug arrest in Colombia, and he had a face that *looked* like a killer's. He was an illegal immigrant, he had a burglary record, and his fingerprints were found on the Ackermans' kitchen door, as well as on their kitchen counters. They had enough for an arrest warrant, but a conviction? Jane wasn't sure.

She said, "We can't count on Teddy to help us build a case against Zapata."

"You've got plenty of time to prepare him," said Crowe.

"He didn't see a face."

"He must have seen something that will help us in court."

"Teddy's a lot more fragile than you realize. We can't expect him to testify."

"He's fourteen, for God's sake," Crowe snapped. "When I was fourteen—"

"Don't tell me. You were strangling pythons with your bare hands."

Crowe leaned forward. "I do not want this case to fall apart. We need to get our ducks lined up."

"Teddy is not a duck," said Jane. "He's a child."

"And a psychologically scarred one at that," said Moore. He opened the folder he'd brought into the meeting. "I spoke again to Detective Edmonds, in the US Virgin Islands. He faxed me their file on the Clock family murders, and—"

"They were killed two years ago," interjected Crowe. "Different jurisdiction, even a different country. Where's the connection to this case?"

"Probably none," admitted Moore. "But this information speaks to the boy's emotional state. To why he's so devastated. What happened to him in Saint Thomas was every bit as horrifying as what happened to him here."

"And that case was never solved?" said Frost.

Moore shook his head. "But it generated a lot of press. I remember reading about it at the time. American family on a dream voyage around the world, murdered aboard their seventy-five-foot yacht. Granted, the US Virgin Islands have a homicide rate about ten times ours, but even there the massacre was shocking. It actually took place in the Capella Islands, which are off Saint Thomas.

The Clock family—Nicholas and Annabelle and their three children—were living aboard their yacht, *Pantomime*. They anchored for the night in a quiet bay, no other yachts around. While the family was sleeping, the killer—or killers—boarded the boat. There was gunfire. Shouts, screams. And then an explosion. That, at least, is what Teddy later told the police."

"How did he manage to survive?" asked Frost.

"The explosion made him black out, so there are holes in his memory. The last thing he remembers is his father's voice, telling him to jump. When he woke up he was in the water, strapped into a life jacket. A dive boat found him the next morning, surrounded by debris from the *Pantomime*."

"And the family?"

"There was an extensive search of the waters. They later found the bodies of Annabelle and one of the girls. What was left of them anyway, after the sharks had done their damage. Autopsy revealed that both had been shot in the head. The bodies of Nicholas and the other daughter were never recovered." Moore passed around copies of the faxed report. "Lieutenant Edmonds said it was the most disturbing crime he'd ever investigated. A seventy-five-foot yacht is a tempting target, so he assumed the motive was robbery. The killer or killers probably stripped the boat of valuables, then blew it up to destroy the evidence, leaving nothing for the police to go on. It remains unsolved."

"And the boy couldn't remember anything useful in that case, either," said Crowe. "Is there something seriously wrong with this kid?"

"He was only twelve years old at the time," said Moore. "And he's certainly intelligent. I called their old next-door neighbor in Providence, where the Clocks were living before they left on their sailboat. She told me that Teddy was considered gifted. He was in his school's accelerated program. Yes, he did have problems making friends and fitting in, but he had at least a dozen IQ points over his peers."

Jane thought of the books she'd seen in Teddy's bedroom, and the wide range of esoteric subjects they covered. Greek history. Ethnobotany. Cryptozoology. Subjects that she doubted most fourteen-year-olds were even acquainted with. "Asperger's syndrome," she said.

Moore nodded. "That's what the neighbor said. The Clocks had Teddy evaluated, and the doctor told them Teddy is high functioning, but he misses certain emotional cues. Which is why it's hard for him to make friends."

"And now he's left with no one," said Jane. She thought of how he had clung to her in the neighbor's solarium. She could still feel his silky hair against her cheek and remembered the sleepy-boy scent of his pajamas. She wondered how he was adjusting to the emergency foster family where Social Services had placed him. Last night, before going home to her own daughter, she'd driven to

Teddy's new home and brought him his glasses. He was now staying with an older couple, seasoned foster parents who had years of experience nurturing children in crisis.

But the look Teddy had given Jane as she'd walked out the door after that visit could break any mother's heart. As if she were the only person who could save him, and she was abandoning him to strangers.

Moore reached into his folder and took out a print of a Christmas card photo with the caption: HAPPY HOLIDAYS FROM THE CLOCKS! "This is the last correspondence the neighbor received from the Clocks. It's an e-card, sent about a month after the family left Providence. They pulled their three kids out of school, put their house on the market, and the whole family set off to sail around the world."

"On a seventy-five-foot yacht? They had money," said Frost. "What did they do for a living?"

"Annabelle was a homemaker. Nicholas was a financial consultant for some company in Providence. The neighbor didn't remember the name."

Crowe laughed. "Yeah, a title like *financial consultant* does sound like money."

"It's kind of a radical move isn't it?" said Frost. "To suddenly pull up roots like that? Leave everything behind and drag your family onto a sailboat?"

"The neighbor certainly thought so," said Moore. "And it happened abruptly. Annabelle never even mentioned it until the day just before they left. It makes you wonder."

"About what?" said Crowe.

"Was the family running from something? Scared of something? Maybe there *is* a link between these two attacks on Teddy."

"Two years apart?" Crowe shook his head. "As far as we know, the Clocks and the Ackermans didn't even know each other. All they had in common was the boy."

"It just troubles me. That's all."

It troubled Jane as well. She looked at the Christmas photo, perhaps the last one that existed of the Clock family. Annabelle Clock's chestnut hair was upswept and casually elegant, reflecting hints of gold. Her face, like sculpted ivory with delicately arching brows, could have adorned a medieval painter's canvas.

Nicholas was blond and athletic looking, his impressive shoulders filling out a lemon-yellow polo shirt. With his square jaw, his direct gaze, he looked like a man built to protect his family from any threat. On the day this photo was taken, when he stood smiling with one muscular arm draped around his wife, he could not have imagined the horrors that lay ahead. A watery grave for himself. The slaughter of his wife and two of their children. At that instant the camera captured a family with no reason to fear the future; their optimism shone brightly in their eyes and smiles, and in the Christmas decorations they had hung on the tree behind them. Even Teddy looked ebullient as he stood beside his younger sisters, three angelic-looking children with matching light brown hair and wide blue eyes. All of them smiling and safe within the bubble of their sheltering family.

And she thought: Teddy will never feel safe again.

*Killing is easy. All you need is access and the proper tool, whether it's a bullet, a blade, or Semtex. And if you plan it right, no cleanup is necessary. But extracting a man like Icarus, who's alive and resisting you, a man who surrounds himself with family and bodyguards, is a far more delicate process.*

*Which is why we devoted most of that June to surveillance and reconnaissance and dry runs. The hours were long, seven days a week, but no one complained. Why would we? Our hotel was comfortable, our expenses covered. And at the end of the day, there was always plenty of alcohol. Not mere plonk, but good Italian wines. For what we were required to do, we believed we deserved the best.*

*It was a Thursday when we got the call from our local asset. He worked as a waiter inside the restaurant La Nonna, and that night two adjacent tables had been reserved for dinner. One table was for a party of four, the other for a party of two. Bottles of Brunello di Montalcino had been requested, to be opened immediately for proper airing upon the patrons' arrival. He had no doubt for whom those tables were reserved.*

*They arrived in separate vehicles, one right behind the other. In the black BMW were the two bodyguards. In the silver Volvo, Icarus was at the wheel. It was one of his quirks: He always insisted on being his own driver, on being in control. Both cars parked directly across the street from La Nonna, where they would be in view throughout the meal. I was already in position, seated at an outdoor café nearby, sipping espresso. From there I had a front-row view of the precision ballet that was about to unfold.*

*I saw the bodyguards get out of their BMW first, and they watched as Icarus emerged from his Volvo. He always drove a Volvo, an unexciting choice for a man who could afford a fleet of Maseratis. He opened the rear door, and out climbed one of the reasons for choosing such a safe vehicle. Little Carlo, the younger son, was eight years old, with large dark eyes and unruly hair like his mother's. The boy's shoelace had come loose, and Icarus bent down to tie it.*

*That was the moment Carlo noticed me, sitting nearby. His eyes fixed on mine so intently that I felt a dart of panic. I thought: The boy knows. Somehow he knows what's about to happen. I did not have children; no one on our team did, so children were a mystery to us. They were like little aliens, unformed creatures who could be ignored. But Carlo's eyes were luminous and wise, and I felt stripped of all pretense, unable to justify what we were about to do to his father.*

*Then Icarus stood up. He took Carlo's hand and*

led his wife and older son across the street, into La
Nonna for their supper.

I breathed again.

Our team moved into action.

A young woman approached, pushing a baby
carriage, her infant hidden under layers of swad-
dling. The baby gave a sudden wail; the woman
stopped to fuss over him. I was the only one close
enough to see her slash the tire of the bodyguards'
vehicle. Her infant fell silent, and the woman continued up the sidewalk.

At that moment, inside La Nonna, wine was
being poured, two little boys twirled spaghetti, and
platters of veal and lamb and pork emerged from
the kitchen.

Outside, on the street, the jaws of a trap were about
to close. Everything was proceeding as planned.

But I could not shake off the image of little
Carlo's face, staring at me. A look that reached into
my chest and clawed at my heart. When you feel a
premonition as powerful as that, it should never be
ignored.

I am sorry that I did.

# <u>SEVEN</u>

MAURA DROVE WITH HER WINDOWS OPEN AND the smell of summer blowing into the car. Hours ago she had left the Maine coast behind and headed northwest, into gently rolling hills where the afternoon sun leafed hay fields in gold. Then the forest closed in, the trees suddenly so dense that it seemed night had instantly fallen. She drove for miles without passing any cars and wondered if she'd taken a wrong turn. Here there were no houses, no driveways, not a single road sign to tell her whether she was headed in the right direction.

She was ready to turn around when the road suddenly ended at a gate. On the archway above it was a single word, spelled in gracefully entwined letters: EVENSONG.

She stepped out of her Lexus and frowned at the locked gate, which was flanked by massive stone pillars. She saw no intercom button, and the wrought-iron fence extended deep into the woods in both directions, as far as she could see. She pulled out her cell phone to call the school, but this deep in the forest she couldn't get a signal. The silence of the woods magnified the ominous whine of a mosquito, and she slapped at the sudden sting on her cheek. Stared down at the alarming smear of blood. Other mosquitoes were closing in on her in a hungry, biting cloud. She was about to retreat into her car when she spotted the golf cart approaching on the other side of the gate.

A familiar young woman stepped out of the golf cart and waved. In her early thirties, dressed in slim blue jeans and a green Windbreaker, Lily Saul looked far healthier and happier than the last time Maura had seen her. Lily's brown hair, pulled back in a loose ponytail, was now streaked with blond, and her cheeks had a healthy glow, so different from the pale, thin face that Maura remembered from that blood-splattered Christmas when they'd met during the course of a homicide investigation. Its violent conclusion had nearly claimed both their lives. But Lily Saul, who'd spent years running from demons both real and imagined, was a canny survivor, and judging by her happy smile Lily had finally outrun her nightmares.

"We expected you here earlier, Dr. Isles," said Lily. "I'm glad you made it before dark."

"I was afraid I'd have to climb this fence," said Maura. "There's no cell signal out here, and I couldn't call anyone."

"Oh, we knew you'd arrived." Lily punched in a code on the gate's security keypad. "There are motion sensors all along this road. And you probably missed them, but there are cameras as well."

"That's a lot of security for a school."

"It's all about keeping our students safe. And you know how Anthony is about security. There's never enough." She met Maura's gaze through the bars. "It's not surprising he feels that way. When you consider what we've all been through."

Staring into Lily's eyes, Maura realized the young woman's nightmares had not entirely been laid to rest. The shadows still lingered.

"It's been nearly two years, Lily. Has anything else happened?"

Lily pulled open the gate and said, ominously, "Not yet."

That was just the sort of statement that Anthony Sansone would make. Crime left permanent scars on survivors like Sansone and Lily, both of them haunted by violent personal tragedies. For them, the world would always be a landscape riddled with danger.

"Follow me," said Lily as she climbed back into the golf cart. "The castle's another few miles up the road."

"Don't you need to close the gate?"

"It will close automatically. If you need to leave, the keypad code this week is forty-five ninety-six, for both the gate and the school's front door. The number changes every Monday, when we announce it at breakfast."

"So the students know it, too."

"Of course. The gate isn't here to keep us in, Dr. Isles. It's to keep the world *out*."

Maura climbed back into the Lexus, and as she drove past the twin pillars, the gate was already starting to swing shut. Despite Lily's assurance that the gate wasn't meant to lock her in, the wrought-iron bars made her think of a high-security prison. It brought back the sound of clanging metal and the sight of caged faces staring at her.

Lily's golf cart led her down a single-lane road carved through dense woods. In the gloom of those trees, a shockingly brilliant orange fungus stood out, clinging to the trunk of a venerable oak. High in the forest canopy, birds fluttered. A red squirrel perched on a branch, its tail twitching. This deep in the Maine woods, what other creatures would emerge once darkness fell?

The forest gave way to open sky, and a lake stretched before her. In the distance, beyond impenetrably dark waters, loomed the Evensong building. Lily had referred to it as *the castle,* and that was exactly what it looked like, mounted on barren granite. Constructed of that same gray rock, the walls rose up as though thrust from the hill itself.

They drove under a stone arch into the courtyard, and Maura parked her Lexus beside a moss-covered wall. Only an hour ago, the day had been summery, but when she stepped out the air felt cold and damp. Looking up at towering granite walls, at the steeply sloping roof, she imagined bats circling the turret high overhead.

"Don't worry about your suitcase," said Lily, taking it out of the Lexus trunk. "We'll just leave it here on the steps, and Mr. Roman will bring it up to your room."

"Where are all the students?"

"Most of the students and staff have left for summer break. We're down to only two dozen kids and a skeleton crew who stay year-round. And next week you and Julian will find it really quiet around here, because we'll be taking the rest of the kids on a field trip to Quebec. Let me give you a quick tour, then I'll bring you to see Julian. He's in class right now."

"How is he doing?" Maura asked.

"Oh, he's really blossomed since he got here! He's still not crazy about classroom work, but he's resourceful, and he notices things that everyone else misses. And he's protective of the younger kids, always watching out for them. A true Guardian personality." Lily paused. "It did take him awhile to trust us, though. You can understand that, after what he went through in Wyoming."

Yes, Maura did understand. Because she and Julian had lived through it together, both of them fighting for their lives, not knowing whom to trust.

"And you, Lily?" Maura asked. "How are you doing?"

"I'm right where I should be. Living in this beautiful place. Teaching these amazing kids."

"Julian told me you built a Roman catapult in class."

"Yes, during our unit on siege warfare. The students really got into that one. Broke a window, unfortunately."

They climbed stone steps and came to a doorway so tall it could have admitted a giant. Lily punched in the security code again. The massive wooden door swung open easily with just a push, and they stepped across the threshold into a hall where soaring archways were framed in old timbers. Hanging overhead was an iron chandelier, and set in the arch above it, like a multicolored eye, was a circular stained-glass window. On this gloomy afternoon, it admitted only a faintly muddy glow.

Maura stopped at the foot of a massive stairway and admired the tapestry hanging on the wall, a faded image of two unicorns resting in a bower of vines and fruit trees. "This really *is* a castle," she said.

"Built around 1835 by a megalomaniac named Cyril Magnus." Lily gave a disgusted shake of the head. "He was a railroad baron, big-game hunter, art collector, and all-around mean bastard, according to most accounts. This was built as his private castle. Designed in the Gothic style that he admired during his trips to Europe. The granite was quarried fifty miles from here. The timbers are good old Maine oak. When Evensong purchased this property thirty years ago, it was still in pretty good shape, so most of what you see here is original.

Over the years, Cyril Magnus kept adding to the building, which makes it a little confusing to navigate. Don't be surprised if you get lost."

"That tapestry," said Maura, pointing to the weaving of the unicorns. "It actually *looks* medieval."

"It is. It comes from Anthony's villa in Florence."

Maura had seen the treasure trove of sixteenth-century paintings and Venetian furniture that Sansone kept in his Beacon Hill residence. She had no doubt that his villa in Florence would be as grand as this building, and the art even more impressive. But these were not the warm, honey-hued walls of Tuscany; here the gray stone radiated a chill that even a sunny day would not dispel.

"Have you been there yet?" Lily asked. "To his home in Florence?"

"I haven't been invited," said Maura. *Unlike you, obviously.*

Lily gave her a thoughtful look. "I'm sure it's only a matter of time," she said, and turned toward what looked like a paneled wall. She pushed against one of the panels; it swung open to reveal a doorway. "This is the passage to the library."

"Are you trying to hide the books?"

"No, it's just one of the peculiar features of this building. I think old Cyril Magnus liked surprises, because it's not the only door in this house that's disguised as something else." Lily led her down a windowless corridor, the gloom accentuated by dark wood paneling. At the far end, they emerged into a room where tall arched windows admitted the last gray light of day. Maura stared up in wonder at gallery upon gallery of bookshelves that soared three stories to a domed ceiling where the plaster had been decorated with a painting of fluffy clouds in a blue sky.

"This is the beating heart of Evensong," said Lily. "This library. Anytime, day or night, the students are welcome to come in here and pull any book from the shelves, as long as they promise to treat it with respect. And if they can't find what they're looking for in the library . . ." Lily crossed to a door and opened it, revealing a room with a dozen computers. "As a last resort, there's always Dr. Google." She shut the door again with a look of distaste. "But really, who wants the Internet when the real treasures are right *here*?" She gestured to three stories of books. "The collected wisdom of centuries, under one roof. It makes me salivate, just looking at them."

"Spoken like a true teacher of the classics," said Maura as she scanned the titles. *Napoleon's Women. Lives of the Saints. Egyptian Mythology.* She paused as one title caught her eye, stamped in gold on dark leather. *Lucifer.* The book seemed to call to her, demanding her attention. She pulled out the volume and stared at the worn leather cover, with its tooled illustration of a crouching demon.

"We believe that no knowledge is off limits," said Lily quietly.

"Knowledge?" Maura slid the book back onto the

shelf and looked at the young woman. "Or superstition?"

"It helps to understand both, don't you think?"

Maura walked down the room, past rows of long wooden tables and chairs, past a series of globes, each representing the world as known in a different age. "As long as you don't teach it as fact," she said, stopping to examine a globe from 1650, the continents misshapen, vast territories unknown and unexplored. "It's superstition. Myth."

"Actually, we teach them *your* belief system, Dr. Isles."

"*My* belief system?" Maura looked at her in puzzlement. "Which one would that be?"

"Science. Chemistry and physics, biology and botany." She glanced at the antique grandfather clock. "Which is where Julian is right now. And his class should just be ending."

They left the library, returning through that dark-paneled corridor to the entrance hall, and climbed the massive stairway. As they passed beneath the tapestry, Maura saw it flutter against the stone wall, as if a draft had just swept into the building, and the unicorns seemed to come alive, trembling beneath the lushly fruited trees. The steps curved past a window, and Maura paused to admire the view of wooded hills in the distance. Julian had told her that his school was surrounded by forest, that it was miles from the nearest village. Only now did she see how isolated Evensong truly was.

"Nothing can reach us here." The voice, so soft,

startled her by its nearness. Lily stood half hidden in the shadow of the archway. "We grow our own food. Raise chickens for eggs, cows for milk. Heat with our own wood. We don't need the outside world at all. This is the first place I've truly felt safe."

"Here in the forest, with bears and wolves?"

"We both know there's a lot of things more dangerous than bears and wolves beyond the gate."

"Hasn't it gotten any easier for you, Lily?"

"I still think about what happened, every single day. What he did to my family, to me. But being here, it's helped me a great deal."

"Has it? Or does this isolation just reinforce your fears?"

Lily looked straight at her. "A healthy fear of the world is what keeps some of us alive. That's the lesson I learned two years ago." She continued up the steps, past a shadowy painting of three men in medieval robes, no doubt another contribution from Anthony Sansone's family collection. Maura thought of unruly students stampeding past this masterpiece every day, and she wondered how many milliseconds this art would survive intact in any other school. She thought, too, of the library with its priceless volumes bound in gold-stamped leather. The students of Evensong must be an unusual group indeed to be entrusted with such treasures.

They reached the second floor and Lily pointed upstairs, toward the third floor. "Living quarters are on the next level. Student dormitories in the east wing, faculty and guests in the west. You'll be staying in the older part of the west wing, where the rooms have lovely stone fireplaces. In the summer, it's the choicest spot in the whole building."

"And in winter?"

"It's not habitable. Unless you want to stay up all night throwing logs on the fire. We close it off when the weather turns cold." Lily led the way down the second-floor hallway. "Let's see if old Pasky's finished yet."

"Who?"

"Professor David Pasquantonio. He teaches botany, cell biology, and organic chemistry."

"Rather advanced subjects for high school students."

"High school?" Lily laughed. "We start those subjects in middle school. Twelve-year-olds are a lot smarter than most people give them credit for."

They walked past open doorways, past deserted classrooms. She glimpsed a human skeleton dangling on a stand, a lab bench and test tube racks, a wraparound wall chart with a time line of world history.

"Since it's summer break, I'm surprised you still have classes in session," said Maura.

"The alternative is two dozen students going stir-crazy with boredom. No, we try to keep those gray cells humming."

They turned the corner and confronted an enormous black dog stretched out in front of a closed door. At the sight of Maura, his head instantly perked up, and he bounded toward her, his tail wagging furiously.

"Whoa! Bear!" Maura laughed as he rose up on hind legs. Two giant paws landed on her shoulders, and a wet tongue slathered her face. "I see your manners haven't improved."

"He's obviously happy to see you again."

"And I'm glad to see you, too," Maura whispered as she gave the dog a hug. He dropped back to all fours, and she could swear he was smiling at her.

"I'll leave you here then," said Lily. "Julian's been anxiously awaiting your arrival, so why don't you go on in?"

Maura waved goodbye, then slipped so quietly into the classroom that no one noticed her entrance. She stood in the corner and watched the bald and bespectacled teacher write the week's schedule on the chalkboard in a thin and skittery hand.

"Eight A.M. sharp, we will gather at the lake," he said. "If you're late, you *will* be left behind. And you'll miss your chance to see a rare specimen of *Amanita bisporigera,* which just popped up after the last rain. Bring boots and rain gear. It could get muddy."

Even from behind, Julian "Rat" Perkins was easy to spot among the two dozen students gathered around Professor Pasquantonio's demonstration table. At sixteen, he was already built like a man, with broad shoulders that had grown even more muscular since she'd last seen him. She'd relied on those same shoulders last winter, when together they'd struggled to survive in the Wyoming mountains, a battle that had forged a deep and lasting bond between them. Julian was as close to a son as she would ever know, and she saw with pride how straight he stood, how attentive he seemed, even as Professor Pasquantonio droned on in a voice that whined like a mosquito.

"I want all your plant toxicity reports turned in by Friday, before most of you leave for the trip to Quebec. And don't forget we have the mushroom identification quiz on Wednesday. Class dismissed."

Turning to leave, Julian glimpsed Maura and his face lit up with a grin. In two steps he crossed to her, his arms already spreading to give her a hug. But at the last instant, aware that his classmates were watching, he seemed to think better of it and she had to settle instead for a quick peck on the cheek, a clumsy clap on the shoulders.

"You finally got here! I've been waiting for you all afternoon."

"Well, now we have two whole weeks together." She brushed the dark forelock off his face and her hand lingered on his cheek, where she was startled to feel the first hint of a beard. He was growing up far too fast.

He blushed at her touch, and she realized that some of the students had not left the room but were standing around, watching. Most teenagers ignored the very existence of adults, but Julian's classmates seemed intrigued by this alien visitor to their world. They ranged from middle school to high school age, and their clothing ran the gamut as well, from a blond girl with torn blue jeans to a boy wearing dress slacks and an oxford shirt. All of them were staring at Maura.

"You're the medical examiner," said a girl in a miniskirt. "We heard you were coming."

Maura smiled. "Julian mentioned me?"

"Like, just about all the time. Are you going to teach a class?"

"A class?" She looked at Julian. "I hadn't planned to."

"We wanted to hear about forensic pathology," piped up an Asian boy. "In biology, we dissected frogs and fetal pigs, but that was just normal anatomy. It's not like the cool stuff you do with dead people."

Maura glanced around at the eager faces. Like so much of the public, their imaginations were probably fueled by too many TV cop shows and crime novels. "I'm not sure that topic would be appropriate," Maura said.

"Because we're kids?"

"Forensic pathology is a subject usually taught to medical students. Even most adults find the subject disturbing."

"We wouldn't," the Asian boy said. "But maybe Julian didn't tell you who we are."

What you are is *odd*, Maura thought as she

watched Julian's classmates exit, their exodus marked by shuffling shoes and creaking floors. In the silence that followed, Bear gave a bored whine and trotted over to lick Julian's hand.

"*Who we are?* What did he mean by that?" asked Maura.

It was the teacher who answered. "Like far too many of his classmates, young Mr. Chinn often engages his mouth before his brain. There's little point trying to decode any deeper meaning to adolescent babbling." The man peered sourly at Maura over his spectacles. "I'm Professor Pasquantonio. Julian told us you would be visiting this week, Dr. Isles." He glanced at the boy, and his lips twitched in a half smile. "He's a fine student, by the way. Needs work with his writing skills, hopelessly bad at spelling. But better than anyone at spotting unusual botanical specimens in the woods."

Laced though it was with criticism, the compliment made Julian grin. "I'll work on my spelling, Professor."

"Enjoy your visit with us, Dr. Isles," said Pasquantonio, gathering his notes and plant specimens from the demonstration table. "Lucky for you, it's quiet this time of year. Not so many noisy feet clomping up and down the stairs like elephants."

Maura noticed the clump of purple flowers the man was holding. "Monkshood."

Pasquantonio nodded. "*Aconitum.* Very good."

She scanned the other plant specimens he'd laid

out on the table. "Foxglove. Purple nightshade. Rhubarb."

"And this one?" He held up a twig with dried leaves. "Extra credit if you can tell me which flowering shrub this comes from."

"It's oleander."

He looked at her, his pale eyes lit up with interest. "Which doesn't even grow in this climate, yet you recognize it." He gave a deferential nod of his bald head. "I am impressed."

"I grew up in California, where oleander's common."

"I suspect you're also a gardener."

"Aspiring. But I am a pathologist." She looked at the botanical specimens arrayed on the table. "These are all poisonous plants."

He nodded. "And so beautiful, some of them. We grow monkshood and foxglove here, in our flower garden. Rhubarb's growing in our vegetable garden. And purple nightshade, with such sweet little blossoms and berries, springs up everywhere as a common weed. All around us, so prettily disguised, are the instruments of death."

"And you're teaching this to children?"

"They have need of this knowledge as much as anyone else. It reminds them that the natural world is a dangerous place, as you well know." He set the specimens on a shelf and scooped up pages of notes. "A pleasure to meet you, Dr. Isles," he said before turning to Julian. "Mr. Perkins, your friend's visit will not serve as an excuse for late homework. Just so we're clear on that matter."

"Yes, sir," said Julian solemnly. He maintained that sober expression until Professor Pasquantonio was well down the hall and out of earshot, then he burst out in a laugh. "Now you know why we call him Poison Pasky."

"He doesn't seem like the friendliest of teachers."

"He's not. He'd rather talk to his plants."

"I hope your other teachers aren't quite as strange."

"We're *all* strange here. That's why it's such an interesting place. Like Ms. Saul says, normal is so boring."

She smiled at him. Touched his face again. This time he didn't shrink away. "You sound happy here, Rat. Do you get along with everyone?"

"Better than I ever did at home."

Home, in Wyoming, had been a grim place for Julian. In school he'd been a D-minus student, bullied and ridiculed, known not for any academic achievement but for his scrapes with the law and his schoolyard fistfights. At sixteen, he'd seemed bound for a future prison cell.

So there was truth to what Julian had just said, about being strange. He was not normal, and he never would be. Cast out by his own family, thrust alone into the wilderness, he'd learned to rely on himself. He had killed a man. Although that killing was in self-defense, the spilling of another's blood

changes you forever, and she wondered how deeply
that memory still haunted him.

He took her hand. "Come on, I want to show
you around."

"Ms. Saul showed me the library."

"Have you been to your room yet?"

"No."

"It's in the old wing, where all the important
guests go. That's where Mr. Sansone stays whenever he visits. Your room has a big old stone fireplace. When Briana's aunt visited, she forgot to
open the flue, and the room filled with smoke. They
had to evacuate the whole building. So you'll remember that, right? About the flue?" *And you
won't embarrass me* was the unspoken message.

"I'll remember. Who's Briana?"

"Just a girl here."

"*Just* a girl?" With his dark hair and piercing
eyes, Julian was growing into a handsome young
man who'd one day catch many a woman's eye.
"Details, please."

"She's no one special."

"Did I just see her in class?"

"Yeah. She had long black hair. A *really* short
skirt."

"Oh. You mean the pretty one."

"I guess."

She laughed. "Come on. Don't tell me you haven't
noticed."

"Well, yeah. But I think she's kind of a jerk. Even
if I do feel sorry for her."

"Sorry for her? Why?"

He looked at her. "She's here because her mom got murdered."

Suddenly Maura regretted how blithely she'd pried into his friendships. Teenage boys were a mystery to her, hulking creatures with big feet and simmering hormones, vulnerable one moment, cold and remote the next. As much as she wanted to be a mother to him, she would never be good at it, would never have a mother's instincts.

She was silent as she followed him down the third-floor hallway, where the walls were hung with paintings of medieval villages and banqueting tables and an ivory-skinned Madonna with child. Her guest room was near the end of the hall; when she stepped inside she saw that her suitcase had already been delivered and was resting on a cherry-wood luggage rack. From the arched window, she could see a walled garden adorned with stone statues. Beyond that wall the forest pressed in, like an invading army.

"You're facing east, so you'll get a nice view of the sunrise tomorrow."

"All the views are beautiful in this place."

"Mr. Sansone thought you'd like this room. It's the quietest."

She remained at the window, her back turned to him as she asked: "Has he been here lately?"

"He came about a month ago. He always comes for meetings of the Evensong school board."

"When is the next one?"

"Not till next month." He paused. "You really like him. Don't you?"

Her silence was far too revealing. She said, matter-of-factly, "He's been a generous man." She turned to face Julian. "We both owe him a great deal."

"Is that really all you have to say about him?"

"What else would there be?"

"Well, you asked me about Briana. I figured I'd ask about Mr. Sansone."

"Point taken," she admitted.

But his question hung in the air, and she didn't know how to answer it. *You really like him, don't you?*

She turned to look at the elaborately carved four-poster bed, at the oak wardrobe. Perhaps they were more antiques from Sansone's home. Though the man himself was not here, she saw his influence everywhere, from the priceless art on the walls to the leather-bound books in the library. The isolation of this castle, the locked gate and private road, reflected his obsession with privacy. The one jarring note in the room hung above the mantelpiece. It was an oil portrait of an arrogant-looking gentleman in a huntsman's coat, a rifle propped over his shoulder, one boot resting on a fallen stag.

"That's Cyril Magnus," said Julian.

"The man who built this castle?"

"He was really into hunting. Up in the attic, there's a ton of mounted animal trophies that he brought back from all over the world. They used to hang in the dining hall until Dr. Welliver said all those stuffed heads ruined her appetite, and she told Mr. Roman to take them down. They got into this big fight about whether the trophies glorified violence. Finally Headmaster Baum had us all vote on it, even the students. That's when the heads got taken down."

She didn't know any of these people he was talking about, a sad reminder that she was not part of his world here, that he now had his own life far away and independent of her. Already she felt left behind.

". . . and now Dr. Welliver and Mr. Roman are fighting about whether students should learn to hunt. Mr. Roman said yes, because it's an ancient skill, but Dr. Welliver says it's barbaric. Then Mr. Roman pointed out that Dr. Welliver eats meat, so that qualifies her as a barbarian, too. Boy, did that get her mad!"

As Maura unpacked jeans and hiking boots, hung up blouses and a dress in the wardrobe, Julian chattered about his classmates and teachers, about the catapult they'd built in Ms. Saul's class, about their wilderness trip when a black bear had sauntered into their camp.

"And I'll bet you were the one who chased that bear away," she said with a smile.

"No, Mr. Roman scared him off. No bear wants to tangle with *him*."

"Then he must be a seriously scary man."

"He's the forester. You'll meet him at dinner tonight. If he shows up."

"Doesn't he have to eat?"

"He's avoiding Dr. Welliver, because of the argument I told you about."

Maura closed the dresser drawer. "And who's this Dr. Welliver, who hates hunting so much?"

"She's our psychologist. I see her every other Thursday."

She turned and frowned at him. "Why?"

"Because I have issues. Like everyone here."

"What issues are you talking about?"

He looked at her in puzzlement. "I thought you knew. That's the reason I'm here, the reason all the students were chosen for Evensong. Because we're different from regular kids."

She thought of the class she'd just visited, the two dozen students gathered around Poison Pasky's demonstration table. They'd seemed like any other cross section of American teenagers.

"What, exactly, is different about you?" she asked.

"The way I lost my mom. It's the same thing that makes all the kids here different."

"The other students have lost parents as well?"

"Some of them. Or they've lost sisters or brothers. Dr. Welliver helps us deal with the anger. The nightmares. And Evensong teaches us how to fight back."

She thought of how Julian's mother had died. Thought of how violent crime ripples through families, through neighborhoods, through generations. *Evensong teaches us how to fight back.*

"When you say the other kids have lost their parents or sisters or brothers," said Maura, "do you mean . . ."

"Murder," said Julian. "That's what we all have in common."

# EIGHT

THERE WAS A NEW FACE IN THE DINING HALL tonight.

For weeks Julian had been talking about this visitor Dr. Isles, and about her work in the Boston medical examiner's office cutting up dead people. He'd never mentioned that she was also beautiful. Dark-haired and slender, with a quietly intense gaze, she looked so much like Julian that they could almost be mother and son. And Dr. Isles looked at Julian the way a mother would look at her own child, with obvious pride, attentive to every word he said.

No one will ever look at me that way again, thought Claire Ward.

Seated at her usual solitary spot in the corner, Claire kept her eye on Dr. Isles, noting how elegantly the woman used a knife and fork to cut her meat. From this table, Claire could see everything that went on in the dining hall. She did not mind sitting alone; it meant she didn't have to engage in pointless conversations and could keep an eye on what everyone else was doing. And this corner was the only place she felt comfortable, with her back to the wall, where no one could creep up behind her.

Tonight on the menu were consommé, a salad of baby lettuces, beef Wellington with roasted potatoes and asparagus, and a lemon tart for dessert. It meant juggling an array of forks and spoons and cutlery, something that had confused Claire when she first arrived at Evensong a month ago. In Bob and Barbara Buckley's house in Ithaca, dinners had been far simpler, involving only a knife, a fork, and a paper towel or two.

There'd never been any beef Wellington.

She missed Bob and Barbara far more than she'd ever imagined she would. Missed them almost as much as she missed her parents, whose deaths two years ago had left her with distressingly foggy memories that were fading fast day by day. But the deaths of Bob and Barbara were still raw, still painful, because it was all her fault. If she hadn't sneaked out of the house that night, if Bob and Barbara hadn't been forced to go searching for her, they might still be alive.

*Now they're dead. And I'm eating a lemon tart.*

She set down her fork and stared past the other students, who mostly ignored her, just as she ignored them. Once again she focused on the table where Julian sat with Dr. Isles. The lady who sliced dead people. Usually Claire avoided looking at adults, because they made her uneasy and they asked too many questions. Especially Dr. Anna Welliver, the school shrink, with whom Claire spent every Wednesday afternoon. Dr. Welliver was nice enough, a big and frizzy-haired grandma type, but she always asked the same questions. Did Claire still have trouble sleeping? What did she remember about her parents? Were the nightmares any better? As if talking about it, thinking about it, would make the nightmares go away.

*And all of us here have nightmares.*

When she looked around the dining hall at her classmates, Claire saw what a casual observer would probably miss. How Lester Grimmett kept glancing at the door, to assure himself that there was an open escape route. That Arthur Toombs's arms were rippled with ugly burn scars. That Bruno Chinn frantically shoveled food into his mouth, so that his phantom abductor wouldn't snatch it away from him. All of us have been marked, she thought, but some of our scars are more apparent than others.

She touched her own. It was hidden beneath her long blond hair, a ridge of scar tissue that marked the spot where the surgeons had sliced her scalp and sawed open her skull to remove blood and bullet fragments. No one else could see the damage, but she never forgot it was there.

Lying awake later that night, Claire was still rubbing that scar, and she wondered what her brain looked like beneath it. Did brains have scars as well, like this knotted ridge of skin? One of the doctors—she didn't remember his name, there'd been so many in that London hospital—told her that children's brains recovered better than adults' did, that she was lucky to be only eleven years old when she was shot. *Lucky* was the word he'd actually used, stupid doctor. He'd been mostly right about her recovery. She could walk and talk like everyone else. But her grades now sucked because she had trouble concentrating on anything for more than ten minutes, and she too quickly lost her temper in ways that scared her, ways that left her ashamed. While she didn't *look* damaged, she knew she was. And that damage was the reason she was now lying wide awake at midnight. As usual.

There was no point wasting her time in bed.

She rose and turned on the light. Her three roommates had gone home for the summer, so she had the room to herself and could come and go without anyone ratting her out. In seconds she was dressed and slipping out into the hall.

That's when she spotted the nasty note taped to her door: *Dain Bramaged!*

It was the bitch Briana again, she thought. Briana, who whispered *retard* whenever Claire passed by, who'd laughed hysterically in class when Claire tripped over some strategically placed foot. Claire had retaliated by sneaking a handful of slimy earthworms into Briana's bed. Oh, the shrieks had been worth it!

Claire yanked the note off the door, went back into her room for a pen, and scrawled: *Better check your sheets.* On her way down the hall, she slapped the note on Briana's dorm room door and kept walking, past rooms where other classmates slept. On the stairway, her shadow flitted along the wall like a twin spirit spiraling down beside her. She stepped out the front door and walked out into the moonlight.

The night was strangely warm and the wind smelled like dry grass, as if it had blown in from a great distance, bringing with it the scent of prairies and deserts and places she would never go. She drew in a deep breath, and for the first time all day, she felt free. Free of classes, of teachers watching her, of Briana's taunts.

She moved down the stone steps, sure of her footing in the bright moonlight. The lake lay ahead, where rippling water sparkled like sequins, calling to her. She started pulling up her T-shirt, eager to glide into that silky water.

"You're out again," a voice said.

Claire spun around to see the figure separate itself from the shadow of the trees. A figure she instantly recognized by the chunky silhouette. Will Yablonski moved into the moonlight, where she saw his chubby-cheeked face. She wondered if he knew that Briana whispered *great white whale* behind his back. *That much Will and I have in common,* she thought. *We're the uncool kids.*

"What are you doing out here?" she said.

"I was looking through my telescope. But the moon's come up now, so I packed up the scope for the night." He pointed toward the lake. "That's a really good spot over there, by the water. Just right for searching the sky."

"What are you looking for?"

"A comet."

"Did you see it?"

"No, I mean a *new* comet. One that's never been reported. Amateurs find new ones all the time. There's this guy named Don Machholz who found eleven of them, and he's just an amateur like me. If I find one, I get to name it. Like Comet Kohoutek. Or Halley or Shoemaker-Levy."

"What would you call yours?"

"Comet Neil Yablonski."

She laughed. "Like *that* has a ring to it."

"I don't think it sounds so bad," he said quietly. "It's in memory of my dad."

She heard the sorrow in his voice and wished she hadn't laughed. "Yeah, I guess that'd be pretty neat. Giving it your dad's name," she said. Even if *Comet Yablonski* did sound stupid.

"I saw you a few nights ago," he said. "What do *you* do out here?"

"I can't sleep." She turned to look at the water and imagined swimming across lakes, across oceans. Dark water didn't scare her; it made her feel alive, like a mermaid returning home. "I hardly sleep. Ever since . . ."

"Do you get nightmares, too?" he asked.

"I just don't sleep. It's because my brain's all messed up."

"What do you mean?"

"I have this scar here, on my head, where the doctors sawed open my skull. They dug out pieces of the bullet and it damaged things inside. So I don't sleep."

"People *have* to sleep or they die. How can you go without it?"

"I just don't sleep as much as everyone else. A few hours, that's all." She took a breath of the summer-scented wind. "Anyway, I like the nighttime. I like how quiet it is. How there are animals that you don't see during the day, like owls and skunks. Sometimes I go walking in the woods, and I see their eyes."

"Do you remember mc, Claire?"

The question, asked so softly, made her turn to him in puzzlement. "I see you every day in class, Will."

"No, I mean do you remember me from somewhere else? Before we came to Evensong?"

"I didn't know you before."

"Are you sure?"

She stared at him in the moonlight. Saw a big head with a moon-like face. That was the thing about Will, he was big all over, from his head to his enormous feet. Big and soft, like a marshmallow. "What are you talking about?"

"When I first got here, when I saw you in the dining hall, I had this weird feeling. Like I met you before."

"I was living in Ithaca. Where were you?"

"In New Hampshire. With my aunt and uncle."

"I've never been to New Hampshire."

He moved closer, so close that his big head eclipsed the rising moonlight. "And I used to live in Maryland. Two years ago, when my mom and dad were alive. Does that mean anything to you?"

She shook her head. "I wouldn't remember. I even have trouble remembering my own mom and dad. What their voices were like. Or how they laughed or smelled."

"That's really sad. That you don't remember them."

"I have photo albums, but I hardly look at them. It's like seeing pictures of strangers."

His touch startled her, and she flinched. She did not like people touching her. Not since she'd awakened in that London hospital, where a touch usually meant another needle prick, another person inflicting pain, however well intentioned. "Evensong's supposed to be our family now," he said.

"Yeah." She snorted. "That's what Dr. Welliver keeps saying. That we're all one big happy *family*."

"It's nice to believe that, don't you think? That we'll all look out for each other?"

"Sure. And I believe in the Tooth Fairy. People don't look out for each other. They only look out for themselves."

A beam of light flickered through the trees. She whirled around, spotted the approaching car, and instantly darted toward the nearest bush. Will followed her, moving like a noisy moose with his giant feet. He dropped down beside her.

"Who's arriving at this time of night?" he whispered.

A dark sedan rolled to a stop in the courtyard, and a man stepped out, tall and lean as a panther. He paused beside his car and scanned the night, as though searching the darkness for what no one else could see. For one frantic instant Claire thought he was looking directly at her, and she ducked lower behind the bush, trying to hide from his all-seeing eyes.

The school's front door swung open, throwing light onto the courtyard, and Headmaster Gottfried Baum stood in the doorway. "Anthony!" Baum called out. "Thank you for coming so quickly."

"These are disturbing developments."

"So it seems. Come, come. Your room's ready, and there's a meal waiting for you."

"I ate on the plane. We should get straight to the matter at hand."

"Of course. Dr. Welliver's been monitoring the situation in Boston. She's ready to intercede if necessary."

The front door swung shut. Claire rose to her feet, wondering who this strange visitor was. And why Headmaster Baum had sounded so nervous. "I'm going to check out his car," she said.

"Claire, no," whispered Will.

But she was already moving toward the sedan. The hood was still warm from the drive, the waxed surface gleaming under moonlight. She moved around the vehicle, her hand caressing the surface. She knew it was a Mercedes because of the hood ornament. Black, sleek, expensive. A rich man's car.

Locked, of course.

"Who is he?" said Will. He'd finally found the courage to emerge from the bush and he now stood beside her.

She looked up at the west wing, where a silhouette briefly appeared in a lit window. Then the curtains abruptly slid shut, cutting off her view.

"We know his name is Anthony."

# NINE

**M**AURA DID NOT SLEEP SOUNDLY THAT NIGHT. Perhaps it was the unfamiliar bed; perhaps it was the stillness of the place, a silence so deep that it seemed the night itself was holding its breath, waiting. When she awakened for the third time, the moon had risen and was shining directly in her window. She'd left the curtains open for fresh air, but now she climbed out of bed to close them against the glare. Pausing at the window, she looked down at the garden below. It was aglow in moonlight, the stone statues as luminous as ghosts.

*Did one of them just move?*

She stood clutching the drape, staring at statues that stood like chess pieces among the clipped hedges. Across that spectral landscape moved a slender figure with long silver-bright hair and limbs as graceful as a nymph's. It was a girl, walking in the garden.

In the hallway outside her door, footsteps creaked past. She heard men's voices.

". . . We're not sure whether the threat is real or imagined, but Dr. Welliver seems convinced."

"The police seem to have the situation in hand. All we can do is wait and see."

*I know that voice.* Maura pulled on a bathrobe and opened her door. "Anthony," she called out.

Anthony Sansone turned to face her. Dressed in black, standing beside the much shorter Gottfried Baum, Sansone seemed a towering, almost sinister figure in that dimly lit hallway. She noticed his wrinkled clothes, the fatigue in his eyes, and understood that his journey here had been a long one.

"I'm sorry if we woke you, Maura," he said.

"I had no idea you were coming to the school."

"Just a few issues to deal with." He smiled, a wary smile that did not reach his eyes. She sensed a troubling tension in that hallway. She saw it in Gottfried Baum's face, and in the cool distance with which Sansone now regarded her. He'd never been an openly warm man, and there had been times when she'd wondered if he even disliked her. Tonight that reserve was more impenetrable than ever.

"I need to talk to you," she said. "It's about Julian."

"Of course. In the morning, maybe? I won't be leaving until the afternoon."

"You're here for such a short time?"

He gave an apologetic shrug. "I wish I could stay longer. But you can always discuss any concerns with Gottfried here."

"*Do* you have concerns, Dr. Isles?" asked Gott-fried.

"Yes, I do. About why Julian's here. Evensong isn't just any boarding school, is it?"

She saw a glance pass between the men.

"That subject would be better left for tomorrow," Sansone said.

"I do need to talk about this. Before you vanish again."

"We will, I promise." He gave a brisk nod. "Good night, Maura."

She closed her door, troubled by his remoteness. The last time they had spoken was only two months ago, when he had stopped at her house to drop off Julian for a visit. They'd lingered on the porch, smiling at each other, and he'd seemed reluctant to leave. *Or did I imagine it? Have I ever been wise about men?*

Her track record was certainly dismal enough. For the last two years she'd been trapped in an affair with a man she could never have, an affair she'd known would end badly, yet she'd been as helpless as a junkie to resist it. That's what falling in love really amounted to, your brain on drugs. Adrenaline and dopamine, oxytocin and serotonin. Chemical insanity, celebrated by poets.

*This time, I swear I'll be wiser.*

She went back to the window to shut the curtains and block the moonlight, said to be yet another source of insanity so praised by those same witless poets. Only as she reached for the drapes did she remember the figure that she'd spotted earlier. Staring down at the garden, she saw statues in a silvery landscape of shadows and moonlight. Nothing moved.

The girl was gone.

OR HAD SHE EVER *been there*? Maura wondered the next morning when she looked out that same window and saw a gardener crouched below, wielding hedge clippers. A rooster crowed, loudly and lustily, proclaiming his authority. It seemed a perfectly normal morning, the sun shining, the cock crowing again and again. But last night, under moonlight, how unearthly everything had seemed.

Someone knocked on her door. It was Lily Saul, who greeted her with a cheerful "Good morning! We're meeting in the curiosities room, if you'd like to join us."

"Which meeting is this?"

"To address your concerns about Evensong. Anthony said you had questions, and we're ready to answer them." She gestured toward the staircase. "It's downstairs, across from the library. There'll be coffee waiting for us."

Maura found far more than just coffee waiting for her when she walked into the curiosities room. Lining the walls were glass cabinets filled with artifacts: carved figurines and ancient stone tools, arrowheads and animal bones. The yellowed labels told her this was an old collection, perhaps owned by Cyril Magnus himself. At any other time she would have lingered over these treasures, but the five people already seated at the massive oak table demanded her attention.

Sansone rose from his chair and said, "Good morning, Maura. You already know Gottfried Baum, our headmaster. Next to him is Ms. Duplessis, who teaches literature. Our botany professor, David Pasquantonio. And this is Dr. Anna Welliver, our school psychologist." He gestured to the smiling, big-boned woman to his right. In her early sixties, with silver hair springing out in a cheerfully undisciplined mane, Dr. Welliver looked like an aging hippie in her high-necked granny dress.

"Please, Dr. Isles," said Gottfried, pointing to the coffee carafe and the tray of croissants and jams. "Help yourself."

As Maura took a seat beside Headmaster Baum, Lily placed a steaming cup of coffee in front of her. The croissants looked buttery and tempting, but Maura took only a sip of coffee and focused on Sansone, who faced her from the far end of the table.

"You have questions about our school and our students," he said. "These are the people who have the answers." He nodded to his associates around the table. "Please, let's hear your concerns, Maura."

His uncharacteristic formality unsettled her; so did this setting, surrounded by oddities in cabinets, and by people she scarcely knew.

She answered him with equal formality. "I don't believe Evensong is the right school for Julian."

Gottfried raised an eyebrow in surprise. "Has he told you he's unhappy, Dr. Isles?"

"No."

"Do you think he's unhappy?"

She paused. "No."

"Then what is the nature of your concern?"

"Julian has been telling me about his classmates. He says that a number of them have lost family members to violence. Is this true?"

Gottfried nodded. "For many of our students."

"Many? Or most?"

He gave a conciliatory shrug. "Most."

"So this is a school for victims."

"Oh, dear, not victims," Dr. Welliver said. "We like to think of them as *survivors*. They come to us with special needs. And we know exactly how to help them."

"Is that why you're here, Dr. Welliver? To address their emotional needs?"

Dr. Welliver gave her an indulgent smile. "Most schools have counselors."

"But they don't keep therapists on staff."

"True." The psychologist looked around the table at her colleagues. "We're proud to say we're unique that way."

"Unique because you specialize in traumatized children." She looked around the table. "In fact, you recruit them."

"Maura," said Sansone, "child protective agencies around the country send children to us because we offer what other schools can't. A sense of safety. A sense of order."

"And a sense of purpose? Is that what you're really trying to instill?" She looked around the table at the six faces watching her. "You're all members of the Mephisto Society. Aren't you?"

"Maybe we could try to stay on topic?" suggested Dr. Welliver. "And focus on what we do here at Evensong."

"I am talking about Evensong. About how you're using this school to recruit soldiers for your organization's paranoid mission."

"Paranoid?" Dr. Welliver gave a surprised laugh. "That's hardly a diagnosis I'd make of anyone in this room."

"The Mephisto Society believes that evil is real. You believe that humanity itself is under attack, and your mission is to defend it."

"Is *that* what you think we're doing here? Training demon hunters?" Welliver shook her head in amusement. "Trust me, our role is hardly metaphysical. We help children recover from violence and tragedy. We give them structure, safety, and a superb education. We prepare them for university or whatever their goals may be. You visited Professor Pasquantonio's class yesterday. You saw how engaged the students are, even with a subject like botany."

"He was showing them poisonous plants."

"And that's precisely why they were interested," said Pasquantonio.

"Because the subtext was murder? Which plants can be used to kill?"

"That's your interpretation. Others would call it a class on safety. How to recognize and avoid what could harm them."

"What else do you teach here? Ballistics? Blood splatters?"

Pasquantonio shrugged. "Neither would be out of place in a physics class. What is your objection?"

"My objection is that you're using these children to advance your own agenda."

"Against violence? Against the evils that men do to one another?" Pasquantonio snorted. "You make it sound like we're pushing drugs or training gangsters."

"We're helping them heal, Dr. Isles," Lily said. "We know what it's like to be crime victims. We help them find purpose in their pain. Just as we do."

*We know what it's like.* Yes, Lily Saul would know; she'd lost her family to murder. And Sansone had lost his father to murder as well.

Maura looked at the six faces and felt a chilling sense of comprehension. "You've all lost someone," she said.

Gottfried gave a mournful nod. "My wife," he said. "A robbery in Berlin."

"My sister," said Ms. Duplessis. "Raped and strangled in Detroit."

"My husband," Dr. Welliver said softly, her head bowed. "Kidnapped and murdered in Buenos Aires."

Maura turned to Pasquantonio, who stared down in silence at the table. He did not answer the question; he didn't need to. The answer was there, in his face. She suddenly thought of her own twin sister, murdered only a few years earlier. And Maura realized: *I belong in this circle. Like them, I mourn someone lost to violence.*

"We understand these children," said Dr. Welliver. "That's why Evensong is the best place for them. Maybe the only place for them. Because they're one of us. We are all one family."

"Of victims."

"Not victims. We're the ones who *lived*."

"Your students may be survivors," said Maura, "but they're also just children. They can't choose for themselves. They can't object."

"Object to what?" said Dr. Welliver.

"To joining this army of yours. That's what you think you are, an army of the righteous. You gather up the wounded and turn them into warriors."

"We nurture them. Give them a way to spring back from adversity."

"No, you keep them in a place where they'll never be allowed to forget. By surrounding them with other victims, you take away any chance of them seeing the world the way other children do. Instead of light, they see darkness. They see evil."

"Because it's there. Evil," Pasquantonio whispered. He sat hunched in his chair, his head still bowed. "The proof of it comes from their own lives. They merely see what they already know exists." Slowly he lifted his head and looked at her with pale and watery eyes. "As do you."

"No," she said. "What I see in my work is the result of violence. This thing you call *evil* is merely a philosophical term."

"Call it what you will. These children know the truth. It's burned into their memories."

Gottfried said, reasonably, "We provide them with the knowledge and skills to make a difference in the world. We inspire them to take action, just as other private schools do. Military academies teach discipline. Religious schools teach piety. College preps emphasize academics."

"And Evensong?"

"We teach resilience, Dr. Isles," Gottfried answered.

Maura regarded the faces around the table, evangelists all. And their recruits were the wounded and vulnerable, children who had not been given a choice.

She rose to her feet. "Julian doesn't belong here. I'll find another school for him."

"I'm afraid that's not your decision," said Dr. Welliver. "You don't have legal custody of the boy."

"I'll petition the state of Wyoming."

"I understand you had the chance to do that six months ago. You declined."

"Because I thought this school was the right place for him."

"It *is* the right place for him, Maura," said Sansone. "To pull him from Evensong would be a mistake. One that you'll regret." Was that a warning in his voice? She tried to read his face, but like so many times before, she failed.

"This is up to Julian, don't you think?" Dr. Welliver said.

"Yes, of course it is," said Maura. "But I'm going to tell him exactly how I feel about this."

"Then I suggest you take the time to understand what we're doing here."

"I *do* understand."

"You just got here yesterday, Dr. Isles," Lily said. "You haven't seen what we offer the children. You haven't walked in our forest, seen our stables and farm, observed all the skills they're picking up here. Everything from archery to growing their own food to learning how to survive in the wilderness. I know you're a scientist. Shouldn't you base your decisions on facts and not emotions?"

This made Maura pause, because what Lily said was true. She had not yet explored Evensong. She had no idea if there was a better alternative for Julian.

"Give us a chance," said Lily. "Take the time to meet our students, and you'll see why Evensong is the one place that can help them. As an example, we've just taken in two new kids. Both of them have survived two separate massacres. First their parents were killed, then their *foster* parents. Imagine how deep *their* wounds must go, to be twice orphaned, twice a survivor." Lily shook her head.

"I don't know of another school that would understand their pain the way we can."

*Twice orphaned. Twice a survivor.* "These children," Maura said softly. "Which ones are they?"

"The names don't matter," said Dr. Welliver. "What matters is that they *need* Evensong."

"I want to know who they *are*." Maura's sharp demand seemed to startle them all.

A silence passed before Lily asked: "Why do their names make a difference?"

"You said there were two of them."

"A boy and a girl."

"Are their cases related?"

"No. Will came to us from New Hampshire. Claire came from Ithaca, New York. Why do you ask?"

"Because I just performed autopsies on a family in Boston, killed in a home invasion. There was one survivor in the house, their foster child. A boy of fourteen. A boy who was orphaned two years ago when his family was massacred." She looked around the table at the stunned faces. "He's just like your two students. Twice orphaned. Twice a survivor."

# TEN

IT WAS A STRANGE PLACE TO MEET.

Jane stood on the sidewalk, eyeing the blacked-out windows where the words ARABIAN NIGHTS were stenciled in flaking gold letters over the painted figure of a buxom woman in harem pants. The door suddenly opened and a man stumbled out. He wobbled for a moment, squinting in the daylight, and headed unsteadily down the street, trailing the sour scent of booze.

As Jane stepped into the establishment, an even stronger whiff of alcohol hit her full in the face. Inside, it was so dim that she could barely make out the silhouettes of two men hunched at the bar, nursing their drinks. Gaudy cushions and camel bells decorated the velvet-upholstered booths, and she half expected a belly dancer to come tinkling by with a tray of cocktails.

"Get ya something, miss?" the bartender called out, and the two patrons swiveled around to stare at her.

"I'm here to meet someone," she said.

"I'm guessing you want that guy in the back booth."

A voice called out: "I'm here, Jane."

She nodded to the bartender and headed to the back booth where her father was sitting, almost swallowed up among poufy velvet cushions. A glass of what looked like whiskey sat on the table in front of him. It wasn't even five P.M. and he was already drinking, something she'd never seen him do before. Then again, Frank Rizzoli had recently done a lot of things she'd never thought he'd do.

Like walk out on his wife.

She slid onto the bench across from him and sneezed as she settled on dusty velvet. "Why the hell are we meeting here, Dad?" she asked.

"It's quiet. Good place to talk."

"*This* is where you hang out?"

"Lately. You want a drink?"

"No." She looked at the glass in front of him. "What's that all about?"

"Whiskey."

"No, I mean what's with drinking before five?"

"Who the hell made up that rule, anyway? What's so magic about five o'clock? Anyway, you know how the song goes. It's always five o'clock somewhere. Smart man, Jimmy Buffett."

"Aren't you supposed to be at work?"

"I called in sick. So sue me." He took a sip of whiskey but didn't seem to enjoy it, and set the glass back down. "You don't talk to me much these days, Jane. It hurts."

"I don't know who you are anymore."

"I'm your father. That hasn't changed."

"Yeah, but you're like a pod person. You do things that my dad—my old dad—wouldn't do."

He sighed. "Insanity."

"That sounds about right."

"No, I mean it. The insanity of lust. Fucking hormones."

"My old dad wouldn't have used that word."

"Your old dad's a lot wiser now."

"Is he?" She leaned back, and her throat itched from the dust puffing up from the velvet upholstery. "Is that why you're trying to reconnect with me?"

"I never cut you off. *You* did."

"It's hard to keep connected when you're shacked up with another woman. There were weeks when you never bothered to call, even once. To check on *any* of us."

"I didn't dare. You were too pissed at me. And you took your mom's side."

"Can you blame me?"

"You have two parents, Jane."

"And one of them walked out. Broke Mom's heart and ran off with a bimbo."

"Your mom doesn't look too heartbroken to me."

"You know how many months it took for her to get to this point? How many nights she spent crying her eyes out? While you were out partying with what's-her-face, Mom was trying to figure out how to survive on her own. And she did it. I've got to hand it to her, she's landed on her feet and is doing fine. Great, in fact."

Those words seemed to hit him as hard as if she'd actually thrown a punch. Even in the gloom of that cocktail lounge she could see his face crumple, his shoulders fold forward. His head dropped into his hands, and she heard what sounded like a sob.

"Dad? Dad."

"You gotta stop her. She can't marry that man, she can't."

"Dad, I—" Jane glanced down at the cell phone vibrating on her belt. A quick glance told her it was a Maine area code, a number she didn't recognize. She let it go to voice mail and refocused on her father. "Dad, what's going on?"

"It was a mistake. If I could just turn back the clock . . ."

"I thought you were engaged to what's-her-name."

He took a deep breath. "Sandie called it off. And she kicked me out."

Jane didn't say a word. For a moment, the only sounds were the clink of ice cubes and the rattle of the cocktail shaker at the bar.

Head drooped, he murmured into his chest. "I'm staying at a cheap hotel around the corner from here. That's why I asked you to meet me here, 'cause this is where I hang out now." He gave a disbelieving laugh. "The fucking Arabian Nights cocktail lounge!"

"What happened between you two?"

He raised his eyes to hers. "Life. Boredom. I don't know. She said I couldn't keep up with her. That I was acting like an old fart, wanting my dinner cooked every night, and what was she, the maid?"

"Maybe now you appreciate Mom."

"Yeah, well, nobody beats your mom's cooking, that's for damn sure. So maybe I *was* unfair, expecting Sandie to measure up. But she didn't have to twist the knife, you know? Calling me *old*."

"*Ouch*. That's gotta sting."

"I'm only sixty-two! Just 'cause she's fourteen years younger doesn't make her some spring chicken. But that's how she sees me, too old for her. Too old to be worth . . ." He dropped his head in his hands again.

Lust fades and then you see your new and exciting lover in the harsh light of day. Sandie Huffington must have woken up one morning, looked at Frank Rizzoli, and noticed the lines in his face, the sag of his jowls. When the hormones were spent, what was left was sixty-two years old, and going flabby and bald. She'd snagged another woman's husband and now she wanted to throw back the catch.

"You gotta help me," he said.

"You need money, Dad?"

His head snapped up. "No! I'm not asking for that! I got a job, why would I need your money?"

"Then what do you need?"

"I need you to talk to your ma. Tell her I'm sorry."

"She should hear that from you."

"I tried to tell her, but she doesn't want to hear me out."

Jane sighed. "Okay, okay. I'll tell her."

"And . . . and ask her when I can come home."

She stared at him. "You're kidding."

"What's that look on your face?"

"You expect Mom to let you move back in?"

"Half the house is mine."

"You'll kill each other."

"A bad idea to have your parents together again? What kind of thing is that for a daughter to say?"

She took a deep breath, and when she spoke, it was slowly and clearly. "So you want to go back to Mom and be the way you were before. Is that what you're saying?" She rubbed her temples. "Holy shit."

"I want us to be a family again. Her, me, you and your brothers. Christmas and Thanksgiving together. All those great times, great meals."

*Mostly the great meals.*

"Frankie's on board," he said. "He wants it to happen. So does Mike. I just need you to talk to her, because she listens to you. You tell her to take me back. Tell her it's the way things were meant to be."

"What about Korsak?"

"Who gives a shit about him?"

"They're engaged. They're planning the wedding."

"She's not divorced yet. She's still my wife."

"It's only a matter of paperwork."

"It's a matter of *family*. A matter of *what's right*. Please, Jane, talk to her. And we can go back to being the Rizzolis again."

*The Rizzolis.* She thought about what that meant. A history. All the holidays and birthdays, together. Memories shared by no one else but them. There was a sacredness to that, something that should not be easily cast aside, and she was sentimental enough to mourn what had been lost. Now it could be reconstructed and made whole, Mom and Dad together again, as they'd always been. Frankie and Mike wanted it. Her dad wanted it.

And her mother? What did she want?

She thought of the pink taffeta bridesmaid's dress that Angela had so happily presented to her. Remembered the last time she and Gabriel had gone to her mother's house for dinner, when Angela and Korsak had giggled like teenagers and played footsie under the table. She looked across at her father and could not remember him ever playing footsie. Or giggling. Or slapping Angela's butt. What she saw was a tired and beaten man who'd gambled on a flaky blonde and lost. *If I were Mom, would I take him back?*

"Janie? Talk to her for me," he pleaded.

She sighed. "Okay."

"Do it soon. Before she gets too tight with that jerk."

"Korsak's not a jerk, Dad."

"How can you say that? He walked in and took what isn't his."

"He walked in because there was a vacancy. You understand, don't you, that things have changed since you left? Mom's changed."

"And I want her back the way she used to be. I'll do whatever it takes to make her happy. You tell her that. Tell her it'll be just like old times."

Jane looked down at her watch. "It's dinnertime. I've gotta go."

"You promise you'll do this for your old dad?"

"Yeah, I promise." She slid out of the booth, glad to escape the dusty cushions. "Take care of yourself."

He smiled at her, the first smile she'd seen since she'd arrived, and a hint of Frank Rizzoli's old cockiness returned. Dad, reclaiming his territory. "I will. Now that I know everything's gonna be okay."

*I wouldn't count on it,* she thought as she walked out of the Arabian Nights. She dreaded the conversation with Angela, dreaded her mother's reaction. Yelling would probably be involved. No matter what her mother decided, someone was going to get hurt. Either Korsak or her dad. And Jane had just gotten accustomed to the thought of Korsak joining the family. He was a big man with a big heart, and he loved Angela, of that there was no doubt. *Who will you choose, Mom?*

The looming conversation plagued her all the way home, darkening her mood through dinner, through Regina's bath time, through their evening rituals of the storybook and five bedtime kisses. When she finally closed Regina's bedroom door and walked to the kitchen to call Angela, it felt like a march to Death Row. She picked up the phone, hung up again, and sank with a sigh into a kitchen chair.

"You do know you're being manipulated," said Gabriel. He closed the dishwasher and started the wash cycle. "You don't have to do this, Jane."

"I promised Dad I'd call her."

"He's perfectly capable of calling Angela himself. It's wrong to put you in the middle of this. Their marriage is their problem."

She groaned and put her head in her hands. "Which makes it my problem."

"I'll just say it. Your dad's a coward. He screwed up big-time, and now he wants you to fix things."

"What if I'm the only one who can?"

Gabriel sat down, joining her at the kitchen table. "By talking your mother into taking him back?"

"I don't know what's best."

"Your mom's going to have to choose."

She lifted her head and looked at him. "What do you think she should do?"

He considered the question as the dishwasher

swished and hummed in the background. "I think she seems pretty happy right now."

"So you'd vote for Korsak."

"He's a decent man, Jane. He's kind to her. He won't hurt her."

"But he's not my dad."

"And that's why you shouldn't get involved. You're being forced to choose sides, and that's wrong for your father to do. Look what he's putting you through."

After a moment, she sat up straight. "You're right. I shouldn't have to do this. I'm going to tell him to call her himself."

"Don't feel guilty about it. If your mom wants your advice, she'll ask you."

"Yeah. Yeah, I'll tell him. Now what the hell's his new phone number?" She reached into her purse and dug out her cell phone to check the contacts list. Only then did she notice the message on her screen: ONE NEW VOICE MAIL. It was the call that had come in while she was talking to her father.

She played the message and heard Maura's voice:

. . . *two children here, a girl named Claire Ward and a boy, Will Yablonski. Jane, their stories are like Teddy Clock's. Real parents killed two years ago. Foster parents killed just last month. I don't know if this is related, but it's damn weird, don't you think?*

Jane replayed the recording twice, then dialed the number that Maura had called from.

After six rings, a woman answered: "Evensong School. This is Dr. Welliver."

"I'm Detective Jane Rizzoli, Boston PD. I'm trying to reach Dr. Maura Isles."

"I'm afraid she's gone for an evening canoe on the lake."

"I'll try her cell phone."

"We don't have a cell signal out here. That's why she used our landline."

"Then have her call me back when she can. Thank you." Jane hung up and stared at her phone for a moment, all thoughts of her parents temporarily forgotten. Instead she thought of Teddy Clock. The unluckiest boy in the world, Moore called him. But now she knew of two others just like him. Three unlucky children. Maybe there were more she didn't know about, foster children in other cities, being hunted even now.

"I have to go out," she said.

"What's going on?" asked Gabriel.

"I need to see Teddy Clock."

"Is there a problem?"

She grabbed her car keys and headed for the door. "I hope not."

It was dark by the time she reached the suburban foster home where Teddy had been temporarily placed. The house was an older but neatly kept white Colonial set back from the street and screened by leafy trees. Jane parked in the driveway and stepped out, into a warm night that smelled of freshly mown grass. It was quiet on this road, with only an occasional car passing by. Through the trees she could barely glimpse the lights of the neighbors next door.

She climbed the porch steps and rang the bell.

Mrs. Nancy Inigo answered, drying her hands on a dish towel. Her smiling face was streaked with flour, and gray hairs had come loose from her braid. The scent of cinnamon and vanilla wafted from inside, and Jane heard the sound of girls' laughter.

"You made it here in record time, Detective," said Nancy.

"I'm sorry if my phone call alarmed you."

"No, the girls and I are having a fine old time baking cookies. We just got the first batch out of the oven. Come on in."

"Is Teddy okay?" Jane asked softly as she stepped into the foyer.

Nancy gave a sigh. "I'm afraid he's hiding upstairs right now. Not really in the mood to join us in the kitchen. That's how he's been since he got here. Eats dinner, then goes into his room and shuts the door." She shook her head. "We asked the psychologist if we should coax him out, maybe take away his computer time and make him join us for family activities, but she said it's too soon. Or maybe Teddy's just afraid to get attached to us, because of what happened to the last . . ." Nancy paused. "Anyway, Patrick and I are taking it slow with him."

"Is Patrick here?"

"No, he's at Trevor's soccer practice. With four kids, there's never a moment to sit still."

"You two are really something, you know that?"

"We just like having kids around, that's all," Nancy said with a laugh. They walked into the kitchen, where two flour-dusted girls of about eight were pressing cookie cutters into a sheet of dough. "Once we got started taking them in, we couldn't seem to stop. Did you know we're already about to attend the fourth wedding? Patrick's walking another foster daughter down the aisle next month."

"That's going to add up to a lot of grandkids for you two."

Nancy grinned. "That's the whole idea."

Jane glanced around the kitchen, where countertops were covered with homework papers and schoolbooks and scattered mail. The happy disorder of a busy family. But she'd seen how instantly *normal* could vanish. She had stood in kitchens transformed by blood splatters, and just for an instant she imagined splatters on these cabinets. She blinked and the blood was gone, and once again she saw two eight-year-olds with sticky hands cutting star-shaped cookies.

"I'm going up to see Teddy," she said.

"Upstairs, second bedroom on the right. The one with the closed door." Nancy slid another cookie sheet into the oven and turned to look at her. "Be sure to knock first. He's particular about that. And don't be surprised if he doesn't want to talk. Just give him time, Detective."

We may not have much time, she thought as she climbed the stairs to the second floor. Not if other foster families were being attacked. She paused outside the boy's room and listened for the sound of a radio or TV, but heard only silence through the closed door.

She knocked. "Teddy? It's Detective Rizzoli. Can I come in?"

After a moment, the button lock clicked and the door swung open. Teddy's owlish pale face regarded her through the gap, blinking rapidly, his glasses askew as if he'd just woken up.

As she entered the room, he stood silent, thin as a scarecrow in his baggy T-shirt and jeans. It was a pleasant room painted lemon yellow, the curtains printed with African savanna scenes. The shelves contained children's books for various age levels, and on the walls hung cheery posters of Sesame Street characters, décor that was certainly too young for a smart fourteen-year-old like Teddy. Jane wondered how many other traumatized children had taken refuge in this room, had found comfort in this secure world created by the Inigos.

The boy had still not spoken.

She sat in a chair by Teddy's laptop computer, where a screensaver traced geometric lines across the monitor. "How are you doing?" she asked.

He shrugged.

"Why don't you sit down, so we can talk."

Obediently he sank onto the bed and sat with shoulders folded inward, as though he wanted to make himself as small and inconsequential as possible.

"Do you like it here with Nancy and Patrick?"

He nodded.

"Is there anything you need, anything I can bring you?"

A shake of the head.

"Teddy, don't you have *anything* to say?"

"No."

At last a word, even if it was only one.

"Okay." She sighed. "Then maybe I should just get to the point. I need to ask you about something."

"I don't know anything else." He seemed to shrink deeper into himself and mumbled into his chest. "I told you everything I remembered."

"And you helped us, Teddy. You really did."

"But you haven't caught him, have you? So you want me to tell you more."

"This isn't about that night. It's not even about you. It's about two other children."

Slowly his head lifted, and he looked at her. "I'm not the only one?"

She stared at eyes so colorless they seemed transparent, as if she could look right through him. "Do *you* think there are other kids like you?"

"I don't know. But you just said there were two other kids. What do they have to do with me?"

The boy might not say much, but obviously he listened and understood more than she realized.

"I'm not sure, Teddy. Maybe you can help me answer that question."

"Who are they? The other kids?"

"The girl's name is Claire Ward. Have you ever heard that name?"

He considered this for a moment. From the kitchen came the sounds of the oven door banging shut, the girls squealing, noises of a happy family. But in Teddy's room there was silence as the boy sat thinking. Finally, he gave a small shake of the head. "I don't think so."

"You're not sure?"

"Anything's possible. That's what my dad used to say. But I can't be sure."

"There's also a boy named Will Yablonski. Does that ring any bells?"

"Is his family dead, too?"

The question, asked so softly, made her heart ache for the boy. She moved close beside him, to place her arm around his pitifully thin shoulders. He sat stiffly beside her, as if her touch was simply something to endure. She kept her arm around him anyway as they sat on the bed, two mute companions joined by a tragedy neither could explain.

"Is the boy alive?" Teddy asked softly.

"Yes, he is."

"And the girl?"

"They're both safe. You are, too, I promise."

"No, I'm not." He looked at her, his gaze clear-eyed and steady, his voice matter-of-fact. "I'm going to die."

"Don't say that, Teddy. It's not true, and—"

Her words were cut off as the lights suddenly went out. In the darkness she heard the boy breathing loud and fast, and felt her own heart banging in her chest.

Nancy Inigo called out from the kitchen: "Detective Rizzoli? I think we must have blown a fuse!"

Of course that's all it is, thought Jane. A blown fuse. Things like this happen all the time.

The crack of shattering glass made Jane leap to her feet. In an instant she had her holster unsnapped, her hand on her Glock.

"Nancy!" she yelled.

Frantic footsteps came thumping up the stairs, and the two girls burst in, followed by the heavier footfalls of Nancy Inigo.

"It came from the front of the house!" said Nancy, her voice almost drowned out by the girls' panicked whimpers. "Someone's breaking in!"

And they were all trapped upstairs. Their only escape was through Teddy's window, which led to a two-story drop.

"Where's the nearest telephone?" Jane whispered.

"Downstairs. In my bedroom."

And Jane's cell phone was in her purse, which she'd left in the kitchen.

"Stay here. Lock the door," Jane ordered.

"What are you doing? Detective, don't leave us!"

But Jane was already headed out of the room. She heard the door close softly behind her, heard

Nancy snap the button lock. That lock was next to useless; it would delay an intruder for only the seconds it would take to kick down the flimsy door.

*First, he has to get past me.*

Gripping her weapon, she crept up the dark hallway. Whoever had broken the window was silent now. She heard only her own heartbeat and the rush of blood through her ears. At the top of the stairs she halted and dropped to a crouch. This was as far as she'd go. Only a fool would try to stalk a killer in the darkness, and her only priority was protecting Nancy and the children. No, she'd wait right here and pick him off as he climbed the stairs. *Come to Mama, asshole.*

Her eyes had finally adjusted to the gloom, and she could just make out the silhouette of the banister spiraling down into shadow. The only light was the faint glow through a downstairs window. Where was he, where was he? She heard no sound, no movement.

*Maybe he's no longer downstairs. Maybe he's already on the second floor, standing right behind me.*

In panic, her head snapped around, but she saw no monster looming behind.

Her attention swiveled back to the stairs just as an approaching car's headlights flared through the window. Car doors slammed shut, and she heard children's voices, footsteps thumping up the steps. The front door swung open and a man stood framed in the doorway.

"Hey, Nancy? What's with the lights?" he called

out. "I've got half the soccer team here, expecting cookies!"

The invasion of little boys sounded like a cattle stampede as they came clomping in, laughing and hooting in the darkness. Still crouched at the top of the stairs, Jane slowly lowered her weapon.

"Mr. Inigo?" she called out.

"Hello? Who's up there?"

"Detective Rizzoli. Do you have your cell phone?"

"Yeah. Where's Nancy?"

"I want you to call nine one one. And get those boys out of the house."

# ELEVEN

THE WINDOW IN THE DOWNSTAIRS STUDY WAS broken, and glass shards glittered like diamonds scattered across the floor.

"This appears to be the intruder's point of entry," said Frost. "We found the back door ajar, which is probably how he exited. The arrival of Mr. Inigo and all those noisy kids must have chased him off. As for dousing the lights, all the perp had to do was walk into the garage, open the fuse box, and flip the master switch."

Jane crouched down to stare at the oak floor, where the intruder's shoe had left a faint imprint of dirt. Through the broken window she heard the voices of the CSU team examining the soil outside for other footwear impressions, and in the driveway a patrol car's radio hissed and crackled. Reassuring sounds. But as she stared at the footprint on the floor, she felt her pulse pounding again, and remembered the smell of her own fear in the darkness. *If only I'd had the chance to take him down.*

"How did he find the boy?" she said. "How the hell did he know Teddy was here?"

"We can't be sure Teddy was his target. This house could have been a random pick."

"Come on, Frost." She looked up at her partner. "You don't really believe that, do you?"

There was a silence. "No," he admitted.

"Somehow he knew the boy was here."

"That info could have leaked out of Social Services. Boston PD. Any number of sources could have accidentally revealed it. Or the perp could've followed *you* here tonight. Anyone who saw you at the crime scene knows you're working the case."

Jane thought about her drive to the Inigos' house, tried to remember if there'd been anything unusual, any set of headlights that stood out in her rearview mirror. But headlights were anonymous and Boston traffic unremitting. If a killer followed me, she thought, then he knows my car. *And he knows where I live.*

Her cell phone rang. She pulled it from her purse, saw the Maine area code, and knew at once who was calling.

"Maura?" she answered.

"Dr. Welliver told me you got my message. It's quite a coincidence, isn't it? Two more children just like Teddy Clock. What do you think?"

"I think we've got a situation here. Someone just came after Teddy."

"*Again?*"

"The intruder actually got into the house. Luckily, I happened to be here."

"Are you all right? Is the boy?"

"Everybody's fine, but the perp took off. Now we've got to find a safer place to park the kid."

"I know a safe place. And it's right here."

A male CSU tech came into the room, and Jane fell silent as he and Frost talked about fingerprints on the back door and windowsill. This attack had left her shaken and suspicious of everyone, even the professionals with whom she worked. If I wasn't followed here, she thought, then someone must have leaked Teddy's location. Someone who might be working the crime scene at this very moment.

She went into a bathroom and closed the door to continue the conversation. "Tell me your situation there," she said. "Is it secure?"

"It's isolated. There's one road in, and it's gated. They have motion sensors along the road."

"Your surroundings?"

"Thirty thousand acres of private woodland. Theoretically someone could hike in, but then he'd have to get into the building itself. The door's massive, with a security keypad. All the windows are well above ground level. Plus, there's the staff."

"A bunch of schoolteachers? Oh, yeah, that's reassuring."

"They have a forester protecting the property and he's armed. The school's self-contained and has its own farm and generator."

"Still, we're talking teachers. Not bodyguards."

"Jane, they're all members of the Mephisto Society."

That made Jane pause. Anthony Sansone's bizarre little group kept track of violent crimes around the world, searching the data for patterns, seeking evidence that evil was real. That humanity itself was under attack. "You never told me they operated the school."

"I didn't know that until I got here."

"They're conspiracy theorists. They see monsters under every rock."

"Maybe this time they have a point."

"Don't get biblical on me. Not you, please."

"I'm not talking about demons. There *is* something going on here that we can't explain, something that connects these children. The school psychologist refuses to share the details because of patient confidentiality. But Lily Saul told me enough about Claire and Will to convince me there's a pattern here. And Evensong may be the one place these three children are safe."

"A school operated by a paranoid organization."

"Which makes them the perfect guardians. They chose this remote site because they can defend it."

There was a knock on the bathroom door. "Rizzoli?" called Frost. "The social worker's here to take the boy."

"Don't let anyone take him!"

"What do I tell her?"

"Hold on, I'll be out in a minute." She turned her

attention back to the phone. "Maura, I'm not sure I trust Sansone and his crowd."

"He's never failed to come through for us, you know that. And these people certainly have more resources than Boston PD could ever scrape together."

And there'd be no information leaks, thought Jane. No better place to keep a boy hidden from the world.

"How do I get there?" she asked.

"It's not easy to find. I'll have to email you the directions."

"Do it. I'll talk to you later." She disconnected and walked out of the bathroom.

In the living room, the social worker stood waiting with Frost. "Detective Rizzoli," she said, "we've arranged another placement for—"

"I've made alternative arrangements for Teddy," Jane said.

The social worker frowned. "But I thought we were going to place him."

"Teddy may have been the target tonight. Which means there could be more attacks. You don't want another foster family killed, do you?"

The woman lifted her hand to her mouth. "Oh God. Do you really think . . ."

"Exactly." Jane looked at Frost. "Can you make sure the Inigos have a safe place to go tonight? I'm going to take Teddy."

"Where?"

"I'll call you later. I'm going upstairs to pack a

bag for him. Then he and I are getting out of Dodge."

"You have to give me an idea, at least."

She glanced at the social worker, who was watching them, her jaw agape. "The fewer people who know, the safer it will be," she said. *For both of us.*

JANE DROVE NORTH INTO the dawn with one eye on the rearview mirror. In the backseat, Teddy slept through the entire journey. They'd stopped at her apartment just long enough for her to throw some clothes and toiletries into an overnight bag, and then they were on the road. Gabriel had wanted her to get a good night's sleep first, to wait until daylight to leave, but she was anxious to get Teddy out of Boston.

And she sure as hell wouldn't let him stay in her home or anywhere near her own family. She'd seen what happened to families who sheltered Teddy. Death seemed to walk in the boy's footsteps, scythe swinging and hacking at whoever happened to be nearby. She did not want that bloody scythe harvesting the two people she loved most.

So she'd bundled the boy back into the car, threw her bag in the trunk, and by one thirty in the morning they were headed north out of Boston. Away from her family.

At that early hour, traffic was light, and she spied only a few headlights following her. She kept track of their progress. Just beyond the town of Saugus, the pair of sleek blue halogens peeled off. Twenty-five miles later, so did the lights belonging to the SUV. By the time she drove over the Kittery bridge into Maine, it was nearly three A.M. and she saw no headlights at all behind her, but she never stopped glancing in the mirror, never stopped scanning for a pursuer.

*The killer was there, in the house.* She'd seen his shoeprint downstairs, knew that he'd walked throughout the first floor, yet she hadn't caught even a glimpse of his shadow as she'd watched from the top of the steps. How long had she crouched, waiting for him to appear on the stairway? When adrenaline is flooding your veins, when you're about to face your own death, a mere sixty seconds can seem like a lifetime. She was certain it had been five minutes, maybe longer. Certainly time enough for him to search the first floor, to turn his attention to the second. Yet he hadn't. What stopped him? Did he sense that a cop was waiting at the top of the stairs? Did he realize that the odds had turned against him, that a simple execution had now become a battle with an equally lethal opponent?

She glanced over her shoulder at the boy. Teddy was curled up, skinny arms and legs tightly folded around himself like an embryo. He slept deeply, as most children do, showing no sign that tonight's terror had invaded his dreams.

When the sun came up, rising through a receding bank of clouds, she was still behind the wheel. She opened the window and smelled damp earth, saw sun-warmed steam rising from the pavement. She stopped only once for gas and coffee and a bathroom break. Teddy slept through it all.

Even with that jolt of caffeine, she had to fight to stay awake, to stay focused on that final stretch of road. She was so exhausted she forgot to call ahead, as Maura had advised her. By the time she remembered to pull out her phone, the cell signal was down to zero bars, and she had no way to alert the school that she'd arrived.

It didn't matter; someone was already waiting for her at the locked gate. The bear-sized man who stood blocking the entrance cut a forbidding figure in his faded jeans and hiking boots. Dangling from his leather belt was an enormous hunting knife, its lethal serrations glittering in the morning sun. She rolled to a stop right in front of him, yet he didn't flinch, didn't step aside, but stood with arms crossed, as immovable as a mountain.

"State your business, ma'am," he said.

She frowned at the compound bow and quiver of arrows that were slung over his shoulder, and wondered if she'd made a wrong turn somewhere. If she'd wandered into dueling-banjos territory. Then she glanced up at the wrought-iron archway and saw the word EVENSONG.

"I'm Detective Jane Rizzoli. The school is expecting me."

He stalked over to the passenger window and stared in at the sleeping boy. "This is young Mr. Clock?"

"Yes. I'm bringing him to the school."

In the backseat, Teddy finally stirred awake, and when he saw the wild man peering in at him, he gave a yelp of alarm.

"It's all right, son." The voice was surprisingly gentle, coming from such a fierce-looking man. "My name's Roman. I'm the school forester. I look after these here woods, and I'll look after you, too."

"Is that *Mr.* Roman?" asked Jane.

"Just Roman's good enough." He grunted and swung open the gate. "Three miles in, you'll get to the lake. The castle's just beyond. They're expecting you." He waved her through. "Go slow. Don't hit the bear."

She assumed he meant Bear the dog, who belonged to Julian Perkins. But a hundred yards down the road, she rounded a bend in the woods and skidded to an abrupt stop as a black bear—a *real* bear—sauntered across the road, followed by her two cubs, their fur bright and glossy in the sunlight.

"What is this place?" Teddy murmured in wonder.

"It sure ain't the big city." She watched the trio disappear into the woods. "I can see the headline now," she muttered: "BOSTON COP EATEN BY BEARS."

"They don't eat people."

"You know that, do you?"

"Black bears are mostly vegetarian."

"Mostly?"

"Mostly."

"*That* is not reassuring." She drove on, wondering what other surprises might pop out of the woods. Wolves. Cougars. Unicorns. In this wild place with its impenetrable forest, it seemed that anything might appear.

In the backseat, Teddy was now alert and staring out the window, as if everything outside was fascinating. Maybe here, deep in the forest, was exactly where the boy should be. This was the first time she'd heard him say more than two spontaneous sentences.

"Will there be other kids here?" he asked.

"Of course. It's a school."

"But it's summertime. Aren't they all on vacation?"

"It's a boarding school. Some of the kids stay year-round."

"Don't they have families to go to?"

She hesitated. "Not all of them."

"So this is where they live all the time?"

She glanced over her shoulder, but he wasn't looking at her; he was focused instead on the thick curtain of greenery outside his window. "This seems like a pretty nice place to me," she said. "What do you think?"

"Yeah," he said. And added softly: "I don't think he can find me here."

# TWELVE

CLAIRE WAS THE FIRST TO SPOT THE ARRIVAL OF the new boy. From the stairwell window, she watched the hatchback drive under the school's stone arch and roll to a stop in the courtyard. The driver climbed out, a compact woman with unruly dark hair, dressed in blue jeans and a Windbreaker. She stood and stretched, as if she'd been driving for a long time, then walked around to the back of the car and pulled out two small suitcases.

The rear passenger door swung open and someone else climbed out of the car: a boy.

Claire pressed up against the glass to study him, and she saw an egg-shaped head with light brown hair topped by a wisp of a cowlick. He reminded her of Pinocchio, all stick arms and legs moving in mechanical jerks and stops. He squinted up at the building, and his face was so pale that Claire thought: That's what a vampire must look like. Or someone who's been shut away too long in a cellar.

"Hey, look. It's the Night Crawler."

Claire's back stiffened at the too-familiar insult. She turned to see Briana and her two snooty girlfriends come sweeping down the staircase on their way to breakfast. These three were the golden girls, the princess posse with glossy hair and perfect teeth.

"What's so interesting out there?" one of the princesses asked.

"Maybe she's looking for a new place to hunt for grubs tonight."

"Hey, Briana. Look," one of the princesses said. "There's the new kid we heard about."

The three girls pushed Claire aside and crowded forward to stare through the window.

"*He's* fourteen?" said Briana.

"You heard about him?" asked Claire.

Briana ignored her. "What a stick boy. He looks like he's about ten."

In the courtyard below, Headmaster Baum and Dr. Isles came out of the building to welcome the new arrivals. From the way the two women greeted each other, it was clear they were already acquainted.

"He looks like an insect," one of the princesses said. "Like some creepy praying mantis."

Briana laughed and looked at Claire. "Hey, Night Crawler. It sounds like your new boyfriend just arrived."

HALF AN HOUR LATER, at breakfast, Claire got another look at him. The boy was sitting at Julian's table, where the older boys sat. That's probably why they'd put him there, so he'd be looked after on his first day. He seemed dazed and a little scared, as if he'd just landed on an alien planet. Somehow he sensed that she was looking at him, and he turned to stare at her. Then he kept on staring, as if Claire was the only one he found interesting. As if he'd just spotted the one other person who was as much a misfit as he was.

The insistent clink of a spoon against a water goblet made everyone look up at the teachers' table. Headmaster Baum rose to his feet with a noisy scrape of his chair.

"Good morning, students," he said. "As I'm sure you've noticed, we have a new student with us today. Starting tomorrow, he'll be attending classes." He gestured toward Pinocchio-boy, who blushed at the sudden attention. "I hope you'll make him feel welcome. And I hope you all remember what it was like when you first arrived, and try to make Teddy's first day here an excellent one."

Teddy, with no last name. She wondered why Headmaster Baum had left out that particular detail. She studied the boy more closely, the same way he was watching her, and she saw his lips curve into a smile so tentative that she wasn't entirely sure it was there. She wondered why, of all the girls in the room, *she* was the one he was looking at. The three princesses were way prettier, and they were sitting closer to him. I'm just the class weirdo, she thought, the girl who always says the wrong thing. The girl with the hole in her head. *So why are you looking at me?*

It made her feel uncomfortable and thrilled at the same time.

"Ooh, look. He's *staring* at her." Briana had sidled up to Claire's table and now bent close to whisper in her ear. "It looks like Mr. Stick Bug has a thing for Ms. Night Crawler."

"Leave me alone."

"Maybe you'll have cute little insect babies together."

Without a word, Claire picked up her glass of orange juice and splashed it on Briana. Juice splattered her rival's sparkly jeans and brand-new ballet flats.

"Did you *see* that?" Briana screamed. "Did you *see* what she just did to me?"

Ignoring the outraged squeals, Claire stood up and headed for the exit. On her way out, she glimpsed Will Yablonski's spotty face grinning at her, and he gave her a sly thumbs-up. Now, *there* was another weirdo, just like her. Maybe that's why Will was always so nice to her. Weirdos had to stick together here at Freak High, where no one could hear you scream.

The new boy was still staring, too. Teddy-with-no-last-name. She felt his eyes follow her every step.

IT WASN'T UNTIL THE next afternoon that she spoke to him. Every Thursday she had stable chores, and today she was grooming Plum Crazy, one of the four Evensong horses. Of all the duties regularly assigned to students, this was one she did not mind at all, even though it meant mucking out stalls and hauling around bales of wood shavings. Horses didn't complain. They didn't ask questions. They just watched her with their quiet brown eyes and trusted her not to hurt them. Just as she trusted them not to hurt her, even though Plum Crazy was a thousand pounds of muscle and sharp hooves, and all he had to do was roll over and he could squash her right here in his stall. Chickens scratched and flapped nearby, and Herman the rooster let loose with an annoying screech, but Plum Crazy stood still and serene through it all, nickering in contentment as Claire ran the currycomb across his flank and down his rear. The *rasp, rasp* of the rubber teeth was hypnotically soothing. She was so focused on the task that she did not at first realize someone was standing behind her. Only when she straightened did she suddenly notice Teddy's face peering at her over the stall door. She was so startled, she almost dropped the currycomb.

"What are *you* doing here?" she snapped. Not exactly the friendliest of greetings.

"I'm sorry! I just wanted to . . . they told me I could . . ." He glanced over his shoulder, as if hoping someone would rescue him. "I like animals," he finally said. "Dr. Welliver told me there were horses."

"And cows and sheep. And these dumbshit chickens." She dropped the currycomb in a hanging bucket, where it landed with a loud thump. It was an angry sound, but she wasn't really angry. She just didn't like being startled. Teddy was already backing away from the stall door.

"Hey," she said, trying to make amends. "You want to pet him? His name's Plum Crazy."

"Does he bite?"

"Naw, he's just a big baby." She gave the horse's neck a gentle pat. "Aren't you, Plum?"

Cautiously Teddy swung open the stall door and stepped inside. As he stroked the horse, Claire retrieved the currycomb and resumed grooming. For a while they did not talk, just shared the stall in silence, inhaling the smells of fresh pine shavings and warm horseflesh.

"I'm Claire Ward," she said.

"I'm Teddy."

"Yeah. I heard that at breakfast."

He touched Plum's muzzle, and the horse suddenly tossed its head. Teddy flinched and pushed his glasses back up the bridge of his nose. Even in the gloom of the stable, she saw how pale he was, and thin, his wrists as delicate as twigs. But his eyes were arresting, wide and long-lashed, and he seemed to be taking in everything at once.

"How old are you?" she asked.

"Fourteen."

"Really?"

"Why do you sound surprised?"

"Because I'm a year younger than you. And you

seem so . . ." *Small* was what she was about to say, but at the last second a kinder word came to mind. "Shy." She peered at him over the horse's back. "So do you have a last name?"

"Detective Rizzoli says I shouldn't go around telling everyone."

"You mean that lady who brought you here? She's a detective?"

"Yeah." He got up the nerve to stroke Plum's muzzle again, and this time the horse accepted the pat and gave a soft nicker.

She stopped combing Plum and gave the boy her full attention. "So what happened to *you*?"

He didn't answer, just looked at her with those wide, transparent eyes.

"It's okay to talk about it here," she said. "Everybody does. It's the kind of school where they want you to get your pain out."

"That's what shrinks always say."

"Yeah, I know. I have to talk to her, too."

"Why do *you* need a shrink?"

She set the currycomb down. "I have a hole in my head. When I was eleven years old, someone killed my mom and dad. And then he shot me in the head." She turned to face him. "That's why I have a shrink. Because I'm supposed to be dealing with the trauma. Even though I can't remember it. Any of it."

"Did they catch him? The man who shot you?"

"No. He's still out there. I think he might be looking for me."

"How do you know that?"

"Because it happened again, last month. My foster parents got killed, and that's why I ended up here. Because it's safe here."

He said, softly: "That's why they brought me here, too."

She stared at him with new understanding, and saw tragedy written in his pale cheeks, in the brightness of his eyes. "Then you're in the right place," she said. "It's the only school for kids like us."

"You mean all the other kids here . . ."

"You'll find out," she said. "If you stay long enough."

A shadow blotted out the light above the stall door. "There you are, Teddy. I've been looking for you," said Detective Rizzoli. She noticed Claire and smiled. "Making new friends already?"

"Yes, ma'am," said Teddy.

"I'm sorry to interrupt, but Dr. Welliver wants to talk to you now."

He looked at Claire, who answered his unspoken question by mouthing: *The shrink*.

"She just wants to ask you a few questions. Get to know you better." Detective Rizzoli opened the stall door. "Come on."

Teddy stepped out, pulling the door shut behind him. Turning back, he whispered to Claire: "It's Teddy Clock."

He looks like a Teddy Clock, thought Claire as she watched him walk away. She left the stall and pushed the wheelbarrow filled with soiled horse bedding out of the stables. In the barnyard, that annoying rooster was causing trouble again, chasing and pecking a beleaguered hen. Even chickens could be cruel. They're as mean as we are, she thought. They attack each other, even kill each other. Suddenly the sight of that poor hen, cowering under Herman the rooster's assault, infuriated her.

"Leave her *alone*!" She aimed a kick, but Herman flapped safely out of reach and darted away, squawking. "Asshole rooster!" she yelled. Turning, she saw one of the princesses laughing at her from the corral. "What?" she snapped.

"He's just a chicken, retard. What's your problem?"

"Like anybody cares," she muttered, and walked away.

*Until the moment it all fell apart, the operation was running perfectly. When disaster strikes, you can usually look back and pinpoint exactly where it starts to unravel, where one unlucky event sets off the sequence leading inevitably to disaster. As the saying goes,* For want of a nail, the shoe was lost, *and it's true; the smallest detail, overlooked, can doom a horse, a soldier, a battle.*

*But on that June evening in Rome, with our target in sight, the battle seemed ours to win.*

*Inside La Nonna, Icarus and his party were finishing up their desserts. We were all in position when they finally emerged, the bodyguards first, followed by Icarus with his wife and sons. A heavy meal, washed down with glasses of excellent wine, had rendered Icarus mellow that evening, and he did not stop to scan his surroundings, but headed directly to his car. He helped his wife, Lucia, and their two sons into the Volvo, then slid behind the steering wheel. Right behind him, the bodyguards climbed into their BMW.*

*Icarus was the first to pull away, into the road.*

*At that instant the produce truck veered into position, lurching to an angled stop that blocked the BMW. The bodyguards climbed out, shouting at the truck driver to move, but he ignored them as he nonchalantly carried a crate of onions into La Nonna's kitchen.*

*That's when the bodyguards realized their tire had been slashed, and they were stranded. An ambush. Icarus saw at once what was happening, and he reacted as we expected he would.*

*He hit his accelerator and roared away, speeding toward the safety of his hilltop home.*

*We were in the car right behind him. A second car, with two more members of our team, waited a hundred yards up the road. It cut into position just in front of Icarus, and the Volvo was now boxed between our two vehicles.*

*The road narrowed as it wound up the hillside, carving hairpin turns. A blind curve was coming up, and the first car braked to slow down the Volvo. Our plan was to force it to a stop, to yank Icarus from the Volvo and bundle him into our vehicle. But instead of slowing, Icarus surprised us. Recklessly he accelerated, squeezing past the first car, with barely an inch to spare.*

*No one saw the oncoming truck until it was too late.*

*Icarus desperately swerved right, but that sent the Volvo into the guardrail. It caromed off and skidded.*

*The truck hit it broadside, crumpling the passenger doors.*

*Even before I scrambled out of my car, I knew that the wife was dead. I was the one who yanked open Icarus's door, the one who first glimpsed the* carnage inside. Lucia's broken body. The destroyed face of the ten-year-old. And little Carlo, still conscious but dying. Carlo looked at me, and I saw the question in his eyes. It is a question that I still struggle to answer: Why?

We dragged Icarus from the Volvo. Unlike his family, he was very much alive and fighting us. Within seconds we had his wrists and ankles bound. We tossed him into the backseat of my vehicle and threw a blanket over him.

The hapless truck driver, dazed and light-headed from the collision, had no idea what had really happened. Later he would tell the police that Good Samaritans had stopped to rescue the Volvo's driver and must have brought him to a hospital. But our destination was a private airstrip fortyeight miles away, where a chartered jet was fueled and waiting.

We had accomplished what we came to do, but this was not the way it should have ended, with three dead innocents. After any other successful mission, we would have celebrated with a round of whiskey and high fives. But that night we were subdued. Anxious about the repercussions to follow.

We had no idea how terrible they would be.

# THIRTEEN

WIND RATTLED THE WINDOWS OF DR. ANNA Welliver's office, and from that lofty perch in the castle's turret Jane saw black clouds rolling in from the mountains, moving inexorably toward them. A summer storm was coming, and the sound of the wind made Jane uneasy as she and Maura watched Dr. Welliver assemble a tray of teacups and saucers. Outside the view looked threatening, but inside the turret it was a cozy space with a floral sofa and incense sticks and crystals hanging in the window, a serene retreat where a traumatized child could curl into the overstuffed chair and safely share his darkest fears. The incense made it seem more like the parlor of an eccentric earth mother than a therapist's office, but then Welliver *was* eccentric, with her wild gray hair and granny dresses and orthopedic shoes.

"I've had about forty-eight hours to observe the boy," said Dr. Welliver. "And I must say, I have concerns." On the side table, the electric kettle began to hiss and burble, and she rose to pour steaming water into a porcelain teapot.

"What problems do you see?" asked Jane.

"Superficially, he seems to be settling in remarkably well. He appeared to enjoy the first day of classes. Ms. Duplessis said he reads well above his grade level. Mr. Roman coaxed him into shooting a few arrows at archery class. And last night, I discovered him in the computer room, surfing You-Tube."

Jane glanced at Maura. "You can't make a cell phone call here, but you can surf the Web?"

"We can't hold back the digital age," said Dr. Welliver with a laugh. She settled heavily back into her chair, her dress puffing up like a tent around her generous body. "Of course we block inappropriate websites, and our students know they're never to reveal any personal information. Not their locations, not their names. It's a matter of safety."

"For these children, in particular," said Maura.

"The point I was trying to make," said Dr. Welliver, "is that Teddy has, to all appearances, adjusted very well to this new environment. He even seems to have made a few friends."

"So what's the problem?" asked Jane.

"At my session with him yesterday, I discovered quite a few things he doesn't remember—or chooses not to remember—about his birth family."

"You do know there's a reason he can't remember the night they died."

"I know they were killed aboard their sailboat

off Saint Thomas. And there was an explosion that made Teddy black out. But I can't help wondering if that explosion is the whole explanation for his memory gaps. When I ask him about his family, he tries to avoid all my questions. He deflects. Says he's hungry or needs to use the bathroom. Occasionally, he still refers to members of his family in the present tense. He simply doesn't want to deal with that loss at all."

"He was only twelve years old," said Maura. "Still a tender age."

"It's been two years. That's time enough for him to have processed his loss, the way our other students have. There's a lot of work to be done with Teddy. To get him past this denial stage. To accept that his family is gone." She looked at Jane. "It's a good thing you brought him here, Detective. I hope you'll let him stay."

"This was an emergency move," said Jane. "It's not my decision where he stays in the long term."

"Last night, the Evensong board unanimously agreed to accept Teddy, all expenses paid. Please convey that to the state of Massachusetts. We do want to be of service."

"I'll tell you how you can really be of service," said Jane. "Tell me about the other two students. Claire Ward and Will Yablonski."

Welliver stood to pour the herbal tea, which had been brewing. In silence she filled the cups and served her visitors, then she sat down and stirred several generous spoonfuls of sugar into her tea.

"This is a delicate matter," she finally said. "Sharing confidential files about our students."

"I've got a delicate matter, too," said Jane. "I'm trying to keep Teddy alive."

"Why do you think there's a connection among these three children?"

Maura said, "The coincidence is eerie. That's why I called Jane, because there are so many parallels. Three different families, the Wards, the Yablonskis, and the Clocks, were all killed the same year. Even the same *week*. Now, two years later, their surviving children are attacked again. Within weeks of one another."

"Yes, I agree it *is* odd."

"It's way more than odd," said Jane.

"But it's merely a coincidence."

Jane leaned forward to look straight into Dr. Welliver's eyes. "How can you so easily dismiss the possibility there's a connection?"

"Because these families were killed in different locations. Teddy Clock's family died on their sailboat off Saint Thomas. Claire's parents were shot to death in London."

"And Will's parents? The Yablonskis?"

"They died when their private plane went down, in Maryland."

Jane frowned. "I thought they were murdered. That sounds more like an accident."

Dr. Welliver turned and looked out the glass door to the rooftop walkway, where mist was swirling in the wind. "I've probably told you far too much already. These are my patients, and they trust me to keep their secrets. I feel bound by rules of confidentiality."

Jane said, "You know, I could just pick up the phone and talk directly to law enforcement. I could get those details myself. Why don't you make my life easier and just tell me. *Was* that plane crash an accident?"

Dr. Welliver was silent for a moment as she weighed her response. "No, it wasn't an accident," she finally said. "The NTSB concluded that the plane was sabotaged. But again, there's no obvious link with the other two families. Except for the manner of their deaths."

"Excuse me for saying this," said Jane, "but drawing that conclusion is *my* job, not yours. Most likely it is a coincidence, but I have to proceed as if it's by design. Because if I miss something, we could end up with three dead kids."

Welliver set down her teacup and studied Jane for a moment, as if trying to gauge her determination. At last, she rose from her chair and shuffled to the filing cabinet, where she rooted inside for a chart. "The Yablonskis' plane went down soon after takeoff," she said. "Neil Yablonski was at the controls when it happened. He and his wife were the only ones aboard. At first, it was presumed to be an accident." She brought Will's file back to the desk and handed it to Jane. "Then the NTSB found forensic evidence of explosives. The investigators searched for a motive, for any reason why this particular couple was targeted. They never came up with an answer. Luckily their son, Will, wasn't on board his parents' plane that day. He'd chosen to spend the weekend with his aunt and uncle, so he could work on a science project."

Jane opened the folder and scanned the Evensong School's intake form.

*Fourteen-year-old white male with no known surviving family members. Referred by the state of New Hampshire after a fire of suspicious origin destroyed the home of his aunt and uncle, Brian and Lynn Temple, who have served as his guardians since his parents' deaths two years ago . . .*

Jane read the next paragraph and looked up at Welliver, who was adding yet a fourth teaspoon of sugar to her cup of herbal tea. "The kid was briefly considered a suspect in the New Hampshire fire?"

"The police had to consider that possibility, because Will was the sole survivor. He told them he was outside looking through his telescope when the house exploded. A passing motorist spotted the flames and stopped to help. She's the one who brought the boy to the emergency room."

"The kid just *happened* to be outside looking through his telescope?"

"Will's father and his uncle were both NASA scientists who worked at Goddard Space Flight Center in Maryland. It's not surprising that Will's an amateur astronomer."

"So the kid's a geek," said Jane.

"You could call him that. Which is why the police considered him a suspect, if only briefly, because he certainly has the intelligence to build a bomb. But he had no motive."

"That they know of."

"From what I've observed, Will is a very well-behaved boy with excellent academic skills, especially math. I see no aggression whatsoever. Socially he's a bit awkward. His aunt and uncle homeschooled him in New Hampshire, so he didn't have much interaction with other children. That may be one of the reasons he's not quick to make friends."

"Why was he homeschooled?" asked Maura.

"He had problems back in Maryland. The poor boy was teased and bullied."

"Why?"

"Because of his weight." Dr. Welliver looked down at her own large frame, only partly disguised by the voluminous dresses she always wore. "Most of my life, I've struggled with my own weight, so I know what it's like to be ridiculed. Children can be especially cruel, zeroing in on the fact that Will's heavy, and also a bit clumsy. Here we intervene at once if we see any bullying going on, but we're not omniscient. Despite any teasing, Will's always cheerful and good-natured. He's kind to the younger children. He's a reliable student who's never in trouble." Welliver paused. "Unlike the girl."

"Claire Ward," said Jane.

Welliver sighed. "Our little nocturnal wanderer." She pushed out of her chair and went back to the filing cabinet to look for Claire's chart. "Now, *this* child has caused us multiple headaches. Most of them related to her neurologic issues."

"What do you mean, *neurologic issues*?"

Welliver straightened and looked at her. "Claire was with her parents the night they were attacked in London. All of them were shot in the head. Only Claire survived."

In the distance, thunder rumbled, and the sky had turned ominously dark. Jane looked down at her own arm and saw that the hairs had lifted, as if a cool wind had just blown across her skin.

Welliver placed Claire's folder in front of Jane. "It happened as the family was walking to their car after dining in a restaurant. Claire's father was Erskine Ward, a foreign service officer who'd worked in London, Rome, and Washington. Her mother, Isabel, was a homemaker. Because of Erskine's job at the US embassy, there was concern that this might have been a terrorist attack, but in the end the police concluded it was a robbery gone wrong. Claire couldn't help the investigation because she couldn't remember the attack. The first thing she does remember is waking up in the hospital, after surgery."

"For a girl who was shot in the head, she seems amazingly normal now," said Jane.

"At first glance, she does look perfectly normal."

Welliver looked at Maura. "Even you didn't immediately spot her deficits, did you, Dr. Isles?"

"No," Maura admitted. "They're subtle."

"When the bullet was fired into her head," said Welliver, "it resulted in what's called diaschisis. It's Greek for 'shocked thought.' At the age of eleven, her brain was still relatively plastic, so she's been able to recover almost all function. Her language and motor skills are virtually normal, as is her memory. Except for that night in London. Prior to the attack, she was an excellent student, even gifted. But I'm afraid she'll never be an academic star now."

"But she can still live a normal life?" said Jane.

"Not entirely. Like many head-injury patients, she's impulsive. She takes risks. She says things without much thought about the consequences."

"Sounds like a typical teenager."

Dr. Welliver gave a knowing laugh. "True. *Teenage brain* is a diagnosis in and of itself. But I don't think Claire's ever going to grow out of this. Impulse control will always be an issue for her. She loses her temper, blurts out what she thinks. It's already caused problems. She has a feud going on with another girl here. It started with some name calling, nasty notes. Accelerated to tripping, shoving. Clothes vandalized, earthworms in the bed."

"Sounds like me and my brothers," said Jane.

"Except you, hopefully, grew out of it. But Claire's always going to leap before she looks. And that's especially dangerous, given her other neurologic issue."

"Which is?"

"Her sleep–wake cycle has been completely disrupted. That happens to many head-injured patients, but most of them suffer from excessive drowsiness. They sleep more than normal. Claire, for some reason, had a paradoxical result. She's restless, especially at night, when she seems to be hyperacute. She seems to need only four hours of sleep a night."

"The night I arrived," said Maura, "I saw her down in the garden. It was well after midnight."

Welliver nodded. "That's when she's most active. She's like a nocturnal creature. We call her our midnight rambler."

"And you allow her to just wander around in the dark?" said Jane.

"When she was living in Ithaca, there was nothing her foster family could do to stop it. They tried medications, locked doors, threats of punishment. This is going to be Claire's baseline behavior for the rest of her life, and she needs to learn to deal with it. She's not a prisoner here, so we decided not to treat her as one."

"By allowing her to run wild at night?"

"Fortunately there aren't many things that can hurt you in the Maine woods. We have no poisonous snakes, no large predators, and our black bears are more terrified of us than we are of them. The biggest danger is that she'll step on a porcupine, or sprain an ankle stumbling into some animal burrow. This is simply Claire's nature, and it's a condition she'll have to live with. Frankly, it's far safer for her to wander here in the woods than in any big city."

Jane could not argue with that statement; she knew only too well where the most dangerous predators were found. "And after she graduates from Evensong? What happens to her then?"

"When that time comes, she'll have to make her own choices. Meanwhile, we're giving her the skills to survive. That's our purpose here, Detective. It's the reason this school exists, so these children can find their places in the world. A world that hasn't been kind to them." Welliver pointed toward the filing cabinet. "We have dozens of students like Claire, some so traumatized when they arrived that they could barely talk. Or they'd wake up every night screaming. But children are resilient. With guidance, they can bounce back."

Jane opened Claire's file. Like Will's, it included an initial psychological evaluation by Dr. Welliver. She turned to a summary of the Ithaca PD investigation. "How did Claire end up living with this particular couple, the Buckleys?"

"Bob and Barbara Buckley were friends of Claire's parents, and her designated guardians in their will. They had no children of their own. When they took in Claire, they certainly got a handful."

Jane stared at the police report summing up the Buckleys' deaths and looked up at Maura. "Someone plowed into their car. Shot them both in the head."

"It certainly looked like a targeted killing," said Dr. Welliver. "But the Buckleys had no known enemies. Which raised the possibility that *Claire* was the target, because she was in the car, too."

"Then why is the girl still alive?" said Jane.

Dr. Welliver shrugged. "Divine intervention."

"Excuse me?"

"Ask Claire, and she'll tell you that's exactly what happened. She was trapped inside the car. Heard the gunshots. Actually saw the killer standing *right there*. And then someone else showed up on the scene. *An angel* is how Claire described her. A woman who helped her out of the vehicle and stayed with her."

"Did the police interview this woman? Did *she* see the killer?"

"Unfortunately, the woman vanished just as the police arrived. No one but Claire ever saw her."

"Maybe she didn't exist," suggested Maura. "Maybe Claire imagined her."

Dr. Welliver nodded. "The police did have doubts about this mysterious woman. But they certainly had no doubt that this was an execution. Which is why Claire was brought to Evensong."

Jane closed the file and looked at the psychologist. "That raises another question. How, exactly, did that happen?"

"She was referred to us."

"I'm sure the state of New York can look after its

own kids. Why send her to Evensong? And how did Will Yablonski end up here, from New Hampshire?"

Dr. Welliver didn't look at Jane; instead she focused on one of the crystals that dangled in the window. On a sunny day, that bit of quartz would scatter rainbows around the room, but on this gray morning, it hung inert, offering no light-bending magic. "Evensong has a reputation," she said. "For many of these children, we offer tuition, room and board, at no cost to the states. Law enforcement agencies all around the country know about the work we do here."

"Because the Mephisto Society is everywhere," said Jane. "And so are your spies."

Welliver's eyes met Jane's. "You and I are on the same side, Detective," she said quietly. "Never doubt that."

"It's the conspiracy theories that bother me."

"Can we agree, at least, that the innocent need protection? That victims need to be healed? At Evensong, we do both. Yes, we track crimes around the world. Like any scientists, we search for patterns. Because we're victims, too, and we've chosen to fight back."

Someone knocked on the door, and they all turned as an Asian boy, small and wiry, popped into the room.

Dr. Welliver greeted him with a motherly smile. "Hello, Bruno. Do you need something?"

"We found something in the woods. On a tree," the boy blurted out.

"The woods are full of trees. What's special about this one?"

"We're not sure what it means, and the girls, they're all screaming . . ." Bruno took a deep breath to calm himself, and Jane suddenly noticed that the boy was shaking. "Mr. Roman says you need to come *right now*."

Dr. Welliver rose to her feet in alarm. "Show us."

# FOURTEEN

THEY FOLLOWED THE BOY DOWN THREE FLIGHTS of stairs in a noisy parade of footsteps. Outside the wind whipped Jane's hair, and she regretted not bringing her jacket. The distant dark clouds that she had seen from the turret were now almost upon them, and she heard the creak and groan of the trees, smelled impending rain in the air. They tramped into the woods, led by the boy, who did not seem to be following any obvious trail. With so many feet snapping twigs and crunching over dead leaves, the birds had gone silent. There was only the sound of their passage and the wind in the branches.

"Are we lost?" asked Jane.

"No, it's just a shortcut," Dr. Welliver answered. Despite her tent-like dress, she managed to move steadily through the woods, lumbering heavily behind the Puck-like boy who scampered ahead of them.

The trees grew denser, the branches blotting out

Jane's view of the sky. Though it was only mid-morning, here in the forest the day had darkened to a twilight gloom.

"Does this kid actually know where he's going?"

"Bruno knows exactly where he's going." Dr. Welliver pointed at a broken branch just above their heads.

"He marked a trail?"

The psychologist glanced back at her. "Don't underestimate our students."

They'd lost sight of the castle. Now all Jane saw, in every direction, were trees. How far had they walked, half a mile, more? And this was supposed to be a shortcut? Her shoelace came loose and she crouched down to tie it again. When she straightened, she saw that the others were already a dozen paces ahead of her and almost out of sight. Left alone here, she might wander for days trying to find her way out. She scrambled to catch up and pushed through a curtain of brush into a small clearing where the others had come to a halt.

Beneath a magnificent willow tree stood Professor Pasquantonio and Roman, the forester. Nearby stood a group of students, huddled together against the wind.

". . . haven't touched a thing. We left 'em just as we found 'em," Roman said to Dr. Welliver. "Damned if I know what this means."

"A sick prank." Pasquantonio snorted. "That's what it is. Children do ridiculous things."

Dr. Welliver moved beneath the willow tree and

stared up into the branches. "Do we know who did this?"

"Nobody's owning up to it." Roman grunted.

"We *all* know she did it," a dark-haired girl said. "Who else would it be?" She pointed at Claire. "She sneaked out again last night. I saw her through the window. *Night Crawler.*"

"I didn't do it," Claire said. She stood off by herself at the edge of the woods, arms crossed over her chest as though to fend off the accusations.

"You *were* out. Don't lie about it."

"Briana," said Dr. Welliver, "we don't accuse people without proof."

Jane eased her way through the gathering to see what had drawn them all to this place. Dangling from a lower branch of the willow tree were three dolls made of twigs and twine, suspended like rustic Christmas ornaments. Stepping closer, Jane saw that one of the dolls had a birch-bark skirt. A female. The twig dolls slowly twisted in the wind like little hangman's victims, all of them splattered with what looked like blood. High in the willow tree, crows cawed, and Jane looked up. Saw the source of those splatters hanging above her head, and caught a whiff of decay. In disgust she backed away, her gaze fixed on the carcass that hung from that high branch.

"Who found it?" asked Dr. Welliver.

"We all did," said Roman. "Every few days, I take 'em down this trail, pointing out how the forest changes. Those girls were the first to spot 'em."

He pointed to Briana and the two girls who always seemed to hover around her. "Never heard such hysterical caterwauling." He pulled out a knife and sliced the rope that suspended the carcass, and the dead rooster plopped to the ground. "You'd think they never ate chicken," he muttered.

"It's Herman," one of the boys murmured. "Someone killed Herman."

Not just killed him, thought Jane. Slit him open. Pulled out his entrails and exposed them to the crows. This was no mere juvenile prank; this turned her stomach.

Dr. Welliver looked around at the students, who stood shivering as the first raindrops began to fall. "Does anyone know anything about this?"

"I didn't hear him crowing this morning," said one of the girls. "Herman always wakes me up. But not this morning."

"I came down the trail yesterday afternoon," said Roman. "Wasn't hanging then. Must've been done last night."

Jane glanced at Claire. *The midnight rambler.* The girl, suddenly aware of Jane's gaze, stared back at her in defiance. A look that dared everyone to prove she had done it.

As raindrops splattered her dress, Dr. Welliver looked around at the circle of students, her arms spread as if offering a hug to anyone who needed one. "If anyone wants to talk to me about this later, my door is always open. I promise, whatever you tell me will stay just between you and me. Now."

She sighed, looking up at the rain. "Why don't you head back?"

As the students left the clearing, the adults remained by the willow tree. Only when the children were out of earshot did Dr. Welliver say softly: "This is very disturbing."

Maura crouched down over the slaughtered rooster. "His neck is broken. That's probably what killed him. But then to gut him? Leave him here, where everyone will see him?" She looked at Dr. Welliver. "There's meaning to this."

"It means you've got one sick puppy here," said Jane. She looked up at the three twig figures. "And what does *that* mean? Like creepy little voodoo dolls. Why did she do this?"

"She?" said Welliver.

"Sure, Claire denied it. But kids lie all the time."

Dr. Welliver shook her head. "That brain injury made her impulsive. But it also made her almost incapable of deception. Claire says exactly what she thinks, even though it gets her into trouble. She denied it, and I believe her."

"Then which of 'em did it?" said Roman.

Behind them, a voice asked: "Why do you think it was a student?"

They all turned to see Julian standing at the edge of the clearing. He had returned so quietly, they hadn't heard him.

"You just assume it's one of us," said Julian. "That's not fair."

Dr. Pasquantonio laughed. "You don't really think a teacher would do this?"

"Remember what you taught us about the word *assume,* sir? That it makes an ass of you and me?"

"Julian," Maura said.

"Well, it *is* what he says."

"Where, exactly, is this leading, Mr. Perkins?" asked Pasquantonio.

Julian stood straighter. "I'd like to take Herman's body."

"It's already rotting," said Roman. He lifted the corpse by its rope and tossed it into the woods. "Crows have already gotten a start on it; let 'em finish."

"Well then, can I have the twig dolls?"

"I'd as soon burn the damn things. Forget this fool business."

"Burning them doesn't make the mystery go away, sir."

"Why do you want them, Julian?" asked Maura.

"Because right now, we're all looking at each other, suspecting each other. Wondering who'd be sick enough to do this." He looked at Dr. Pasquantonio. "This is evidence, and the Jackals can analyze it."

"What are the Jackals?" said Jane. She looked at Maura, who shook her head, just as bewildered.

"It's the school forensics club," said Dr. Welliver. "Founded decades ago by a former student named Jack Jackman."

"Which is why it's called the Jackals," said Julian. "I'm the new president, and this is just the kind of project our club does. We've studied blood splatters, tire tracks. We can analyze *this* evidence."

"Oh, I get it." Jane laughed and shot a glance at Maura. "It's *CSI High School*!"

"All right, boy," said Roman. He reached up with his hunting knife and sliced the dolls from the branch. Held them out to Julian. "They're yours. Go to it."

"Thank you, sir."

Thunder rumbled, and Roman looked up at the sky. "Now we'd best get inside," he said. "I smell lightning coming this way. And there's no telling where it'll strike."

# FIFTEEN

**"D**ID YOU DO IT?"

Claire had been expecting the question. Back at the clearing, when they'd all stood gaping at what hung from the willow tree, she'd caught Will looking at her and had read the question in his eyes. He'd been discreet enough not to say a word at the time. Now that they'd lagged behind the other kids on the trail, he sidled up to whisper: "The others, they're saying it was you."

"They're idiots."

"That's what I told them. But you *were* out again last night."

"I told you, I don't sleep. I can't sleep."

"Next time, why don't you wake me up? We could hang out together."

She halted beside the streambed. Raindrops plopped onto their faces and drummed tattoos on the leaves. "You want to hang out with *me*?"

"I checked the weather forecast, and the sky's supposed to be clear tomorrow night. You could look through my telescope, and I'll show you some really cool galaxies. I'm sure you'd like seeing those."

"You hardly know me, Will."

"I know you better than you think."

"Oh, sure. Like we're best friends forever." She hadn't meant to sound sarcastic, but once the words were out, she couldn't take them back, and she wished she could. There were a lot of things she wished she'd never said. She tramped a few more paces up the trail and realized that Will was no longer beside her. Turning, she saw he'd stopped and stood staring at the stream, where water splashed and rippled across rocks.

"Why couldn't we be?" he said quietly, and looked at her. "We're not like everyone else. You and I, we're both . . ."

"Screwed up."

"That's not what I meant."

"Well, *I'm* screwed up, anyway," she said.

"Why do you say that?"

"Everyone says so, including my shrink. You want proof?" She grabbed his hand and pressed it against the scar on her scalp. "Feel that? That's where they sawed open my skull. That's why I stay awake all night, like a vampire. Because I'm brain-damaged."

He made no attempt to pull free, as she'd expected. His hand lingered in her hair, caressing the scar that marked her freakdom. He might be fat and spotty with acne, but she suddenly noticed that he had nice eyes. Soft and brown, with long lashes. He kept looking at her, as if trying to see what she was really thinking. All the things she was afraid to tell him.

She shoved his hand aside and walked away. Kept walking until the trail ended at the edge of the lake. There she stopped and stared across rain-dappled waters. Hoping Will would follow her.

And there he was, standing right beside her. A frigid wind blew off the lake, and she hugged herself, shivering. Will didn't seem to notice the cold, even though he wore only jeans and a damp T-shirt that clung to every unflattering bulge of his pillowy torso.

"Did it hurt?" he asked. "Getting shot?"

Automatically she reached up to touch the spot on her skull. The little indentation that marked the end of her life as a normal kid, a kid who slept through the night and got good grades. A kid who didn't say all the wrong things at the wrong times. "I don't know," she said. "The last thing I remember is having dinner in a restaurant with my mom and dad. They wanted me to try something new, but I wanted spaghetti. I kept insisting on spaghetti, spaghetti, and my mom finally told the waiter just to get me what I wanted. That's what I remember last. That my mom was annoyed with me. That I disappointed her." She swiped a hand across her eyes, leaving a streak of warmth on her cheeks.

On the pond a loon cried, a lonely, unearthly sound that made tears well up in her throat.

"I woke up in the hospital," she said. "And my mom and dad were dead."

His touch was so soft that she wasn't sure if she imagined it. Just a featherlight stroke of his fingers on her face. She lifted her head to look into Will's brown eyes.

"I miss my mom and dad, too," he said.

"THIS IS A CREEPY school with creepy kids," said Jane. "Every single one of them is peculiar."

They sat in Maura's room, their chairs pulled close to the hearth, where a fire was burning. Outside, rain lashed the windows and wind rattled the glass. Although she'd changed into dry clothes, the dampness had penetrated so deeply into Jane's bones that even the heat of the flames failed to warm her. She pulled her sweater tighter and looked up at the oil painting that hung above the mantelpiece. It was a gentleman hunter, rifle propped over his shoulder as he posed proudly beside a fallen stag. Men and their trophies.

"The word I would use," said Maura, "is *haunted*."

"The children, you mean?"

"Yes. They're haunted by crime. By violence. No wonder they strike you as odd."

"You put a bunch of kids like that together, kids who have serious emotional issues, and all it does is reinforce their weirdness."

"Maybe," said Maura. "But it's also the one

place where they find acceptance. With people who understand them."

That was not what Jane had expected her to say. The Maura she saw now, sitting by the fire, seemed like a different woman. The wind and humidity had transformed her usually sculpted black hair into a tangled thatch. Her plaid flannel shirt was untucked, and the cuffs of her blue jeans were stained with dried mud. Only a few days in Maine, and she'd been transformed into someone Jane did not quite recognize.

"You told me earlier that you wanted to pull Julian out of this school," said Jane.

"I did."

"So what changed your mind?"

"You can see how happy he is here. And he refuses to leave. That's what he told me. At sixteen, he already knows exactly what he wants." Maura sipped from a cup of tea and regarded Jane through the curling steam. "Remember what he was like in Wyoming? A wild animal who always got into fights, whose only friend was that dog. But here, in Evensong, he's found friends. This is where he belongs."

"Because here they're *all* oddballs."

Maura smiled at the fire. "Maybe that's why Julian and I bonded. Because I am, too."

"But in a good way," Jane quickly added.

"Which way would that be?"

"Brilliant. Determined. Reliable."

"I'm starting to sound like a German shepherd."

"And honest." Jane paused. "Even when it means losing friends because of it."

Maura stared into her teacup. "I'm going to pay for that sin forever. Aren't I?"

For a moment they didn't speak; the only sounds were the rain hitting the window and the hiss of the fire. Jane could not remember the last time they had sat together and quietly talked, just the two of them. Her bag was already packed and she was expected back in Boston tonight, but Jane made no move to leave. Instead she remained in the armchair, because she did not know when they would have this chance again. Life was too often a series of interruptions. Phone calls, family crises, other people always interrupting, whether it was in the morgue or at the crime scene. On this gray afternoon there were no ringing phones, no one knocking on the door, yet silence hung between them, heavy with all that had been left unsaid these past weeks, ever since Maura's testimony had sent a cop to prison. Boston's finest did not easily forgive such acts of treason.

Now, at every crime scene, Maura was forced to walk a gauntlet of chilly silence and hostile stares, and the strain was apparent in her face. In the firelight, her eyes seemed hollow, her cheeks thinner.

"Graff was guilty." Maura's fingers tightened around the teacup. "I would testify to that again."

"Of course you would. That's what you do, you tell the truth."

"You make it sound like a bad habit. A tic."

"No, it takes courage to tell the truth. I should have been a better friend."

"I wasn't sure if we *were* friends anymore. Or if I'm capable of holding on to *any* friends." Maura stared at the fire, as if all the answers could be found in those flames. "Maybe I should just stay here. Become a hermit and live in the woods. It's so beautiful. I could spend the rest of my life in Maine."

"Your life's in Boston."

"It's not as if Boston ever embraced me."

"Cities don't embrace you. People do."

"And it's people who let you down." Maura blinked at the firelight.

"That could happen anywhere, Maura."

"There's a hardness to Boston. A coldness. Before I moved there, I'd heard about chilly New Englanders, but I didn't really believe it. Then I got to Boston, and I felt like I had to chip through ice just to know people."

"Even me?"

Maura looked at her. "Even you."

"I had no idea we gave off those vibes. I guess it ain't sunny California."

Once again, Maura's gaze was on the flames. "I should never have left San Francisco."

"You have friends in Boston now. You have me."

A smile twitched up the corner of Maura's mouth. "You, I would miss."

"Is Boston really the problem? Or is it one Bostonian in particular?"

They didn't need to say his name; they were both thinking of Father Daniel Brophy, the man who'd brought both joy and sorrow into Maura's life. The man who had probably suffered just as deeply from their ill-considered affair.

"Just when I think I'm over him," said Maura, "when I think I've finally crawled out of the hole and back into the sunlight, I'll see him at a crime scene. And the wound rips right open again."

"It's hard to avoid him when death scenes are what you both do."

Maura gave a rueful laugh. "A healthy way to build a relationship! On tragedy."

"It is over between you, isn't it?"

"Yes." Maura paused. "And no."

"But you're not together."

"And I can see how much he's suffering because of it. It's written all over his face."

*And on your face, too.*

"Which is why I *should* leave Boston. Go back to California, or . . . anywhere."

"And that will solve everything?"

"It could."

"You'd be two thousand miles away from him, but you'd also be two thousand miles from every tie you've built over the last few years. Your home, your colleagues. Your friends."

"Friend. As in singular."

"You didn't see the memorial service we held for you when we thought you were dead. When we thought the body in that coffin was yours. The room was packed, Maura, with people who respect you. Who care about you. Yeah, maybe we're no good at showing our feelings. Maybe these long winters make us all crabby. But we do have feelings. Even in Boston."

Maura kept staring at the fireplace, where the flames were slowly dying, leaving only the glow of ashes.

"Well, I know someone who'll be really sorry if you go back to California," said Jane. "Does he know you're thinking about this?"

"He?"

"Oh, geez, don't play dumb. I've seen how he looks at you. It's the one reason Sansone and Brophy dislike each other so much. Because of *you*."

Surprise flickered in Maura's eyes as she looked at Jane. "Anthony Sansone was never on your list of favorite people."

"Talk about oddballs. And he's part of this weird Mephisto group."

"Yet now you're telling me he's a reason for me to stay in Boston."

"He's worth considering, isn't he?"

"Wow. He's come a long way in your estimation."

"At least he's available." *Unlike Daniel Brophy* was what Jane didn't have to add. "And he has a thing for you."

"No, Jane." Maura slumped back into the armchair. "He doesn't."

Jane frowned. "How do you know?"

"A woman knows." Her gaze drifted off again, pulled like a moth back to the moribund flames. "The night I got here, Anthony showed up, too."

"And what happened?"

"Nothing. The next morning we had a meeting with the faculty. And then he was gone again, off to London. Just a phantom who flits in and out of my life."

"Sansone's been known to do that kind of thing. It doesn't mean he's not interested."

"Jane, *please*. Don't try to talk me into another bad affair."

"I'm trying to talk you into not leaving Boston."

"Because Anthony's *such* a good catch?"

"No, because Boston needs you. Because you're the smartest ME I've ever worked with. And because . . ." Jane sighed. "I'd friggin' miss you, Maura."

The last remnants of the birch log collapsed, sending up a puff of glowing ashes. That, and the steady patter of rain, were the only sounds in the room. Maura sat very still, so still that Jane wondered whether Maura had registered what she'd just said. Whether it made any difference at all to her. Then Maura looked at her, eyes bright with tears, and Jane knew that her words might make all the difference in the world.

"I'll take that under consideration," Maura said.

"Yeah, you do that." Jane glanced again at her watch. "I should get going."

"Do you really need to leave today?"

"I want to dig deeper into the Ward and Yablonski cases, which means dealing with multiple jurisdictions, multiple agencies. And I'll be doing it mostly on my own, since Crowe doesn't want to waste any manpower on it."

"Detective Crowe has a pathetic lack of imagination."

"You noticed that, too?" Jane stood. "I'll be checking in every day, to make sure Teddy's okay. You call me if there are any problems."

"Relax, Jane. This is the safest place he could be."

Jane thought about the gated road, the isolation. The thirty thousand acres of wooded wilderness. And she thought of the ever-alert guardians who watched over it all, the Mephisto Society. What safer place to hide a threatened child than with people who knew how dangerous the world could be?

"I'm satisfied with what I've seen," she said. "I'll see you back in Boston."

On her way out of the castle, Jane stopped to check on Teddy one last time. He was sitting in class, and she didn't disturb him, just watched from the doorway as Lily Saul, with swoops and slashes, demonstrated the advantages of the Spanish sword used by the Roman legions. Teddy looked enthralled, body angled forward as though to spring out of his chair and join the battle. Lily caught sight of Jane and gave a nod, a look that said: *He'll be fine. Everything is under control.*

That was all Jane needed to see.

Outside, she scurried through the rain to her car, tossed her overnight bag into the backseat, and slid in behind the wheel. Swiping water from her face, she reached in her pocket for the four-digit security code she'd need to exit the gate.

*Everything is under control.*

But as she pulled out of the courtyard and drove under the archway, something in the distance caught her eye, something in the woods. A man standing among the trees. He was so far away that she could not make out his face, only his shape. His clothes were the same mottled gray-brown as the tree trunks around him.

The road brought her in that direction, and as she drew closer she kept her eye on the man, wondering why he stood so still. Then a curve in the road briefly cut off her view, and when the clump of trees came back into sight, she saw no one standing there. It was just the stump of a dead oak, its bark mottled with lichen and pocked with woodpecker holes.

She stopped at the side of the road and rolled down her window. Saw leaves dripping with rain, branches bobbing in the wind. But there was no watcher in the woods, just that lifeless tree stump, masquerading as a menace.

*Everything is under control.*

Yet her uneasiness remained as she passed through the gate and drove south through forest and then farmland. Perhaps it was the unrelenting rain and the dark clouds hanging low on the horizon. Perhaps it was the lonely road, with its abandoned houses with sagging porches and boarded-over windows. This place felt like the end of the world, and she might be the last human alive.

Her ringing cell phone shattered that illusion. I'm back in civilization again, she thought as she rooted around in her purse for the phone. Reception was weak, barely enough to carry on a conversation, but she could make out Frost's fragmented voice.

"Your last email . . . spoke to Hillsborough PD . . ."

"Hillsborough? Is this about Will Yablonski's aunt and uncle?"

" . . . says it's weird . . . wants to discuss . . ."

"Frost? Frost?"

Suddenly his voice popped out loud and clear. The miracle of a good cell signal at last. "He has no idea what it all means."

"You spoke to the Hillsborough cop?"

"Yeah. A Detective David G. Wyman. He said the case struck him as weird from the beginning. I told him about Claire Ward, and his attention *really* perked up. He didn't know there were other kids. You need to talk to him."

"Can you meet me in New Hampshire?" asked Jane.

There was a pause; then his voice dropped. "No way. Crowe wants us focused on finding Andres Zapata. I'm on stakeout tonight. The housekeeper's apartment."

"Crowe's still going with robbery as the motive?"

"On paper Zapata looks good. Burglary priors in Colombia. He had access, opportunity. And his fingerprints are on the kitchen door."

"But this is bugging me, Frost. These three kids."

"Look, we're not expecting you here till tomorrow. You've got time to make a little detour."

She'd planned to be home tonight for dinner with Gabriel, and a good-night kiss for Regina. Now it seemed she was headed to New Hampshire. "Don't say a word to Crowe."

"Wasn't planning to."

"One more thing. Run a VICAP search on unsolved family massacres. Specifically the same year the Wards, the Yablonskis, and the Clocks were killed."

"What do you think we're dealing with?"

"I don't know." She stared ahead at the rain-slicked road. "But whatever it is, it's starting to scare me."

# SIXTEEN

B Y THE TIME JANE PULLED INTO THE DRIVEWAY, the rain had stopped, but clouds hung on, gray and oppressive, and the trees continued to drip moisture. No other vehicles were in sight. She stepped out of her car and approached the remains of what had once been the farmhouse of Will's aunt and uncle, Lynn and Brian Temple. A dozen yards away the barn stood untouched, but the residence was now nothing more than a pile of charred timbers. Standing alone by the ruins, the sound of water dripping all around her, she could almost smell the stench of smoke still rising from the ashes.

Tires crunched across gravel, and she turned to see a dark blue SUV pull to a stop behind her Subaru. The man who stepped out was wearing a yellow rain slicker, which hung like a four-man tent on his hefty frame. Everything about him seemed large, from his bald head to his meaty hands, and although she was not afraid of him, in this isolated spot she was acutely aware of his physical advantage over her.

"Detective Wyman?" she called out.

He strode toward her, boots splashing through puddles. "And you must be Detective Rizzoli. How was your drive down from Maine?"

"Wet. Thanks for meeting me." She looked at the ruins. "This is what you wanted me to see?"

"I thought we should meet here first, while there's still daylight. So you could take a look around."

For a moment they stood together, regarding the destroyed house in silence. In the field beyond it, a deer wandered into view and stared at them, unafraid. It was not yet acquainted with the crack of a rifle, the punch of a bullet.

"They seemed like decent citizens," Detective Wyman said. "Quiet. Kept the property in good order. Never came to our attention." He paused and gave an ironic shake of the head. "That's one definition of *decent citizen*, I guess."

"So you didn't personally know the Temples."

"I heard there was a new couple who were renting the old McMurray place, but I never met them. They didn't appear to have regular jobs, so not many folks in town got to know them, except for their rental agent. They told her they were looking for a quiet life in the country, someplace where their nephew could enjoy the outdoors, breathe fresh air. Gas station, grocery store clerks saw them around town, but to everyone else the Temples were pretty much invisible."

"What about their nephew, Will? He must have had friends around here."

"Homeschooled. Never got a chance to mix in with any local kids. Besides which, I got the feeling he was sort of different."

"How so?"

"Kind of big and clumsy. A real nerd, if you know what I mean. The night it happened, he told me he was standing out in that field there." Wyman pointed to the pasture, where the lone deer was leisurely grazing. "He had this fancy telescope set up, and he was looking at the stars or something. Oh, I remember now. He was searching for comets." Wyman laughed. "Now, I got two teenage boys of my own. And on a Saturday night, the last thing they'd want to do is stand out in a field with no TV and no Facebook."

"So Will's just standing out here by himself in this field, looking at the sky. And the house blows up."

"That's about it. I assumed it was just an accident. Furnace, propane tank, something like that. Then the fire chief checks it out, and finds what look like incendiary devices. That's when we called in the State Police Major Crime Unit. It's all in my report. I've brought a copy for you. It's in the truck."

"Their nephew, Will. What did you think of him? I mean, beyond the fact he's a nerd."

"I took a long look at the kid, of course. Wondered if maybe he had issues with his aunt and uncle, maybe wanted to get out from under their thumbs. But we're pretty sure he couldn't have done it."

"You just told me he's a smart kid. He could probably figure out how to build a bomb."

"Not like this one."

"What's special about it?"

"Semtex, to start with."

That startled her. "Plastic explosives?"

"Highly sophisticated design. According to the FBI, the components were French. That's not what a fourteen-year-old kid would use to murder his aunt and uncle."

Jane frowned at the blackened timbers. Came to the only possible conclusion. *A professional did this.* "Tell me about the Temples," she said.

"They were the boy's only surviving relatives. Lynn Temple was his mother's sister. She worked as a librarian near Baltimore. Brian Temple was a physicist, worked at NASA-Goddard in Greenbelt, Maryland, where Will's father Neil Yablonski also worked. The two men were friends and colleagues, and the couples were pretty close. After the boy's parents were killed in the plane crash, Lynn and Brian got custody of Will. What happened after that is kind of a puzzle."

"What do you mean?"

"Days after the boy's parents died in the crash both Brian and Lynn quit their jobs. Just like that, Brian leaves a twenty-year career with NASA. They pack up, put their furniture in storage, and leave Baltimore. Few months later, they settled here."

"Without jobs? How did they support themselves?"

"Another good question. The Temples died with five hundred thousand dollars in their bank account. Now, I don't know how well NASA pays, but that's quite a nice nest egg, even for a physicist."

Daylight was fading. From the woods, two more deer emerged, a doe and her fawn, but they were cautious, eyeing the two humans as they ventured out, step by step, into the field. Come hunting season, that caution might be the extra margin of safety that would keep them alive. *But nothing will save you once you catch the hunter's eye.*

"What were the Temples running from?" she said.

"I don't know, but it's pretty obvious they *were* running. Maybe they knew something about that plane crash."

"Then why not go to the police?"

"I have no idea. The Maryland detective I spoke to, the one who investigated the Yablonskis' deaths, sounded as baffled as I am."

"Did Will know why his aunt and uncle moved him here?"

"They told him Baltimore was a dangerous town, and they wanted to live someplace safer. That's it."

"And this is where they end up," she said, thinking of collapsing timbers, searing flames. A hellish death at the edge of a quiet wood.

"The thing is, this *is* a safe town," said Wyman. "We get our OUIs, our stupid teens doing stupid stuff. Maybe a burglary, or some family hauling off at each other. That's our police blotter. But this?" He shook his head. "I've never dealt with anything like it. And I hope I never will again."

In the field, more silhouettes appeared. A whole herd of deer, moving silently through the twilight. For a city girl like Jane it was a magical sight. Here, where wild deer felt secure enough to wander into view, the Temples must have thought they'd found their own sanctuary. A place where they could settle, unknown and unnoticed.

"It's just a matter of luck that the boy survived," said Wyman.

"And you're sure it was just luck?"

"Like I said, I did briefly consider him a suspect. I had to, just as a matter of routine. But that boy, he truly was shaken up. We found his telescope still out in the field, where he said he'd left it. It was a crystal-clear sky that night, just the kind of night you'd set up a telescope. And he got singed pretty good, trying to save his aunt and uncle."

"I understand a passing motorist brought him to the hospital."

Wyman nodded. "A woman was driving by and she saw the flames. She drove the kid to the ER."

Jane turned to look at the road. "The last house

I saw was about a mile from here. Does that woman live around here?"

"I don't think so."

"You don't know?"

"We never spoke to her. She dropped off the boy and left. Told the nurse her phone number, but there was some kind of mix-up. When we called the number, some guy in New Jersey picked up, had no idea what we were talking about. At that point, we weren't thinking this was a crime at all. We thought it was an accident, so hunting for witnesses wasn't a priority. It was only later, after we heard about the Semtex, that we realized we were dealing with a homicide."

"She might have seen something that night. Maybe even passed the killer on the road."

"We had no luck tracking her down. Both the boy and the ER nurse described her as blond and slim, in her forties. Matches the glimpse we caught of her in the hospital surveillance video." Wyman looked up as a light rain began to fall. "So that's the puzzle we're left with. This thing is like an iceberg, with only a piece showing above the water. And a whole deeper story that we can't see." He pulled the hood over his head against the rain. "I got that file for you in my truck. Why don't you look it over, call if you have questions."

She took the thick bundle of papers he handed her. "Actually, I do have another question. About how Will ended up at Evensong."

"I thought you were just there. Didn't they tell you?"

"The school psychologist said Will was referred there from your state agency."

"Fastest damn placement I ever saw. Day after the fire, while the kid's still in the hospital, I got a call from the governor's office. They put the boy under special protection. Then some guy in an unmarked car arrives, scoops up the kid, and off they go."

"Some guy?"

"Tall, dark-haired fellow. Dressed all in black, like a vampire."

All in black. *Anthony Sansone.*

# SEVENTEEN

"I NOW CALL TO ORDER THIS MEETING OF THE Jackals," announced Julian.

Maura watched as six boys took their seats in the chemistry classroom. Because they sat together at Julian's table in the dining hall, Maura had come to know all their names. In the second row there was Bruno Chinn, who never seemed to sit still for a minute, and even now was fidgeting and twitching in his chair. Beside him, Arthur Toombs sat perfectly still, his burn-scarred hands clasped together on the desk. Those scars, she'd been told, were the ugly souvenirs of a fire set by his own father. Near the door sat Lester Grimmett, a boy obsessed with quick escape routes. A quick escape out a window had once saved his life, and he always, always chose a seat near the exit. And in the front row sat the two newest members of the Jackals, Will Yablonski and Teddy Clock. Their stories, Maura knew all too well.

Six boys, six tragedies, Maura thought. But life

went on and here they were, some of them scarred, all of them survivors. This club was their way of dealing with the losses, the bad memories, a way for even these powerless children to feel like warriors.

But as crime fighters, they seemed a rather unimpressive lot.

Only Julian stood out, tall and commanding, a club president who looked the part. Although Jane had dismissed the Jackals as nothing more than *CSI High School,* it was clear that Julian took his role as club president seriously. And the other boys in the room looked every bit as serious.

"Today, Jackals, we have a *real* forensic investigator joining us," said Julian. "Dr. Isles works at the medical examiner's office in Boston, where she performs autopsies. She's a medical doctor. A forensic pathologist. A scientist. And . . ." He looked at her with pride. "She's my friend."

*My friend.* Two such simple words, yet the way he'd said them held a far deeper meaning for both of them. She stood up, smiling, and addressed the club with the same respect that they regarded her.

"Thank you for the introduction, Julian. As he told you, I'm a pathologist. I work with the dead. I examine human remains on the autopsy table, and I look at tissues under the microscope, to understand why people die. Whether it was the natural result of a disease process. Or whether it was caused by trauma or toxins. Poisons. Since my scientific background is medicine, I can advise you on . . ." She paused, glimpsing movement in the hallway. A flash of blond hair. "Claire?" she called out. "Would you like to join us?"

All the boys turned at once to look at the doorway. Claire could hardly slip away unnoticed, so she gave a shrug, as if she had nothing better to do anyway. She walked straight to the front row and dropped indifferently into the chair next to Will. All the boys were still staring at this exotic creature who'd just wandered into their midst. Indeed, thought Maura, Claire Ward *was* a strange girl. With her white-blond hair and pale eyelashes, she looked otherworldly, like some forest nymph. But her bored expression and slouched shoulders radiated pure American teenager.

Claire looked around at the speechless boys. "Do you guys actually *do* something at these meetings, or do you just stare?"

Julian said, "We're about to discuss what we found in the willow tree."

"Which I had nothing to do with. No matter what anyone says."

"We just follow the evidence, Claire. Wherever it leads us." He looked at Maura. "I thought, since you're the medical expert, you could start by telling us the cause of death."

Maura frowned. "Cause of death?"

"The rooster's," called out Bruno. "We already know the manner of his death was homicide. Or chicken-cide, I guess you'd call it. But *how* did he die?"

Maura looked around at the faces watching her. They're serious, she thought. They're actually treating this as a death investigation.

"You did examine him," said Arthur. "Didn't you?"

"Only briefly," Maura admitted. "Before Mr. Roman discarded the remains. And based on the angle of his neck, I'd say it was clearly broken."

"So would that be death from strangulation or spinal cord trauma?"

"She just said the neck was snapped," said Bruno. "I'd call that neurologic, not vascular."

"And what about the time-of-death estimate?" said Lester. "Do you know what the postmortem interval was?"

Maura looked from face to face, startled by the rush of questions. "Time of death is always tricky, if there are no witnesses. In humans, we look at a number of indicators. Body temperature, rigor mortis, livor mortis—"

"Have you ever tried doing vitreous potassium on a bird?" asked Bruno.

She stared at him. "No. No, I can't say that I have. I admit, I don't know much about chicken pathology."

"Well, at least we have a cause of death, then. But what was the point of cutting him open? Why pull out his guts and hang him in the tree?"

*Precisely the question I asked in the clearing.*

"That issue gets into profiling," said Julian. "For now, we'll stick to the physical evidence. I went back into the woods to try and find the body, but I think some scavenger made off with it, so we don't have the remains to examine. I also searched for footwear impressions around the chicken coop, but I'm sorry to say the rain pretty much wiped those out. So I guess we'll move on to what you guys found." He looked at Bruno. "Do you want to go next?"

As Bruno moved to the front of the class, Maura sat down, feeling like the student who hadn't done her homework. She had no idea what the bouncy, twitchy little Bruno would have to share. He pulled on latex gloves and reached into a brown paper sack. Out came the three twig dolls, still attached to their twine nooses, and he laid them on the stainless-steel lab counter. Such trivial things, she thought, looking at them now. Under the classroom's bright fluorescent lights, the reddish brown splatters looked like mud stains, not blood at all. Dangling from the willow tree and twisting in the wind, they'd seemed unholy. Now they had lost their power, reduced to nothing more than what they were: bundles of twigs.

"Here we have exhibits A, B, and C," said Bruno. "Human figurines that appear to represent two males and one female. They're made up of various twigs and bark, tied together with twine. It's the twine I looked at. I determined that it's made of jute. I also found samples of the same kind of twine in the barn, where it's used to tie up bales of hay for the horses." He reached in his pocket and pulled out a sample of string. "See? Identical. From our own barn!" He sat back down.

"Arthur, you want to go next?" said Julian.

"I identified the twigs," said Arthur, rising to his feet. "The bark skirt was easy. It's *Betula papyrifera*, the American white birch. The twigs weren't as easy to figure out, and there are two different kinds. Based on the smooth green bark and the pointed buds, I think some of them are *Fraxinus nigra*, the black ash. The other twigs I was able to identify because of their star-shaped pith. I think they're balsam poplar. You can find all these trees down by the stream."

"Good work," said Julian.

Maura stared at Arthur as he sat down, and she thought: That fifteen-year-old knows more about trees than I ever will. *CSI High School* was turning out to be far more impressive than she'd imagined.

Lester rose from his chair, but he didn't move to the front of the classroom. He stayed right by the exit, where he felt safe. "I looked at the rope that was used to hang the victim from that high branch. I had to go back and climb the tree to get the sample, since we couldn't find Herman—the victim—in the woods."

"And what did you find out about the rope?" said Julian.

"It's quarter-inch white nylon, diamond braid. All-purpose, good tensile strength. Resists rot and mildew." Lester paused. "I searched all over the place, to see if I could find the source. And I found a whole roll of it in the toolshed." He sat down.

"We've established that all the materials needed to make these dolls can be found right here, on the school grounds. The twigs. The twine. The rope." Julian looked around the room. "So now comes the hard part, answering the question that Bruno asked earlier: Why? Why would someone kill a rooster, slice him open, and gut him? Why hang him up along a trail that we walk almost every day? A place where we'd be sure to come across it?" He waited for an answer.

Arthur said, "Someone wants attention."

"Or hates roosters," said Bruno, looking pointedly at Claire.

"A religious rite," suggested Will. "Like Santería. They kill chickens, don't they?"

"A psychopath kills animals for fun," said Lester. "Maybe he enjoyed it. Maybe he got a thrill, which means he'll do it again." Lester paused. "Next time, it might not be a chicken."

That made the room fall silent.

It was Teddy who broke the hush. "I think it's a message," he said.

"What kind of message?" asked Julian.

"He's trying to tell us something. Trying to warn us." Teddy's voice faded to a whisper. "Does anyone else wonder why there are three dolls?"

Maura looked at the twig dolls. Then she looked at Claire, sitting in the front row, flanked by Will and Teddy.

*Two males. One female.*

# EIGHTEEN

"**I**'M A LITTLE HAZY ON MY GEOGRAPHY, RIZZOLI, so help me out here," said Detective Crowe. "The last time I checked, New Hampshire was not in our jurisdiction."

Jane looked around the table at the detectives who'd gathered for the team conference. Frost and Moore sat facing her, but neither one seemed eager to butt heads with Crowe this morning. The whole team, in fact, looked weary of conflict. Crowe had beaten them all down, and she was the only one prepared to challenge him. The only one who actually relished a knock-down, drag-out battle.

"I just listed all the parallels to the Ackerman case," she said. "Two years ago, the Yablonskis die when a bomb takes down their private plane."

"Which crashed in Maryland," pointed out Crowe.

"Also two years ago, Claire Ward's parents are shot to death—"

"In London." Crowe laughed. "A different *country,* for Chrissakes."

"—and both events take place the *very same week* that Teddy Clock's family is attacked in Saint Thomas. Three families, Crowe. All killed within days of each other. Now it's two years later, and the sole survivors of those families are all attacked again. It's like someone's determined to wipe out the bloodlines. And these three kids will be the last to die."

"What do you propose, Rizzoli? You want to fly to Maryland and run their investigation for them?"

"Flying to Maryland would be a start."

"What's next, London? Boston PD will be *thrilled* to foot that bill. Oh, and let's not forget Saint Thomas. Someone needs to check out *that* incident."

Frost raised a hand. "I volunteer for Saint Thomas."

"I'm not asking for junkets to London and Saint Thomas," said Jane. "I'd just like to spend some time on this. I think there are connections that we just aren't seeing. Something that ties together the Wards, the Yablonskis, and the Clocks."

"A vast international conspiracy," said Crowe. "Right."

"It warrants a deeper look."

"No. We stay focused on Andres Zapata. Suddenly he's nowhere to be seen, which sounds like a guilty man to me." Crowe looked at Frost. "What do we have on his phone calls?"

Frost shook his head. "Hasn't used his cell phone

since the Ackermans were killed. I'm guessing he tossed it, or he's already back in Colombia. Maria's phone calls don't trip any alarms for me."

"Then she has some other way she contacts him. Email. A go-between. So we move on to friends of friends. Any new tips since this morning's broadcast?"

Moore nodded. "We're trying to keep up with all of them."

"You know what Master Yoda says. *There's no try, only do.*" Crowe glanced at his watch and abruptly stood up, straightening his tie. "Got a reporter waiting for me," he said and walked out of the room.

"Do you think we should widen that doorway now?" said Jane. "Before his head gets too big to fit through?"

"I think it's too late," said Moore. Legendary for his patience, even he looked disgusted as he gathered his papers and stuffed them into his briefcase. Lately he'd been talking a lot about retirement; this might be the case that finally pushed him out the door.

"What do you think about Zapata?" Jane asked him.

"Andres Zapata has everything that Crowe loves in a suspect. Access, opportunity, a rap sheet. And no green card."

"You don't sound convinced."

"Neither do I have a convincing argument to rebut it. For now, Zapata's our man." Moore snapped the briefcase shut and trudged out the door like a weary bureaucrat.

"Geez," she said to Frost. "What happened to *him*?"

"You don't know what it's been like around here the past few days," said Frost. "You haven't had the pleasure of Crowe's company."

She sat tapping her pen on the files she'd brought into the meeting. Thought about all the hours she'd devoted to researching the Wards and Yablonskis. "Tell me I've got a point, Frost. Tell me there's something weird about it all."

"There's something weird."

"Thank you."

"But that doesn't mean it ties in here. I did that VICAP search. Looked at hundreds of family annihilations across the country. I'm sorry to say, these three families have a lot of company."

"But it's the *second* attacks that make these three stand out. It's like the Grim Reaper won't give up until He finishes the job. How do we explain it?"

"Not every crazy thing has an explanation. Sometimes it just is."

"I never liked that answer. It's the kind of thing I tell my kid."

"And Regina's okay with it, right?"

"Doesn't mean I am."

Her cell phone rang. She saw Crowe's number on the display and groaned. Rolled her eyes at Frost as she answered: "Rizzoli."

"They spotted Zapata, an apartment in Roxbury.

Surveillance tails Maria there, and the fucking moron shows up. Get here now, we're moving in."

TEN MINUTES LATER JANE and Frost pulled up next to a chain-link fence and scrambled out of their car. Crowe was already there, strutting like General MacArthur exhorting his troops, which consisted of Detectives Arbato and Moore and two patrolmen.

"Front entrance is around the corner," said Arbato, pointing to the four-story redbrick apartment building. "Cahill's watching the front door. Hasn't seen the suspect come out yet."

"Are we sure it is Zapata?" asked Moore.

"If not, then he's got a double. Maria stepped off the bus two blocks from here, walked straight to this address. Half an hour later, Zapata cuts across that parking lot, enters the building."

"You got a list of the tenants?" asked Jane.

"Yeah. There are twenty-four apartments, five of them vacant."

"Any Hispanic names?" said Crowe. "We'll check those first."

One of the patrolmen laughed. "Hey, man, that's profiling!"

"So sue me."

"Can I see that list?" Frost asked, and he scanned down the names. "There's a Philbrook living here."

"Yeah, that's *real* Hispanic," the patrolman said.

"Maria has a sister." Frost looked up. "She's married to a Philbrook."

"That's gotta be it," said Crowe. "Which apartment?"

"It says Two Ten."

"That'd be the rear of the building," said Arbato. "Security code for the entrance keypad is one two seven."

"Arbato," snapped Crowe, "you and these two officers stay on the exits. Rest of us, *in*."

Anyone who spotted them would know something was about to go down as Crowe and Moore, Frost and Jane moved together toward the front entrance. But those in Apartment 210, which faced the rear of the building, would be blind to what was coming their way. Crowe punched 1-2-7 on the entrance keypad, and the lock clicked open. As Jane followed him inside, her heart was thumping, her hands starting to sweat. This could go down easy, or it could turn into a bloody disaster. Which meant these might be the last seconds she'd ever register, her shoes moving up scuffed stairs, the weight of the Glock in her hands. Frost's back was just ahead of her, his Kevlar vest bulging beneath his shirt. All these details she took in with click-click efficiency, a dozen impressions at once.

They reached the second-floor landing. Apartment 210 was down the hall. Behind her, a door suddenly opened and Jane whirled, weapon swinging around. A young woman stared back, baby clutched in her arms, dark eyes wide with terror.

"Stay inside!" Jane hissed. Instantly the woman retreated and the door slammed shut.

Crowe was already at Apartment 210. He paused, shot his team a glance. "Rizzoli," he whispered. "Your show. Get us in there."

She knew why he'd chosen her. Female face and voice, not as threatening. She took a breath and rang the door buzzer. Stood close enough to the peephole that she'd fill the view. Unfortunately that also made it easier for anyone inside to blow off her head. She spied a flicker of movement in the peephole; someone was staring at her.

The door swung open. A Hispanic woman appeared, round-faced, in her forties, with a strong enough resemblance to the Ackerman's housekeeper that Jane knew this must be Maria's sister.

"Mrs. Philbrook?" said Jane.

The woman spotted the other detectives in the hall and screamed: "Maria!"

"Go, go!" barked Crowe as he shoved past Jane and burst into the apartment.

Too many things happened at once. Detectives barreling through the apartment. Maria's sister shouting, wailing in Spanish. As Jane ran through, toward the next room, she caught glimpses of a stained carpet, a striped sofa, a playpen.

*Kids. There are kids in this apartment.*

Jane darted into a bedroom, where heavy curtains cast a gloom so deep she almost missed the huddled shapes in the corner. A woman was hugging two toddlers, her body curled around the children as though insulating them from harm with her own flesh.

*Maria.*

Footsteps clanged on metal.

Jane ducked through another doorway, into a second bedroom where Moore was scrambling through the open window, onto the fire escape.

"Zapata?" Jane asked.

"Headed up the ladder!"

*Why up?*

She stuck her head out the window and saw Arbato and Cahill standing in the alley below, their weapons drawn. She looked up, spotted her three teammates clambering up the ladder in pursuit.

She sprinted back through the apartment and dashed for the stairwell. If Zapata made it to the roof, that's where she'd intercept him. She took the steps two at a time, saw a door pop open and slam shut as she hurtled past, up the final flight, her heart whomping, her chest heaving.

She burst through the door to the rooftop and emerged into the glare of midday. Saw Zapata scramble over the edge and land with both feet onto the roof.

"Freeze!" she yelled. "Police!"

He halted, staring at her. He was empty-handed. Faded blue jeans, wrinkled button-down shirt with a ripped sleeve. For a few seconds it was just the two of them on that rooftop. She saw desperation in his eyes, watched it harden to grim determination.

"Hands in the air!" Crowe shouted as he and Frost dropped onto the rooftop behind Zapata.

There was nowhere for him to run. One cop in front of him, two behind him, all of them armed. Jane saw Zapata's legs wobble, thought he was about to drop to his knees in surrender. His next move shocked her.

He sprang to his left and ran toward the roof's far edge. Toward the narrow alley that cut between buildings. Only an Olympic-class leap could take a man safely across that gulf.

Yet leap he did, flinging himself from the roof's edge toward the next building. For a moment he seemed to hang in midair, his body stretched out in a swan dive that almost carried him across the chasm.

Jane scrambled to the edge. Saw Zapata clinging desperately to the rain gutter of the other building as his legs scissored above a four-story drop.

"Jesus, is he nuts?" said Frost.

"Arbato, get next door!" Crowe yelled down at the street, and the two detectives on the ground sprinted across the alley.

Still dangling from the rain gutter, Zapata tried to pull himself up, feet fighting for purchase against the wall. He swung up one leg, missed. Swung again. Just as his shoe made it up over the edge, the gutter tore away from the roof.

Jane closed her eyes, but she couldn't shut out the squeal of collapsing metal, or the thud of Zapata's body hitting the pavement.

Somewhere, a woman was screaming.

# NINETEEN

MARIA SALAZAR SAT HUNCHED AT THE INTER-
view table, head drooping as she wiped tears
from her eyes. As a young woman, Maria would
have been strikingly beautiful. At forty-five she was
still handsome, but through the one-way mirror
Jane could see the gray roots peeking through on
the crown of Maria's head. Her arms, propped up
on the table, were heavy but solid with muscles
built up from years of housework. While she had
scrubbed and polished and swept other people's
houses, what resentments had bubbled up inside
her? As she'd dusted the Ackermans' antique furniture, vacuumed the Persian carpets, had it ever oc-
curred to her that just one of their paintings, one
emerald necklace from Mrs. Ackerman's jewelry
box, could make all her financial woes disappear?

"Never," Maria moaned in the next room. "I
never steal anything!"

Crowe, playing bad cop to Moore's good cop,
leaned in close, his teeth bared with undisguised

aggression. "You disarmed the security system for your boyfriend."

"No."

"Left the kitchen door unlocked."

"No."

"Gave yourself a rock-solid alibi, babysitting your sister's kids, while Andres slipped into the Ackermans' house. Was he just going to rob them that night, or was murder always the plan?"

"Andres, he never hurt anyone!"

"His fingerprints are on the kitchen door. They're *inside* the kitchen." Crowe bent even closer and Maria shrank away. Jane almost felt sorry for the woman because there were few sights uglier than Darren Crowe's snarl, shoved into your face. "He was in the house, Maria. Just walked through that kitchen door."

"He brought my cell phone! I left it home that morning, so he comes to the house."

"And left his fingerprints inside the kitchen?"

"I give him coffee. I clean the stove, and he sits for a minute."

"And Mrs. Ackerman's okay with that? A strange man, sitting in her kitchen?"

"She don't mind. Mrs. Ackerman, she's always nice to me."

"Come on. Weren't the Ackermans like every other rich asshole? Paid you almost nothing, while you're on your knees scrubbing their toilets."

"No, they treat me good."

"They had all the money in the world, and look

at you, Maria. Struggling to pay your bills. It's so unfair. You deserve more, don't you think?"

She shook her head. "You make this up. It's not the truth."

"The *truth* is, Andres had a criminal record in Colombia. Drug smuggling. Burglary."

"He never hurt anyone."

"There's always a first time. Gotta be tempting when we're talking about people as rich as the Ackermans. All those nice things, there for the taking." He pulled an evidence bag out of the box he'd brought into the room. "We found these in your apartment, Maria. Nice pearl earrings. How did you afford these?"

"Mrs. Ackerman, she gave them to me. For Christmas."

"*Gave* them to you? Sure."

"She *did*."

"They're worth about five hundred bucks. Pretty nice bonus."

"She didn't want them anymore. Said I could have them."

"Or did she suddenly find out you'd stolen them? Maybe that's the reason Andres had to kill them. To keep them quiet so you wouldn't get arrested."

Maria's head came up, her eyes swollen and damp, her face flushed with rage. "You are a *devil*!"

"I'm just trying to keep this city safe."

"By making up lies? You don't know me. You don't know Andres."

"I know he was a criminal. I know he ran from us. That tells me he was guilty."

"He was *afraid*."

"Of what?"

"Colombia. He couldn't go back to Colombia. They would kill him there."

"So he chose to die here, instead?"

Maria dropped her face in her hands. "He wanted to live," she sobbed. "He wanted to be left alone."

"Tell the truth, Maria."

"That *is* the truth."

"Tell the truth, or . . ." Crowe paused at Moore's touch on his shoulder. Though no words were exchanged between the two men, Jane saw the look that passed between them. Saw Moore's disapproving shake of the head, answered by Crowe's glare.

Abruptly Crowe straightened. "Think about it, Maria," he said, and walked out of the room.

"Man," Frost muttered beside Jane. "That's one asshole on steroids."

Through the one-way mirror, Jane watched as Moore sat with Maria. He offered no comforting touch, no reassuring words, as the woman continued to sob, hugging herself as though to stop her shaking.

"There's not enough evidence here," said Jane.

"The fingerprints on the kitchen door?" said Frost. "The fact that he ran from us?"

"Give me a break. You sound like Crowe."

"And those earrings. Who gives their housekeeper an expensive gift like that?"

"Maybe it's true. Maybe Mrs. Ackerman was a generous woman. We can't disprove it. And think about that house, all the things Zapata could have stolen, if this really was a robbery. Even the jewelry box was left."

"He got spooked. Ran before he could take anything."

"Does that sound plausible? It's gotta bother you. It sure as hell bothers me."

In the next room, Maria slowly rose to her feet, steadied by Moore's hand. As he guided the housekeeper out the door, Jane said quietly: "It bothers Moore, too."

"The trouble is, you don't have anything else to go on. Just a bad feeling."

That wasn't enough, but it was also something she couldn't ignore. A bad feeling was your subconscious telling you you'd missed something, a vital detail that could change the course of an investigation.

It could change lives.

Her phone rang. When she looked at the caller's name, she had another bad feeling. "Frankie," she answered with a sigh.

"I've called you twice and you didn't pick up."

"I've been busy." *Chasing suspects. Watching a man die.*

"Yeah, well, now it's too late. It's all hitting the fan."

"What's going on?"

"We're at Mom's, and Korsak's just arrived."

"*We*? You mean Dad's there, too?"

"Yeah. They're all yelling at each other."

"Jesus, Frankie. You've gotta keep Dad and Korsak apart. And get one of them out of there."

"I swear they're gonna kill each other, Jane."

"Okay, okay. I'll be right there." She hung up.

"Remember, there's nothing more dangerous than a domestic call," said Frost, spectacularly unhelpful.

"I just hope I won't have to call a lawyer."

"For your dad?"

"For me. After I kill him."

# TWENTY

As JANE STEPPED OUT OF HER CAR, SHE COULD already hear the shouting. She hurried past three familiar vehicles parked at crazy angles in front of her mother's house and banged on the front door. Banged again when no one answered, probably because they'd gone deaf inside from the racket.

"Finally, the police arrive," said a cranky voice behind her.

Jane turned to see Angela's next-door neighbor, Mrs. Kaminsky, glaring at her from the sidewalk. The woman had looked ancient twenty years ago, and the passage of decades had changed nothing, as if she'd been frozen in time, her face forever cemented in a scowl.

"This neighborhood's gone all to pot," said Mrs. Kaminsky. "All this running around with strange men."

"Excuse me?" said Jane.

"Your mother used to be respectable. A good married woman."

"My dad left her."

"So that's an excuse to run wild?"

"Wild? My mom?"

The front door opened. "Thank God you're here!" said Korsak. "It's two against one!" He grabbed Jane's hand. "Come help me."

"You *see*?" said Mrs. Kaminsky, pointing at Korsak. "*He's* what I'm talking about!"

Jane followed Korsak into the house, relieved to close the front door against the neighbor's disapproving stare. "What do you mean, two against one?"

"I'm all on my own here. Your dad and Frankie keep hammering away, trying to get your mom to dump me."

"What does Mom say?"

"Who knows what she'll do? Any minute now, she's gonna snap."

Kicking all these guys out of her house would be a good first step, thought Jane as she followed the sound of voices toward the kitchen. Of course this battle *would* have to be in the kitchen, where a sharp knife was always handy.

"It's like you've been taken over by pod people, and now you can't think for yourself," Jane's father said.

"Ma, we don't know you anymore," Frankie chimed in.

"I just want my old Angela back. My wife and me together, the way we used to be."

Angela was sitting at the table, clutching her head as though to shut out the voices assaulting her.

"Dad, Frankie," said Jane, "leave her alone."

Angela looked up at her daughter with desperate eyes. "What do I do, Janie? They're making me so confused!"

"There's no confusion here," said Frank. "We're married, and that's that."

"Last week, you were getting divorced," said Korsak.

"That was a misunderstanding."

"And her name was Sandie," muttered Angela.

"She meant nothing!"

"Not what I heard," said Korsak.

"This has nothing to do with you," said Jane's brother. "Why are you still here, asshole?"

" 'Cause I love this woman, okay? After your dad walked out, I was the one who stood by her. I was the one who made her laugh again." Korsak placed a possessive hand on Angela's shoulder. "Now your dad needs to move on."

"Don't touch my wife." Frank slapped Korsak's hand away from Angela.

Korsak bristled. "Did you just hit me?"

"What, you mean that little tap?" Frank gave Korsak's arm a hard shove. "Or did you mean *that*?"

"Dad, don't," said Jane.

Korsak's face flushed a dangerous red. With both hands he shoved Frank Rizzoli backward against the kitchen counter. "*That* was assaulting a police officer."

Jane's brother shoved himself between the two older men. "Hey. *Hey.*"

"You ain't a police officer now!" Frank Senior yelled. "And no wonder! Fat ass with a bad ticker!"

"*Dad,*" Jane pleaded as she swept the nearby wood block of kitchen knives out of his reach. "Stop it. *Both* of you!"

Korsak gave his shirt collar a tug. "I'll overlook what just happened here, for Angela's sake. But don't think I'll ever forget it."

"Get outta my house, asshole," said Frank Senior.

"Your house? You walked out on her," pointed out Korsak. "That makes this *her* house."

"Which I've been paying the mortgage on for the past twenty years. Now you think you can just horn in on my property?"

"Property?" Angela suddenly snapped straight, as if that word had driven a spear down her spine. "*Property?* Is that what I am to you, Frank?"

"Ma," said Frankie, "Dad didn't mean it that way."

"He most certainly did."

"No, I didn't," said Frank. "I'm just saying . . ."

Angela shot him a thousand-volt look. "I am nobody's property. I am my own woman."

"You tell him, babe," said Korsak.

Frank and Frankie snapped simultaneously: "*You* shut up."

"I want you out of here," Angela said, rising from her seat at the table, a Valkyrie ready for battle. "Go," she ordered.

Frank and Korsak looked at each other uncertainly.

"Well, you heard her," said Korsak.

"I mean both of you. *All* of you," said Angela.

Korsak shook his head in bewilderment. "But Angie—"

"You're giving me a headache with all this tugging and yelling. It's my kitchen, my house, and I want it back. *Now*."

"Ma, that sounds like a good idea," said Frankie. "A great idea." He gave his father a pat on the back. "Come on, Dad. Give her time and she'll come back to her senses."

"*That,*" said Angela, "will not help your father's case." She glared at the interlopers in her kitchen. "Well, what are you all waiting for?"

"*He* leaves first," said Frank, pointing at Korsak.

"Why should it be me?"

"We're *all* leaving, Ma," said Jane. She took Korsak's arm and pulled him toward the front door. "Frankie, you get Dad out of here."

"Not you, Jane," said Angela. "You stay."

"But you just said—"

"I want the *men* to leave. They're the ones giving me this headache. I want you to stay, so we can talk."

"Take care of this, Janie," said Frankie, and she couldn't miss the threatening note in his voice. "Remember, we're a *family*. That doesn't change."

Sometimes to my regret, she thought as the men left the kitchen, trailing a cloud of hostility so thick she could almost smell it. She didn't dare say a word, didn't move a muscle, until she heard the front door shut, then the sound of three car engines simultaneously revving up. Sighing with relief, she slid the block of kitchen knives back to its usual space on the counter and looked at her mother. Now, this was a strange turn of events. Frankie was the child Angela always seemed proudest of, her Marine Corps son who could do no wrong, even while he was tormenting his siblings.

But today Angela hadn't asked for Frankie, she'd asked for Jane, and now that they were alone together Jane took the time to study her mother. Angela's face was still flushed from her outburst, and with that color in her cheeks, the fire in her eyes, she didn't look like any man's property. She looked like a woman who should be clutching a spear and a battle-ax, steam hissing from her nostrils. But as they heard the three cars drive away, that warrior seemed to wilt, leaving only a weary middle-aged woman who slumped into her chair and buried her head in her hands.

"Mom?" said Jane.

"All I wanted was another chance at love. Another chance to feel alive again."

"What do you mean, alive? You didn't feel that way?"

"I felt invisible, that's what I felt. Every night, putting dinner in front of your father. Watching him suck it down without a single compliment. I thought that's how it's supposed to be when you're married for thirty-five years. How was I supposed to know things could be different? I figured that was that. My kids are grown, I have a house with a nice backyard. Who am I to complain?"

"I never knew you were unhappy, Mom."

"I wasn't. I was just . . ." Angela shrugged. "Here. Breathing. You, you're still a newlywed. You and Gabriel, you probably don't know what I'm talking about, and I hope you never do. It's a terrible feeling, to think the best years of your life are over. He made me feel that way."

"But you were so upset when he left."

"Of course I was upset! He left me for another woman!"

"So . . . you didn't want him. But you didn't want her to get him, either."

"Why's that so hard to understand?"

Jane shrugged. "I guess I get it."

"And *she's* the one who ended up being sorry. The bimbo." Angela laughed, a loud, cynical cackle.

"I think they're both sorry. That's why Dad wants to come home. I'm guessing it's a little late for that?"

Angela's lip trembled, and she looked down at the table where her hands rested. Decades of cooking, of burns from hot grease and nicks from kitchen knives, had left battle scars on those hands. "I don't know," she murmured.

"You just told me how unhappy you were."

"I was. Then Vince came along, and I felt like a new woman. A young woman. We did crazy things together, things I never dreamed I'd do, like shooting a gun. And skinny-dipping."

"TMI, Mom." *Way* too much information.

"He takes me dancing, Janie. Do you remember the last time your father took me dancing?"

"No."

"Neither do I. That's the point."

"Okay." Jane sighed. "Then we'll deal with this. It's your decision, and whatever it is, I'll back you up." Even if it meant wearing a pink clown dress to the wedding.

"That's just it, Janie. I *can't* decide."

"You just told me how happy Vince makes you."

"But Frankie said the magic word. *Family.*" Angela looked up with tormented eyes. "That means something. All those years together. Having you and your brothers. Your father and I, we have a *history,* and that's something I can't just walk away from."

"So *history* is more important than what makes you happy?"

"He's your father, Jane. Does that mean so little to you?"

Jane gave a confused shake of the head. "This

has nothing to do with me. It's about you and what you want."

"What if what I want makes me feel guilty? What if I marry Vince and spend the rest of my life regretting that I didn't give our family a second chance? Frankie, for one, will never forgive me. And then there's Father Flanagan and everyone at church. And the neighbors . . ."

"Forget the neighbors." *They're a lost cause.*

"So you see, there's a lot to consider here. It was so much easier when I was the wronged woman, and everyone was saying *You go, girl!* Now it's all flipped around and I'm the one breaking up the family. You know how hard that is for me? Being the scarlet woman?"

Better scarlet, thought Jane, than depressed and gray. She reached across the table to touch her mother's arm. "You deserve to be happy, that's all I can say. Don't let Father Flanagan or Mrs. Kaminsky or Frankie talk you into doing anything you don't want to do."

"I wish I could be like you, so sure of yourself. I look at you and I think, how did I raise such a strong daughter? Someone who makes breakfast, feeds her baby, and then takes down perps?"

"I'm strong because you made me that way, Ma."

Angela laughed. Ran a hand across her eyes. "Yeah, right. Look at me, a babbling mess. Torn between my lover and my family."

"This member of the family wants you to stop worrying about us."

"Impossible. When they say your family is flesh and blood, that's exactly what it means. If I lose Frankie because of this, it'll be like cutting off my own arm. When you lose your family, you lose everything."

THOSE WORDS ECHOED IN Jane's head as she drove home that evening. Her mother was right: If you lost your family, you lost everything. She'd seen what happened to people who lost husbands or wives or children to murder. She'd seen how grief shriveled lives, how faces aged overnight. As hard as she might try to offer them comfort, to promise them closure through justice, she did not really know, or want to know, the depths of their suffering. Only another victim would truly understand.

Which was why a school like Evensong existed. It was a place for the wounded to heal, among those who understood.

She'd spoken with Maura that morning, but had not updated her about Zapata's fate. With their prime suspect dead, and Teddy presumably no longer in danger, they had to decide whether it might be time to bring him back to Boston. She pulled into her apartment parking lot and was about to call Maura's cell phone when she remembered there was no reception at Evensong. Scrolling down her call log, she found the landline number that Maura had last called from, and dialed it.

Six rings later, a tremulous voice answered: "Evensong."

"Dr. Welliver, is that you? It's Detective Rizzoli." She waited for an answer. "Hello, are you there?"

"Yes. Yes." A startled laugh. "Oh, my God, they're so beautiful!"

"What's beautiful?"

"I've never seen birds like those. And the sky, such strange colors . . ."

"Um, Dr. Welliver? May I speak to Dr. Isles?"

"I don't know where she is."

"Could you ask her to call me back? You'll be seeing her at dinner, right?"

"I'm not going. Everything tastes funny today. Oh! Oh!" Welliver gave a squeal of delight. "If you could just see these birds! They're so close, I could touch them!"

Jane heard her set down the receiver. Heard footsteps walking away.

"Dr. Welliver? Hello?"

There was no answer.

Jane frowned as she disconnected, wondering what species of bird could have so enchanted the woman. She had a sudden vision of pterodactyls swooping in over the Maine woods.

In the world that was Evensong, anything seemed possible.

# TWENTY-ONE

**C**HICKEN KILLER.

Though no one said it to her face, Claire knew what they were whispering as they leaned their heads together and shot glances at her from the other dining tables. *She's the one.* Everyone knew that Claire had tried to kick Herman a few days ago, outside the stables. Which made her the chief suspect. In the court of gossip, she'd already been tried and convicted.

She speared a brussels sprout and it tasted as bitter as her resentment, but she ate it anyway, chewing mechanically as she tried to ignore the whispers, the stares. As always, Briana was the ringleader, backed up by her princesses. The only one who regarded Claire with any obvious sympathy was Bear the dog, who rose from his usual place at Julian's feet and trotted over to her. She slipped him a morsel of meat under the table and blinked away tears when he gave her a grateful lick on the hand. Dogs were so much kinder than humans. They accepted you just the way you were. She reached down and buried her hand in Bear's thick fur. At least he would always be her friend.

"Can I sit at your table?"

She looked up to see Teddy holding his dinner tray. "Be my guest. But you know what'll happen if you do."

"What?"

"You'll never be one of the cool kids."

"Never was anyway." He sat down, and she looked at his meal of boiled potatoes, brussels sprouts, and lima beans.

"What are you, a vegetarian?"

"I'm allergic."

"To what?"

"Fish. Shrimp. Eggs." He used his fingers to count down his list of allergies. "Wheat. Peanuts. Tomatoes. And maybe, but I'm not sure, strawberries."

"Geez, how do you not starve to death?"

"I'm as carnivorous as you are."

She looked at his pale face, his matchstick arms, and thought: You are the least carnivorous-looking boy I've ever met.

"I like meat. Yesterday, I ate the chicken." He paused, and his cheeks suddenly suffused with pink. "Sorry," he murmured.

"I didn't kill Herman. No matter what they're all saying about me."

"They're not *all* saying that."

She slapped her fork on the table. "I'm not stupid, Teddy."

"Will believes you. And Julian says a good investigator always avoids snap judgments."

She glanced at the other table and caught Briana's sneer. "Bet *she's* not defending me."

"Is it because of Julian?"

She looked at Teddy. "What?"

"Is that why you and Briana hate each other? Because you both like Julian?"

"I don't know what you're talking about."

"Briana says you've got a crush on him." Teddy looked at Bear, who wagged his tail, hoping for another morsel of food. "And that's why you're always fussing over his dog, to make Julian like you."

Was that what everyone thought? She gave Bear a sudden shove and snapped, "Stop bothering me, stupid dog."

The whole dining room heard it and turned to look at her as she stood up.

"Why are you leaving?" said Teddy.

She didn't answer. Just walked out of the dining hall, out of the building.

Outside it was not yet dark, but another lingering summer twilight. The swallows were whirling and looping in the sky. She walked the stone path around the building, halfheartedly scanning the shadows for the telltale flashes of fireflies. The crickets were chirping so loudly that at first she did not hear the clatter overhead. Then something tumbled down and thudded right at her feet. A chunk of slate.

*That could have hit me!*

She looked up and saw a figure perched on the

edge of the roof. Silhouetted against the night sky, arms spread wide like wings, it seemed poised to take flight.

No, she wanted to scream, but nothing came out of her throat. *No.*

The figure leaped. Against the darkening sky, the swallows continued to circle and soar, but the body plummeted straight down, a doomed bird stripped of its wings.

When Claire opened her eyes again, she saw the black pool spreading on the path, widening like a corona around Dr. Anna Welliver's shattered skull.

THE CHIEF MEDICAL EXAMINER in the state of Maine was Dr. Daljeet Singh, whom Maura had met years earlier at a forensic pathology conference. At every conference since then, they'd made it a tradition to meet for dinner, where they'd discuss odd cases and share photos of vacations and family. But it was not Daljeet who emerged from the white SUV with the ME placard; instead a young woman stepped out, dressed in boots, cargo pants, and a fleece jacket, as if she'd come straight from a hiking trail. She strode past the Maine State Police vehicles with the confident gait of someone who knew her way around a death scene, and walked straight toward Maura.

"I'm Dr. Emma Owen. And you're Dr. Isles, right?"

"Good guess," Maura said as they automatically shook hands, although it felt strange to do so with another woman. Especially a woman who looked scarcely old enough to have finished college, much less a pathology fellowship.

"Not a guess, really. I saw your photo in that article you wrote last year in *Journal of Forensic Pathology*. Daljeet talks about you all the time, so I feel like I already know you."

"How is Daljeet?"

"He's in Alaska this week, on vacation. Otherwise he'd be here himself."

Maura said, with an ironic laugh, "And this was supposed to be *my* vacation."

"That's got to suck. Come to Maine and the dead bodies follow you." Dr. Owen pulled shoe covers out of her pocket and, with the grace of a dancer, easily slipped them on while balancing on one leg, then the other. Like so many young female physicians now transforming the face of the medical profession, Dr. Owen seemed smart, athletic, and sure of herself. "Detective Holland already briefed me over the phone. Did you see this coming? Notice any signs of suicidal ideation, depression?"

"No. I'm as shocked as everyone else here. Dr. Welliver seemed perfectly fine to me. The only thing different today is that she didn't come down to dinner."

"And the last time you saw her?"

"At lunchtime. I believe she had her last student appointment of the day at one o'clock. No one saw her after that. Until she jumped."

"Do you have any theories? Any idea why she'd do this?"

"Absolutely none. We're all baffled."

"Well," the woman said, "if an expert like Dr. Isles is in the dark, then we've *really* got a mystery." She pulled on a pair of latex gloves. "Detective Holland told me there was a witness."

"One of the students saw it happen."

"Oh God. That'll give the kid nightmares."

As if Claire Ward didn't already have her share of them, thought Maura.

Dr. Owen looked up at the building, the windows lit up against the night sky. "Wow. I've never been out here before. I didn't even know this school existed. It looks like a castle."

"Built in the nineteenth century as a railroad baron's estate. Judging by the Gothic architecture, I think he fancied himself as royalty."

"Do you know where she jumped from?"

"The roof walk. It leads off the turret, where her office is located."

Dr. Owen stared up at the turret, where Welliver's office lights were still shining. "That looks like it's about seventy feet, maybe even higher. What do you think, Dr. Isles?"

"I'd agree."

As they followed the path around the side of the building, Maura wondered when she'd assumed the role of Senior Authority, a status made apparent whenever the young woman addressed her as *Dr. Isles*. Up ahead were the flashlight beams of the two Maine State Police detectives. The body lying at their feet was covered with a plastic sheet.

"Evening, gentlemen," said Dr. Owen.

"Ain't it always the shrinks who do this sort of thing?" one of the detectives said.

"She was a shrink?"

"Dr. Welliver was the school psychologist," said Maura.

The detective grunted. "As I was saying. I guess there's a reason they choose the field."

As Dr. Owen lifted up the sheet, both cops aimed their flashlights to illuminate the body. Anna Welliver lay on her back, face exposed to the glare, her hair splayed about her head like a wiry gray nest. Maura glanced up at the third-floor dormitory windows and saw the silhouettes of students staring down at a sight that children should never have to see.

"Dr. Isles?" Dr. Owen offered Maura a pair of gloves. "If you'd like to join me."

It was an invitation Maura didn't particularly welcome, but she pulled on the gloves and crouched down beside her younger colleague. Together they palpated the skull, examined the limbs, tallied up the obvious fractures.

"All we want to know is: accident or suicide?" said one of the detectives.

"You've already ruled out homicide, have you?" said Dr. Owen.

He nodded. "We talked to the witness. Girl named Claire Ward, age thirteen. She was outside, standing right here when it happened, and she didn't see anyone else on the roof but the victim. Said the woman spread her arms and took a dive." He pointed up toward the brightly lit turret. "The door leading from her office was wide open, and we saw no signs of a struggle. She stepped out onto the roof walk, climbed over the railing, and jumped."

"Why?"

The detective shrugged. "That I'll leave to the shrinks. The ones who *haven't* jumped."

Dr. Owen quickly rose back to her feet, but Maura felt her own age as she stood up more slowly, her right knee stiff from too many summers of gardening, from four decades of inevitable wear and tear on tendons and cartilage. It was yet another creaky reminder that a new generation always stood waiting in the wings.

"So, based on what the witness told you," said Dr. Owen, "this doesn't sound like an accidental death."

"Unless she *accidentally* climbed over the railing and *accidentally* flung herself off the roof."

"Okay." Dr. Owen stripped off her gloves. "I have to agree. Manner of death is suicide."

"Except we never saw it coming," said Maura. "There was no warning at all."

In the dark, she could not see the expressions of the two cops, but could imagine them both rolling their eyes.

"You want a suicide note?" one detective said.

"I want a reason. I knew the woman."

"Wives think they *know* their husbands. And parents *know* their kids."

"Yes, I hear the same thing all the time after suicides. *We had no warning.* I'm fully aware that families are sometimes clueless. But this . . ." Maura paused, aware of three pairs of eyes watching her, the distinguished ME from Boston, trying to defend something as illogical as a hunch. "You have to understand, Dr. Welliver's job was to counsel damaged children. To help them heal after severe emotional trauma. It was her life's work, so why would she traumatize them further by making them see this? By dying in such a spectacular way?"

"Do you have an answer?"

"No, I don't. Neither do her colleagues. No one on the faculty or staff understands this."

"Next of kin?" asked Dr. Owen. "Anyone who might provide insight?"

"She was a widow. As far as Headmaster Baum knows, she has no family left."

"Then I'm afraid it's just one of those unknowns," said Dr. Owen. "But I will do an autopsy, even though the cause of death seems apparent."

Maura looked down at the body and thought: Determining cause of death will be the easy part. Slice open skin, examine ruptured organs and shattered bones, and you'll find answers. It was the questions she could not answer that troubled her. The motives, the secret torments that drove human beings to kill strangers or take their own lives.

After the last official vehicle finally left that night, Maura made her way upstairs to the faculty common room, where most of the staff had gathered. A fire was burning in the hearth, but no one had turned on any of the lamps, as if none of them could bear any bright light on this tragic night. Maura sank into a velvet armchair and watched firelight flicker on the faces. She heard a soft clink as Gottfried poured a glass of brandy. Without a word he set it down on the table beside Maura, surmising that she, too, could use a stiff drink. She gave a nod and gratefully took a sip.

"Someone here must have a clue why she did it," said Lily. "There had to be some sign, something we didn't realize was significant."

Gottfried said: "We can't check her emails because I don't have her password. But the police searched her personal effects, looking for a suicide note. Nothing. I spoke to the cook, the gardener, and they saw nothing of significance, not a single sign that Anna was suicidal."

"I saw her in the garden this morning, snipping roses for her desk," said Lily. "Does that sound like something a suicidal woman would do?"

"How would we know?" Dr. Pasquantonio muttered. "*She* was the psychologist."

Gottfried looked around the room at his colleagues. "You've all spoken to the students. Do any of them have an answer?"

"No one," said Karła Duplessis, the literature teacher. "She had four student sessions scheduled today. Arthur Toombs was her last appointment, at one P.M., and he said she seemed a little distracted, but nothing else. The children are as bewildered as we are. If you think this is difficult for us, imagine how hard it is for them. Anna was tending to *their* emotional needs, and now they find out she was the fragile one. It makes them wonder if they can count on us. If adults are strong enough to stand by them."

"Which is why we can't look weak. Not now." The gruff words came from a shadowy corner of the room. It was Roman the forester, the only one who was not indulging in a comforting glass of brandy. "We have to go about our business as we always do."

"That would be unnatural," said Karla. "We all need time to process this."

"*Process?* Just a fancy word for moping and wailing. The lady killed herself, there's nothing to be done but just move on." With a grunt he rose and walked out of the room, trailing the scent of pine and tobacco.

"There's the milk of human kindness for you," Karla said under her breath. "With Roman setting the example, no wonder we've got students killing chickens."

Gottfried said, "But Mr. Roman does bring up a valid point, about the importance of maintaining routine. The students need that. They need time to mourn, of course, but they also need to know that life goes on." He looked at Lily. "We are going ahead with the field trip to Quebec?"

"I haven't canceled anything," she said. "The hotel rooms are booked, and the children have been talking about it for weeks."

"Then you should take them as promised."

"They're not all going, are they?" said Maura. "Given Teddy's situation, I think it's too dangerous for him to be out in public and exposed."

"Detective Rizzoli made that perfectly clear," said Lily. "He'll stay here, where we know he's safe. Will and Claire will stay behind as well. And of course, Julian." Lily smiled. "He told me he wants more time alone with you. Which is quite the compliment, Dr. Isles, coming from a teenager."

"This still feels wrong, somehow," said Karla. "To take them on a fun field trip when Anna's just died. We should stay here, to honor her. To figure out what drove her to this."

"Grief," said Lily quietly. "Sometimes it catches up with you. Even years later."

Pasquantonio harrumphed. "That happened, what? Twenty-two years ago?"

"You're talking about the murder of Anna's husband?" asked Maura.

Pasquantonio nodded and reached for the brandy bottle to refill his glass. "She told me all about it. How Frank was snatched from his car. How his company paid the ransom, but Frank was executed anyway, and his body was dumped days later. No arrest was ever made."

"That must have enraged her," said Maura. "And anger turned inward results in depression. If she carried that rage all these years . . ."

"We all do," said Pasquantonio. "It's why we're here. Why we choose this work. Rage is the fuel that keeps us going."

"Fuel can also be dangerous. It explodes." Maura looked around the room, at people who had all been scarred by violence. "Are you certain *you* can handle it? Can your students? I saw what was hanging from that willow tree. Someone here has already proven he—or she—is capable of killing."

There was an uncomfortable moment of silence as the teachers looked at one another.

Gottfried said, "It is something that concerns us. Something that Anna and I discussed yesterday. That one of our students may be deeply disturbed, perhaps even—"

"A psychopath," said Lily.

"And you have no idea which one?" said Maura.

Gottfried shook his head. "That was what bothered Anna the most. That she had no idea which student it might be."

A PSYCHOPATH. DEEPLY DISTURBED.

That conversation left Maura uneasy as she climbed the stairs later that night. She thought about damaged children and how violence can twist souls. She thought about what sort of child would kill a rooster for amusement, slice it open, and display it with entrails hanging in a tree. She wondered in which room, in this castle, that child now slept.

Instead of returning to her room, she kept climbing the stairs to the turret. To Anna's office. She had visited the room earlier that evening, with the state police detectives, so when she stepped into the office and flipped on the lights she expected no surprises, no new revelations. Indeed, the room appeared as they'd left it. The quartz crystals, dangling in the window. The stubs of incense sticks, burned down to gray ash. On the desk was a stack of charts, the top one still open to a police report from St. Thomas. It was Teddy Clock's file. Nearby was the vase of roses that Anna had cut that morning. Maura tried to imagine what might have gone through Anna's head as she snipped the stems and inhaled the perfume. *This is the last day I will smell flowers?* Or had there been no thoughts of time running out, no farewells to life, just an ordinary morning in the garden?

What made this day turn out so tragically different?

She circled the room, seeking any lingering trace of Anna. She did not believe in ghosts, and those who refuse to believe will never encounter one. But she paused in the room anyway, inhaling the scent of roses and incense, breathing the same air that Anna had only recently breathed. The roof walk door through which Anna had stepped out was now closed against the night chill. The tray with the teapot and china cups and covered sugar bowl was on the side table, where it had been the morning that Jane and Maura had sat in this office. The teacups were clean and stacked, the pot empty. Anna had taken the time to rinse and dry the teapot and cups before she'd ended her life. Perhaps it was a final act of consideration to those who'd have to tidy up in the aftermath.

Then why had she chosen such a messy way to die? An exit that had splattered blood on the path and forever stained the memories of students and colleagues?

"It doesn't make sense. Does it?"

She turned to see Julian standing in the doorway. As usual, the dog was at his feet, and like his master Bear looked subdued. Weighed down by sorrow.

"I thought you'd gone to bed," she said.

"I can't sleep. I went to talk to you, but you weren't in your room."

She sighed. "I can't sleep, either."

The boy hesitated in the doorway, as though to step into Anna's office would be disrespectful to the dead. "She never forgot a birthday," he said. "A kid would come down to breakfast and find some funny little gift waiting. A Yankees cap for a boy who liked baseball. A little crystal swan for a girl who got braces. She gave me a present even when it wasn't my birthday. A compass. So I'd always know where I was going, and would always remember where I've been." His voice thinned to a whisper. "It's what always happens to people I care about."

"What does?"

"They leave me." *They die* was what he meant, and it was true. The last of his family had perished last winter, leaving him alone in the world.

*Except for me. He still has me.*

She pulled him into her arms and held him. Julian was as close to a son as she'd ever have, yet in so many ways they were still strangers to each other. He stood stiffly in her arms, a wooden statue embraced by a woman who was equally uneasy with affection. In this way they were sadly alike, hungry for connection, yet untrusting of it. At last she felt the tension go out of him, and he returned the hug, melting against her.

"I won't leave you, Rat," she said. "You can always count on me."

"People say that. But things happen."

"Nothing will happen to me."

"You know you can't promise that." He pulled away and turned toward Dr. Welliver's desk. "She said we could count on *her*. And look what happened." He touched the roses in the vase; one pink petal dropped off, fluttering down like a dying butterfly. "Why did she do it?"

"Sometimes there are no answers. I struggle with that question far too often in my own job. Families trying to understand why someone they love committed suicide."

"What do you tell them?"

"Never to blame themselves. Not to feel guilty.

Because we bear responsibility for our own actions alone. Not for anyone else's."

She didn't understand why her answer made his head suddenly droop. He ran a hand across his eyes, a quick, embarrassed swipe that left a glistening streak on his face.

"Rat?" she asked softly.

"I *do* feel guilty."

"No one knows why she did it."

"Not about Dr. Welliver."

"Then who?"

"Carrie." He looked at her. "It's her birthday next week."

His dead sister. Last winter, the girl had perished, along with their mother, in a lonely Wyoming valley. He seldom talked about his family, seldom talked about anything that had happened during those desperate weeks when he and Maura had fought to stay alive. She thought he'd put the ordeal behind him, but of course he hadn't. He is more like me than I realized, she thought. We both bury our sorrows where no one can see them.

"I should have saved her," he said.

"How could you? Your mother wouldn't let her leave."

"I should have *made* her leave. I was the man in the family. It was my job to keep her safe."

A responsibility that should never fall on the shoulders of a mere sixteen-year-old boy, she thought. He might be as tall as a man, with a man's broad shoulders, but she saw a boy's tears on his face. He swiped them with his sleeve and glanced around for tissues.

She went into the adjoining bathroom and unspooled a wad of toilet paper. As she tore it off, a sparkle caught her eye, like glittering bits of sand scattered on the toilet seat. She touched it and stared at white granules adhering to her fingers. Noticed that there were more granules sparkling on the bathroom tiles.

Something had been emptied into the toilet.

She went back into the office and looked at the tea tray on the side table. Remembered how Anna had brewed herbal tea in that china pot and poured three cups. Remembered that Anna had added three generous teaspoons of sugar to her own cup, an extravagance that had caught Maura's eye. She lifted the lid to the sugar bowl. It was empty.

Why would Anna pour the sugar into the toilet?

The telephone rang on Anna's desk, startling both her and Julian. They glanced at each other, both rattled that someone was calling a dead woman.

Maura answered it. "Evensong School. This is Dr. Isles."

"You didn't call me back," said Jane Rizzoli.

"Was I supposed to?"

"I left a message with Dr. Welliver hours ago. Figured I'd better try again before it got too late."

"You spoke to Anna? When?"

"Around five, five thirty."

"Jane, something awful's happened, and—"

"Teddy's okay, right?" Jane cut in.

"Yes. Yes, he's fine."

"Then what is it?"

"Anna Welliver is dead. It looks like a suicide. She jumped off the roof."

There was a long pause. In the background, Maura could hear the sound of the TV, running water, and the clatter of dishes. Domestic sounds that made her suddenly miss her own home, her own kitchen.

"Jesus," Jane finally managed to say.

Maura looked down at the sugar bowl. Pictured Anna emptying it into the toilet and walking back into this room. Opening the roof door and stepping outside, to take a short walk to eternity.

"Why would she commit suicide?" asked Jane.

Maura was still staring at the empty sugar bowl. And she said: "I'm not convinced she did."

# TWENTY-TWO

"ARE YOU SURE YOU WANT TO BE HERE FOR THIS, Dr. Isles?"

They stood in the morgue anteroom, surrounded by supply cabinets filled with gloves and masks and shoe covers. Maura had donned a scrub top and pants from the locker room, and she was already tucking her hair into a paper cap.

"I'll send you the final report," said Dr. Owen. "And I'll order a comprehensive tox screen, as you suggested. You're welcome to stay, of course, but it seems to me . . ."

"I'm only here to observe, not interfere," said Maura. "This is entirely your show."

Beneath her bouffant paper cap, Dr. Owen flushed. Even under harsh fluorescent lights it was a youthful face with enviably smooth skin that had no need for all the camouflaging creams and powders that had started to creep into Maura's bathroom cabinet. "I didn't mean it that way," said Dr. Owen. "I'm just thinking about the fact that you knew her personally. That has to make this hard for you."

Through the viewing window, Maura watched Dr. Owen's assistant, a burly young man, assembling the instrument tray. On the table lay the corpse of Anna Welliver, still fully dressed. How many cadavers have I sliced open, she wondered, how many scalps have I peeled away from skulls? So many that she had lost track. But they were all strangers, with whom she shared no memories. She had known Anna, though. She knew her voice and her smile and had seen the gleam of life in her eyes. This was an autopsy any pathologist would avoid, yet here she was, donning shoe covers and safety glasses and mask.

"I owe this to her," she said.

"I doubt there'll be any surprises. We know how she died."

"But not what led up to it."

"This won't give us that answer."

"An hour before she jumped, she was acting strangely on the phone. She told Detective Rizzoli that food didn't taste right. And she saw birds, strange birds, flying outside her window. I'm wondering if those were hallucinations."

"That's the reason you asked for the tox screen?"

"We didn't find any drugs in her possession, but there's a chance we missed something. Or she hid them."

They pushed through the door into the autopsy room, and Dr. Owen said: "Randy, we've got a distinguished guest today. Dr. Isles is from the ME's office in Boston."

The young man gave an unimpressed nod and asked: "Who's going to cut?"

"This is Dr. Owen's case," said Maura. "I'm just here to observe."

Accustomed to being in command in her own morgue, Maura had to resist the urge to claim her usual place at the table. Instead she stood back as Dr. Owen and Randy positioned instrument trays and adjusted lights. In truth, she did not want to move any closer, did not want to look into Anna's face. Only yesterday she had seen awareness in those eyes, and now the absence of it was a stark reminder that bodies are merely shells, that whatever constituted a soul was fleeting and easily extinguished. Emma Owen was right, she thought. *This isn't an autopsy I should watch.*

She turned instead to the preliminary X-rays hanging on the light box. As Dr. Owen and her assistant undressed the corpse, Maura stayed focused on images that had no familiar face. Nothing in these films surprised her. Last night, just by palpation, she had detected depressed fractures of the left parietal bone, and now she saw the evidence in black and white, a subtle spider's web of cracks. She turned next to the rib cage where, even through the vague shadows of clothing, she spotted massive fracturing of ribs two through eight on the left. The force of free fall had fractured the pelvis as well, compressing the sacral foramen and cracking apart the ramus of the pubic bone. Exactly what one would expect to see in a body dropped from a height. Even before they sliced open the chest, Maura could predict what they would find in the thoracic cavity because she had seen the results of free fall in other bodies. While a fall might crack ribs and crush a pelvis, what ultimately killed was the force of abrupt deceleration tugging on heart and lungs, ripping delicate tissues and tearing great vessels. When they sliced open Anna's chest, they would most likely find it filled with blood.

"How the hell did she get these?" Randy said.

Dr. Owen called out: "Dr. Isles, you'll want to look at this."

Maura crossed to the table. They had unbuttoned the top of Anna's dress, but had not yet peeled it off the hips. The corpse was still wearing a bra, a practical white D-cup with no lace, no frills. They all stared at the exposed skin.

"These are the weirdest scars I've ever come across," said Dr. Owen.

Maura stared, stunned by what she saw. "Let's get the rest of her clothes off," she said.

With three of them working together, they quickly removed the bra, pulled the dress down. As they peeled the underwear waistband over the hips, Maura remembered the pelvic fractures that she had just seen on X-ray and grimaced at the thought of those bony fragments grinding together. Thought of the screams she'd once heard in the ER from a young man whose pelvis had been crushed in a barge accident. But Anna was beyond pain, and she surrendered her clothes without a whimper. Stripped naked, she now lay exposed, her body bruised and deformed by broken ribs and skull and pelvis.

Yet it was the marks on her skin that they stared at. Marks that were invisible to the X-ray machine, and revealed only now. The scars were spread across the front of her torso, an ugly grid of knots on her breasts, her abdomen, even her shoulders. Maura thought about the modest Mother Hubbard gowns that Anna wore even on warm days, dresses chosen not because of her eccentric sense of style, but for concealment. She wondered how many years it had been since Anna had donned a bathing suit or sunbathed on a beach. These scars looked old, permanent souvenirs of some unspeakable ordeal.

"Could these be some kind of skin grafts?" asked Randy.

"These aren't skin grafts," said Dr. Owen.

"Then what are they?"

"I don't know." Dr. Owen looked at Maura. "Do you?"

Maura didn't answer. She turned her attention to the lower extremities. Reaching up for the light, she redirected it to the shins, where the skin was darker. Thicker. She looked at Randy. "We need detailed X-rays of the legs. The tibias in particular, and both ankles."

"I already did the skeletal survey," said Randy.

"The films are hanging there right now. You can see all the fractures."

"I'm not concerned about new fractures. I'm looking for old ones."

"How does this help us with cause of death?" said Dr. Owen.

"It's about understanding the victim. Her past, her state of mind. She can't talk to us, but her body still can."

Maura and Dr. Owen retreated to the anteroom, where they watched through the viewing window as Randy, now garbed in a lead apron, positioned the body for a new set of X-rays. *How many scars were you hiding, Anna?* The marks on her skin were obvious, but what of the emotional wounds that never heal, that cannot be closed over with fibrosis and collagen? Was it old torments that finally drove her to step out onto the roof walk and surrender her body to gravity and the hard earth?

Randy clipped a new set of films onto the light box and waved to them. As Maura and Dr. Owen reentered the lab, he said: "I don't see any other fractures on these views."

"They'd be old," said Maura.

"No scar formation, no deformities. You know, I *can* recognize those."

There was no missing the irritation in his voice. She was the interloper, the high-and-mighty expert from the big city who'd questioned his competence. She chose not to engage him and focused instead on the X-rays. What he had said was correct: At first glance, there were no obvious old fractures of the arms or legs. She moved closer to study first the right tibia, then the left. The darker skin on Anna's shins had raised her suspicions, and what she saw on these films confirmed her diagnosis.

"Do you see this, Dr. Owen?" Maura pointed to the outline of the tibia. "Notice the layering and the thickness."

The young pathologist frowned. "It is thicker, I agree."

"There are endosteal changes here as well. Do you see them? These are highly suggestive." She looked at Randy. "Can we see the ankle films now?"

"Suggestive of what?" he asked, still unconvinced by this expert from Boston.

"Periostitis. Inflammatory changes of the membrane covering the bone." Maura pulled down the tibia X-rays. "Ankle films, please."

Tight-lipped, he shoved the new X-rays under the clips, and what Maura saw in those films swept away any doubts she'd had. Dr. Owen, standing beside her, murmured a troubled: *"Oh."*

"These are classic bony changes," said Maura. "I've seen them only twice before. Once in an immigrant from Algeria. The second was a corpse that turned up in a freighter, a man from South America."

"What are you looking at?" said Randy.

"The changes in the right calcaneus," said Dr. Owen. She pointed to the right heel bone.

Maura said, "You can see them in the left calcaneus, too. Those deformities are from multiple old fractures that have since healed."

"*Both* her feet were broken?" said Randy.

"Repeatedly." She stared at the X-rays and shuddered at their significance. "Falaka," she said softly.

"I've read about it," said Dr. Owen. "But I never thought I'd see a case in Maine."

Maura looked at Randy. "It's also known as bastinado. The feet are beaten on the sole, which breaks bones, ruptures tendons and ligaments. It's known in many places around the world. The Middle East. Asia. South America."

"You mean someone *did* this to her?"

Maura nodded. "And those changes in the tibias that I pointed out are also from repeated beatings. Something heavy was slammed against the shins. It may not be enough to actually fracture bone, but it leaves permanent changes in the periosteum from repeated hemorrhages." Maura went back to the table, where Anna's broken body lay. She understood, now, the significance of that grid of scars on the breasts, the abdomen. What she did not understand was *why* any of this had been done to Anna. Or when.

"It still doesn't explain why she killed herself," said Dr. Owen.

"No," Maura admitted. "But it makes you wonder, doesn't it? If her death is somehow connected to her past. To what caused these scars."

"You're now questioning whether this was a suicide?"

"After seeing this, I question everything. And now we have another mystery." She looked at Dr. Owen. "Why was Anna Welliver tortured?"

*A jail cell diminishes any man, and so it was with Icarus.*

*Viewed through the bars, he seemed smaller, inconsequential. Now stripped of his Italian suit and his Panerai wristwatch, he wore a lurid orange jumpsuit and rubber flip-flops. His solitary cell was furnished only with a sink, a toilet, and a concrete shelf bed with a thin mattress, on which he was now sitting.*

*"You know," he said, "that every man has his price."*

*"And what would yours be?" I asked.*

*"I have already paid it. Everything I ever valued has been lost." He looked up at me with bright blue eyes, so unlike the soft brown eyes of his dead son Carlo. "I was speaking of your price."*

*"Me? I can't be bought."*

*"Then you are merely a simpleminded patriot? You do this for love of country?"*

*"Yes."*

*He laughed. "I've heard that before. All it means is that the alternative offer was not high enough."*

*"There isn't any offer high enough to make me sell out my country."*

*He gave me a look akin to pity, as if I were feebleminded. "All right, then. Go back to your country.*

But you do know, you'll go home poorer than you need to be."

"Unlike some people," I taunted him, "at least I can go home."

He smiled, and that smile made my hands suddenly go cold. As if I were looking into the face of my future. "Can you?"

# TWENTY-THREE

JANE HAD TO ADMIT, DARREN CROWE LOOKED good on TV. Sitting at her desk in the homicide unit, she watched the interview on the department's TV, admiring Crowe's sharp suit, blow-dried hair, and those dazzling teeth. She wondered if he'd bleached his teeth himself with a drugstore whitening kit, or if he'd paid a professional to polish up the pearly whites.

"Reuben with double sauerkraut," said Frost, setting a sandwich bag on her desk. He dropped into the chair beside hers and unwrapped his usual lunch, a turkey on white, no lettuce.

"Look how that reporter's ogling him," Jane said, pointing to the blond correspondent interviewing Crowe. "I swear, any second now she's gonna rip off her blazer and scream, *Take me, Officer!*"

"No one ever says that to me." Frost sighed, resignedly biting into his sandwich.

"He's milking this like a pro. Oh, look, here he comes with the *deep thoughts* expression."

"I saw him practicing that look in the john."

"Deep thoughts?" She snorted as she unwrapped her Reuben sandwich. "Like he has any. The way he's staring at that chick, he's thinking more along the lines of *deep throat*."

They sat eating their sandwiches as they watched Crowe on TV describing the Zapata takedown. *Could have surrendered, but chose to run . . . We exercised restraint at all times . . . clearly the actions of a guilty man . . .*

Her appetite suddenly gone, Jane put down her Reuben.

*Illegal aliens like Zapata who bring their violence to this country will be dealt with. That's my pledge to the good citizens of Boston.*

"This is bullshit," she said. "Just like that, he's got Zapata tried and convicted."

Frost didn't say anything, simply kept eating his turkey sandwich as if nothing else mattered, and that annoyed her. Usually she appreciated her partner's unflappability. No drama, no meltdowns, just a maddeningly even-keeled Boy Scout who now reminded her of a cow calmly chewing grass.

"Hey," she said. "Doesn't this bother you?"

He looked at her, his mouth full of turkey. "I know it bothers you."

"But you're okay with it? Closing the book when we've got no murder weapon, nothing in Zapata's possession that ties him to the Ackermans?"

"I didn't say I was okay with it."

"Now Cop Hollywood's on TV there, wrapping it all up like a Christmas present. A present that stinks. It should piss you off."

"I guess."

"Does *anything* piss you off?"

He took another bite of turkey and chewed, thinking over the question. "Yeah," he finally said. "Alice."

"Ex-wives are supposed to do that."

"You asked."

"Well, this case should, too. Or bug you, at least, the way it's bugging me and Maura."

At the mention of Maura's name, he finally set down his sandwich and looked at her. "What *does* Dr. Isles think?"

"Same thing I do, that these three kids are somehow connected. Their psychologist has just jumped off a roof, and Maura's wondering, What is it about these kids that kills everyone close to them? It's as if they're cursed. Everywhere they go, someone dies."

"And now they're all together in one place."

*Evensong.* She thought of dark woods where willow trees were hung with blood-splattered ornaments. Thought of a castle where the occupants themselves were haunted, all of them living in the shadow of violence. Both Teddy and Maura were there behind locked gates, with children who were all too well acquainted with bloodshed.

"Rizzoli." The voice startled her, and she snapped

around in her chair to see Lieutenant Marquette standing behind her. At once she grabbed the remote and shut off the TV.

"Not enough to do around here?" Marquette said. "You two watching soap operas now?"

"Biggest soap opera of them all," she said. "Detective Crowe telling the good people of Boston how he single-handedly took down the evil genius Zapata."

Marquette cocked his head. "I need you in my office."

She saw Frost's look of *uh-oh* as she stood up, and she followed Marquette in a brisk march into his office. He closed the door. She waited until he'd settled into his own chair before she sat down. Tried to keep her gaze steady as he stared at her across his desk.

"You and Crowe are never going to agree on anything, are you?" he said.

"What's his complaint about me now?"

"The lack of a unified front on the Ackerman case. The fact that you keep raising questions about a rush to judgment."

"Guilty as charged," she conceded. "I think it is a rush to judgment."

"Yeah, I've heard all your objections. But you have to see how this looks, if the press gets wind of what you're saying. It'd be a PR nightmare. This case has already gotten everyone's attention. Wealthy family, dead kids, everything that Nancy Grace loves. It also has a villain that half of America loves to hate, an illegal immigrant. Zapata was everyone's dream perp. Best of all, he's dead and the case is closed. A fairy-tale ending."

"If nightmares were fairy tales," she said.

"After all, they do call them the Brothers Grimm."

"The public's satisfied, so you're saying I should shut up and be satisfied, too?"

He leaned back in his chair. "Sometimes, Rizzoli, you really are a pain in the butt."

"I've been hearing that a lot lately."

"Which is why you make a good investigator. You poke and you prod. You go digging holes where no one else wants to. I read your report on the three kids. Semtex in New Hampshire? A plane bombed in Maryland? This thing is looking like one hell of a big graveyard." He paused, fingers tapping his desk as he studied her. "So go ahead. Do your thing."

She wasn't sure what he was saying. "My thing?"

"Dig. Officially, the Ackerman case is closed. Unofficially, I've got doubts, too. But you're the only one who knows it."

"Can I bring Frost aboard? I could use him."

"I cannot commit any more resources to this. I'm not even sure I should let *you* spend time on it."

"So why are you?"

He leaned forward, his eyes on hers. "Look, I'd love to close this case right now and call it a win. I want our statistics to look good, of course I do. But just like you, I've got instincts. Sometimes we're forced to ignore those gut feelings, and when it turns out we were right all along, we kick ourselves. I don't want it someday shoved in my face that I shut this down too fast."

"So we're covering our asses."

"Anything wrong with that?" he snapped.

"Not a thing."

"Okay." He leaned back again. "What's your plan?"

She had to think about this for a moment, consider which of the unanswered questions demanded priority. And she decided that her number one question was: What did the Wards, the Yablonskis, and the Clocks have in common, aside from the manner of their deaths? Did they know one another?

She said: "I need to go to Maryland."

"Why Maryland?"

"Will Yablonski's father worked at NASA-Goddard. So did Will's uncle, Brian Temple. I want to talk to their colleagues at NASA. Maybe they know why that plane went down. And why Brian and his wife were so quick to get their nephew out of Maryland and move him to New Hampshire."

"Where their farmhouse blows up."

She nodded. "This whole thing's starting to look very big and very bad. Which is why I want Frost along, to help me sort it out."

After a moment, he nodded. "Okay, you got Frost. I'll give you three days on this."

"We're on it. Thank you." She stood up.

"Rizzoli?"

"Yes, sir?"

"Keep it quiet. Don't tell anyone in the unit, especially Crowe. As far as the public is concerned, the Ackerman case is closed."

"You know how that old saying goes, *It doesn't take a rocket scientist*?" said Frost as they drove through the Goddard Space Flight Center campus. "Well, now we're going to be hanging out with real rocket scientists! That's so amazing. I mean, look out the window and just think about the average IQ of these guys you see walking around here."

"What does that make us, birdbrains?"

"All that math and chemistry and physics they've gotta know. I wouldn't have the faintest idea how to launch a rocket."

"You mean you never shot up one of those toy rockets with vinegar and baking soda?"

"Yeah, right. Like that's how we got to the moon."

She pulled into a parking stall in front of the Exploration Sciences Building, and they both clipped on the NASA visitor badges that they'd picked up at the entrance gate.

"Man, I hope I get to keep this," he said, fondling his badge. "It'd be such a cool souvenir."

"Can you dial down the geek worship a little bit? You sound like a Trekkie, and frankly, that is *so* embarrassing."

"I *am* a Trekkie." As they stepped out of the car,

he raised his hand in a Vulcan salute. "Live long and—"

"*Don't* do that while we're in there, okay?"

"Hey, look at that!" He pointed to the bumper sticker on one of the cars in the parking lot. "BEAM ME UP, SCOTTY!"

"So?"

"So these are *my people*!"

"Then maybe they'll keep you," she muttered as she stretched the kinks from her back. They had caught an early-morning flight to Baltimore, and as they walked into the building, she glanced around hoping to spot a coffee machine. Instead she saw an enormous man waddling their direction.

"You the folks from Boston?" he asked.

"Dr. Bartusek?" said Jane. "I'm Detective Rizzoli. This is my partner, Detective Frost."

"Call me Bert." Grinning, Bartusek grabbed her hand and gave it an enthusiastic shake. "Big-city homicide detectives! I bet you folks have really interesting jobs."

"Not as interesting as yours," said Frost.

"Mine?" Bartusek snorted. "Nowhere as cool as hunting down killers."

"My partner here thinks it's way cooler to work for NASA," said Jane.

"Well, you know what they say about the grass on the other side of the fence," Bartusek said with a laugh as he waved them down the hall. "Come on, let's go sit in my office. The guys upstairs gave me full clearance to talk to you. 'Course, what else am I going to do, when a cop asks me questions? If I don't answer, you might arrest me!" He led them down the corridor, and Jane imagined she could almost feel the building shake with each ponderous step he took. "I've got a lot of questions myself," he said. "Me and my colleagues, we all want to know what happened to Neil and Olivia. You speak to Detective Parris yet?"

"We're meeting with him this evening," said Jane. "Assuming he gets back from Florida in time."

"Parris seemed like a smart cop when I met him. Asked me just about every possible question. But I don't think he ever came up with an answer." He glanced at Jane. "Two years later, I'm wondering if you'll be able to."

"You have any theories about that plane crash?"

He shook his head. "Never made sense to any of us, why anyone would want to kill Neil. A good guy, a really good guy. We talked about it a lot here, and we went over all the possible reasons. Did he owe someone money? Did he tick off the wrong people? Was it a crime of passion?"

"Is that a possibility, a crime of passion?" asked Frost. "He or his wife having an affair?"

Bartusek stopped outside a doorway, his massive girth blocking any view into the room. "I didn't think it was possible at the time. I mean, they were such *regular* people. But then, you never know what's really going on in a marriage, do you?" He gave a sad shake of the head and stepped into his office. On his walls hung a gallery of stunning photos of galaxies and nebulae, like multicolored amoebas.

"Wow. The Horsehead Nebula," said Frost, admiring one of the photos.

"You know your night sky, Detective."

Jane glanced at her partner. "You really are a Trekkie."

"Told you so." Frost moved on to another photograph. "I see your name here, Dr. Bartusek. You took these?"

"Astrophotography's a hobby of mine. You'd think, after spending my day studying the universe, I'd go home and take photos of birds or flowers. But no, I keep my eye on the sky. Always have." He squeezed in behind his desk and sank into a massive chair, setting off a loud groan of the springs. "You might call it an obsession."

"Is that true for all rocket scientists?" asked Frost.

"Well, technically speaking, I'm not really a rocket scientist. Those are the guys who light the candles and blow stuff up. They'd tell you they have the fun jobs."

"And your job?"

"I'm an astrophysicist. In this building, we're focused on the research side. My colleagues and I, we formulate a scientific question, and we figure out what kind of data we need to answer it. Maybe we want to sample dust from a passing comet, or we want to do a wide-field infrared survey of the sky. To get that data, we need to launch a special telescope. That's when we turn to the rocket scientists, who help us get that scope up and into position. We define the purpose of a mission. The rocket engineers design a way to do it. Truth is, we kinda talk different languages. They're gearheads. They think of us as eggheads."

"Which was Neil Yablonski?" asked Jane.

"Neil was most definitely an egghead. He and his brother-in-law Brian Temple were the smartest guys around here. Which may be why they were friends. Such good friends, in fact, they were planning a joint trip to Rome with their wives. That's where Neil and Olivia first met, and they wanted to visit their old romantic haunts."

"Hardly sounds like a romantic trip if you're bringing another couple along."

"Not just any other couple. See, Lynn and Olivia were sisters. Neil and Brian were best friends. So when Lynn and Brian got married, presto, they turned into the four amigos. Brian and Neil had to go to Rome for a meeting anyway, so they thought they'd bring their wives. Man, was Neil looking forward to that trip! Tortured me with all his talk about pasta! Pizza! Fritto misto!" He looked down at his bulging stomach, which suddenly gave a growl. "I think I gained weight just saying those words."

"But they never made it to Rome?"

Bartusek gave a sad shake of the head. "Three weeks before they were supposed to leave, Neil and Olivia took off for their weekend cottage on the

Chesapeake. Neil had a little Cessna he liked to fly down there. Their son, Will, had a science project he needed to work on, so the boy stayed with the Temples. Lucky for the kid, because three minutes after takeoff that Cessna went down in flames. The weather was perfect, and Neil was a very careful pilot. We all assumed it was mechanical. Until Detective Parris and the FBI showed up here a week or so later and started asking a lot of questions. That's when I realized there was more to the crash than we thought. Parris never came right out and told me, but I read about it later in the newspaper. That the crash was suspicious. That there may have been a bomb aboard that Cessna. Since you folks are now asking about it, I assume it's true."

"We'll discuss that with Detective Parris tonight," said Jane.

"So it wasn't an accident. Was it?"

"It appears not."

Bartusek slumped back against his chair and shook his head. "No wonder Brian freaked out."

"What do you mean?"

"The day after Neil's plane went down, Brian came into work white as a sheet. Picked up some of his research papers, said he was going to work from home for a few days, because Lynn and their nephew didn't want to be alone. A week later, I heard he'd resigned from NASA. That really shocked me, because he loved this job. After twenty-some years, I can't imagine what would make him just pick up and quit. He didn't tell any of us where he was going. I didn't even know they'd moved to New Hampshire until we heard that he and Lynn died in that house fire."

"So Brian didn't give you any clue why he left town?"

"Not a word. As I said, he looked pretty shook up, but at the time I thought it was only natural. His best friend and his wife's sister just got killed, and now he had Neil's kid to raise." Bartusek fell silent for a moment, fleshy face drooping at the memory. "Poor boy's had some damn tough breaks in life. To lose your parents when you're only twelve." He shook his head. "You know, I never mentioned this to Detective Parris, but some of us had a theory that it was all a mistake. Maybe the killer put a bomb aboard the wrong Cessna. Couple of big-business types keep their planes at that field. So do a few politicians, and Lord knows some of us would love to bring down *their* planes." He paused. "That was a joke. Really." He looked back and forth at the two detectives. "But I can see you don't appreciate the humor."

"We've been focusing on Neil, but what about his wife?" said Frost. "Is there any reason she might have been the target?"

"Olivia? No way. She was a sweet gal, but also a bit bland. Whenever I saw her at NASA parties, she'd be standing off in a corner, looking lost. I used to try my best to give her some attention, 'cause she was such a wallflower. But frankly, nothing she ever said was memorable. She had some boring job as a sales rep for medical equipment."

Frost glanced at his notebook. "Leidecker Hospital Supplies."

"Yeah, that was it. She didn't talk much about it. The only time she got animated was when she talked about Will. The kid's some sort of genius, just like Neil."

"Okay, let's go back to Neil," said Jane. "Did he have any conflicts here at work? Any colleagues he didn't get along with?"

"Just the usual stuff."

"Meaning?"

"A scientist proposes a theory, stakes out a position. Sometimes he gets emotionally attached to that position when others disagree."

"Who disagreed with Neil?"

"I can't even remember, that's how normal it was. He and Brian, they were always having spirited debates, but it was never hostile, you know? It was more like this egghead game between them. You get the two of them talking about debris disks, and *whoosh!* They're like two rambunctious kids playing in the sandbox, tossing toys at each other."

Frost looked up from the notes he'd been jotting. "Debris disks? What are those?"

"That was the subject of their research. It has to do with interstellar cloud cores. When they collapse, angular momentum causes them to form these spinning disks of gas and dust around baby stars."

"They got into arguments about that?" said Jane.

"Hey, we get into arguments about everything. It's what makes science so damn engaging. Yeah, sometimes the debates might turn personal, but we can deal with it here. We're all big boys." He looked down at his belly and added with an ironic sigh, "Some of us bigger than others."

"What kind of arguments would you get into over a dirt disk?"

"Debris disks. There's a lot of controversy about how these rings of dust and gas transform into solar systems with planets. Some say the planets form because of multiple collisions, but what makes those debris particles stick together? How does mass accumulate? How do you turn a bunch of swirling particles into a Mercury, Venus, and Earth? It's a question we can't answer yet. We do know ours isn't the only solar system. There are countless planets in this galaxy alone, and many of them are in the habitable zone."

Frost, who might as well have had TREKKIE tattooed on his forehead, rocked forward with sudden interest. "You mean we could colonize them?"

"Maybe. *Habitable zone* means that life in *some* form could exist there. At least, the carbon-based life we're familiar with. Data from the Kepler Mission identifies a number of what we call Goldilocks planets. Not too hot, not too cold, but just right. In fact, that's why Neil and Brian were going to Rome. To present their data to the team at the Vatican observatory."

Frost gave a surprised laugh. "The Vatican has an observatory?"

"Quite well regarded, part of the Pontifical Academy of Sciences." He saw Frost's raised eyebrow. "Yeah, I know, it sounds strange that this is the same church that attacked Galileo for believing the Earth revolves around the Sun. But their academy has some impressive astronomers. They were anxious to look over Neil and Brian's latest research, because it has major implications. Certainly for the Vatican."

"Why would this research concern the Catholic Church?" asked Jane.

"Because we're talking about astrobiology, Detective Rizzoli. The study of life in the universe. Think about it. What does it mean to our perceived place in that universe if we find life on another planet? What happens to the concept of divine creation and *Let there be light*? It overturns humankind's most cherished belief, that we are unique. That God made us. It could topple the central pillar of the Church."

"Topple? Did Yablonski and Temple actually have the data to do that?"

"I don't know that I'd call it proof, exactly."

"They shared it with you?"

"I saw their initial analysis of data from infrared and radio telescopes. It came from one of those Goldilocks planets I was telling you about. There was carbon dioxide, water, ozone, and nitrogen.

Not just the building blocks of life, but also molecules that indicate photosynthesis is taking place."

"Which means plant life," said Frost.

Bartusek nodded. "It was highly suggestive."

"How come we haven't heard about this?" said Frost. "Where was the press conference, the big White House announcement?"

"You can't just come out and announce this stuff without being absolutely certain, or you'll look like an idiot. You *know* you'll be attacked. You *know* there'll be wacko deniers of every stripe coming after you. We'd need contingency plans to deal with all the nuts who'd try to drive truck bombs into our buildings here." He stopped to take a calming breath. "So, no. We do not make announcements, not until we can prove anything beyond a shadow of a doubt. Hell, ET himself would need to land on the White House lawn before some people would be convinced. But Neil and Brian, they felt they had enough evidence. In fact, that was one of the last things Neil told me, before he died."

Jane stared at him. "That he had proof?"

Bartusek nodded. "Of extraterrestrial life."

# TWENTY-FOUR

JANE AND FROST WERE SILENT AS THEY DROVE toward Columbia, both of them stunned and trying to process what they had just heard. After their visit to NASA, this was an anticlimactic journey down a mundane highway toward the unexciting office where Olivia Yablonski had worked as a medical equipment sales rep.

"I'm wondering if we had it wrong," said Frost. "I don't think the boy was the target in New Hampshire."

Jane glanced at her partner, who was squinting ahead, as though trying to peer through fog. "You're thinking it was the boy's uncle. Brian Temple."

"Both men are about to reveal something earth-shattering. Neil gets taken out. Brian panics, flees with his wife and nephew to New Hampshire. The bad guys come after *him*."

"Trouble is, we don't know who the bad guys are."

"You heard Bartusek. Finding ET would shake

up the world. It would make people question everything they learned in Sunday school."

"So, what, we've got some albino assassin monk killing NASA scientists?" She laughed. "I think that was a movie."

"Consider what religious zealots already do to defend their beliefs. Those climate scientists at MIT, they're always getting threats. This is gonna *really* bring out the crazies. If it ever gets announced." He frowned. "Interesting that NASA hasn't."

"Sounds like the proof isn't there yet."

"Is that really true, or is this too hot for them— for anyone—to handle?"

*Extraterrestrial life.* She spun that possibility in her head, trying to see it from every angle, imagine every repercussion. A motive for assassination? The murders of the Yablonskis and the Temples were definitely the work of professionals who knew their way around Semtex. "There's a problem with this theory," she said. "It doesn't explain Claire Ward's family. Her father was a diplomat, working for the State Department. What's his connection with NASA?"

"Maybe they're unrelated cases. We're just linking them because both kids ended up at Evensong."

She gave a sigh. "Now you sound like Crowe. Different kids, different cases. Just a coincidence they ended up in the same school."

"Although it is interesting . . ."

"What?"

He pointed to a road sign for the turnoff to Washington. "Didn't Erskine Ward also work in DC for a while?"

"And Rome. And London."

"At least we've got a geographic connection between the Wards and the Yablonskis. They lived within the same fifty-mile radius."

"But not Teddy Clock's family. Nicholas Clock's job was in Rhode Island."

"Yeah." Frost shrugged. "So maybe we're trying to connect things that have no connection, and we're just making it all too complicated."

She spotted the address they were searching for and turned into the parking lot. It was yet another strip mall, indistinguishable from thousands of others across the country. Was there some universal strip mall design they taught you in architecture school, photocopied blueprints passed around to every builder in America? She pulled into a parking spot and eyed the usual mix of businesses. A drugstore, a dress shop for big sizes, a dollar store, and a Chinese buffet. That was the one constant you could always count on, the Chinese buffet.

"I don't see it," said Frost.

"Must be at the far end." She pushed open her door. "Let's stretch our legs and walk."

"You sure this is the right address?"

"I confirmed it with the manager this morning. She's expecting us." Her cell phone rang, and she recognized the Maryland number of the detective who had investigated the Yablonski case. "Rizzoli," she answered.

"It's Detective Parris. Did you make it to Baltimore?" he asked.

"We're here now. Can you still meet us tonight?"

"Yes, ma'am. I'm on the road right now, but I should be back in town by dinnertime. How about we meet at the LongHorn Steakhouse around seven thirty? It's on Snowden River Parkway. By then, I'll be ready for some red meat. I'd rather not meet at my residence."

"I understand. I don't like to mix business and family, either."

"No, it's more than that. It's this case."

"What about it?"

"We'll talk about it later. Did you bring your partner?"

"Detective Frost is right here with me."

"Good. It always helps to have someone watch your back."

She hung up and looked at Frost. "That was a weird call."

"What hasn't been weird about this case?" He eyed the strip mall, with its unexciting array of shops. "From NASA to this place." He sighed. "Let's do it."

Leidecker Hospital Supplies was located at the far end of the mall, behind a storefront window displaying two wheelchairs and a quad cane. Stepping inside, Jane expected to find a showroom filled with medical equipment. Instead they found an office with five desks, beige carpet, and two potted palms. At one of the desks, a middle-aged woman with shellacked blond hair was talking on the phone. She spotted the visitors and said, "I'll call you back later about that order, Mr. Wiggins." Hanging up, she smiled at her visitors. "May I help you?"

"Ms. Mickey? Detectives Rizzoli and Frost," said Jane. "We spoke earlier."

The woman rose to greet them, revealing a slim figure in a well-cut gray pantsuit. "Please, call me Carole. I really hope I can help you. It still haunts me, you know. Every time I look over there, at her desk, I think about her."

Jane glanced around at the unoccupied desks. "Are Olivia's other colleagues around? We'd like to talk to them, as well."

"I'm afraid everyone else is out of town right now, on sales calls. But I knew Olivia longer than anyone here, so I should be able to answer your questions. Please, sit down."

As they all settled into chairs, Frost said: "I'm guessing you've been asked these questions before."

"Yes, a detective was here several times. I've forgotten his name."

"Parris?"

"That's him. A week after the accident, he called here, asking . . ." She paused. "But I guess we know now it wasn't an accident."

"No, ma'am."

"He asked me if Olivia had any enemies. Any old boyfriends. Or any *new* boyfriends."

"And did you know of any?" Jane asked.

Carole Mickey gave a vigorous shake of her head, but not a hair moved in her perfect blond helmet. "Olivia wasn't that kind of person."

"Lots of regular people have affairs, Ms. Mickey."

"Well, she wasn't just a *regular* person. She was the most reliable sales rep we had. If she said she'd be in London on Wednesday, she'd be in London on Wednesday. Our clients always knew they could rely on her."

"And these clients," said Frost, "These are hospitals? Medical offices?"

"Both. We sell to institutions around the world."

"Where are your products? I don't see much on display here."

Carole reached into a drawer and pulled out a heavy catalog, which she thumped onto the desk in front of them. "This is just our satellite sales office. The catalog shows our extensive range of products. They're shipped out of warehouses in Oakland, Atlanta, Frankfurt, Singapore. Plus a few other locations."

Jane flipped through the catalog and saw hospital beds and wheelchairs, commodes and gurneys. A glossy compilation of everything she hoped she'd never need. "Mrs. Yablonski was on the road a lot?"

"All of our sales reps are. And this office is home

base, where I try to keep everything under control."

"You don't go out on the road yourself?"

"Someone has to hold down the fort." Carole looked around the room with its beige carpet and fake palm trees. "But sometimes it sure does get claustrophobic in here. I should spiff things up, shouldn't I? Maybe put in some travel posters. It would be nice to stare at a tropical beach for a change."

Frost said, "Do your reps make their sales calls solo, or do they travel with associates?"

Carole gave him a puzzled look. "Why do you ask?"

"I just wondered if Olivia had a particularly close friendship with any of her colleagues."

"Our five reps travel alone. And no, there were no inappropriate friendships in this office. For heaven's sake, this is *Olivia* we're talking about. A happily married woman with a son. I babysat Will a few times, and you learn a lot about people just by seeing the sort of children they raise. Will's a wonderful boy, very polite and well behaved. Obsessed with astronomy, like his father was. I just thank God he wasn't aboard their plane that day. To think of the whole family being wiped out . . ."

"What about Will's aunt and uncle, the Temples? Did you know them as well?"

"No, I'm afraid I didn't. I heard they took Will

and moved away, probably to escape all these sad memories. Give the boy a fresh start."

"You do know that Lynn and Brian Temple are dead?"

Carole stared at her. "Oh, my God. How did it happen?"

"Their farmhouse burned down in New Hampshire. Will wasn't in the house at the time, so he escaped."

"Is he all right? Is he staying with other relatives?"

"He's in a safe place" was all Jane would say.

Clearly shocked by the news, Carole sank back in her chair and murmured: "Poor Olivia. She'll never see him grow up. You know, she was eight years younger than I am, and I never imagined I'd outlive her." Carole looked around the office as if truly seeing it for the first time. "Two years later, and what have I done with *my* extra time? Here I am, in exactly the same place, and I haven't changed a thing. Not even those stupid fake palms."

The phone rang on the desk. Carole took a deep breath and forced a smile to her lips as she answered it brightly: "Oh hello, Mr. Damrosch, so nice to hear from you again! Yes, of course we can update that order for you. Is this for multiple items, or just that one in particular?" She reached for a pen and began jotting down notes.

Jane had no interest in hearing a conversation about canes and walkers, and she rose from the chair.

"Excuse me, Mr. Damrosch, can you hold on a minute?" Carole cupped a hand over the receiver and looked at Jane. "I'm sorry. Did you want to ask me anything else?"

Jane looked at the glossy catalog on the desk. Thought of Olivia Yablonski, hauling that heavy catalog from city to city, appointment to appointment, selling wheelchairs and bedpans. "We have no more questions," she said. "Thank you."

DETECTIVE PARRIS LOOKED LIKE a man who loved his beef and booze. They found him already seated at the LongHorn Steakhouse, sipping a martini as he studied the menu. His burly frame was so tightly wedged into the booth that Jane waved him back into his seat when he began to rise as she and Frost settled into the seat across from him. He set down his martini and gave them a typical cop's once-over, the same cool survey that Jane was simultaneously conducting of him. In his early sixties, probably on the cusp of retirement, he'd long ago lost his boyish figure as well as most of his hair. But judging by that penetrating stare, there was still a cop's brain behind those eyes, and he was sizing up Jane and Frost before he committed to the conversation.

"I've been wondering when someone would finally come asking about that case," he said.

"And here we are," said Jane.

"Hmph. Boston PD. You just never know which direction this thing is gonna twist next. You folks hungry?"

"Yeah, we could eat," said Frost.

"I just spent a very long week with my vegan daughter in Tallahassee. So you can bet I'm not here for any frigging salad." He picked up his menu again. "I'm going for the porterhouse. Twenty ounces with a loaded potato and stuffed mushrooms. That should make up for suffering through a week of broccoli."

He ordered his steak rare, and another martini. His week in Tallahassee, thought Jane, must have been quite the ordeal. Only after he took a sip of his second drink did he seem ready to get down to business.

"You read the whole file?" he asked.

"Everything you emailed us," said Jane.

"Then you know what I know. At first glance, it looked like just another small aircraft accident. Single-engine Cessna Skyhawk goes down shortly after takeoff. Debris scattered across a wooded area. Pilot was described as a real nitpicker about safety, but you know how it is. It's almost always human error, either the pilot's or the mechanic's. I didn't get involved in the case until I got the call from NTSB. In the recovered debris, they'd found signs of penetration by high-velocity fragments. That led them to test for explosive residue. Don't quote me on the chemistry details, but they used liquid chromatography and mass spectrometry. Found something called hexahydro blah blah blah. Otherwise known as RDX."

"Research Department Explosive," said Frost.

"So you did read the report."

"That part interested me. It's used by the military and it's more powerful than TNT. Mix it with wax, and you can shape it. It's part of what makes up Semtex."

Jane looked at her partner. "Now I know why you wanted to be a rocket scientist. So you can blow stuff up."

"And that's exactly what happened to the Yablonskis' little Skyhawk," said Parris. "It got blown up. The RDX was lit up via radio control. Not a timer, not altitude-triggered. Someone was on site, saw the plane take off, and pressed a button."

"So this was not a mistake," said Jane. "Not the wrong plane."

"I'm almost certain the Yablonskis were the intended target. That's probably not what you heard from Neil's NASA colleagues. They refuse to believe anyone would want to kill him. I never bothered to enlighten them."

"Yes, that's exactly what we heard from Dr. Bartusek," said Jane. "That it had to be a mistake. That Neil had no enemies."

"Everyone has enemies. But the kind who play around with RDX?" He shook his head. "We're talking scary shit, military-grade explosives. Scary enough to make me wonder if . . ." He suddenly stopped as the waitress brought their meals. Compared with the huge slab of meat on Parris's platter, Jane's seven-ounce filet and Frost's chicken breast looked like appetizers. Only after the waitress had left did Jane prompt Parris to finish his sentence.

"It made you wonder what?" she asked.

"If I was the next one who'd turn up dead," he muttered, and shoved a dripping chunk of meat into his mouth. Bloody juices pooled on his plate as he cut another chunk, took another gulp of his martini. Jane remembered what he'd said on the phone earlier that afternoon: *I'd rather not meet at my residence.* She'd thought it was merely to keep his job separate from his personal life. Now his statement had an ominous new meaning.

"This scared you that much?" she said.

"Damn right." He looked at her. "You'll start to understand if you keep chasing this."

"What are you afraid of?"

"That's just it, I don't know. I'll never know if I was being paranoid and imagining things. Or if there really *was* someone tapping my phone. Tailing my car."

"Whoa." Jane laughed. "You're serious?"

"As a heart attack." He set down his knife and fork and stared at her. "That's why I'm glad you came with your partner here. Someone to watch your back. I'm old school enough to think ladies need to be looked after, even if they're cops."

"Looked after?" Jane said to Frost. "You've been falling down on the job."

"Detective Parris," said Frost, "where do you think this, uh, threat is coming from?"

"I can hear it in your voice. You don't believe me.

But you'll find out soon enough. So here's my advice: Keep looking over your shoulder. Everywhere you go, pay attention to the faces, and you'll notice that some of them start to look familiar. The guy in the coffee shop. The gal in the airport. Then one night, you'll notice the van parked outside your house. The van that just stays there."

Frost shot a glance at Jane, and it was not missed by Parris.

"Yeah, okay. You think I'm nuts." He shrugged and reached for his martini. "Just keep digging and things will start squirming out of the mud."

"What things?" said Jane.

"You've probably already got 'em stirred up, just by coming here and asking questions."

"Having to do with Neil or with Olivia?"

"Forget Olivia. Poor gal was just in the wrong plane at the wrong time." Parris waved at the waitress and pointed at his empty martini glass. "If you don't mind," he called out.

"You think the motive was professional?" asked Frost.

"When you rule out jealous lovers and pissed-off neighbors and greedy relatives, you're kind of down to the workplace."

"You know what his research was at NASA, right?"

Parris nodded. "Alien life. Word is, he and his buddy Brian Temple thought they might've found it, even if no one at NASA will go on the record and say it."

"Because they're suppressing it?" asked Frost. "Or because it's not true?"

Parris leaned forward, his face flushed from the alcohol. "You don't get blown up when you're wrong. It's when you're *right* that things get dangerous. And I have a feeling . . ." He suddenly stopped, his gaze fixed on something behind Jane. She started to turn, and he whispered: *"Don't."*

"What is it?"

"Guy with glasses, white shirt, blue jeans. Seated at six o'clock. I think I saw him at a highway rest stop two hours ago."

Jane let the napkin slide off her lap onto the floor. She bent to pick it up and caught a look at the man in question, just as a woman with a toddler in hand slid into the booth beside him.

"Unless they're hiring three-year-olds as spies," said Jane, straightening, "I don't think you need to worry about the guy with the glasses."

"Okay," Parris admitted. "So I got that one wrong. But there've been other things."

"Like vans outside your house," she said, voice neutral.

He stiffened. "I know how it sounds. When this started, I couldn't believe it, either. I kept fishing for a logical explanation, but stuff kept happening. Voice mails got lost. Things on my desk got moved, files went missing. That went on for months."

"And it's still going on?"

Parris paused as the waitress returned with a third martini. He stared at his drink, as if weighing the wisdom of dumping any more alcohol into his bloodstream. At last he picked it up. "No. The weird stuff stopped happening around the same time the case ran out of steam. Government agencies we were working with—NTSB, FBI—told me their investigation was at a standstill. I guess they had other priorities. It all went quiet. The strange vans went away, and my life went back to normal. Then, a few weeks ago, I heard from the New Hampshire police about the Temples' farmhouse, blown up with Semtex." He paused. "Now *you're* here. And I'm just waiting for the vans to show up again."

"You have any idea who's sending them?"

"I don't want to know." He slumped back against the seat. "I'm sixty-four. Should've retired two years ago, but I need the income to help out my daughter. This is my job, but it's not my *life,* you know?"

"The trouble is," said Jane, "there may be other lives at stake here. Neil and Olivia's son, for one."

"That'd make no sense, to go after a fourteen-year-old boy."

"Makes no sense to go after two other kids, either."

Parris frowned. "What kids?"

"During your investigation, did you ever come across the names Nicholas and Annabelle Clock?"

"No."

"What about Erskine and Isabel Ward?"

"No. Who are these people?"

"Other victims. Other families who were murdered the same week Neil and Olivia died. In each of those families, a child survived. And now those three kids have been attacked again."

Parris stared at her. "Those other names never came up in my investigation. This is the first I've heard of them."

"The parallels are eerie, aren't they?"

"Is there a connection with NASA? Can you tie them together that way?"

"Unfortunately, no."

"So what *do* you have linking these kids?"

"That's what we hoped you could tell us. What the connection is."

He sat back, eyeing them over his empty dinner plate, now pooled with blood. "You know as much as I do now, about the Yablonskis. So tell me about the Wards."

"They were shot to death in a London alley, appeared to be a mugging gone awry. He was an American diplomat, she was a homemaker. Their eleven-year-old daughter was shot as well, but managed to survive."

"Ward was a diplomat, Yablonski a NASA scientist. What's the connection? I mean, astrobiology isn't exactly a hot diplomatic issue."

Frost suddenly sat up straight. "If ET's intelligent, we'd have to establish diplomatic relations, wouldn't we?"

Jane sighed. "No more *Star Trek* for you."

"No, think about it! Neil Yablonski and Brian

Temple are about to fly to Rome, to meet with Vatican scientists. Erskine Ward was once assigned to Rome, so he had connections there, at the embassy. He probably spoke fluent Italian."

"What about the Clock family?" said Parris. "You haven't told me about them. Do they have a link to any of this?"

"Nicholas Clock was a financial consultant in Providence, Rhode Island," said Jane. "He and his wife, Annabelle, were killed aboard their yacht off Saint Thomas."

Parris shook his head. "I'm not seeing any connection with the Yablonskis or the Wards. Nothing that ties these three families together."

*Only that their children are all in the same school.* A fact that Jane didn't reveal, because it made her uneasy. A killer needed only to track them down to Evensong, and it would be one-stop slaughter.

"I don't know what any of this means," said Parris. "All I can say is, this scares the hell out of me. RDX brought down the Yablonskis' plane. Semtex blew up the Temple farmhouse in New Hampshire. These are not amateurs. Killers like that, they don't give a damn that we're cops. They're operating on a whole different level, with special training and access to defense-grade explosives. You and me, we're just cockroaches to them. Remember that." He drained his martini and set down the glass. "And that's about all I have to tell you." He waved to the waitress. "Check, please!"

"We'll take care of dinner," said Jane.

Parris nodded. "Much appreciated."

"Thanks for meeting with us."

"Not that I could add much," he said, rising from the chair. Despite the three martinis, he seemed perfectly steady on his feet. "In fact, I should thank *you*."

"Why?"

The look he gave her was one of sympathy. "This gets me off the hook. Now they'll be watching you."

JANE TOOK A HOT shower and flopped onto her motel bed to stare up at the darkness. The cup of coffee with dinner had been a mistake. Caffeine, plus the day's events, kept her wide awake, mind churning over what she and Frost had learned, and what it all meant. When at last she fell asleep, the turmoil followed her straight into her dreams.

It was a clear, clear night. She was holding Regina as she stood amid a crowd, gazing up at the sky where stars glittered. Some of those stars began to move like fireflies, and she heard the crowd murmur in wonder as those stars grew brighter, traveling across the heavens in geometric formation.

They weren't stars.

In horror, she realized what those lights really meant, and she pushed her way through the crowd, desperately searching for a place to hide. A place where the alien lights could not find her. *They are coming for us.*

She lurched awake, her heart slamming so hard

she thought it might leap out of her chest. She lay sweating as the terror of the nightmare slowly faded. This was what happened when you had dinner with a paranoid cop, she thought. You dreamed about alien invasions. Not friendly ETs, but monsters with spaceships and death rays. And why wouldn't aliens come to earth as conquerors? *They would probably be as bloodthirsty as we are.*

She sat up on the side of the bed, her throat parched, the sweat cooling her skin. The motel's bedside clock glowed two fourteen A.M. In only four hours, they had to check out and catch their flight back to Boston. She rose in darkness and felt her way toward the bathroom to get a drink of water. As she passed the window, a pinpoint beam of light flickered through the curtain and vanished.

She moved to the window and nudged aside the drape to peer out at the unlit parking lot. The motel was completely booked, every parking stall filled. She searched the darkness, wondering where that flashlight beam had come from, and was about to let the curtain fall shut again when a dome light suddenly went on inside one of the vehicles.

*That's our rental car.*

She hadn't packed a weapon for this trip; neither had Frost. They were unarmed, without backup, against what? She snatched up her cell phone and hit speed dial. A few rings later, Frost answered, voice still groggy with sleep.

"Someone's screwing around with our car," she

whispered as she pulled on her blue jeans. "I'm going out there."

"What? Wait!"

She zipped up her fly. "Thirty seconds and I'm out the door."

"Hold on, hold on! I'm coming."

She grabbed her flashlight and keycard and stepped barefoot into the hallway, just as Frost emerged from his room next door. No wonder he'd managed such a quick exit; he was still wearing his pajamas. Red-and-white-striped PJs that hadn't been in fashion since Clark Gable.

He saw her staring at him, and said: "What?"

"Those make my eyes hurt. You're like walking neon," she muttered as they headed for the side exit at the end of the hall.

"What's the plan?"

"We find out who's in our car."

"Maybe we should call nine one one."

"By the time they respond, he'll be long gone."

They slipped out the exit into the night and darted behind a parked car. Peering around the rear bumper, she stared down the row, toward the stall where their rental vehicle was parked. The dome light was no longer shining.

"You sure about what you saw?" he whispered.

She didn't like the doubt she heard in his voice. At this hour of night, with the gritty pavement biting into her bare feet, the last thing she needed was to have her eyesight questioned by Mr. Neon PJs.

She crept toward their rental car, not knowing or

caring if Frost was behind her, because now she was starting to doubt herself. Starting to wonder if the light she'd seen was just a remnant from her nightmare. Aliens in her dreams, and now aliens in the parking lot.

The car was one stall away.

She paused, her sweating palm pressed against the rear bumper of a pickup truck. All she had to do was take another two steps and she'd be touching their own bumper. Crouching in the darkness, she listened for movement, for any sound at all, but she heard only the hiss of distant traffic.

She rocked forward and stared between the two vehicles. Saw empty space. That doubtful note she'd heard in Frost's voice echoed in her head, even louder now. It sent her scrambling around the rear of their rental car, to peer down the passenger side.

No one there, either.

She rose to her feet and felt the night breeze against her face as she scanned the parking lot. If anyone was watching them, he would see her now, fully exposed. And now here came Frost, an even more blatant target in his red-and-white pajamas.

"No one," he said. Not a question, just stating the obvious.

Too irritated to respond, she turned on her penlight and circled the car. Saw no scratches in the finish, nothing on the pavement around it except a trampled cigarette butt that looked like it had been lying there for weeks. "My room is right there," she said, pointing to her window. "I saw a light through the curtains. A flashlight. While I was watching, the dome light went on. Someone got into our car."

"Did you actually see anyone?"

"No. He must've been crouching too low."

"Well, if he got into our car, then it should be . . ." Frost paused. "Unlocked."

"What?"

"It's not locked." He gave the driver's handle a tug and the dome light came on inside. They both stared into the lit car, neither one of them moving.

"I locked it tonight," she said.

"Are you sure?"

"Why do you keep questioning me? I *know* I locked the frigging door. You ever seen me *not* lock my car?"

"No," he admitted. "You always do." He looked down at the handle he'd just touched. "Shit. Finger-prints."

"I'm more concerned about *why* someone was in our car. And what they were looking for."

"What if they weren't looking for anything?" he said.

She stared through the window into the front seat and thought about Neil and Olivia Yablonski climbing aboard their Cessna Skyhawk. She thought about RDX and Semtex and a New Hampshire farmhouse that exploded into flames.

"Let's take a look under the car," she said quietly. She didn't have to explain a thing; he had already

backed away from the driver's door and was following her to the rear bumper. She got down on
her hands and knees and felt grit biting into her
palms as she leaned in to study the undercarriage.
Her flashlight beam skimmed across the muffler and
tailpipe and floor pans. Nothing caught her eye or
looked out of place.

She stood, her neck sore from the awkward position. Massaging her sore muscles, she circled to the
front of the vehicle and once again dropped to her
hands and knees to search the undercarriage.

No bomb.

"Shall I pop the trunk?" said Frost.

"Yeah." *And hope that doesn't blow us sky-high.*

He hesitated, clearly sharing her anxiety, then
reached under the dashboard and pulled the release
lever.

Jane lifted the trunk and shone her flashlight into
the empty space. No bomb. She peeled back the
floor carpet and peered into the well with the spare
tire. No bomb.

*Maybe I did dream it all,* she thought. *Maybe I
forgot to lock the car. And we're standing out here
at three A.M., with Frost in those god-awful PJs,
losing half a night's sleep for nothing.*

She closed the trunk and gave a huff of frustration. "We need to look inside the car."

"Yeah, yeah, I'll do it," muttered Frost. "Might
as well make a whole night of it." He crawled
onto the front seat, his pajama-clad rear end poking out the open door. Who would have guessed

he'd go for the candy-cane convict look? As he rifled through the glove compartment, she knelt down and shone her flashlight up into the left rear wheel well. Of course, she saw nothing. She moved to the front of the car, repeated her examination of the left and right wheels, and circled back to the right rear wheel. Dropping to her knees, she aimed the flashlight into the space above the tire.

What she saw instantly made her freeze.

Frost called out: "I found something!"

"So did I." She crouched, staring into the wheel well as a chill clawed its way up her back. "You'd better come look at this," she said quietly.

He climbed out of the car and dropped down beside her. The device was no larger than a cell phone and affixed to the underside of the wheel well.

"What the hell is it?" she said.

"It looks like a GPS tracker."

"What did you find inside?"

He took her by the arm and pulled her a few feet away. Whispered: "It's under the passenger seat. They didn't even bother to tape it in place. I'm guessing whoever put it there had to take off in a hurry." He paused. "That's why he left the car door unlocked."

"It can't be because he spotted us. He was gone before we even got out here."

"You called me on your cell phone," said Frost. "That had to be the tip-off."

She stared at him. "You think our phones are being monitored?"

"Think about it. There's a bug under the seat and a GPS tracker in our wheel well. Why wouldn't they tap our phones?"

They heard the sound of an engine and turned just in time to see a car suddenly swerve out of the parking lot. They stood barefoot beside their bugged and tracked rental car, wide awake now, and too shaken to return to bed.

"Parris wasn't paranoid," said Frost.

She thought about burned farmhouses. About massacred families. "They know who we are," she said. *And where we live.*

# TWENTY-FIVE

THE EVENSONG DINING HALL WAS STRANGELY hushed this morning, students and teachers talking in murmurs over the muted clink of china-ware. Dr. Welliver's now vacant seat was flanked by Dr. Pasquantonio and Ms. Duplessis, who both scrupulously avoided glancing at the empty chair that their late colleague had occupied only days earlier. Is that what happens when you die? Claire wondered. Does everyone suddenly pretend you never existed?

"Is it okay if we sit here, Claire?"

She looked up to see Teddy and Will standing above her with their breakfast trays. This was new and different; now *two* people wanted to join her. "Whatever," she said.

They sat at her table. On Will's tray was a hearty portion of eggs and sausage. Teddy had only a sad little mound of potatoes and a single slice of dry toast. They couldn't be more unlike, even down to their meal choices.

"Is there anything you're *not* allergic to?" she asked Teddy, pointing to his breakfast.

"I'm not hungry today."

"You're never hungry."

He pushed his glasses higher on his pale nose and pointed to the sausage on her plate. "That contains toxins, you know. Processed meat cooked at high temperatures has carcinogens from heterocyclic amines."

"Yum. No wonder it tastes so good." She popped the last chunk of sausage in her mouth, just to be contrary. When you'd been shot in the head, it gave you a different perspective on dangers as minor as carcinogens.

Will leaned in close and said softly: "There's going to be a special meeting, right after breakfast."

"What meeting?"

"The Jackals. They want you to come, too."

She focused on Will's pimply moon face, and a word suddenly sprang into her head: *endomorph*. She'd learned it from their health textbook, a term that was far kinder than what Briana called Will behind his back. *Fatboy. Spotted pig.* Claire and Will had that much in common; so did Teddy. They were the three misfits, the kids who were too weird or fat or nearsighted to ever be invited to the cool kids' table. So they would make this table their own: the table for outcasts.

"Will you come?" asked Will.

"Why do they want me at their stupid meeting?"

"Because we need to put our heads together and talk about what happened to Dr. Welliver."

"I've already told everyone what happened," said Claire. "I told the police. I told Dr. Isles. I told—"

"He means what *really* happened," said Teddy.

She frowned at him. Teddy, the ectomorph, another word she'd learned from that health book. *Ecto* as in *ectoplasm,* pale and wispy as a ghost. "Are you saying I didn't tell the truth?"

"That's not at all what he meant," said Will.

"That's what it sounded like."

"We're just wondering—the Jackals are wondering—"

"Are you talking behind my back? You and the club?"

"We're trying to understand how it happened."

"Dr. Welliver jumped off the roof and she went splat on the ground. That's not so hard to understand."

"But *why* did she do it?" said Will.

"Half the time, I can't even tell you why *I* do the things I do," she said, and rose to her feet.

Will reached across the table and grabbed her hand, to stop her from leaving. "Does it make *any* sense to you, why she'd jump off the roof?"

She stared down at his hand, touching hers. "No," she admitted.

"That's why you should come," he said urgently. "But you can't talk about it. Julian says it's only for the Jackals."

She glanced across the dining hall at the table where glossy-haired Briana sat gossiping with the other cool kids. "Is *she* going to be there? Is this some kind of practical joke?"

"Claire, it's *me* asking you," said Will. "You know you can trust me."

She looked at Will, and this time she didn't focus on his pimples or his pale moon face, but his eyes. Those gentle brown eyes with long lashes. She'd never known Will to do or say anything unkind. He was goofy, sometimes annoying, but never hurtful. *Unlike me.* She thought of the times she'd pointedly ignored him or rolled her eyes at something he said, or laughed, along with everyone else, about the monster cannonballs he splashed up jumping into the lake. *Somewhere, a farmer is missing his hog,* the other girls had said, and Claire had not challenged that cruel comment. It shamed her now as she looked into Will's eyes.

"Where are we meeting?" she asked.

"Bruno will show us the way."

THE PATH THAT TOOK them up the hillside behind the school was steep and rocky, a direction that Claire had not yet explored on her midnight rambles. The route was so poorly marked that without Bruno Chinn to lead them, she might have gotten lost among the trees. Like Claire, Bruno was thirteen and yet another misfit, but a relentlessly cheerful one who seemed fated to always be the shortest kid in the group. He scampered like a mountain goat up a boulder and cast an impatient glance at his three lagging classmates.

"Does anyone want to race me to the top?" he offered.

Will halted, his face flushed bright pink, his T-shirt plastered to his doughy torso. "I'm dying here, Bruno. Can't we rest?"

Bruno waved them forward, a grinning little Napoleon leading his charge up the hill. "Don't be such a lazybones. You need to get in shape like me!"

"Do you want to kill Bruno?" muttered Claire. "Or should I?"

Will wiped the sweat from his face. "Just give me a minute. I'll be okay," he gasped. He certainly didn't look okay as he plodded ahead, panting and wheezing, his enormous shoes slipping and sliding on moss.

"Where are we going?" Claire called out.

Bruno halted and turned to his three classmates. "Before we go any farther, you all have to promise."

"Promise what?" said Teddy.

"That you won't reveal this location. It's *our* place, and the last thing we want is that grumpy old Mr. Roman telling us it's off limits."

Claire snorted. "You think he doesn't already know?"

"Just promise. Raise your right hands."

With a sigh, Claire raised her hand. So did Will and Teddy. "We promise," they said simultaneously.

"All right, then." Bruno turned and pushed aside a clump of bushes. "Welcome to the Jackals' Den."

Claire was the first to step into the clearing. Seeing stone steps, slippery with moss, she realized this was no natural opening in the trees, but something man-made. Something very old. She mounted the steps to a circular terrace built of weathered granite and entered a ring of thirteen giant boulders, where her classmates Lester Grimmett and Arthur Toombs now sat. Nearby, in the shadow of trees, was a stone cottage, its roof green with moss, the shutters closed, its secrets locked away.

Teddy moved to the center of the ring and slowly turned to survey the thirteen boulders. "What is this place?" he asked in wonder.

"I tried to look it up in the school library," said Arthur. "I think Mr. Magnus built this when he built the castle, but I can't find a reference to it anywhere."

"How did *you* find this place?"

"We didn't. Jack Jackman did, years ago. He claimed it for the Jackals, and it's been ours ever since. The stone house there, it was all falling down when Jackman first saw it. He and the first Jackals fixed it up, put on the roof and shutters. When it gets cold, we meet in there."

"Who'd put a house way up here in the middle of the woods?"

"It's kind of strange, isn't it? Like these thirteen boulders. Why *thirteen*?" Arthur's voice dropped. "Maybe Mr. Magnus had a cult or something."

Claire looked down at where clumps of grass had pushed through the cracks between the stones. In time saplings and eventually trees would do their part to camouflage this foundation, to lift and separate and shatter the granite. Already the years had wrought their damage. But on this summer morning, with the haze hanging in the distance, it seemed to her that this place was timeless, that it had always been this way.

"I think this is way older than the castle," she said. "I think it's been here a really long time."

She walked to the edge of the terrace. Through a gap in the trees, she looked down into the valley. There was the Evensong School with its many chimneys and turrets, and beyond it the dark waters of the lake. From here, she thought, I can see the whole world. Two canoes being paddled across the lake, sketching wakes on the water. Students on horseback, moving dots on the pin scratch of a trail. Standing here, with the wind in her face, she felt all-seeing and omnipotent. Queen of the universe.

The sound of a barking dog told her that Julian was approaching. She turned to see him stride up the steps to the stone terrace, Bear at his heels as always. "You all made it," he said, and looked at Claire. "You took the pledge?"

"We promised not to talk about this place, if that's what you mean," she said. "It's not like you're some secret order. Why do we have to meet up here?"

"So we can feel free to say exactly what we think. No one else can hear us. And what's said here, stays here." Julian looked around at the circle of students, now seven of them in all. A fine collection they were, thought Claire. Bruno, the cheerful little mountain goat. Arthur, who tapped everything five times before he used it. Lester, whose nightmares sometimes ended in screams that woke everyone in the dorm. Claire was the only girl in the group, and even among these oddballs she felt conspicuous.

"Something strange is happening," Julian said. "They're not telling us the truth about Dr. Welliver."

"What do you mean, the truth?" asked Teddy.

"I'm not convinced she killed herself."

"I saw her do it," Claire said.

"That may not be what actually happened."

Claire bristled. "Are you calling me a liar?"

"I saw Maura bag up Dr. Welliver's sugar bowl and send it to the crime lab. And the night after she came back from watching the autopsy, she had a long meeting with some of the teachers. They're worried, Claire. I think they're even scared."

"What's this got to do with the three of us?" asked Will. "Why did you ask us to be here?"

"Because," said Julian, turning to look at Will, "you three are somehow at the center of this. I heard Maura talking on the phone with Detective Rizzoli, and your names all came up. Ward. Clock. Yablonski." He looked from Claire to Teddy to Will. "What do you three have in common?"

Claire looked at her two companions and shrugged. "We're weird?"

Bruno let out one of his annoying giggles. "Like *that* wasn't the obvious answer."

"There's also their files," said Arthur.

"What about our files?" asked Claire.

"The day Dr. Welliver died, I was her one o'clock appointment. When I walked into her office, I saw that she had three files open on her desk, like she'd been reading them. Your file, Claire. And Will's and Teddy's."

Julian said, "That night, after she killed herself, those three files were still on her desk. Something about *you three* caught her attention."

Claire looked around at the expectant faces. "You already know why. It's because of our families." She turned to Will. "Tell them how your parents died."

Will looked down at his feet, those enormous feet in their enormous sneakers. "They said it was just an accident. A plane crash. But I found out later . . ."

"It wasn't an accident," said Julian.

Will shook his head. "It was a bomb."

"Teddy," said Claire. "Tell them what you told me. About your family."

"I don't want to talk about it," Teddy whispered.

She looked at the other students. "They were murdered, like Will's parents. Like mine. That's what you all wanted to hear, isn't it? *That's* what we have in common."

"Tell them the rest of it, Claire," said Julian. "What happened to your foster families."

Everyone's eyes turned back to Claire.

She said, "You *know* what happened. Why are you doing this? Because it's fun to screw around with the weird kids' heads?"

"I'm just trying to understand what's happening here. To you, and to the school." Julian looked at the other Jackals. "We talk about being investigators someday, and how we'll make a difference in the world. We spend all our time learning about blood types and blowflies, but it's all just theoretical. Now we have a *real* investigation going on around us, right here. And *these three* are at the center of it."

"Why don't you just ask Dr. Isles?" said Will.

"She says she can't talk about it." He added on a faintly resentful note, "Not to me, anyway."

"So you're going to run your own investigation? A bunch of kids?" Claire laughed.

"Why can't we?" Julian moved toward her, so close she had to look up to meet his eyes. "Don't you wonder about it, Claire? You, too, Will and Teddy? Who wants you dead? Why do they want it so badly that they'd *twice* try to kill you?"

"It's like that creepy movie *Final Destination*," Bruno said, far too cheerfully. "About those kids who are supposed to die in a plane crash, but they escape. And Death keeps coming after them."

"This is not a movie, Bruno," said Julian. "We're not talking about the supernatural. Real people are doing this, and for a reason. We need to figure out why."

Claire gave a dismissive laugh. "Listen to you! You think you can figure out what the police can't? You're just a bunch of kids with your microscopes and chemistry sets. So tell me, Julian, how are you going to fit all this amazing police work in between classes?"

"I'm going to start by asking *you*. You're the one this is happening to, Claire. You must have some idea what connects the three of you."

She looked at Will and Teddy. The endomorph and the ectomorph. "Well, we sure aren't related, 'cause we don't look anything like each other."

"And we were all living in different places," said Will. "My mom and dad were killed in Maryland."

"Mine were killed in London," said Claire. *Where I almost died, too.*

"Teddy?" asked Julian.

"I told you, I don't want to talk about it," he said.

"This could be important," said Julian. "Don't you want answers? Don't you want to know why they died?"

"I *know* why they died! Because we were on a boat. On my dad's *stupid* boat in the middle of nowhere. If we hadn't been on it, if we'd just stayed home . . ."

"Tell them, Teddy," Claire prompted gently. "Tell them what happened on the boat."

For a long time Teddy didn't say a thing. He

stood with head drooping as he stared down at the stones. When at last he did speak, it was so quietly they could barely hear him.

"There were people with guns," he whispered. "I heard screaming. My mother. And my sisters. And I couldn't help them. All I could do was . . ." He shook his head. "I hate the water. I never want to be in a boat again."

Claire went to Teddy and wrapped her arms around him. Felt his heart fluttering like a bird's against his frail chest. "It's not your fault," she murmured. "You couldn't save them."

"I lived. And they didn't."

"Don't blame yourself. Blame the people who did it. Or the shitty world. Or even your dad, for taking you on that boat. But never blame yourself, Teddy."

He jerked out of her arms and backed away from the circle. "This is stupid. I don't want to play this game."

"It's not a game," said Julian.

"To *you* it is!" Teddy shot back. "You and your stupid club. Don't you get it? For us, this is real life. It's *our* lives."

"Which is why you're the ones who have to figure it out, the three of you," said Julian. "You need to put your heads together. Find out what you have in common. Your families, your parents, where you went to school. It's about finding that one link, that person who ties you together."

"Person?" Will asked quietly. "You mean, the killer."

Julian nodded. "It all gets down to that. There's someone who's passed through your lives, or your parents' lives. Someone who might be searching for you right now."

Claire looked at Will and remembered what he'd said to her: *I feel like I've met you.* She had no memory of him. She had no recollection of a lot of things, but that was because she'd been shot in the head. A lot of things could be blamed on that bullet, from her mediocre grades to her insomnia to her freakishly bad temper.

And now the old headache was back. She blamed the bullet for that, too.

She went to a boulder and sat down to massage her scalp, fingers worrying at the old defect in her skull. It was a permanent reminder of everything that she'd lost. At her feet, a skinny sapling had grown between the stones. Even granite can't stop the inevitable, she thought. Someday the tree will break through, cracking and lifting that rock. Even if I snip this sapling, another will pop up.

The way killers do.

CLAIRE OPENED HER CLOSET and reached up for the battered cardboard box on the shelf. She had not taken it out since she'd arrived at Evensong, and could scarcely remember what was in it. Two years ago, she and Barbara Buckley had packed it with a few mementos from her parents' London apartment. Since then, the box had traveled with her, from London to Ithaca and now here, but not once had she looked inside. She'd been afraid to see their faces again, afraid it would make her remember all that she had lost. She sat down on her bed and set the box beside her. Took a moment to brace herself before she lifted the cardboard flaps.

A porcelain unicorn lay on top. Izzy, she thought. I remember its name. It belonged to her mother, a silly little trinket that Isabel Ward had picked up in a flea market somewhere; she'd called it her good-luck charm. *The luck ran out, Mom. For all of us.*

Gingerly, Claire set the unicorn on her nightstand and reached into the box for the next items. A velvet drawstring bag with her mother's jewelry. Her parents' passports. A silk scarf that smelled faintly of perfume, something bright and lemony. Finally, at the bottom, two photo albums.

She took out the albums and set them on her lap. It was obvious which one was the most recent; it still had a few empty pages at the end. This volume she opened first, and she saw her own face smiling up from the first page of photographs. She was wearing a fluffy yellow dress and holding a balloon in front of the Disney World entrance. She didn't remember the dress, nor did she remember going to Disney World. How old was she in this photo, three? Four? She was no good at judging kids' ages. Had this photo not existed, she would not have known she'd ever set foot in the Magic Kingdom.

Another memory I've lost, she thought. She

wanted to tear that page from the album, rip that lying photograph to pieces. If she didn't remember it, then it might as well never have happened. This album was a book of lies, some other girl's childhood, some other girl's memories.

"Can I come in, Claire?" said Will, peeking through her open doorway. He seemed afraid to step in, and he hung back in the hall, his head ducked as though she might throw something at him.

"I don't care," she said. She meant it as an invitation, but when he backed away, she called out: "Hey, where are you going? Don't you want to come in and check out my room?"

Only then did he enter, but he hesitated just inside the door and looked around nervously at the bookshelves, the desks, the dressers. He avoided looking at any of the beds, as if one of them might leap up and bite him.

"My roommates are packing for Quebec," he said. "It sucks, that we can't go with them tomorrow."

"Like I'd want to be stuck on a bus for hours and hours? I'd rather stay here," she said, even though that wasn't really true; it *did* suck, being left behind. She turned a page in the album and saw another photo of herself, this time dressed in a cowboy hat, sitting on a depressed-looking pony.

"Is that you?" He laughed. "You're really cute."

Annoyed, she slapped the album shut. "I'm just doing research, like Julian asked us to."

"I'm doing research, too." He reached into his pocket and unfolded a sheet of paper. "I'm working on a time line of our lives. All the things that've happened to you and me and Teddy, and how they might relate. I'm trying to see if anything intersects between us. I still need to get Teddy's exact dates, but I've got yours here. You want to check them?"

She took the sheet of paper and focused on the two event markers that represented her personal tragedies. The first was the date she and her parents were shot in London, an event so hazy in her memory that it might have happened to another girl, not her. But the second event was still fresh enough to make her stomach churn with guilt. She had stubbornly avoided thinking about it these past few weeks, but seeing that date on Will's time line brought it back in a sickening rush of memories. How blithely she had slipped out of the Buckleys' house that night. How tired and worried Bob and Barbara had looked when they'd fetched her in their car. *They died because of me. Because I was a thoughtless jerk.*

She thrust the time line back at Will. "Yeah. The dates are okay."

He pointed to the photo albums. "Did you find anything?"

"Just pictures."

"Can I see?"

She didn't want to reveal any more embarrassing photos of herself, so she set aside the more recent album and opened her parents' album instead. On the first page, she saw her father, Erskine, tall and handsome, wearing a suit and tie. "That's my dad," she said.

"That's the Washington Monument behind him! I've been there. My dad took me to the Air and Space Museum when I was eight. It's *such* a cool place."

"Whoop-de-do."

He looked at her. "Why do you do that, Claire?"

"Do what?"

"Put me down all the time."

A denial reflexively bubbled to her lips; then she saw his face and realized what he'd said was true. She did put him down all the time. She sighed. "I don't really mean to."

"So it's not because you think I deserve it? Like I'm disgusting or something?"

"No. It's because I'm not thinking at all. It's a stupid habit."

He nodded. "I have stupid habits, too. Like how I'm always using the word *like*."

"Just stop it, then."

"Let's agree we'll both stop it. Okay?"

"Sure. Whatever." She turned more pages in the album, saw more photos of her handsome dad posing in different settings. At a picnic with friends under the trees. Wearing a swimsuit on a beach with palm trees. She came to a photo of both her mom and dad, their arms entwined, standing in front of the Roman Colosseum.

"Look. That's my mom," she said softly, stroking

a finger across the image. Suddenly the scent of the perfume on that scarf cut through the fog of lost memories, and she could smell her mother's hair, feel her mother's hands on her face.

"She looks like you," said Will in wonder. "She's really beautiful."

They were both beautiful, thought Claire, gazing hungrily at her mother and father. They must have thought the whole world was at their feet when this picture was taken. They had striking good looks and a lifetime ahead of them. And they were living in Rome. Did they ever stop to think, did they ever imagine, how prematurely their future would end?

"This was taken nineteen years ago," said Will, noting the date that Claire's mom had written in the album.

"They were just married then. My dad worked at the embassy. He was a political secretary."

"In Rome? Cool. Is that where you were born?"

"My birth certificate says I was born in Virginia. I guess my mom came home to have me."

They turned more pages, saw more images of the same handsome couple smiling at a dinner, holding up champagne glasses at a cocktail party, waving from a motorboat. Living *la dolce vita,* her mother used to say. The sweet life. And that's what Claire saw in these photos, a record of what seemed to be a never-ending string of good times with colleagues and friends. But that's what photo albums were meant to show, the best moments in life. The moments you wanted to remember, not the ones you wanted to forget.

"Look. That's gotta be you," said Will.

It was a photo of Claire's mother, smiling from her hospital bed as she cradled an infant. She saw the handwritten date and said, "Yeah, that's the day I was born. My mom said it happened really fast. She said I was in a hurry to get out and she almost didn't make it to the hospital in time."

Will laughed. "You're still in a hurry to get out."

She turned the pages, past more boring baby photos. In a stroller. In a high chair. Clutching a bottle. None of this helped her remember anything because these were all taken before her memories had been laid down. It could just as well be another child's album.

She reached the last page. In the final two photos, Claire did not appear. These featured yet another cocktail party, another set of smiling strangers holding wineglasses. That was the burden of the diplomat's wife, her mom used to joke. *Always smiling, always pouring*. Claire was about to shut the album when Will's hand suddenly closed over hers.

"Wait," he said. "That picture."

"What about it?"

He took the album from her and leaned in close to study one of the party photos. It showed Claire's dad, cocktail glass in hand, caught in midlaugh with another man. The handwritten caption said, 4TH OF JULY. HAPPY BIRTHDAY, USA!

"This woman," murmured Will. He pointed to a

slim brunette standing to the right of Erskine Ward. She was wearing a low-cut green dress with a gold belt, and her gaze was fixed on Claire's father. It was a look of unabashed admiration. "Do you know who she is?" Will asked.

"Should I?"

"*Look* at her. Try to remember if you've ever seen her."

The harder she stared, the more familiar the woman seemed, but it was just a wisp of a memory, one she couldn't be sure of. One that might not even exist, except through a trick of effort. "I don't know," she said. "Why?"

"Because I *do* know her."

She frowned at him. "How could you? This is *my* family album."

"And that," he said, pointing to the woman in the photo, "is my mother."

# TWENTY-SIX

ANTHONY SANSONE ARRIVED AT EVENSONG under cover of darkness, as he had before.

From her window, Maura saw the Mercedes park in the courtyard below. A familiar figure climbed out, tall and cloaked in black. As he swept past, beneath the courtyard lantern, he briefly cast a long, sinister shadow across the cobblestones and then disappeared.

She left her room and headed downstairs to intercept him. At the second-floor landing she paused and looked down into the shadowy entrance hall, where Sansone and Gottfried were speaking in hushed voices.

". . . still unclear why she did it," said Gottfried. "Our contacts are deeply troubled. There's too much we didn't know about her, things we *should* have been told."

"You believe it *was* a suicide?"

"If not suicide, how do we explain . . ." Gottfried

froze at the creak of a step. Both men turned to see Maura standing above them, on the stairs.

"Dr. Isles," said Gottfried, instantly forcing a smile. "Having a touch of insomnia?"

"I want to hear the truth," she said. "About Anna Welliver."

"We're as baffled about her death as you are."

"This isn't about her death. It's about her life. You said you had no answers for me, Gottfried." She looked at Sansone. "Maybe Anthony does."

Sansone sighed. "I suppose it is time to be honest with you. I owe you that much, Maura. Come, let's talk in the library."

"Then I'll say good night to you both," said Gottfried, and he turned to the stairs. There he paused and looked back at Sansone. "Anna's gone, but that doesn't break our promise to her. Remember that, Anthony." He climbed the steps, disappearing into shadow.

"What does that mean?" Maura asked.

"It means there are some things I cannot tell you," he said as they entered the gloomy passage leading to the library.

"What's the point of all the secrecy?"

"The point is trust. Anna revealed things to us under the strictest confidence. Details we're unable to share." He paused at the end of the passageway. "But now we wonder if even *we* knew the truth about her."

During the day, sunlight flooded the library's Palladian windows and gleamed on polished wood tables. But now shadows cloaked the room, transforming alcoves into dark little caves. Anthony switched on a single desk lamp, and in intimate gloom they sat facing each other across a table. All around them loomed rows and rows of bookcases in scholarly formation, two millennia's worth of knowledge. But it was this man she now struggled to read, a man as unknowable as a closed book.

"Who *was* Anna Welliver?" Maura asked. "I saw her autopsy. Her body is covered with old scars from torture. I know her husband was murdered, but what happened to Anna?"

He shook his head. "Will it always be this way between us?"

"What do you mean?"

"Why can't we have normal conversations, like other people? About the weather, the theater? Instead we talk about your work, not the most pleasant of subjects. But I suppose that is what keeps bringing us together."

"Death, you mean?"

"And violence." He leaned forward, his eyes as intense as lasers. "We're so much alike, you and I. There's a darkness in you, and that's the bond we share. We both understand."

"Understand what?"

"That the darkness is real."

"I don't want to see the world that way," she said.

"But you see the evidence every time a corpse

lands on your autopsy table. You know the world isn't all sunshine, and so do I."

"And that's what we bring to this friendship, Anthony? Doom and gloom?"

"I sensed it in you the first time we met. It runs deep in you, because of who you are."

*Who I am.* Queen of the dead. The daughter of monsters. The darkness extended as deep as the blood in her veins, because it was the same blood that ran in her mother, Amalthea, a killer who would spend the rest of her life in prison.

His gaze was so intent that she could not bear to maintain eye contact. She focused, instead, on his briefcase. They had known each other for almost two years, yet with just a look, he could still throw her off balance and make her feel like a specimen under glass, examined and exposed.

"I'm not here to talk about myself," she said. "You promised you'd tell me the truth about Anna."

He nodded. "What I *can* tell you, anyway."

"Did you know that she was a victim of torture?"

"Yes. And we knew she was still deeply haunted by what happened to her and her husband in Argentina."

"Yet you hired her. Brought her onto your staff as a counselor to vulnerable children."

"The Evensong school board hired her."

"You must have personally approved it."

He nodded. "Based on her references, her academic qualifications. Her dedication to crime victims. And she was one of *us*."

"A member of the Mephisto Society."

"She, too, was personally scarred by violence. Twenty-two years ago, Anna and her husband were working for an international firm in Argentina when they were abducted. Both Anna and her husband were tortured. Her husband, Frank, was executed. The killers were never captured. That experience taught Anna that justice is unreliable. That monsters are always with us. She left the company she'd been working for, went back to graduate school, and become a counselor for crime victims. Sixteen years ago, she joined us."

"You're not exactly in the Yellow Pages. How did she learn about the society?"

"The way all our members do. Through an intermediary."

"She was recruited?"

"Her name was proposed to the society by a member who served in law enforcement. Anna came to his attention because of her excellent work as a counselor. He knew that she'd lost her husband to violence. That she was especially effective with childhood victims, and she had multiple contacts within law enforcement and child protective agencies around the country." He lifted the briefcase he'd carried into the library and set it on the table. "After I got news of her death, I reviewed her membership file."

"Every member has a file?"

"Compiled at the time of proposal. I've redacted

the sensitive information, but here's what I can share with you."

"I can't be trusted with the complete file?"

"Maura." He sighed. "Even though I trust you, some information can be shared only among members."

"Then why show this to me at all?"

"Because you've made yourself part of the investigation. You attended the autopsy. You requested a comprehensive tox screen on Anna's blood, so I assume you have doubts it was a suicide. When you raise questions, I listen. Because I know how good you are at your job."

"I have no evidence yet to support my doubts."

"But something's triggered your instincts. Something in your subconscious has picked up details that you're not even aware of yet. It's telling you something is wrong." He leaned closer, studying her face. "Am I correct?"

She thought of the empty sugar bowl. And the baffling phone conversation between Jane and Anna. She looked down at the file that Sansone had slid to her, and opened the folder.

The first page was a photo of Anna, before her hair had turned silver. It was taken sixteen years earlier, when she'd been proposed for the society. As always, she wore a modest dress with long sleeves and high collar, a wardrobe choice that made her seem eccentric, but which Maura now understood was meant to hide the scars of torture.

Nothing in Anna's smile, in her eyes, spoke of old torments or a future suicide.

Maura turned the page to a dry compilation of biographical data. Born in Berlin to a US Army officer and his wife. Earned a degree in psychology from George Washington University in DC and married Franklin Welliver. Along with her husband, she worked for an international headhunting firm with offices in Mexico, Chile, and Argentina.

She turned the page and saw newspaper articles about the couple's abduction and Franklin's subsequent murder in Argentina. A second clipping stated that the killers were never apprehended.

"Anna personally experienced the failure of justice," said Sansone. "That made her one of us."

"Not the sort of membership qualification anyone wants to have."

"None of us joined the society because we *wanted* to, the way you want to join a country club. We were each compelled to join because of personal tragedies that left us angry or hopeless or in despair. We understand what ordinary people don't."

"Evil."

"That's one word for it." He pointed to the file. "Certainly Anna understood. After her husband's death, she quit her job and returned to the US to go back to school. Earned her degree in counseling. In her own way, she was trying to fight evil, by working with the families of victims. We offered her the chance to be even more effective, to reshape a whole generation of lives. Not just as a counselor, but as our admissions scout. With her contacts within child protective agencies and law enforcement, she could identify prospective students all over the country."

"By trawling through murder cases? Targeting the wounded?"

"We've had this conversation before, Maura. I know you don't approve."

"Because it smacks of recruitment for your cause."

"Look at Julian and how he's blossomed. Tell me this school hasn't been good for him."

She didn't respond because she had no rebuttal. Evensong was exactly where Julian should be. In just these few months he'd gained both muscle and confidence.

"Anna knew he would do well here," said Sansone. "If you judged him only by his school records in Wyoming, no one would consider him a promising candidate. He was failing half his classes, getting into fights, committing petty crimes. But Anna saw in his file that he was a survivor. She knew he'd kept you alive in those mountains for no other reason but compassion. And that's how she knew he was a student we wanted."

"So she made that decision?"

"Anna's approval was key. She handpicked half the students you see here." He paused and added: "Including Claire Ward and Will Yablonski."

She considered that last piece of information for a moment. Thought about the meeting that she and Jane had held in Anna's office about these children, and whether there was a connection among them. Anna had told them it was merely a coincidence, and not worth pursuing. Yet on the day Anna died, she had been studying the files of those same three children.

The room was so quiet Maura could hear her own heartbeat. The silence magnified the sound of approaching footsteps, and she turned as four figures emerged from the shadows and walked into the glow of the lamp.

"We need to talk to you," said Julian. Beside him stood three companions. *The* three. Will and Teddy and Claire, the trio whose tragedies seemed to have no end to them.

Although it was approaching eleven P.M., and these children should all be in bed, Sansone regarded them with the same respect he'd give any adult. "What do you have on your mind, Julian?" he asked.

"The Jackals had a meeting this morning, about Dr. Welliver," the boy said. "And these three members have since uncovered a lead. But we need your help to pursue it."

Maura sighed. "Julian, I know you want to be helpful, but it's late. Mr. Sansone and I have things to—"

"We want to see our files," Claire cut in. "We want to know everything the police know about us and our parents. *All* the reports."

"I don't have that information, Claire."

"But you can get it, right? Or Detective Rizzoli can."

"These are ongoing investigations. Which means that information isn't meant for the public."

"We're not the public," said Claire. "This is about us, about *our* lives, and we have a right to know."

"Yes, you do have a right to know, when you get older. But these are official documents, and there are details that you might not understand."

"Because we're too young to handle the truth? That's what you're saying, isn't it? That thirteen-year-olds can't possibly deal with it. It's like you have no idea who we are, or what we've been through."

"I do know, Claire," Maura said quietly. "I understand."

"Understand what? *She got shot in the head?* That's what you know about me, but you have no idea what that really means. Waking up in a hospital, not remembering how you got there. Not knowing your mom and dad are dead. Feeling like you'll never again be able to read a whole book or sleep through the night or even hold on to a single damn thought." She pressed her hand to her head. "When they blasted this hole in my skull, they blew up my life, too. I'll never be like everyone else. I'll always be the weirdo. So don't tell me you know me, or anything about me."

The boys, stunned by that outburst, stared at her in astonishment. Perhaps even admiration.

"I'm sorry," said Maura. "You're absolutely

right, Claire, I don't know." She looked at Will and Teddy. "Just like I don't know what your lives have been like, not really. I cut open bodies and see what's inside, but that's all I can do. You three, well, you'll just have to tell me what the files can't. About your lives and who you are."

"Like Claire says, we're the weirdos," said Will, and Teddy gave a sad nod of agreement. "We're the ones no one wants to be around. It's like everyone can sense we're bad luck, and they don't want anything to do with us, in case it rubs off." Will's head drooped. "And they end up dead, like Dr. Welliver."

"There's no proof that Dr. Welliver's death was anything but a suicide."

"Maybe," said Will, "but our files were on her desk the day she died. It's like she opened them and got cursed."

"Maura," said Julian, "we want to help the investigation. We have information."

"The Jackals are a fine group, Julian. But there are professionals at work investigating everything that's happened."

"This one's only for pros, is that it?"

"Yes, as a matter of fact."

"What if we found something the professionals didn't?" He looked at Claire. "Show them."

Only then did Maura notice that Claire was holding a book. "This is my family album," said Claire, handing the volume to Maura.

Maura opened the book to a photograph of a young man and woman standing before the Roman

Colosseum, both blond, both stunningly attractive. "Your parents?" she asked.

"Yeah. My dad worked at the embassy. He was a political officer."

"They were a handsome couple, Claire."

"But that's not what I wanted to show you." Claire flipped the album to the last page of photos. "It's this picture, the cocktail party. That's my dad there, talking to that guy. And you see this woman standing off to the side here, in the green dress? Do you know who she is?"

"Who?"

"That's my mother," said Will.

Maura turned to him in surprise. "Are you sure? It could be someone who looks like her."

"It *is* my mother. I recognize the dress. She always wore it to parties. It was green, with a gold belt, and she told me it was the most expensive dress she'd ever bought, but that quality always pays for itself. That was her motto, what she used to say to me all the time." Will's voice faded and his shoulders slumped as he said softly: "That's my mom."

Maura looked at the caption: 4TH OF JULY. HAPPY BIRTHDAY, USA! "There's no year. We don't know when this picture was taken."

"The point is," said Julian, "They were *together,* at the same party. And you know who else was there?"

"Him," said Claire. She pointed to the blond

man photographed in conversation with Erskine
Ward. Captured in profile, he was taller than Ward,
broad-shouldered and powerfully built. In a room
filled with people drinking wine, he was the only
one holding a can of beer.

"It's my father," said Teddy.

"*There's* the connection," said Julian. "It still
doesn't tell us why they were killed, or why someone wants to hurt their children all these years
later. But this is the evidence you were looking for.
Claire's dad. Teddy's dad. Will's mom. They *knew*
each other."

THE SCANNED IMAGE GLOWED on Frost's computer
screen, a photo of guests dressed in party clothes,
some seated, some standing, most with a drink in
hand. The central figures in the tableau were Erskine
Ward and Nicholas Clock, who stood facing each
other, but with their faces partly turned to the camera, as though someone had just called out: "Smile,
gentlemen!" Will's mother, Olivia, stood in the pe-
riphery beside another woman, but her gaze was
turned toward Erskine Ward. Jane scanned the other
faces, searching for the spouses of these three, but
did not spot them amid the well-heeled and clearly
well-lubricated gathering.

"That," said Frost, pointing to Olivia, "is the expression of a woman who has the hots for Ward."

"That's what you see in her face?"

"Not that anyone ever looks at me like that."

"It could be just the look of an old friend. Some-one who knows him well."

"Then it's funny we can't find anything else to tie Olivia and Erskine together. If they knew each other that well."

Jane leaned back in her chair and stretched the kinks from her neck. It was nearly midnight, and everyone else in the homicide unit had left the build-ing for the night. So should we, she thought, but these scanned photos, which Maura had emailed to Boston PD, had kept Jane and Frost at their desks for the last hour. Maura had sent eight photos from the Ward family album, images of barbecues and black-tie parties, of gatherings indoors and out-doors. In none of the other photos had Jane spotted either Olivia Yablonski or Nicholas Clock; this was the only image where the two appeared along with Erskine Ward. A Fourth of July party, year unspeci-fied, in a room with at least a dozen other people visible in the shot.

Where and when had this photo been taken?

Frost clicked through the other seven images and stopped at a photo of the Ward family, seated on a white sofa. Claire looked about eight years old. They were dressed in their best, Erskine in a gray suit, Isabel in a well-cut dress and blazer. Be-hind them was an elaborately decorated Christmas tree.

"This is the same room as the cocktail party," said Frost. "See the hearth there, on the right?

It's in the other photo as well. And here . . ." He zoomed in on a corner of the room. "Does that look like the same crown molding?"

"Yeah, it does," said Jane. She squinted to read the handwritten caption from the album: OUR LAST CHRISTMAS IN GEORGETOWN. LONDON, HERE WE COME! She looked at Frost. "This was taken in DC."

"So that's where the cocktail party was. The question is, why did Nicholas Clock and Olivia Yablonski get invited to a diplomat's party? Nicholas was in finance. Olivia was a medical equipment sales rep. How and where did these three people meet?"

"Go back to the other photo," she said.

Frost pulled up the image of the cocktail party, which they now knew was in Washington.

"They look younger here," said Jane. She swiveled around to grab the Ward family's file from her desk and flipped it open to Erskine Ward's curriculum vitae. "Foreign service officer, served in Rome for fourteen years, Washington for five. Then stationed in London, where he was killed a year later."

"So this cocktail party was held sometime during the Wards' five-year stay in DC."

"Right." She closed the file. "How did these three meet? It must have been in Washington. Or . . ." She looked at Frost just as the same thought seemed to spring into his head.

"Rome," said Frost, and he sat up straight in

excitement. "Remember what that guy at NASA told us? Neil and Olivia were looking forward to their trip to Rome—where they first met each other."

Jane swiveled around again to grab her file on the Yablonskis. "All this time, we've focused on Neil and *his* job. Kept chasing that stupid NASA and aliens shit, when it was *Olivia* we should have been looking at." Bland Olivia with the boring job, who stood around looking lost at her husband's NASA gatherings. Olivia, who regularly traveled overseas to sell medical equipment. *What were you really selling, Olivia?*

Jane found the page she was searching for. "Here it is. Date of marriage, Olivia and Neil Yablonski. Fifteen years ago. She met her future husband in Rome, which would place her there during the same time Erskine Ward was working at the embassy."

"What about this guy?" Frost pointed at Teddy's father, Nicholas Clock, who cut a striking and athletic figure, a man confident enough in his own skin to drink beer when everyone else was sipping wine, to sport Dockers and a golf shirt among a jacket-and-tie crowd. "Can we place Nicholas Clock in Rome around that same time? Were all three of them there?"

Jane flipped through the file. "We don't know enough about Clock. Most of what we've got is what the Saint Thomas police sent us."

"He was just a tourist in Saint Thomas. Down there, no one would know him."

"But they would know him in Providence, where he worked." She paged through the file. "Here. Financial consultant at Jarvis and McCrane, Chapman Street." She looked up. "Our next stop."

# TWENTY-SEVEN

I DIDN'T WANT TO GO TO QUEBEC ANYWAY.

Claire sulked in the courtyard as she watched her excited classmates climb aboard the field trip bus. She had told Will she didn't want to be stuck on any bus for hours, but this was a sleek new bus, not some ratty yellow clunker like most schools used. Bruno added insult to injury by shouting out the bus window, announcing all the onboard luxuries.

"Hey, everyone, it's got TVs! Headphones! WiFi!"

Now Briana and the princesses came out of the building, wheeling their cute little carry-ons, which they rolled across the cobblestones in a royal procession. As they passed her, Claire heard one of them sneer, under her breath: *Night Crawler.*

"Loser," Claire shot back.

Briana wheeled around. "I'm just going to say it right here, loud and clear, so everyone hears it. My room is *locked.* If I find anything missing when I get back—*anything*—we'll all know who did it."

"Get on the bus, Briana," Ms. Saul said with a sigh as she and Ms. Duplessis tried to shepherd their students aboard. "We have to get going now if we want to make it there by lunchtime."

Briana shot a poisonous glance at Claire and climbed aboard the bus.

"Are you okay, Claire?" Ms. Saul asked gently.

Of all the teachers at Evensong, Ms. Saul was her favorite, because she looked at you as if she really saw you, and cared. And what she saw now must be obvious: that as much as Claire denied wanting to go with them, she hated being left behind.

"It's only because you're still so new to Evensong," said Ms. Saul. "You'll get to go on our next trip. And won't it be nice this weekend, just the four of you, having the whole school to yourselves?"

"I guess," moped Claire.

"Mr. Roman's set up the hay bales for you, if you want to shoot a few arrows. You'll be an expert archer by the time we get back."

*Aren't you afraid I'll kill another chicken?* was what Claire thought, but she kept her mouth shut as Ms. Saul climbed aboard and the doors closed. With a puff of diesel smoke, the bus pulled away and drove under the stone archway. She heard barking behind her, saw a flash of black fur as Julian's dog shot past, chasing after the bus.

"Bear!" Claire yelled. "Come back here!"

The dog ignored her and tore out of the courtyard. Claire followed him all the way to the edge of the lake where he suddenly halted, his nose lifted to the air. No longer did he seem interested in the bus, which continued driving down the road and disappeared around the bend. Instead Bear turned and took off in a different direction.

"Now where are you going?" she called out. With a sigh, she followed him around the building, toward the trail that led up the ridge. Already he was picking his way through the scrub, moving faster now, so fast that she had to scramble to keep up. "Bear, come *back here*," she commanded. Watched in frustration as he slipped away into the underbrush. So much for obedience; she couldn't get even a dog to show her any respect.

Halfway up the ridge, she gave up chasing him and plopped down on a boulder. From here, she could just look over the school's rooftop. It was not as spectacular a view as up at the Jackals' Den, but this was good enough, especially on this bright morning, with the sun glittering on the lake. By now the bus would be out of the gate and on its way to Quebec. By noon, they'd be eating at some fancy French restaurant—that's what Briana had bragged about, anyway—and there'd be a trip to the Quebec Experience museum, and a ride on an outdoor elevator that went up a cliff.

*Meanwhile, I get to sit on this stupid rock.*

She broke off a chip of lichen and tossed it over the edge. Wondered if Will and Teddy were finished with breakfast yet. Maybe they'd want to shoot arrows with her. But instead of heading back down the ridge, she flopped onto her back, stretching out like a snake warming itself on the boulder, and closed her eyes. Heard a dog's whine and felt Bear brush up against her jeans. She stroked his back, taking comfort from the touch of his fur. What was it that made a dog's company so comforting? Maybe the fact that you never had to hide your feelings from them, never had to fake a smile for their benefit.

"Good old Bear," she murmured, and opened her eyes to look at him. "What did you bring back for me?"

The dog had something in his mouth, something he did not seem willing to surrender. Only when she gave a tug on it did he finally let it drop. It was a leather glove, black. Where in these woods had Bear found a glove? It smelled bad, and it glistened with the dog's saliva.

Grimacing, she picked it up and felt a heaviness to it. Peeking inside, she saw something white gleaming within. She turned the glove upside down, gave it a hard shake. What came tumbling out made her scream and scramble backward, away from the object that lay stinking on the boulder.

A hand.

"IT'S ALWAYS THE DOGS that find them," said Dr. Emma Owen.

Maura and the Maine medical examiner stood in the dappled shade of the woods, insects buzzing around their faces, the air thick with the stench of cadaver. Maura thought of other bodies she'd examined over the years, also unearthed by dogs, whose noses are always on the alert for such ripe treasures. Although these remains were hundreds of yards up the slope, Bear had caught the scent and tracked it to this thicket, where dense underbrush partially concealed the body. The man, who appeared to be well muscled and fit, was dressed in camouflage cargo pants, a dark green Windbreaker, a T-shirt, and hiking boots. A serrated knife was still strapped to his ankle, and a rifle with a telescopic sight was perched on a nearby boulder. He lay on his left side, exposing his right face and neck to the elements. Scavengers had been at work, greedily stripping away the scalp and face, gnawing at nasal cartilage, and digging into the right orbit, which now gaped empty, the socket scooped clean. Canids, thought Maura, noting the teeth marks on the remaining skin, the punctures in the thin orbital bone. Coyotes most likely. Or, in this remote area, perhaps wolves. Even in this tangle of vines, the cause of death was easy to spot: an aluminum arrow, its tip embedded deep in the left eye, its tail feathers dyed a deep green.

Under other circumstances, Maura might have assumed this was just an unlucky hunter, brought down in the woods by another hunter's carelessness. But this man had been trespassing on Evensong property, and from the boulder where his rifle was positioned, he would have had a commanding view of the valley and the school below. He could have observed who arrived on the property, and who departed.

Inured as she was to foul smells, Maura had to turn away as the body was rolled onto a plastic sheet, stirring up a stench so foul that she gagged and lifted her arm over her nose. Dr. Owen's staff was fully garbed and masked, but Maura, standing here as a mere observer, had settled for gloves and shoe covers, the big-city ME trying to prove she was too seasoned to let a rotting corpse defeat her.

Dr. Owen crouched down over the body. "There's barely persistent rigor mortis here," she said, testing the limbs for range of motion.

"It was fifty-one degrees last night," one of the state police detectives said. "Balmy."

The medical examiner lifted the edge of the victim's T-shirt to expose the abdomen. The changes from autolysis were obvious even from where Maura stood. Death sets off a cascade of changes in soft tissues as leaking enzymes digest proteins and disintegrate membranes. Blood cells break apart and leak through vessel walls, and in that soup of nutrients, bacteria feast, filling the abdomen with gases. Braving the stench, Maura crouched down beside Dr. Owen. She saw blue veins marbling the bloated belly and knew that if they rolled down the pants, they would find the scrotum swollen with those same gases.

"Forty-eight to seventy-two hours," said Dr. Owen. "You agree?"

Maura nodded. "Based on the relatively minor

amount of damage by scavengers, I'd favor the lower end of that postmortem interval. The attacks are confined to the head and neck and . . ." Maura paused, glancing at the bony stump poking from the jacket sleeve. ". . . the hand. The wrist must have been exposed. That's how they got at it." She wondered if Bear had sampled a taste before bringing his putrid prize to Claire. *A friendly lick won't be so welcome after this.*

Dr. Owen patted the victim's jacket and cargo pants. "There's something here," she said, and withdrew a thin billfold from the cargo pocket. "And we have ID. Virginia driver's license. Russell Remsen, six foot one, a hundred ninety pounds. Brown hair, blue eyes, thirty-seven years old." She eyed the cadaver. "Could be. Let's hope he has dental X-rays on file."

Maura stared at the victim's face, half of it gnawed away, the other half swollen and streaked with purge fluid. A postmortem bulla had ballooned the intact eyelid into a bulging sac. On the right side, scavengers had stripped the neck of skin and muscle; the damage extended all the way down to the neckline of his clothing, where sharp teeth had already punctured and frayed the fabric, trying to tear into the thoracic outlet. Evisceration would have been next, heart and lungs, liver and spleen dragged out and feasted on. Limbs would be ripped from joints, portable prizes to be carried off to dens and pups. The forest would do its part as well, vines twisting around ribs, insects delving, devouring. In a year, she thought, Russell Remsen would be little more than bone fragments, scattered among the trees.

"This guy wasn't carrying your usual hunting rifle," the state police detective said, examining the weapon perched on the boulder. With gloved hands, he brought it over to show Dr. Owen, turning it to reveal the manufacturer's stamp on the lower receiver.

"What kind of rifle is that?" asked Maura.

"An M one ten. Knight's Armament, semiautomatic with a bipod." He looked at her, clearly impressed. "This one's got excellent optics, twenty-round box magazine. Fires a three oh eight or a seven six two, NATO. Effective range of eight hundred meters."

"Holy cow," said Dr. Owen. "You could shoot a deer in the next county."

"Wasn't designed for hunting deer. It's military issue. A very nice and very expensive sniper rifle."

Maura frowned at the dead man. At the camouflage pants. "What was he doing up here with a sniper rifle?"

"Well, a deer hunter *might* use one of these. It's a pretty handy weapon if you want to drop a deer at long range. But it's kind of like using a Rolls-Royce to make a run to the grocery store." He shook his head. "I guess this is what you'd call irony. Here he was, equipped with top-of-the-line gear, and he's taken down by something as primitive as an arrow." He glanced at Dr. Owen. "I take it that's going to be the cause of death?"

"I know cause of death seems obvious, Ken, but let's wait until the autopsy."

"I knew you'd say that."

Dr. Owen turned to Maura. "You're welcome to join me in the morgue tomorrow."

Maura thought of slicing into that belly, ripe with decay and foul gases. "I think I'll pass on this autopsy," she said and stood up. "I'm supposed to be on a holiday from Death. But He keeps finding me."

Dr. Owen rose to her feet as well, and her thoughtful gaze made Maura uncomfortable. "What's going on here, Dr. Isles?"

"I wish I knew."

"First a suicide. Now this. And I can't even tell you what *this* is. Accident? Homicide?"

Maura focused on the arrow protruding from the dead man's eye. "This would take an expert marksman."

"Not really," said the state detective. "The bull's-eye on an archery target is smaller than an eye socket. A decent archer could hit that from a hundred, two hundred feet, especially with a crossbow." He paused. "Assuming he *meant* to hit this target."

"You're saying this might have been an accident," said Dr. Owen.

"I'm just throwing out scenarios here," said the cop. "Say two buddies come hunting on this land without permission. The guy with the bow spots a deer, gets excited, and lets an arrow fly. Oops, down goes his buddy. Guy with the bow freaks out and runs. Doesn't tell anyone, 'cause he knows they were trespassing. Or he's on probation. Or he just doesn't want the trouble." He shrugged. "I could see it happening."

"Let's hope that *is* the story," said Maura. "Because I don't like the alternative."

"That there's a homicidal archer running around these woods?" said Dr. Owen. "That is not a comforting thought, so close to a school."

"And here's another disturbing thought. If this man wasn't hunting for deer, what was he doing up here with a sniper rifle?"

No one responded, but the answer seemed obvious when Maura gazed down at the valley below. If I were a sniper, she thought, this is where I would wait. Where I'd be camouflaged by this underbrush, with a clear view of the castle, the courtyard, the road.

But who was the target?

That question dogged her as she scrambled down the trail an hour later, across bare boulders, through sun and shade and sun again. She thought of a marksman poised on the hill above her. Imagined a target hatch mark trained on her back. A rifle with an eight-hundred-meter range. Half a mile. She would never realize anyone was watching her, aiming at her. Until she felt the bullet.

At last she stumbled out of a tangle of vines onto

the school's back lawn. As she stood brushing twigs and leaves from her clothes, she heard men's voices, raised in argument. They came from the forester's cottage at the edge of the woods. She approached the cottage, and through the open doorway she saw one of the detectives she'd met earlier up on the ridge. He was standing inside with Sansone and Mr. Roman. None of them acknowledged her as she stepped inside, where she saw an array of out-doorsmen's tools. Axes and rope and snowshoes. And hanging on one wall were at least a dozen bows, as well as quivers filled with arrows.

"There's nothing special about these arrows," Roman said. "You can find 'em in any sporting goods store."

"Who has access to all this equipment, Mr. Roman?"

"All the students do. It's a school, or haven't you noticed?"

"He's been our archery instructor for decades," said Sansone. "It's a skill that teaches them discipline and focus. Valuable skills relevant to all their subjects."

"And all the students take archery?"

"All those who choose to," Roman said.

"If you've been teaching for decades, you must be pretty good with a bow," the detective said to Roman.

The forester grunted. "Fair enough."

"Meaning?"

"I hunt."

"Deer? Squirrels?"

"Not enough meat on a squirrel to make 'em worth the trouble."

"The point is, you could hit one?"

"I can also hit your eye at a hundred yards. That's what you want to know, isn't it? Whether I took down that fella up on the ridge."

"You had a chance to examine the body, did you?"

"Dog took us straight to him. Didn't have to examine the body. Clear as day what killed him."

"That can't be an easy shot to make, an arrow through the eye. Anyone else at this school able to do it?"

"Depends on the distance, doesn't it?"

"A hundred yards."

Roman snorted. "No one here but me."

"None of the students?"

"No one's put in enough time. Or had the training."

"How did you get your training?"

"Taught myself."

"And you hunt with only a bow? Never a rifle?"

"Don't like rifles."

"Why not? Seems like a rifle would be a lot easier when you're hunting deer."

Sansone cut in: "I think Mr. Roman's told you what you wanted to know."

"It's a simple question. Why won't he use a rifle?" The detective stared at Roman, waiting for a response.

"You don't need to answer any more questions, Roman," said Sansone. "Not without a lawyer."

Roman sighed. "No, I'll answer it. Seems to me he already knows about me, anyway." He met the cop's gaze head-on. "Twenty-five years ago, I killed a man."

In the silence that followed, Maura's sharp intake of breath made the cop finally look at her. "Dr. Isles, would you mind stepping outside? I'd like to continue this interview in private."

"Let her stay, I don't care," said Roman. "Better to have it all out right now, so there's no secrets. Never wanted to keep it a secret anyway." He looked at Sansone. "Even though you thought it best."

"You know about this, Mr. Sansone?" the cop asked. "And you employ him here anyway?"

"Let Roman tell you the circumstances," said Sansone. "He deserves to be heard, in his own words."

"Okay. Let's hear it, Mr. Roman."

The forester crossed to the window and pointed at the hills. "I grew up there, just a few miles past that ridge. My grandfather was the caretaker here, looked after the castle since way back, before it became a school. No one was living here then, just an empty building, waiting for a buyer. Naturally, there were trespassers. Some of 'em just came in to hunt and leave. They'd bag their deer and go. But some of 'em, they came to make trouble. Smash windows, set the porch on fire. Or worse. You run

RIZZOLI & ISLES: LAST TO DIE 345

into 'em, you didn't know which kind you were dealing with . . ."

He took a breath. "I ran into him over there, coming out of the woods. There was no moon that night. He just suddenly appeared. Big fella, carrying a rifle. We saw each other and he raised his gun. I don't know what he was thinking. I'll never know. All I can tell you is, I reacted on pure instinct. Shot him in the chest."

"With a gun."

"Yes, sir. Shotgun. Took him right down. He was probably dead within five breaths." Roman sat down, looking a decade older, his hands resting on his knees. "I'd just turned eighteen. But I guess you knew that."

"I called in a background check."

Roman nodded. "No secret around these parts. Thing is, he was no saint, even if he was a doctor's kid. But I killed him, so I went to jail. Four years, manslaughter." Roman looked down at his hands, scarred from years of outdoor labors. "I never picked up a shotgun again. That's how I got so good with a bow."

"Gottfried Baum hired him straight out of prison," said Sansone. "There's no better man."

"He still has to come into town to sign a statement." The cop turned to the forester. "Let's go, Mr. Roman."

"Headmaster Baum will make some calls, Roman," said Sansone. "He'll meet you in town. Don't say a word, not until he gets there with an attorney."

Roman followed the cop to the door and suddenly stopped to look at Sansone. "I don't think I'll be making it back here tonight. So I want to warn you that you've got a big problem here, Mr. Sansone. I know I didn't kill that man. Which means you better find out who did."

# TWENTY-EIGHT

SUMMER FOG CLOAKED THE HIGHWAY TO PROVIdence, and Jane craned forward, peering from behind the wheel at cars and trucks that glided ahead of them like ghosts in the mist. Today she and Frost were chasing yet another ghost, she thought, as the wiper swept the gray film from her windshield. The ghost of Nicholas Clock, Teddy's father. Born in Virginia, graduate of West Point with a degree in economics, avid outdoorsman and sailor. Married with three children. Worked as a financial consultant at Jarvis and McCrane, a job that required frequent travel abroad. No arrests, no traffic tickets, no outstanding debts.

At least that was what Nicholas Clock looked like on paper. Solid citizen. Family man.

The mist swirled on the road ahead of them. There was nothing solid, nothing real. Nicholas Clock, like Olivia Yablonski, was a ghost, flitting quietly from country to country. And what did that mean, exactly, *financial consultant*? It was one of those vague job descriptions that conjured up businessmen in suits carrying briefcases, speaking the language of dollar signs. Ask a man what he does, and those two words, *financial consultant,* could make your eyes glaze over.

The same way *medical supply sales rep* could.

Beside her in the passenger seat, Frost answered his ringing cell phone. Jane glanced at him when he said, a moment later: "You're kidding me. How the hell did *that* happen?"

"What?" she said.

He waved her off, kept his focus on the phone call. "So you never finished the analysis? There's nothing else you can tell us?"

"Who is that?" she asked.

At last he hung up and turned to her, a stunned expression on his face. "You know that GPS tracker we pulled off the rental car? It's vanished."

"That was the lab calling?"

"They said it disappeared from the lab sometime last night. They got only a preliminary look at it. There was no manufacturer's stamp, totally untraceable. State-of-the-art equipment."

"Jesus. Obviously *too* state-of-the-art to stay in Boston PD's hands."

Frost shook his head. "Now I'm getting *seriously* freaked out."

She stared at the spectral swirls of mist on the highway. "I'll tell you who else is freaked out," she said, her hands tightening on the steering wheel. "Gabriel. Last night he was ready to tie me up and throw me in the closet." She paused. "I sent Regina to stay with my mom this week. Just to be safe."

"Can I hide with your mom, too?"

She laughed. "That's what I like about you. You're not afraid to admit you're afraid."

"So you're not scared? Is that what you're saying?"

She drove for a moment without answering, the wipers sweeping back and forth as she peered at a highway as misty as the future. She thought about planes falling from the sky, bullets shattering skulls, and sharks feeding on bodies. "Even if we are freaked out," she said, "what choice do we have? When you're already in neck-deep, the way out is to forge ahead and get to the end of this."

By the time they reached the outskirts of Providence, the mist had thickened to drizzle. The address for Jarvis and McCrane was in the southeast corner of town, near the industrial waterfront, a bleak neighborhood of abandoned buildings and deserted streets. When they arrived at the address, Jane was already prepared for what they would find.

The two-story brick warehouse was flanked by vacant parking lots. She eyed faded swoops of graffiti and boarded-over first-floor windows and knew that this building had been vacant for months, if not years.

Frost surveyed the broken glass on the sidewalk. "Nicholas Clock financed a seventy-five-foot yacht working *here*?"

"Obviously this was not his primary place of business." She pushed open her door. "Let's take a look, anyway."

They stepped out of the car, into a drizzle that made Jane zip her jacket and turn up her collar. The clouds hung so low, it seemed as if the sky itself was pressing down, trapping them in gloom. They crossed the street, broken glass crunching beneath their shoes, and found the entrance locked.

Frost backed up and surveyed the upper windows, most of them shattered. "I don't see any sign for Jarvis and McCrane."

"I checked the tax records. They are the listed owners for this property."

"Does this look like a real business to you?"

"Let's go around back."

They rounded the corner, past broken crates and an overflowing Dumpster. At the rear of the building, she found an empty parking lot where weeds were forcing their way up through cracks in the pavement.

The rear door latch had been pried open.

She nudged the door with her shoe and it creaked ajar, revealing a cavernous darkness within. She paused at the threshold, feeling the first prickles of alarm.

"Ho-kay," Frost whispered, his voice so close it startled her. "So now we have to search the scary building."

"This is why I brought you along. So you wouldn't miss all the fun."

They glanced at each other and simultaneously drew their weapons. This was not their jurisdiction, not their own state, but neither one dared to venture unarmed into that gloom. She clicked on her flashlight and swept the darkness. Saw a concrete floor, a crumpled newspaper. Felt her heart kick into a faster tempo as she stepped across the threshold.

It felt even chillier inside, as if these brick walls had trapped years of dankness where anything could be incubating. Waiting. She heard Frost close behind her as they moved deeper into the building, their flashlight beams skittering past pillars and broken crates. Frost accidentally kicked a beer can, and the rattle of aluminum over concrete was as startling as gunfire. They both froze as the echoes faded to silence.

"Sorry," whispered Frost.

Jane heaved out a breath. "Well, now the cockroaches all know we're here. But it doesn't look like there's anyone else . . ." She stopped and her head snapped up toward the ceiling.

Above them, the floorboards groaned.

Suddenly her heart was thumping faster as she listened for more movement above. Frost was right behind her as she made her way toward a metal staircase. At the bottom of the steps she paused, peering up at the second floor, where gray light seeped through a window. That sound they'd heard could mean nothing. Just the building settling. Wooden floorboards contracting.

She started up the metal staircase, and each step sent off a faint clang that made the darkness hum and announced: *Here we come*. Near the top of the steps she crouched, palms sweating, and slowly lifted her head to peer over the second-floor landing.

Something hurtled toward her from the shadows. She flinched as it whistled past her cheek. Heard glass shatter on the wall behind her as she saw a crab-like figure retreat into the gloom.

"I see him, I see him!" she yelled to Frost as she scrambled up onto the landing. "Police!" she called out, her gaze fixed on the dark shape hulking in the corner. He was folded into himself, his black face obscured in shadow. "Show me your hands," she ordered.

"I got here first," a voice growled. "Go away." The figure raised an arm, and Jane saw another bottle in his hand.

"Drop it *now*!" she commanded.

"They said I could stay here! They gave me permission!"

"Put down the bottle. We just want to talk!"

"About what?"

"This place. This building."

"It's mine. They gave it to me."

"Who did?"

"The men in the black car. Said they didn't need it anymore, and I could stay here."

"Okay." Jane lowered her weapon. "Why don't we start over? First, what's your name, sir?"

"Denzel."

"Last name?"

"Washington."

"Denzel Washington. Really." She sighed. "I guess that's as good a name as any. So Denzel, how about we both put away our weapons and relax." She slid the gun into her holster and held up both hands. "Fair?"

"What about him?" Denzel said, pointing to Frost.

"Soon as you put down the bottle, sir," Frost said.

After a moment, Denzel set the bottle down between his feet with an emphatic thud. "Only take me an instant to throw it," he said. "So you better behave."

"How long have you been living here?" said Jane.

Denzel struck a match and leaned over to light a candle. By the glowing flame, she saw a trash-strewn floor, the splintered remains of a broken chair. He planted himself beside the candle, a disheveled African American man in ragtag clothes. "Few months," he said.

"How many?"

"Seven, eight. I guess."

"Anyone else ever come by to check out the place?"

"Just the rats."

"You live all alone here?"

"Why do you want to know?"

"Denzel," Jane said, and felt ridiculous just saying that name, "we're trying to find out who really owns this building."

"I told you. Me."

"Not Jarvis and McCrane?"

"Who's that?"

"What about Nicholas Clock? You ever heard that name? Ever met the man?"

Denzel suddenly turned and barked at Frost: "What are you doing over there? You trying to steal my stuff?"

"There's nothing here to steal, man," said Frost. "I'm just looking around. See a lot of iron shavings here on the floor. This must have been some old toolmaking factory . . ."

"Look, Denzel, we're not here to hassle you," said Jane. "We just want to know about the business that was here two, three years ago."

"Wasn't nothing here."

"You knew the building back then?"

"This is my neighborhood. I got eyes."

"You know a man named Nicholas Clock? Six foot two, blond hair, well built? About forty-five and good looking."

"Why you asking *me* about good-looking guys?"

"I'm just asking if you've seen Nicholas Clock around. This address was listed as his place of business."

Denzel snorted. "Must have been *real* successful." His head swiveled toward Frost and he snapped:

"You really don't pay attention, do you? I told you to stop looking around my place."

"What the fuck," Frost said, staring out the broken window. "Someone's in our car!"

"What?" Jane crossed to the window and looked down at her Subaru, saw the passenger door was ajar. She reached for her weapon and snapped, "Let's go!"

"No, you won't," Denzel said as a gun barrel suddenly pressed against the back of Jane's head. "You are going to drop your weapons. Both of you." His voice, no longer a careless drawl, was now cold and crisp.

Jane let her Glock fall to the floor.

"You, too, Detective Frost," the man ordered.

*He knows our names.*

The second gun thudded to the floor. Denzel grabbed Jane's jacket and shoved her down to her knees. The gun was still pressed to her skull, shoved so hard against her scalp that it felt like a drill bit about to punch a hole through bone. Who would find their bodies in this blighted building? It could be days, even weeks before anyone noticed her abandoned car. Before anyone thought to trace its owner.

Frost thumped down to his knees beside her. She heard the beeps of a cell phone being dialed, then Denzel said: "We've got a problem. You want me to finish it?"

She glanced sideways at Frost and saw terror in his eyes. If they were going to fight back, this was their last chance. Two of them against an armed man. One of them would almost certainly take a bullet, but the other might make it. *Do it now, while he's on the phone and distracted.* Muscles tensing, she took a breath, maybe her last. *Twist, grab, deflect . . .*

Footsteps clanged on the stairway and the gun barrel suddenly lifted from her scalp as Denzel stepped away, beyond her reach. Beyond any hope of wrestling the weapon from him.

The footsteps ascended to the top of the stairs and moved toward them, heels clipping sharply against the wooden floor.

"Well, this *is* a problem," said a shockingly familiar voice. A woman's voice. "You can both get up, Detectives. I guess it's time to drop all pretenses."

Jane rose to her feet and turned to face Carole Mickey. But this was not the lacquered blonde who'd claimed to be Olivia Yablonski's colleague at Leidecker Hospital Supplies. This woman wore sleek blue jeans and black boots, and instead of a matronly blond helmet shellacked with hairspray, her blond hair was gathered in a tight ponytail that emphasized a model's jutting cheekbones. Once, she would have been a stunning beauty, but middle age was now etched in that face, in the creases fanning out from her eyes.

"I take it there's no such company as Leidecker Hospital Supplies," said Jane.

"Of course there is," said Carole. "You saw our

catalog. We carry the latest in wheelchairs and shower seats."

"Sold by sales reps who never seem to be in the office. Do they actually exist, or are they all like Olivia Yablonski, running operations around the world for the CIA?"

Carole and Denzel glanced at each other.

"That's a very big leap of logic, Detective," Carole finally said, but that two-beat pause told Jane she'd hit the target.

"And your name isn't really Carole, is it?" said Jane. "Because I *know* his isn't Denzel."

"Those names will do for now."

Denzel said, "They asked me about Nicholas Clock."

"Naturally. They're not idiots." Carole picked up the fallen weapons and offered them back to Jane and Frost. "That's why I've decided it's time we worked together. Don't you think?"

Jane took back her Glock and considered, just for an instant, turning the gun on Carole and telling her to screw that *working together* crap. These people had drawn a gun on her, had forced her and Frost to kneel with the full expectation of death. That was not something you easily kissed and made up over. But she choked back her temper and shoved the gun in her holster. "How did you just happen to be here?"

"We knew you were headed this way. We've been keeping an eye on you."

"This is like the Leidecker company," said Frost.

"Another fake business, this one used as Nicholas Clock's cover."

"And this is where they'd come looking for him," said Carole.

"But Clock's dead. He died aboard his yacht."

"*They* don't know that. For weeks, we've been leaking rumors that Clock is alive, that his appearance has been altered by plastic surgery."

"Who's looking for him?" asked Jane.

Carole and Denzel exchanged looks. After a moment, she seemed to come to a decision and said to Denzel: "I need you outside to watch the street. Leave us."

With a brisk nod, he left the room, and they heard his footsteps clanging down the stairs. Carole watched from the window and didn't say a word until she spotted her associate outside.

She turned to Jane and Frost. "Boxes within boxes. That's how the Company controls information. He knows what's in his own little box, but nothing outside it. So now I'm going to give you a box, which belongs to just you two. Not to be shared. You understand?"

"And who knows it all?" asked Jane. "Who owns all the boxes?"

"I can't tell you."

"Can't or won't?"

"That's not part of your box."

"So we get no idea of where you stand in this hierarchy."

"I know enough to run this operation. Enough to

know that having you two mucking around in this threatens everything I've worked for."

"The CIA's not authorized to run operations on US soil," pointed out Frost. "This is illegal."

"It's also necessary."

"Why isn't the FBI handling this?"

"This was not their mess. It was ours. We are simply cleaning up what should have been finished years ago."

"In Rome," Jane said, quietly.

Carole didn't answer, but her sudden stillness confirmed what Jane believed. Rome was where it started. Where the lives of Nicholas and Olivia and Erskine had intersected in some catastrophic event that was still casting ripples in the lives of their children.

"How did you know?" Carole finally said.

"Sixteen years ago, they were all there in Rome. Erskine, working as a foreign service officer. Olivia, working as a so-called sales rep." Jane paused, made an educated guess. "And Nicholas, traveling as a consultant for Jarvis and McCrane. A company that exists only on paper."

She saw confirmation in Carole's face. The woman stared out the window and sighed. "They were so cocky. So goddamn sure of themselves. We'd pulled it off before, so what could possibly go wrong?"

*We.* "You were there, too," said Jane. "In Rome."

Carole paced away from the window, her boots clicking across the wood. "It was a straightforward operation. Only Olivia was new to the team. The rest of us had worked together before. We knew Rome well, especially Erskine. That was his home base, and he had all the local assets lined up. People in place. All we had to do was swoop in, snatch our target, and get him out of the country."

"You mean . . . a *kidnapping*?"

"You sound so judgmental."

"About kidnapping? Yeah, I tend to be."

"You wouldn't be, if you knew the subject in question."

"You mean your victim."

"A criminal who's responsible, both directly and indirectly, for the deaths of hundreds of people. We're talking Americans, Detective. Our fellow citizens, killed in multiple countries. Not just military personnel, but also innocents abroad. Tourists, businessmen, families. Some monsters simply need to be exterminated, for the good of society. Surely you both understand that, considering your jobs. It is, after all, what *you* do. Hunt down monsters."

"But we do it within the law," said Frost.

"The law has no teeth."

"The law tells us when we're over the line."

Carole snorted. "Let me guess, Detective Frost. You were a Boy Scout."

Jane glanced at her partner. "Well, *that* was right on the money."

"We do what needs to be done," said Carole. "Everyone knows that extreme measures are sometimes necessary, but no one wants to admit it. No one wants to own it." She moved toward Jane, close enough to be intimidating. "If you want a safer world, you need someone to do your dirty work. That someone would be us. We were there to take a monster out of circulation."

"You're talking about extraordinary rendition," said Frost.

"That makes it sound so clinical. But yes, that's what it's called. Sixteen years ago, our mission was to scoop him up, whisk him to a private airstrip, and fly him to a detention facility in a cooperative country."

"For interrogation? Torture?" said Jane.

"It's a lot less than what he did to his victims. This man wasn't driven by politics or religious convictions. He was in it for the money, and he'd made a fortune at it. Wire him enough cash, and he'd arrange to bomb a nightclub in Bali. Or take down a jumbo jet from Heathrow. His fortune made him untouchable—at least, through normal channels. We knew he'd never face justice in Italy. So we had to deliver justice another way. We had one chance, and only one chance, to snatch him. If we fucked up, if Icarus slipped away, he'd go underground. With his resources, we'd never get another shot at him."

"Icarus?"

"Only a code name. His real name isn't important."

"I'm guessing it didn't go well," said Jane.

Carole went back to the window and peered out

through cracked panes. "Oh, we accomplished the mission. Waited outside his favorite restaurant, where he dined with his wife and children and two bodyguards. When they came out, we were ready for them. One team boxed in the bodyguards' vehicle. The other team pursued the car with Icarus and his family." She turned to look at them. "Have you ever driven a mountain road there?"

"I've never been to Italy," said Jane.

"And I'll never be able to go back. Not after what happened."

"You said you accomplished your mission."

"Yes. In spectacularly bloody fashion. We were in pursuit. Four of us, in two cars, winding up killer curves. We almost had him when the truck came around the bend. Icarus hit the guardrail and skidded. The truck hit him broadside." Carole shook her head. "It was a fucking mess. His wife and the older son crushed on impact. The younger son taking his last breaths."

"And Icarus?" said Frost.

"Oh, he was alive. Not just alive but fighting us. Nicholas and Erskine got him restrained and threw him in one of our vehicles. Six hours later he was on a plane, handcuffed and sedated. He woke up behind bars. You know the first thing he said, when he saw me? *You're dead. All of you.*"

"You did kill his family," pointed out Jane.

"That was unfortunate. Collateral damage. But we accomplished our mission. The truck driver was too shaken up to give the Italian police any useful details about us. Erskine continued in his post at the embassy. Nicholas went back to his cover story as a financial consultant."

"And Olivia went back to selling nonexistent bedpans."

Carole laughed. "At least Olivia went home with a souvenir. She stayed on in Italy for a few weeks. Met a dorky tourist named Neil Yablonski. By candlelight, in a Rome restaurant, I guess even a dork looks good. A year later, she married him."

"And you all went on with your lives."

"That's how it *should* have been."

"What went wrong?"

"Icarus escaped."

In the silence that followed, Jane put it all together. The reason why three families were massacred. "Vengeance," she said.

Carole nodded. "For what we did to him, and to his family. Those thirteen years he spent in prison made him even more of a monster. It gave him time to nurse his hatred, to feed it, grow it, until it consumed him. The escape was an inside job, that's the only way it could have happened. I'm sure he offered a king's ransom to whoever helped him. After he slipped out of sight, we had no idea where he went, or even what he looked like. We never did locate all his secret accounts, so he still controlled a fortune. I'm sure he bought a new face. And new friends in high places."

"You said he spent thirteen years in prison," said Frost.

"Yes."

"So he escaped three years ago." He looked at Jane. "That must be why Nicholas Clock and his family packed up and left on the sailboat."

Carole nodded. "After Icarus escaped, Nicholas got nervous. We all did, but he was the only one worried enough to pull up roots and actually ditch the Company. I didn't think it would be easy for Icarus to track us down. Until the Italian government got involved."

"Why?" said Jane.

"Blame it on politics, on WikiLeaks, whatever. Word got out to the press that the CIA had committed an act of extraordinary rendition on Italian soil. Suddenly the Italians were pissed. Violation of sovereignty. A CIA operation that killed three innocent civilians. Our names were redacted from all the reports, but money opens doors. Especially if it's a lot of money." She went back to the window and looked out, a lean silhouette framed in gray light. "Erskine and his wife were killed first. Shot, in a London alley. Days later Olivia and her husband were dead, too, after their plane went down. I tried to get word to Nicholas, but the message didn't reach him in time. In the span of one week, all three of my colleagues were dead."

"How were you lucky enough to stay alive?" said Jane.

"Lucky?" Carole's laugh was bitter. "That's hardly the word I'd choose to describe my life. More like *doomed*. To keep looking over my shoulder. To always sleep with one eye open. For two years I've been living this way, and even though the Company does what it can to keep me safe, it will never feel like enough. And it won't be enough to keep those three children alive."

"Icarus would go that far? He'd kill children?"

"Who else would be hunting them? He killed Nicholas and Olivia and Erskine, all dead within a week of each other. Now he's hunting their children, exterminating the family lines right down to the last survivor. Don't you see, it's all about making a point. It's a message directed to anyone who dares oppose him in the future. *Cross me, and I will massacre you and everyone you love.*" She paced back toward Jane, and her face seemed etched even more deeply with exhaustion. "He will try again."

The sound of a car passing on the street made Carole turn around to the window. She watched as the vehicle passed. Long after the sound of the engine had faded, she was still standing there, searching for, expecting, the coming attack.

Jane pulled out her cell phone. "I'm going to call the Maine State Police. Ask them to dispatch a team—"

"We can't trust them. We can't trust *anyone.*"

"Those children need protection *now.*"

"What I've told you is classified. You can't share any of these details with law enforcement."

"Or what, you'll have to kill us?" Jane said, and snorted.

Carole moved toward her, no trace of humor in her face. "Make no mistake. If I have to, I will."

"Then why are you telling us all this? If it's so top secret?"

"Because you're already deep in this. Because your interference could screw up everything."

"Screw up what, exactly?"

"My best, maybe my only chance, to nail Icarus. That was my plan, anyway. Place all three children in one location, and he won't be able to resist the target."

Jane and Frost glanced at each other in astonishment. "You *planned* it this way?" she said. "You arranged to put those kids at Evensong?"

"It started as a precaution, not a plan. The Company believed they were safe in their various locations, but I had doubts. I was monitoring them. And when the first attack came, on the girl—"

"*You* were the Good Samaritan. The mystery blonde who magically showed up on the scene. And then vanished."

"I stayed with Claire long enough to make sure she'd be safe. When the police arrived, I slipped out of sight. Arranged to move her straight to Evensong, where we already had one of our people in place."

"Dr. Welliver."

Carole nodded. "Anna retired from the Company years ago, after her husband was killed in Argentina. But we knew we could trust her. We also knew Evensong was remote enough and secure enough to keep the girl safe. Which is why we sent the next child to Evensong, too."

"Will Yablonski."

"It was sheer luck that he wasn't in the house when that bomb went off. I arrived just in time to whisk him away."

"So what went wrong with Teddy Clock? You knew what was coming. You knew he'd be targeted next."

"That attack shouldn't have happened. The house was secure, the system was armed. Something went terribly wrong."

"You think?" Jane retorted.

"I had agents stationed outside the residence, around the clock. But that night, they were ordered to abandon their posts."

"Who ordered them?"

"They claimed I called them off. Not true."

"They lied?"

"Everyone has a price, Detective. You just have to keep bidding higher and higher until you reach it." Carole began to pace a restless circle around the room. "Now I don't know whom to trust, or how far up the chain this goes. All I know is, *he's* behind it and he's not finished. He wants those three children. And he wants me." She stopped, swiveled to look at Jane. "I have to be the one to end this."

"How? If you can't trust your own people."

"That's why I've gone *outside* the Company. I'm

doing this my way, with handpicked people I know I can count on."

"And you're telling us all this because you trust *us*?" Jane glanced at Frost. "That's a change."

"You two, at least, haven't been corrupted by Icarus."

"How do you know?"

Carole laughed. "Two homicide detectives, and one of you a Boy Scout." She looked at Frost. "Oh, I did a background on you. I wasn't joking when I called you one." She looked at Jane. "And you have something of a reputation."

"Do I?" said Jane.

"If I use the word *bitch*, don't take offense. It's what they call women like us. Because we don't compromise, we don't go halfway. We kick that ball all the way to the end zone." She gave a slight bow. "There is honor among bitches."

"Geez, I'm flattered."

"My point," said Carole, "is that it's time we work together. If you want to keep those children alive, then you need me, and I need you."

"Do you have an actual plan in mind, or is this just one of those *in principle* alliances?"

"I wouldn't be alive if I didn't make plans. We're going to make Icarus reveal himself."

"How?"

"It involves the children."

"Okay," said Frost, "I'm not liking what I'm hearing."

"You haven't heard it."

"You mentioned the kids. There's no way we'll agree to put them in any danger."

"They're *already* in danger, don't you get it?" Carole snapped. "I'm the only reason Claire and Will are alive right now. Because I was there to save them."

"And now you want to use them?" Frost looked at Jane. "You know that's what she's planning."

"Give her a chance to talk," said Jane, her gaze fixed on Carole. She knew nothing about this woman, not even her real name, and Jane had not decided if she could trust her. *Honor among bitches* only worked if you knew the other bitch. All Jane knew was what she saw: an athletic blonde in her forties, wearing expensive boots and an even more expensive wristwatch. A woman who had about her the faint air of desperation. If what Carole had told them was true, then she'd been a Company operative since her midtwenties. For the past two years, she'd been continually on the move, under different names, which would have been difficult if she'd had a family tagging along. She's a lone wolf, thought Jane. A survivor, who'd do what was necessary to stay alive.

"I know you're concerned about the children," said Carole. "But if we don't end this, they'll never be safe. As long as they live, they represent failure to Icarus. He needs to show the world that he can't be fucked with. That if you cross him, he will be relentless. Think about what their lives will be like if we don't kill him. Every year, they'll need new identities, new homes. Running, always running. I know what that's like, and it's no life for a kid. Certainly not for teenagers hungry for friends and stability. This is their best chance for a normal life, and they don't even have to know about it."

"How are you going to keep this from them?"

"They're already where they need to be. A defensible location. A monitored access road. A school staffed by teachers who will defend them."

"Wait. Are you telling us that Anthony Sansone knows about this?"

"He knows only that they're in danger and they need protection. I asked Dr. Welliver to share that much with him, but not the specifics."

"So he doesn't know about this operation?"

Carole's gaze slipped away. "Even Dr. Welliver didn't know."

"And now she's dead. How did that happen?"

"I don't know why she killed herself. But I already have an agent on the property, and more are coming. These are the last surviving children of my colleagues, and I *will* keep them safe. I owe it to them."

"Is this really about the kids?" asked Jane. "Or is it all about you?"

The truth was there, in Carole's face, and in the wry arch of her eyebrow, the faint tilt of her head. "Yes, I want my life back. But it won't happen until I take him down."

"If you even recognize him when you see him."

"Any armed intruder will be brought down. We can sort out the bodies later."

"How do you know that Icarus himself will show up?"

"Because I understand him. These children are high-value targets for him. So am I. He wants the satisfaction of personally seeing us die. With all of us in one location, he won't be able to resist the bait." She looked at her watch. "I'm wasting time here. I need to get to Maine."

"What do you expect from us?" asked Jane.

"To stay out of it."

"Teddy Clock is *my* responsibility. And lady, you are *way* out of your jurisdiction."

"The last thing I need is clueless cops shooting at their own shadows." She glanced down as her cell phone rang. Turning away, she answered it with a brusque: "Talk to me."

Though Jane could not see the woman's face, she saw her spine suddenly stiffen, her shoulders snap straight. "We're on our way," she said, and disconnected.

"What happened?" asked Jane.

"I had an agent in place. At the school."

"Had?"

"His body has just been found." Carole looked at Jane. "It seems we've come to the final act."

# TWENTY-NINE

"WE SHOULD EVACUATE," SAID SANSONE AS HE unlocked the safe in the curiosities room. He swung open the safe to reveal a handgun stored inside. Maura watched him swiftly load nine-millimeter bullets into the magazine, and was startled by his obvious familiarity with the weapon. She had never even seen him hold a gun before; clearly he was not only comfortable with the weapon but also prepared to use it. "If we wake up the kids now," he said, "we could be on the road within ten minutes."

"And where would we take them?" said Maura. "Outside those gates, we're vulnerable. You've turned this castle into a fortress, Anthony. You have a security system, unbreachable doors." And a gun, she thought, watching him slide the magazine into place. "Jane told us to batten down and wait till she gets here. That's what we should do."

"As secure as I've made this castle, we're still a stationary target."

"Safer inside than out there. Jane was very clear on the phone. *Stay together. Stay in the building. Trust no one.*"

He tucked the gun in his belt. "Let's make one last perimeter check," he said and left the curiosities room.

Nightfall had brought a new chill to the air, and as she followed him into the entrance hall, the temperature seemed to drop even more. She hugged herself as she watched him check the front door, as he scanned the electronic security panel and confirmed that the system was armed, all zones secure.

"Detective Rizzoli could have told us more on the phone," Sansone said as he moved on to the dining hall where he inspected windows, tested locks. "We don't know what the hell we're fighting."

"She said she wasn't allowed to tell us more. We just have to do exactly what she told us."

"Her judgment isn't infallible."

"Well, I trust her."

"And you don't trust me." It wasn't a question, but a statement, one they both knew was true. He turned to face her, and she felt an unsettling thrill of attraction. But she saw too many shadows in his eyes, too many secrets. And she thought about the startling ease with which he'd handled the gun, yet another detail she had not known about him.

"I don't even know who you are, Anthony," she said.

"Someday," he said with a faint smile, "maybe you'll want to find out."

They left the dining hall and moved on to the library. With most of the students and faculty gone, the castle was eerily silent, and at this late hour it was easy to believe that they were utterly alone. The last inhabitants of an abandoned citadel.

"Do you think you could ever learn to trust me, Maura?" he asked as he walked from window to window, a somber guardian moving through the gloom. "Or will there always be this tension between us?"

"You could start by being more open with me," she said.

"We could both take that advice." He paused. "You and Daniel Brophy. Are you still together?"

At the mention of Daniel's name, she halted in her tracks. "Why do you ask?"

"You must have an answer." He turned to her, the shadows from the overhanging alcove hiding his eyes.

"Love isn't cut and dried, Anthony. It's messy and it's heartbreaking. Sometimes there are no endings."

In the gloom, she could just make out his knowing smile. "Yet another reason you and I are alike. Beyond our personal tragedies, beyond the work we do. We're both lonely," he said softly.

In the silence of that library, the sudden ringing of the telephone was all the more startling. As he crossed the room to pick up the extension, she stood rooted to the spot, unsettled by what he'd just said. And shaken by the truth of it. *Yes, we are lonely. Both of us.*

"Dr. Isles is right here," she heard him say into the phone.

*Jane's calling* was Maura's first thought. But when she took the receiver, it was the Maine medical examiner on the line.

"I just wondered if you ever got my message. Since I didn't hear back from you," said Dr. Emma Owen.

"You called? When?"

"Around dinnertime. I spoke to one of the teachers. Some grumpy-sounding guy."

"That would be Dr. Pasquantonio."

"That's his name. I guess he forgot to tell you. I'm about to climb into bed, and I thought I'd give you another call, since you did ask me to expedite this."

"Is this about the tox screen?"

"Yes. Now, I've got to ask you. Was Dr. Welliver *really* a shrink?"

"She was a clinical psychologist."

"Well, she was doing a little mind bending on her own. The tox screen turned up lysergic acid diethylamide."

Maura turned and stared at Sansone as she said, "That can't be right."

"We still have to confirm it with HPLC-fluorescence, but it looks like your Dr. Welliver was tripping out on LSD. Now, I know some shrinks consider it therapeutic. A way to open your mind to spiritual experiences, yada yada. But she was working in a school, for God's sake. Dropping acid is not exactly role-model behavior."

Maura stood very still, the phone pressed so tightly to her ear she could hear her own pulse. "That fall from the roof . . ."

"Very possibly a result of hallucinations. Or acute psychosis. You remember that CIA experiment years ago, when they gave some poor guy LSD and he jumped out the window? You can't predict how a subject will react on the drug."

Maura thought about the stray crystals on the bathroom floor, scattered when someone had emptied the sugar bowl into the toilet. *Disposing of the evidence.*

". . . I'm going to have to reclassify this death as an accident. Not suicide," said Dr. Owen. "Fall from a height after ingestion of hallucinogens."

"LSD can be synthesized," cut in Maura.

"Um, yeah. I suppose. Wasn't it first isolated from some fungus grown on rye plants?"

*And who knows more about plants than Professor David Pasquantonio?*

"Oh my God," Maura whispered.

"Is there a problem?"

"I have to go." She hung up and turned to Sansone, who stood right beside her, his eyes filled with questions. "We can't stay," she said. "We have to get the children and leave *now.*"

"Why? Maura, what's changed?"

"The killer," she said. "He's already inside the castle."

# THIRTY

"WHERE ARE THE OTHERS?" MAURA ASKED.

Julian squinted at them from his doorway, eyes still dazed with sleep. He stood bare-chested, wearing only boxer shorts, his hair standing up in all directions. A sleepy teenager who clearly wanted only to crawl back into bed. Yawning, he rubbed his chin, where the first dark stubble of a beard had sprouted. "Aren't they in bed?"

"Will and Teddy and Claire aren't in their rooms," said Sansone.

"They were there when I checked on them."

"When was that?"

"I don't know. Ten thirty, maybe." Julian suddenly focused on the gun tucked into Sansone's waistband, and he straightened in alarm. "What's going on?"

"Julian," said Maura. "We need to find them *now*. And we need to be quiet about it."

"Hold on," he said, ducking back into his room. A moment later he reemerged dressed in blue jeans and sneakers. With Bear at his heels, he headed down the hall and stepped into Will and Teddy's room.

"I don't get it," he said, frowning at the empty beds. "The boys were both in here, already in their pajamas."

"They didn't say anything about going out?"

"They *know* they're supposed to stay inside tonight. Especially tonight." Julian spun around and headed across the hall. Maura and Sansone followed him into Claire's room, where they all stood surveying the books spread haphazardly on the desk, the sweatshirt and dirty socks lying in a heap in the corner. Nothing alarming here, just the typical disorder of a teenager's room. "It doesn't make sense that they'd leave," said Julian. "They're not stupid."

Suddenly Maura was aware of how deep the silence was. As deep as the earth, as deep as the grave. If any other souls were in the castle, she could not hear them. She dreaded the thought of searching every room, every alcove and stairway, in a fortress that had already been breached by a killer.

The dog's whine startled her. She looked down at Bear, who returned the look with an eerie gleam of intelligence in his eyes. "He can help us search," she said. "He just needs their scent."

"He's not a bloodhound," Julian pointed out.

"But he is a dog, with a dog's sense of smell. He can track them, if we make him understand what we're searching for." She glanced at the mound of

Claire's discarded clothes. "Give him a whiff of those," she said. "Let's see where he takes us."

Julian pulled a leash from his pocket, clipped it to Bear's collar, and led him to the pile of dirty laundry. "Here, boy," he urged. "Take a good sniff. That's what Claire smells like. You know Claire, don't you?" He cupped the dog's enormous head in his hands and stared straight into Bear's eyes. The connection between them was something deep, even sacred. It had been forged in the Wyoming mountains, where boy and dog had learned to rely on each other, where survival had meant complete trust between them. Maura watched in wonderment as understanding seemed to light the dog's eyes. Bear turned toward the door and barked.

"Come on," said Julian. "Let's go find Claire."

Bear tugged on the leash, leading the boy out of the room. But instead of heading toward the main stairway, the dog moved down the corridor, toward the deserted wing of the building where the shadows were deeper, where doors gaped open, revealing empty rooms with sheet-draped furniture. They passed an oil portrait of a woman in red, a woman with eyes that seemed to stare at Maura with strangely metallic brightness, as though lit from within by some secret knowledge.

"He's headed toward the old servants' staircase," said Sansone.

Bear halted and stared down the steps, as if pondering the wisdom of descending into that gloom. He glanced back at Julian, who nodded. Bear started down the narrow stairs, claws clicking on wood. Unlike the banister in the grand staircase, this oak railing was unadorned with elaborate carvings, the wood rubbed smooth over the decades by the hands of multiple servants who had quietly kept the castle tidy and its guests fed. A chill seemed to cling to the air, as if the ghosts of those long-dead servants still lingered in this passage, forever flitting up and down with brooms and breakfast trays. Maura could almost feel one of those ghosts whisper past her like a cold breeze, and she glanced over her shoulder but saw only deserted stairs ascending into the gloom.

They moved down two flights and still they kept descending, toward the basement level. Maura had never been down this far, into the deepest part of Evensong. These steps seemed to lead into the heart of the mountain itself, into closed spaces. She could smell it in the air, could feel it in the dampness.

They arrived at the bottom of the steps and walked into the cavernous kitchen, where Maura saw massive stainless-steel stoves, a walk-in refrigerator, and ceiling racks where pots and pans hung. So this was where their morning eggs were fried and their bread was baked. At this hour the kitchen was deserted, the crockery and utensils stowed until morning.

Bear suddenly froze, staring at a cellar door. The ruff of his neck stood up and he growled, a sound that sent fear screaming up Maura's spine. Something was behind that door, something that alarmed the dog, made him drop to a crouch, as though preparing for attack.

Metal clanged, loud as a cymbal crash.

Maura jumped, heart slamming, as the echoes faded in the kitchen. She felt Sansone holding her arm, but she didn't remember when he'd grasped it. It was simply there, as if he had always been there to steady her.

"I think I see him," Sansone said quietly. Calmly. He released Maura's arm and started across the kitchen.

"Anthony—"

"It's okay. It's okay." He rounded the kitchen island and knelt down, dropping from view. Though she couldn't see him, she heard his voice, murmuring gently. "Hey, you're safe. We're here, son."

She and Julian glanced uneasily at each other, then followed Sansone around the corner of the island. There they found him crouched over a trembling Teddy Clock. The boy was curled into a tight ball, knees shoved up to his chest, arms hugging himself.

"He seems to be fine," said Sansone, glancing up at her.

"He's not fine," she said. Dropping down beside Teddy, she pulled him into her arms and rocked him to her chest. He was chilled, his skin like ice, and shaking so hard that she could hear his teeth rattle. "There, there," she murmured. "I've got you, Teddy."

"He was here," the boy whispered.

"Who?"

"I'm sorry, I'm so sorry," he moaned. "I shouldn't have left them there, but I was scared. So I ran . . ."

"Where are the others, Teddy?" said Julian. "Where are Claire and Will?"

The boy pressed his face against Maura's shoulder, as though trying to burrow his way into some safe place where no one could find him.

"Teddy, you have to talk to us," said Maura, and she peeled him away from her. "Where are the others?"

"He put them all in the room . . ." The boy's fingers were like claws digging desperately into her arms.

She pried away his fingers, forced him to look at her. "Teddy, where are they?"

"I don't want to go back to that room!"

"You have to show us. We'll stay right beside you. Just point us to the place, that's all you have to do."

The boy took a shaky breath. "Can I—can I hold the dog? I want the dog to stay with me."

"Sure, kid," Julian said. Kneeling down, he handed Teddy the leash. "You hold on to him and he'll protect you. Bear's not afraid of anything."

That seemed to give Teddy the dose of courage he needed. He rose unsteadily to his feet, clutching the dog's leash as if it were a lifeline, and moved across the kitchen to the door. Taking a deep breath, he opened the latch. The door swung open.

"That's the old wine cellar," said Sansone.

"It's down there," Teddy whispered, staring into the gloom. "I don't want to go."

"It's okay, Teddy. You can wait right here," said Sansone. He glanced at Maura, then led the way down the stairs.

With every step they descended, the air felt thicker, danker. Bare lightbulbs hung overhead, casting a yellowish glow on rows and rows of empty wine racks that once must have held thousands of bottles, no doubt only the best French vintages for a railroad tycoon and his guests. The wine had long since been consumed, and the racks stood abandoned, a silent memorial to a golden age of extravagance.

They came to a heavy door, its hinges bolted solidly into stone. An old storeroom. Maura glanced at Julian. "Why don't you go up to the kitchen and wait with Teddy?"

"Bear's with him. He'll be fine."

"I don't want you to see this. Please."

But Julian remained stubbornly by her side as Sansone lifted the latch. In the kitchen above, Bear began to howl, a high, desperate sound that sent dread screaming up her spine as Sansone swung open the door. That's when Maura caught the scent from inside that dark room. The smell of sweat. The reek of terror. What she feared most lay before her in the gloom. Four bodies, propped up against the wall.

*The children. Dear God, it's the children.*

Sansone found the light switch and flipped it on.

One of the bodies lifted its head. Claire stared at them wide-eyed and gave a frantic whimper, muffled by duct tape. The others stirred, Will and the cook and Dr. Pasquantonio, all of them bound with duct tape and struggling to speak.

*They're alive. They're all alive!*

Maura dropped down beside the girl. "Julian, do you have your knife?"

The dog's howls were wilder, more frantic, as if pleading with them to *hurry, hurry!*

With an efficient click, Julian swung open his pocketknife and knelt down. "Sit still, Claire, or I can't cut you free," he ordered, but the girl was squirming, her eyes wide with panic as if fighting to breathe. Maura peeled the tape off her mouth.

"It's a trap!" Claire screamed. "He hasn't left! He's right . . ." Her voice died, her gaze fixed on something—someone—standing behind Maura.

Blood roaring in her ears, Maura turned and saw a man towering in the doorway. Saw broad shoulders and glittering eyes in a face smeared black with paint, but it was the gun in his hand she focused on. The silencer. When he fired, there would be no deafening blast; death would come with a muted thud, heard only in this stone room buried deep within the mountain.

"Drop your weapon, Mr. Sansone," he ordered. "Do it *now*."

*He knows our names.*

Sansone had no choice; he eased the gun out of his waistband and let it thud to the floor.

Julian, already kneeling beside Maura, reached out and grabbed her hand. Only sixteen, so very young, she thought, as they held hands, squeezing hard.

Bear howled again, a cry of rage. Of frustration.

Julian suddenly looked up, and she saw his bewildered expression. Realized, just as he did, that this did not make sense. *If Bear's still alive, why isn't he defending us?*

"Kick it toward me," the man said.

Sansone nudged the gun with his shoe, and it slid across the floor. Stopped just short of the doorway where the man stood.

"Now down on your knees."

So this is how it ends for us, thought Maura. All of us on our knees. A bullet to each head.

*"Do it!"*

Sansone's head dipped in surrender as he dropped toward the floor. But it was only the windup to one last, desperate move. Like a sprinter exploding from the starting block, Sansone leaped straight at the gunman.

They both tumbled through the doorway, grappling desperately in the gloom of the wine cellar.

Sansone's gun was still lying on the floor.

Maura scrambled to her feet, but before she could scoop up the weapon, another hand closed around the grip. Lifted the barrel to her head.

"Get back! *Get back!*" Teddy screamed at Maura. His hands were trembling, but his finger was already on the trigger as he aimed at Maura's head. He yelled over his shoulder: "I'll shoot her, Mr. Sansone. I swear I will!"

Maura dropped to the floor again. Knelt there, stunned, as Sansone was shoved back into the room and forced to his knees beside her.

"Is the dog secured, Teddy?" the gunman asked.

"I tied him to the kitchen cabinet. He can't get loose."

"Bind their hands. Do it quick," the man said. "They'll be getting here any minute, and we need to be ready."

"Traitor!" Claire spat out as Teddy unpeeled strips of duct tape and bound Sansone's wrists behind his back. "We were your *friends*. How can you do this to us?"

The boy ignored her as he moved on to Julian's hands.

"Teddy tricked us into coming down here," Claire said to Maura. "Told us you were waiting for us, but it was all a trap." She stared at the boy, her voice thick with disgust. Doomed as she was, the girl was fearless, even reckless. "It was you. It was *always* you. Hanging those *stupid* twig dolls."

Teddy peeled off another strip of tape and wound it tightly around Julian's wrists. "Why would I do that?"

"To scare us. To freak us out."

Teddy looked at her with frank surprise. "I didn't do that, Claire. Those dolls were meant to scare *me*. To make *me* call for help."

"And Dr. Welliver, how could you do that to her?"

A flash of regret registered in Teddy's eyes. "It wasn't supposed to kill her! It was just supposed to confuse her. She was working for *them*. Always watching me, waiting to see when I'd—"

"Teddy," the man snapped. "Remember what I taught you? What's done is done, and we have to move on. So finish the job."

"Yes, sir," the boy answered, cutting off another strip of tape. He wrapped it so tightly around Maura's wrists that no amount of twisting or struggling would free her.

"Good boy." The man handed Teddy a pair of night-vision binoculars. "Now get up there and watch the courtyard. Tell me when they arrive, and how many there are."

"I want to stay with you."

"I need you out of the line of fire, Teddy."

"But I want to help!"

"You've helped me enough." The man laid his hand on the boy's head. "Your job is on the roof. You're my eyes." He glanced down at his belt as an alarm beeped. "She's reached the gate. Headset on, Teddy. *Go.*" He pushed the boy out of the room and followed him out.

"I was your *friend*!" Claire screamed as the door swung shut. "I trusted you, Teddy!"

They heard the padlock thud into place. Up in the kitchen Bear was still barking, still howling, but the door muffled the sound, made it seem as distant as a coyote's cry.

Maura stared at the closed door. "It was *Teddy*," she murmured. "All this time, I never imagined . . ."

"Because he's just a kid" was Claire's bitter observation. "No one pays attention to us. No one gives us credit. Until we surprise you." She looked up toward the ceiling. "They're going to kill Detective Rizzoli."

"She's not coming alone," said Maura. "She told me she's bringing people. People who know how to defend themselves."

"But they don't know the castle like this man does. Teddy's been letting him in after dark. He knows every room, every stairway. And he's ready for them."

In the kitchen, Bear had stopped howling. Even he must have grasped the futility of their situation.

*Jane. It's all up to you.*

# THIRTY-ONE

**T**HE CASTLE LOOKED ABANDONED.

Jane and Frost pulled into the Evensong parking lot and stared up at dark windows, at the jagged rooftop looming against the starlit sky. There'd been no one to meet them at the gate, and no one had answered the phone when she'd called from the road half an hour ago, using the last weak blip of a cell signal. A black SUV pulled up beside them, and through the windows Jane saw the silhouettes of Carole and her two male associates. One was Denzel, the other was a buff and silent man with a shaved head. When they'd all stopped for gas an hour earlier, neither man had said a word; it was clear that Carole was running this show.

"Something's wrong," Jane said. "We would've tripped the sensors on the road, so Maura's got to know we've arrived. Where is everyone?"

Frost glanced at Carole's SUV. "I'd feel a lot

better if we had Maine State Police backup. We should've called them anyway. Screw the CIA."

Car doors thumped shut, and Carole and her men stepped out. To Jane's alarm, they were all strapping on weapons. Already Denzel was moving toward the building.

Jane scrambled out of her car. "What do you people think you're doing?"

"Time for you to get us inside the building, Detective," said Carole as she slipped on a communications headset. "Now go to the front door and speak into the intercom. Let them hear your voice, so they'll know it's okay to let us in."

"We came just to collect the kids and get them to a safe place. That's what we agreed on. Why do you have all this Rambo gear?"

"Change of plans."

"Since when?"

"Since I decided we need to search the building first. Once we're in the front door, you wait in your vehicle until we give you the all-clear."

"You said this was *just* an evacuation. That's the only reason we agreed to help you get inside. Now it looks like you're launching an assault."

"A necessary precaution."

"Fuck that. *Children* are in there. I'm not going to let you shoot up the place."

"The front door, Detective. *Now.*"

"It's not locked," said Denzel, returning from the building. "We don't need them."

Carole turned to him. "What?"

"I just checked it. We can walk right in."

"Now I *know* something's wrong," said Jane. She turned toward the building.

Carole instantly blocked her way. "Get back in your vehicle, Detective."

"My friend is in there. I'm going in."

"I don't think so." Carole raised her gun. "Take their weapons."

"*Whoa!*" said Frost as Denzel forced him and Jane to their knees. "Can we all bring this down a notch?"

"You know what to do with them," Carole snapped to Denzel. "If I need you inside, I'll be on com."

Jane looked up as Carole and the man with the shaved head strode off toward the building. "Lady, you are *so* fucked!" she yelled.

"Like she cares," Denzel laughed. He planted his foot against the small of her back and gave her a push. Jane landed facedown onto the cobblestones. He yanked her hands behind her back, and she felt plastic zip-cuffs suddenly bite into her wrists.

"Asshole," she spat out.

"Awww. Say more sweet things to me." He moved on to Frost, securing his wrists with startling efficiency.

"Is this how you guys always operate?" she said.

"It's how *she* operates. The Ice Queen."

"And you don't have a problem with that?"

"Gets the job done. Everybody's happy." He straightened and paced a few steps away as he said into his com unit, "All secure out here. Yes, I copy. Just tell me when."

Jane rolled onto her side to look at the building, but Carole and the other man had already vanished inside. Now they were roaming those dark halls, adrenaline pumping, instincts primed to fire at any shadow. This mission wasn't about saving lives; the children were merely pawns in a war waged by a woman with one objective in mind. A woman with ice in her veins.

Denzel's footsteps moved back toward her, and she looked up to see him standing just above. Silhouetted by the starry sky, his weapon appeared to be an extension of his hand, a black wand of death. She thought of what Carole had said to him, *You know what to do,* and those words suddenly held a new and frightening meaning. Then Denzel took another step, away from her. He wasn't looking at her at all. His head swiveled left, then right, searching the darkness, and she heard him whisper: "What the hell?"

Something whistled in the wind, like a knife slitting through silk.

Denzel toppled across her chest, landing so hard that the air rushed from her lungs. Crushed by his weight, she struggled to take a breath. Felt his body twitching in its death throes as something warm and wet soaked through her blouse. She heard Frost yelling her name, but she could not move under that deadweight, could do nothing but stare as footsteps approached. Slow, deliberate.

She looked up at the night sky. At stars, so many stars. The Milky Way was more brilliant than she'd ever seen it before.

The footsteps halted. A man towered above her, eyes glowing in a face smeared with black. She knew what would happen next. Denzel's body, dripping blood onto hers, told her all she needed to know.

*Icarus is here.*

# THIRTY-TWO

IT WAS THE DOG WHO ALERTED THEM. THROUGH
the door of their cell, Claire heard Bear start to
howl again, loud enough to echo through the wine
cellar and funnel up the stairs. She did not know
what had set him off. Maybe he understood that
their time had run out, that Death was even now
making His way down the steps to claim them.

"He's coming back," Claire said.

In that airless room, she could smell the fear,
sharp and electric, the scent of animals awaiting
slaughter. Will pressed closer to her, his flesh moist
with sweat. He had finally worked the tape off his
mouth, and now he leaned in and whispered to her:
"Get behind me and stay down, Claire. Whatever
happens, just play dead."

"What are you doing?"

"I'm trying to protect you."

"Why?"

"Don't you know why?" He looked at her, and
even though this was the same chubby, spotty Will

she knew so well, she saw something new in his eyes, something she hadn't noticed before. It was shining there so brightly it could not be missed. "I won't get another chance to say this," he whispered. "But I want you to know that . . ."

The padlock clanged. They both froze as the door squealed open and they saw the barrel of a gun, clutched in gloved hands. The weapon swept an arc around the room, as though seeking a target, and not finding it.

A man with a shaved head stepped into the room and called out, "He's not in here! But the others are."

Now a woman entered, sleek and graceful, her hair hidden under a watch cap. "That dog had to be howling at something down here," she said. They stood side by side, two invaders clad all in black, surveying the room of bound prisoners. The woman's gaze fell on Claire, and she said: "We've met before. Do you remember, Claire?"

Staring up at the woman, Claire suddenly thought of headlights rushing toward her. Remembered the night turning upside down and the sound of shattering glass and gunshots. And she remembered the guardian angel who had magically appeared to pull her from that ruined car.

*Come with me, Claire. If you want to live.*

The woman turned to Will, who was staring openmouthed. "And we've met, too, Will."

"You were there," he murmured. "You're the one . . ."

"Someone had to save you." She pulled out a knife. "Now I need to know where that man is." She held up the blade, as though offering it as a reward for their cooperation.

"Cut me free," snapped Sansone, "and I'll help you take him down."

"Sorry, but this game's not for civilians," the woman said. She looked around at the faces. "What about Teddy? Does anyone know where he is?"

"Screw Teddy," said Claire. "He's a traitor. He led us into this trap."

"Teddy doesn't know what he's doing," the woman said. "He's been lied to, corrupted. Help me save him."

"He won't come out. He's hiding."

"Do you know where?"

"On the roof," said Claire. "That's where he's supposed to wait."

The woman glanced at her partner. "Then we'll have to go up and get him." Instead of freeing Sansone, the woman knelt down behind Claire and sliced her bonds. "You can help us, Claire."

With a gasp of relief, Claire rubbed her wrists, felt the welcome rush of blood into her hands. "How?"

"You're his classmate. He'll listen to you."

"He won't listen to any of us," said Will. "He's helping that man."

"*That man,*" the woman said, turning to Will, "is here to kill you. To kill all of us. I've spent three years trying to catch him." She looked at Claire. "How do we get to the roof?"

"There's a door. In the turret."

"Take us there." The woman yanked Claire to her feet.

"What about them?" Claire said, pointing to the others.

The woman tossed the knife on the floor. "They can cut themselves free. But they have to stay here. It's safer."

"What?" Claire protested as the woman pulled her out of the room.

"I can't have them getting in the way." The woman swung the door shut.

Inside the room, Sansone was cursing, shouting. *"Open the door!"*

"It's not right," insisted Claire. "Leaving them all locked up."

"It's what I need to do. It's best for them, best for everyone. Including Teddy."

"I don't care about Teddy."

"But I do." The woman gave Claire a hard shake. "Now take us to the turret."

They climbed out of the wine cellar into the kitchen, where Bear was barking again, looking pitiful and half strangled as he struggled to free himself from the leash. Claire wanted to untie him, but the woman dragged her away toward the servants' stairway. The man took the lead, his gaze constantly sweeping the steps above them as he climbed. Never had Claire known people who could move as quietly as these two. They were like cats, their footsteps silent, their eyes always moving. Sandwiched between them, Claire had no view forward or backward, so she focused on the steps, on moving as soundlessly as this man and woman. They were some kind of secret agents, she thought, here to save them. Even to save Teddy, the traitor. She'd had a lot of time to think about it while sitting in that room with her hands bound, listening to the cook's whimpers, to Dr. Pasquantonio's nasal whistles as he breathed. She'd thought about all the clues she'd missed. How Teddy never let anyone see his computer screen, but always hit ESCAPE as soon as she walked in the room. He was sending the man messages, she thought. All this time, he'd been helping the man who'd come to kill them.

She just didn't know why.

They were on the third floor now. The man paused and glanced back at Claire for guidance.

"There," she whispered, pointing to the spiral staircase that led to the turret. To Dr. Welliver's office.

He moved up the stone steps, and Claire crept up behind him. The stairs were steep here, and all she could see of him was the back of his hips and the commando knife dangling from his belt. It was so quiet she could hear the soft rasp of their clothes as they moved step by step.

The door to the turret was ajar.

The man gave it a nudge and reached in to flick

on the light switch. They saw Dr. Welliver's desk, her filing cabinet. The sofa with the flowery upholstery and the plump cushions. It was a room Claire knew well. How many hours had she sat on that very sofa, telling Welliver about her sleepless nights, her headaches, her nightmares? In this room that smelled of incense, decorated in soft pastels and magic crystals, Claire had felt safe enough to reveal secrets. And Dr. Welliver had listened patiently, nodding her head of frizzy silver hair, a cup of herbal tea always beside her.

Claire stood near the door as the man and woman quickly searched the office and the adjoining bathroom. They checked behind the desk, opened the closet. No Teddy.

The woman turned to the door that led outside, to the roof walk. The same door Welliver had exited to take her fatal plunge. As the woman stepped outside, the summer wind blew in, warm and sweet with the scent of pine trees. Claire heard running footsteps, then a cry. Seconds later the woman came back in, dragging Teddy by his shirt, and the boy sprawled onto the floor.

Teddy looked up at Claire. "You told them! You ratted me out."

"Why wouldn't I?" Claire shot back. "After what you did to us."

"You don't understand who these people are!"

"I know what *you* are, Teddy Clock." Claire aimed a kick at him, but the woman grabbed her shoulder and dragged her into the corner. "Stay there," she commanded, then turned to Teddy. "Where is he?"

Teddy folded himself into a ball and shook his head.

"What's his plan? Tell me, Teddy."

"I don't know," the boy moaned.

"Of course you do. You know him better than anyone. Just tell me, and everything will be fine."

"You'll kill him. That's why you're here."

"And you don't like to see people killed. Do you?"

"No," Teddy whispered.

"Then you wouldn't want to see this, either." The woman spun around and pressed her gun to Claire's forehead. Claire froze, too shocked to say a word. Teddy was stunned just as silent, his eyes wide in horror.

"Tell me, Teddy," the woman said. "Or I'll just have to splatter your friend's brains all over this nice sofa."

The woman's partner looked just as shocked by this turn of events. "What the fuck are you doing, Justine?"

"Trying to get some cooperation here. So, Teddy, what do you think? Do you want to see your friend die?"

"I don't know where he is!"

"I'll count to three." The gun dug deeper into Claire's forehead. "One . . ."

"Why are you doing this?" Claire cried. "You're supposed to be the *good guys*!"

"Two."

"You said you were here to help us!"

"Three." The woman lifted the weapon and fired into the wall, sending a drizzle of plaster onto Claire's head. With a snort of disgust, the woman turned back to Teddy.

At once Claire scrambled away and dropped down behind the desk, trembling. *Why is this happening? Why have they turned against us?*

"Since that didn't work," the woman said, "maybe you really don't know where he is. So we go to plan B." She grabbed Teddy's arm and dragged him toward the roof walk.

Her partner said, "This is fucked up. These are just kids."

"It needs to be done."

"We came for Icarus."

"Our *target* is whoever I say it is." She yanked off Teddy's communications headset and dragged him out the door, onto the exposed roof walk. "Now we dangle some bait," she said, and swung him over the railing.

Teddy screamed, frantically scrambling for a toehold on the steep slate roof. All that kept him from plummeting to his death was the woman, gripping his arm.

She spoke into the boy's headset. "No, this isn't Teddy talking to you. Guess who I've got hanging off the roof? Such a sweet boy, too. All I have to do is let go, and he'll be nothing but a stain on the ground."

"The kid's not part of this," her partner protested.

The woman ignored him and kept talking into Teddy's com unit. "I know you're on this frequency. And you know what's happening. You also know how to stop it. I never liked children anyway, so it's no big deal to me. And he's getting heavy."

"This is way over the line," the man said, moving toward her. "Pull the kid back."

"Stand down," she ordered him. And she barked into Teddy's microphone: "Thirty seconds! That's all you've got! Show yourself or I let go!"

"Justine," the man said. "Pull the kid back. *Now.*"

"Jesus Christ." The woman yanked Teddy back over the railing and set him down. Then she aimed at her partner and fired.

The force of the bullet sent him flying backward. He collapsed against the desk and slid off, his head thudding to the floor right next to where Claire was cowering. She stared down at the hole above his left eye. Saw blood streaming out, soaking into Dr. Welliver's rose-colored rug.

*She killed him. She killed her own man.*

Justine bent down, scooped up her dead colleague's weapon, and tucked it into her waistband. Then she tossed aside Teddy's headset and spoke into her own com unit. "Where the fuck are you? The target's on his way up to the turret. I need you here *now.*"

Footsteps were moving up the stairs.

Instantly the woman hauled Teddy to his feet and held him in front of her, a human shield against the man who now stepped through the doorway. The same man whom Claire had earlier thought was the enemy. But nothing made sense anymore, because Claire had thought this woman was their rescuer. And she'd thought this man who'd tied her up, with his black-smeared face and camouflage clothes, had come to kill them. *Which one is my friend?*

The man advanced slowly, his weapon trained on the woman. But Teddy stood in the line of fire, pale-faced and trembling in the woman's grip.

"Let him go, Justine. This is between you and me," he said.

"I knew I could make you finally surface."

"These kids have nothing to do with it."

"They're my trump card, and here you are. Still looking fit, I see. Although I liked your old face better." She pressed the barrel of her gun harder against Teddy's temple. "Now you know what to do, Nick."

"You'll kill him anyway."

"But there's always the chance I won't. As opposed to a sure thing, which you'd have to watch." She fired and Teddy screamed, blood trickling from his bullet-torn ear. "Next time," she said, "it will be his chin. So drop it."

Teddy sobbed, "I'm sorry, Dad. I'm so sorry." *Dad?*

The man dropped his gun and now stood unarmed before her. "Do you really think I'd walk into this without a fail-safe, Justine? Kill me, and it all blows up in your face."

Claire stared at the man, searching for any resemblance to the Nicholas Clock she'd seen in the photo with her father. He had the same broad shoulders, the same blond hair, but this man's nose and chin were different. Plastic surgery. Hadn't Justine said it? *I liked your old face better.*

"You're supposed to be dead," Claire murmured.

"I thought for certain you'd show yourself after Ithaca," said Justine. "That you'd make *some* move to save Olivia's boy. But in the end, I guess it all came down to saving just your own flesh and blood."

Claire understood suddenly that this woman had ordered the murders of Bob and Barbara. She'd killed Will's aunt and uncle, all to make Nicholas Clock come back from the dead. Now this woman would send him back to the dead. She'd send them all.

*Do something.*

Claire looked down at the man Justine had just shot. The woman had taken his gun, but he'd also had a knife. Claire remembered it dangling from his belt as she'd followed him up the stairs. Justine wasn't watching her; her complete focus was on Clock.

Claire leaned over the dead man's belt. Tunneled her hand under his body, feeling for the knife.

"If you kill me," said Clock, "I guarantee you'll

go down. Every major news agency will find a video file in their in-box. All the evidence I've been collecting against you these past few years, Justine. Everything that Erskine and Olivia and I managed to pull together. The Company will shut you in a black hole so deep you'll forget what the sky looks like."

Justine kept her grip on Teddy, the gun at his jaw, but uncertainty made her hesitate. By killing him, was she about to set off a disastrous chain of events?

Claire gripped the knife handle. Tried to pull it from the belt, but the dead man's weight pinned it against the floor.

Nicholas Clock said quietly, reasonably: "You don't have to do this. Let me take my boy. Let us both disappear."

"And I'll spend the rest of my life wondering when you'll pop up and start talking."

"The truth will certainly come out if I'm dead," said Clock. "How you helped Icarus escape from prison. How you raided his accounts. The only unanswered question is, Where did you dump his body after you tortured him for his access codes?"

"You have no proof."

"I have enough to make it come crashing down on you. We finally put it together, the three of us. You killed your own people, Justine, all for the money. You know what happens next."

From the stairwell came the sound of running footsteps.

*Do it now. It's your last chance.*

Claire yanked the knife free and lunged. Aimed for the closest target she could reach: the back of Justine's thigh. The blade sliced straight through fabric and sank deep into flesh, almost to the hilt.

Justine shrieked and staggered sideways, releasing Teddy. In an instant, Nicholas Clock was diving for the floor. For his fallen weapon.

Justine fired first. Three pops. Blood misted the wall behind Clock, bright red spray exploding from a gunshot that sent him sprawling. He collapsed on his back, awareness already fading from his eyes.

"Dad!" Teddy screamed. *"Dad!"*

Face white with pain and fury, Justine turned to Claire, the girl who'd dared to fight back. The girl who'd twice cheated Death, only to meet Him now, here. Claire watched the silencer lift to her head. Saw Justine's arms straighten as she steadied the weapon to fire. It was the last image Claire saw before she closed her eyes.

The explosion rocked her back against the desk. Not a mere pop this time, it was a thunderclap that made her ears ring. She waited for the pain. For something to hurt, but all she registered was her own frantic breathing.

And Teddy's voice screaming in desperation: "Help him! Please, help my dad!" She opened her eyes and saw Detective Rizzoli crouched over Nicholas Clock. Saw Justine lying on her back, eyes open and staring, a pool of blood spreading beneath her head.

"Frost!" Rizzoli yelled. "Get Maura up here! We have a man down."

"Daddy," begged Teddy, pulling on Clock's arm, oblivious to his own pain, his own blood, still dripping from his ripped ear. "You can't die. Please don't die."

Justine's blood kept spreading, moving like an amoeba toward Claire, threatening to engulf her. With a shudder, Claire rose to her feet and stumbled to a corner, away from all the bodies. Away from the dead.

More footsteps came racing up the stairs and Dr. Isles swept into the room.

"It's Teddy's father," said Rizzoli quietly.

Dr. Isles dropped to her knees and pressed fingers to the man's neck. Yanked open the shirt, revealing the Kevlar vest beneath it. But the bullet had sliced into flesh just above the vest, and Claire saw a river of blood streaming from the wound, forming a lake where Dr. Isles was kneeling.

"You can save him!" Teddy screamed. "Please. Please . . ."

He was still sobbing that word as the last gleam of consciousness faded from his father's eyes.

# THIRTY-THREE

NICHOLAS CLOCK DID NOT REGAIN CONSCIOUS-
ness.

The vascular surgeons at Eastern Maine Medical
Center repaired his torn subclavian vein, evacuated
the hemothorax from his lung, and deemed the operation a success, but Clock did not awaken from
anesthesia. He was breathing on his own, and his
vital signs remained stable, but with every passing
day that he remained in a coma, Jane heard the
deepening pessimism in the doctors' voices. *Severe
blood loss with hypoperfusion of the brain. Permanent neurologic deficits.* No longer were they talking of recovery; instead the discussion was of
long-term care and nursing home transfer, of Foley
catheters and feeding tubes and other products that
Jane had glimpsed in the fake catalog of Leidecker
Hospital Supplies.

Comatose though he was, Nicholas Clock still
found a way to tell the world the truth.

Seven days after the shooting, the video surfaced.

Al Jazeera was the first to broadcast it, launching it into the ether where it could never again be contained. Within another forty-eight hours, Nicholas Clock was on computer screens and televisions around the world, calmly and methodically recounting the events that took place sixteen years earlier in Italy. He described the surveillance and capture of a terrorist financier whose code name was Icarus, in a case of extraordinary rendition. He revealed the details of Icarus's imprisonment and the enhanced interrogation methods they had used against him. And he spoke of Icarus's escape from the high-security black site in North Africa, an escape aided by a rogue CIA operative named Justine McClellan. None of that should have surprised or impressed a world long turned cynical.

But the murder of American families, on American soil, made the country take notice.

In the conference room at Boston PD, the six detectives who had investigated the Ackerman slayings sat watching the CNN evening news, a broadcast that went a long way toward explaining what had really happened to the Ackermans. The family had not been murdered by a Colombian immigrant named Andres Zapata; they had been executed for the same reason the other two families were: to make Nicholas Clock believe his son, Teddy, was in imminent danger. To force Clock out of hiding.

*As long as Justine believed I was dead, Teddy was safe. She had no reason to attack him. If I took him and we ran, Justine would never stop hunting us. We'd always be looking over our shoulders. Teddy knows I'm alive. He understands why I've chosen to stay invisible. It's for him; it's all for him.*

*But now everything has changed. Justine must have intercepted one of our messages, and she knows I'm alive. I don't have much time. This may be my only chance to share the evidence I've been gathering these past two years. Evidence that Justine Elizabeth McClellan aided in the escape of the terrorist known as Icarus. That she almost certainly murdered Icarus, after obtaining his account numbers and passwords. That she, or her paid agents, were responsible for the murders of the Wards and the Yablonskis and my own family. Because we were asking questions about her sudden wealth. We'd started an investigation, and she had to stop us.*

*Our families were merely innocent bystanders.*

*These three surviving children—Claire and Will and Teddy—are now pawns in the hunt. Justine has gathered these children together as bait, to draw me out. She's using all her resources, both official and unofficial, and she's led the CIA to believe that Icarus is still alive. That he's her target.*

*But I'm the one she wants.*

*If anyone is watching this video, it means that Justine has succeeded. It means I'm speaking to you from the grave. But the truth doesn't die with me. And I, Nicholas Clock, swear that everything I've said here is, indeed, the truth . . .*

Jane looked around at the other detectives seated at the table. Crowe was tight-lipped and scowling, and no wonder: His public triumph as lead investigator of the Ackerman case had just been smashed with a sledgehammer, and every crime reporter in Boston knew it. That rush to judgment against Andres Zapata would always blight his record. Crowe caught her looking at him, and the glare he returned could vaporize water.

For Jane, it should have felt like a moment of victory, a vindication of her instincts, but this brought no smile to her lips. Nicholas Clock was now lying in a coma that could well be permanent, and Teddy was once again fatherless. She thought of how many people had died: the Clocks, the Yablonskis, the Wards. The Ackermans, the Temples, and the Buckleys. Dead, all dead, because one woman could not resist the lure of immeasurable wealth.

The broadcast ended. As the other detectives rose to leave the room, Jane remained in her chair, thinking about justice. About how the dead never benefited from it. *For them, it always comes too late.*

"That was good work, Rizzoli," said Lieutenant Marquette.

She looked up to see him standing in the doorway. "Thank you."

"So why do you look like your best friend just died?"

"It's just not satisfying, you know?"

"You're the one who brought down Justine Mc-Clellan. How can it get more satisfying than that?"

"Maybe if I could bring back the dead?"

"Above our pay grade. We're just the cleanup crew." He scowled at his ringing cell phone. "Looks like the press is going bonkers. Which is a problem, because this story's as sensitive as hell."

"Rogue agent? Dead Americans?" She snorted. "No kidding."

"The feds slapped a muzzle on us. So for now, it's *no comment*, okay?" He cocked his head. "Now get outta here. Go home and have a beer. You deserve it."

That was the nicest thing Marquette had ever said to her. A beer did sound good. And she did deserve it. She gathered up her files, left them at her desk, and walked out of the station.

But she did not go home.

Instead she drove to Brookline, to the home of someone who'd be equally depressed by that broadcast. Someone who had no one else to turn to. When she arrived at the house, she was relieved to see that no TV vans had arrived yet, but the press would certainly be there soon. Every reporter in Boston knew where Dr. Maura Isles lived.

The lights were on inside, and Jane heard classical music playing, the plaintive strains of a violin. She had to ring the bell twice before the door finally opened.

"Hey," said Jane. "Did you see it on TV? It's all over the Internet!"

Maura gave a weary nod. "The fun is just beginning."

"Which is why I came over. I figured you might need the company."

"I'm afraid my company's not going to be much fun. But I'm glad you're here."

Jane followed Maura into the living room, where she saw an open bottle of red wine and a nearly empty glass on the coffee table. "When you bring out the whole bottle, there's some serious drinking planned."

"Would you like a glass?"

"Can I get a beer out of your fridge instead?"

"Be my guest. There should still be a bottle in there from your last visit."

Jane went into the kitchen and saw pristine countertops, with not a single dirty dish in sight. It looked clean enough in there to perform surgery, but that was Maura for you. Everything in its place. It suddenly struck Jane how bleak it all looked without clutter, without even a hint of disorder. As if no human really lived there. As if Maura had scrubbed her life so clean, she had sterilized the joy out of it.

She found the bottle of Adam's ale, probably months old, and uncapped it. Went back to the living room.

The violin music was still playing, but with the volume turned down. They sat on the sofa. Maura sipped wine and Jane took a swig of beer, careful not to spill a drop on Maura's spotless upholstery or the pricey Persian rug.

"You must feel thoroughly vindicated after this," said Maura.

"Yeah. I look like a real genius. The best part was taking Crowe down ten notches." She took another sip of beer. "But it's not enough, is it?"

"What isn't?"

"Closing a case. Knowing we got it right. It doesn't change the fact that Nicholas Clock is probably never going to wake up."

"But the children are safe," said Maura. "That's what matters. I spoke to Julian this morning, and he says Claire and Will are doing fine."

"But not Teddy. I'm not sure he'll ever be fine," said Jane, looking down at her beer. "I saw him at his foster home last night. We brought him back to the Inigos, the family who looked after him before. He wouldn't say a word to me, not one word. I think he blames me." She looked at Maura. "He blames all of us. You, me. Sansone."

"Nevertheless, Teddy's always welcome back at Evensong."

"You've spoken to Sansone about it?"

"This afternoon." Maura reached for the glass of wine, as though needing to fortify herself for this subject. "He made me an interesting offer, Jane."

"What kind of offer?"

"To work for the Mephisto Society as a forensic consultant. And to be part of Evensong, where I could 'shape young minds,' as he put it."

Jane raised an eyebrow. "Don't you think he's really offering you something more personal?"

"No, that's exactly what he said. I have to judge him by his words. Not by my interpretation of those words."

"Jesus." Jane sighed. "The two of you are dancing around each other like you're both blind."

"If I weren't blind, what exactly would I be seeing?"

"That Sansone's a much better choice for you than Daniel ever was."

Maura shook her head. "I don't think I should be choosing *any* man right now. But I am considering his offer."

"You mean, leave the ME's office? Leave Boston?"

"Yes. That's what it would mean."

The violin music soared to a high, sad note. A note that seemed to pierce straight to Jane's chest. "You're seriously thinking about it?"

Maura reached for the CD remote and abruptly shut off the music. Silence hung, heavy as a velvet drape, between them. She looked around the living room at the white leather sofa, at the polished mahogany. "I don't know what's next for me, Jane."

Lights flared through the window, and Jane rose to peek through the curtains. "Unfortunately, I *do* know what's next for you."

"What?"

"TV van just pulled up. Damn hyenas can't even

wait for the press conference. They gotta show up on your doorstep."

"I've been told not to talk to them."

Jane turned with a frown. "Who told you that?"

"I received a call half an hour ago. The governor's office. They're getting pressure from Washington to keep this under wraps."

"Too late. It's already on CNN."

"That's what I said to him."

"So you're not gonna talk to the press at all?"

"Do we have a choice?"

"We always have a choice," said Jane. "What do *you* want to do?"

Maura rose from the sofa and went to stand beside Jane at the window. They both watched as a cameraman began to haul out equipment from the van, preparing for the invasion of Maura's front lawn.

"The easy choice," said Maura, "is to simply tell them *no comment*."

"No one can force us to talk."

Maura mulled this over as they watched a second TV van arrive. "But isn't that how all of this happened?" she asked. "Too many secrets. Too many people not telling the truth. When you shine a bright light, a secret loses all its power."

The way Nicholas Clock did with his video, thought Jane. Shining the light of truth had cost him his life. But it had saved his son.

"You know, Maura, that's exactly what you're so

good at. You shine a light, and you make the dead give up their secrets."

"The trouble is, *the dead* are the only relationships I seem to have. I need someone whose body temperature is a little warmer than ambient. I don't think I'm going to find him in this city."

"I'd hate it if you left Boston."

"You have a family here, Jane. I don't."

"If you want a family, I'll give you my parents. Let them drive *you* crazy. And I'll even throw in Frankie, so you can share the joy."

Maura laughed. "That particular joy is yours, and yours alone."

"The point is, a family doesn't automatically make us happy. Doesn't your work matter, too? And . . ." She paused. Added quietly: "And your friends?"

On the street outside, yet another TV van pulled up, and they heard the sound of slamming vehicle doors.

"Maura," said Jane, "I haven't been a good enough friend. I know that. I swear, I'll do better next time." She went to the coffee table for Maura's wineglass, for her own bottle of beer. "So let's drink to friends being friends."

Smiling, they clinked glass against bottle and sipped.

Jane's cell phone rang. She pulled it from her purse and saw a Maine area code on the display. "Rizzoli," she answered.

"Detective, this is Dr. Stein, Eastern Maine Medical Center. I'm the neurologist taking care of Mr. Clock."

"Yes, we spoke the other day."

"I'm, uh, not exactly sure how to tell you this, but . . ."

"He's dead," Jane said, already guessing the purpose of this call.

"No! I mean . . . I don't *think* so."

"How can you not know?"

There was a sheepish sigh on the other end. "We really can't explain how it happened. But when the nurse went into his room this afternoon to check his vital signs, his bed was empty, and the IV line was disconnected. We've spent the last four hours searching the hospital grounds, but we can't find him."

"Four *hours*? He's been missing that long?"

"Maybe longer. We don't know exactly when he left the room—"

"Doctor, I'll call you right back," she cut in, and hung up. Immediately she dialed the Inigos' residence. It rang once. Twice.

"What's going on, Jane?" Maura asked.

"Nicholas Clock's gone missing."

"*What?*" Maura stared at her. "I thought he was comatose."

On the phone, Nancy Inigo answered: "Hello?"

"Is Teddy there?" Jane said.

"Detective Rizzoli, is that you?"

"Yes. And I'm concerned about Teddy. Where is he?"

"He's in his room. He came home after school and went straight upstairs. I was about to call him down for dinner."

"Please check on him for me. Right now."

Nancy Inigo's footsteps creaked up the stairs as she asked Jane over the phone: "Can you tell me what's going on?"

"I don't know. Not yet."

Jane heard Nancy knock on the door and call out: "Teddy, can I come in? Teddy?" A pause. Then an alarmed: "He's not here!"

"Search the house," ordered Jane.

"Wait. Wait, there's a note here, on the bed. It's Teddy's handwriting."

"What does it say?"

Over the phone, Jane heard the rustle of paper. "It's addressed to you, Detective," said Nancy. "It says, *Thank you. We'll be fine now.* That's all there is."

*Thank you. We'll be fine now.*

Jane imagined Nicholas Clock, miraculously rising from his coma, untethering his own IV line, and walking out of the hospital. She pictured Teddy, placing the note on his bed before he slipped out of the Inigos' house and disappeared into the night. Both of them knew exactly where they were going, because they were bound for the same destination: a future together, as father and son.

"Do you have any idea what this note means?" asked Nancy.

"Yes. I think I know exactly what it means," Jane said softly, and hung up.

"So Nicholas Clock is alive," said Maura.

"Not just alive. He finally has his son." Jane gazed out the window at the TV news vans and the growing pack of reporters and cameramen. And even though she was smiling, the lights of all those vehicles suddenly blurred through her tears. She tipped her beer bottle in a toast to the night and whispered: "Here's to you, Nicholas Clock."

*Game over.*

# THIRTY-FOUR

**B**LOOD IS MORE EASILY WASHED AWAY THAN memories, thought Claire. She stood in Dr. Welliver's office, surveying the brand-new rugs and furniture. Sunlight gleamed on spotless surfaces, and the room smelled of fresh air and lemons. Through the open window she heard the laughter of students rowing on the lake. Saturday sounds. Looking around the room, it was hard to believe that anything terrible had ever happened here, so thoroughly had the school transformed it. But no amount of scrubbing could erase the images seared in Claire's mind. She looked down at the pale green carpet, and superimposed on that pattern of vines and berries, she saw a dead man staring up at her. She turned toward the wall, and there was Nicholas Clock's blood splattered across it. She looked at the desk and could still picture Justine's body lying nearby, brought down by Detective Rizzoli's gunshots. Everywhere she looked in this room, she saw bodies. The ghost of Dr. Welliver still lingered here as well, smiling across her desk, sipping her endless cups of tea.

So many ghosts. Would she ever stop seeing them?

"Claire, are you coming?"

She turned to Will, who stood in the doorway. No longer did she see the pudgy, spotty Will; now she saw *her* Will, the boy whose last impulse when he thought they were going to die was to protect her. She wasn't sure whether that was love, exactly; she wasn't even sure what she felt about *him*. All she knew was that he'd done something no other boy had ever done for her, and that meant something. Maybe it meant everything.

And he had beautiful eyes.

She cast a final look around the room, said a silent goodbye to the ghosts, and nodded. "I'm coming."

Together they walked down the stairs and stepped outside, where their classmates were enjoying that bright Saturday, splashing in the lake, lolling on the grass. Shooting arrows at the targets that Mr. Roman had set up that morning. Claire and Will headed up the path they both knew well now, a path that brought them up the hillside, winding through the trees across lichen-covered boulders, past scrubby juniper bushes. They came to the stone steps and climbed to the terrace, and the circle of thirteen boulders.

The others were waiting. She saw the usual faces: Julian and Bruno, Arthur and Lester. On that fair morning, a chorus of birds sang in the trees, and Bear the dog dozed on a sun-warmed rock. She went to the edge of the terrace and looked down at the castle's jagged rooftop. It seemed to rise from the valley below like an ancient mountain range. Evensong. *Home.*

Julian said. "I now call to order this meeting of the Jackals."

Claire turned and joined the circle.

# ACKNOWLEDGMENTS

After more than two decades as a writer, what I've come to value most are the enduring friendships I've made in this business, and a writer could have no better friends than my terrific literary agent, Meg Ruley, and my superb editor, Linda Marrow. Through thick and thin, you've been there for me, and I tip my martini glass to you both! Thanks also to Gina Centrello, Libby McGuire, and Larry Finlay for believing in me through the years, to Sharon Propson for making book tours such a pleasure, to Jane Berkey and Peggy Gordijn for infallibly spot-on guidance, and to Angie Horejsi for her wit and wisdom.

In researching *Last to Die,* I relied on trusted sources for my information. Thanks to my son Adam for his expertise on firearms; to Peggy Maher, Enidia Santiago-Arce, and their wonderful colleagues at NASA's Goddard Space Flight Center for patiently answering this old Trekkie's questions; and to Bob Gleason and Tom Doherty for so generously including me on that spectacularly fun field trip.

Most of all, I thank my husband, Jacob. After all these years, you're still the one.

# JOHN DOE

A Rizzoli & Isles Short Story

## TESS GERRITSEN

# ONE

**D**r. Maura Isles did not enjoy cocktail parties. Circulating in a room filled with strangers was her idea of an excruciating evening, yet here she was, glass of champagne in hand, standing beneath *Tyrannosaurus rex*. Dinosaur bones did not expect her to smile and come up with small talk, something Maura was singularly bad at. Sheltered in the undemanding company of *T. rex*, she read the informational plaque for the tenth time, glad that for once she wasn't competing with the hordes of children who always gathered at the feet of dinosaurs. Tonight was an adults-only affair, a formal reception to thank the donors to Boston's Museum of Science, and as a member of the benefit committee, Maura could hardly slip away before the speeches started. She smiled stoically and sipped champagne as men in tuxedos and women in evening gowns glided past, chatting and crowd-hopping with an ease that Maura had never acquired.

"You and *T. rex* seem awfully chummy," a male voice said.

Maura turned to see an attractive dark-haired man smiling at her. Although she was wearing four-inch high heels, he was taller than her, fit and trim in a well-tailored tuxedo. She glanced at his name tag and saw his name was Eli Kilgour. The gold dot pasted above his name told her Mr. Kilgour was a high-level donor to the museum.

"I see you're on the benefit committee," he said, reading her name tag, just as she had read his. "Excellent event tonight, Dr. Isles."

She smiled back. "I can't take any credit. All I did was write a check and lend my name to the cause." She shook his hand. "Thank you for *your* generous donation to the museum. We need to get every kid in town fired up about science."

"And that title *Doctor* I see in front of your name," he said, pointing to her tag. "Would that be MD or PhD?"

"MD. I'm a forensic pathologist. And you?"

He gave a modest shrug. "Nothing nearly as impressive. I suppose my full-time job is supporting causes that matter to me."

Which explained the gold dot on his name tag. He didn't have an occupation because he obviously had money.

"And which causes do matter to you?" she asked.

"Inspiring young scientists, for one. Which is why we're both here tonight, wearing our dancing shoes."

"Dancing?" She winced. "More like limping. These are my two-hour shoes."

He looked down at her high heels. "What happens after two hours?"

"Either I kick them off, or someone has to carry me home."

"Both prospects sound pretty exciting."

She laughed, surprised to find herself flirting with an attractive stranger, and she quickly confirmed that he wore no wedding ring. The evening had turned interesting: The champagne tasted more delicious, and a pleasant warmth flushed her cheeks.

"So are you alone here tonight?" he asked, glancing around the room, searching for her escort.

"Yes. Here to do my civic duty."

"And is there a Mr. Dr. Isles?"

She sighed. "Unfortunately, no. You?"

"Unless you count my mother, there is no Mrs. Kilgour. Which turns out to be a good thing tonight, because I can enjoy a guilt-free chat with a beautiful woman in a stunning gown."

"That," she said with a smile, "sounds like a line you've used before."

"But tonight I actually *mean* it." He looked down at her empty champagne glass. "Let me refill that for you. If you promise not to disappear."

She handed him the glass. "Thanks for saving me the pain of hobbling to the bar."

"Back in a flash. Tell *T. rex* to behave himself."

Off he went with her champagne glass, striding with the confidence of a man who knew his way among the tuxedoed crowd. Just as she lost sight of him, the PA system hummed to life.

"Good evening, ladies and gentlemen! I'm George Gilman, chairman of the benefit committee. I'm delighted to see so many people here who care about this museum and all the ways it enriches our city, inspires our children, and awakens our wonder in science . . ."

Maura's two-hour shoes had just about reached their limit. She leaned against a pillar, trying to take the pressure off her numb toes, as George Gilman finished his introductions. The museum director took the microphone and began to talk about their mission as educators and scientists, all things Maura deeply believed in. Her eyes stayed on the speaker, but she scarcely registered his words because she was distracted by the buzz of the crowd, the flushing of her own skin. And by the attentions of a certain stranger.

Suddenly he was back beside her. "Here you go," he whispered, placing a full champagne glass in her hand. "What did I miss?"

"The introductions."

"*T. rex* didn't make a pass?"

"He's been a very good boy," she said as she sipped.

"Have you eaten dinner?"

"The canapés were a meal in themselves."

"I arrived too late to sample any. So . . ."

"So?" She looked at him.

"When the speeches are over, let me take you someplace for dessert."

He was staring at her as if he thought *she* were dessert. The champagne made her feel bold, even reckless, but something she glimpsed in his eyes made her hesitate. She took another sip, giving herself a moment to weigh his invitation.

"We've only just met, Eli."

"True. But I have the special gold dot," he said, tapping his name tag. "Does that count for something?"

Now she had to smile. If ever there was a place to meet a respectable man, it would be a Museum of Science reception. Whatever she'd earlier glimpsed in his eyes, whatever had pinged some internal alarm, was no longer visible.

"After the speeches," she said.

"Of course. That *is* why we're here."

"And then I want to hear more about you. What else you do besides supporting causes."

"Over dessert. And I know just the place. A French café, right in this neighborhood. Strawberry tarts as good as any in Paris. And it's close enough to walk to."

"Ouch." She looked down at her shoes. "Don't even say that word."

He nodded sympathetically. "I can arrange alternative transportation. Pumpkin. Limousine. Stretcher."

"Even the pumpkin sounds good."

Now the evening's featured speaker took the microphone. A distinguished climate scientist from

MIT. Maura drained her champagne to steel her-self for the doom-and-gloom lecture sure to come. Shrinking polar ice caps and disappearing phyto-plankton. Even though she wore only a silk halter gown, the room felt warm and suddenly airless.

". . . and how can we as a country sensibly re-spond to these global challenges, given our schools' latest test scores in science?"

Maura looked at the other attendees. Was no one else feeling overheated? All around her were women in jewel-colored gowns, appearing cool and collected.

She felt a steadying hand on her arm, and looked up into Eli's face.

He took her empty champagne glass and set it on a nearby tray. "I think you need some air," he said.

". . . and that is where we find ourselves today, in a nation rapidly being eclipsed by scientific powerhouses now rising in Asia, where . . ."

THE SUN BURNED THROUGH her eyelids. Maura turned her head, trying to escape the glare, but it shone down on her face like a heat lamp, hot enough to scorch her skin. Her mouth was dry, so dry, and her head hurt. And the damn phone kept ringing and ringing.

She opened her eyes and squinted at the sunlight blazing through the living room window. *Why am I not in bed?* She struggled to focus on her sur-roundings and saw her coffee table, the Persian rug, the bookcase. Everything where it usually was.

*Except for me. How did I end up falling asleep on the sofa?*

The phone stopped ringing.

Groaning, she sat up and immediately had to drop her head as the room seemed to rock. Doubled over, her face resting in her hands, she realized she was still wearing her evening gown from the Museum of Science reception. The silk was thoroughly wrinkled from being slept in, and one high-heeled shoe was lying under the coffee table. Where the other shoe was, she could not remember.

She could not remember a lot of things. How she'd gotten home. How she'd made it through her front door.

Slowly she straightened again, and this time the room stayed steady. She spotted her purse on the floor, with her keys lying beside it. *I must have driven myself home,* she thought. *Unlocked my front door, and collapsed onto the sofa.*

*Why can't I remember any of it?*

She stood up, reeling like a drunken woman, and stumbled down the hall into the kitchen. There she drank two full glasses of water, gulping it so greedily it dribbled down her chin and splattered her silk dress. She didn't care. Thirst quenched at last, she propped herself against the countertop, feeling steadier. Stronger. Her head still throbbed, but she was awake enough now to feel the first prickles of fear. The kitchen clock read eleven thirty-five. It was a Sunday, but even on weekends she never slept this late.

*What happened to me last night? Why can't I remember?*

She looked down at her dress. Except for the wrinkled fabric and the fresh water stains, it appeared intact. She was still wearing her pantyhose, although a fat run had streaked its way up her left stocking. She hadn't been robbed, since her purse and keys were in the . . .

*My purse.*

She hurried back to the living room and scooped up her evening bag. Inside it, she found her business card case, lipstick, and wallet. The wallet was unsnapped. With a rising sense of panic she flipped it open and was relieved to see all her credit cards; only her driver's license was missing. No, there it was, lying loose at the bottom of the purse.

The doorbell rang.

She turned, heart suddenly pounding. Could the answers be waiting on her front porch? Though she had just downed two glasses of water, her throat felt parched again, this time from anxiety, as she opened the door.

Detective Jane Rizzoli pulled off sunglasses and frowned up and down at Maura's evening gown. "Isn't there some rule about formal wear before noon?" she asked.

Maura lifted a hand to her throbbing head. "Oh, God, Jane. I'm so confused."

"What's wrong?"

"I don't know. I don't know what's wrong."

Jane stepped into the house and shut the door.

"You look like you need to sit down," she said, guiding Maura to the sofa. "I've been calling you for the last hour. Where were you?"

"Here." Maura looked down at the white cushions and suddenly gave a laugh. "*Right* here, in fact. This is where I woke up."

"On the sofa? Must've been a wild night."

Maura closed her eyes against the headache. She didn't have to look to know that Jane was eyeing her with a cop's unrelenting stare, exactly what Maura didn't want to face right now. Head in her hands, Maura said, "Why are you here?"

"You didn't answer your phone."

"It's Sunday. I'm not on call."

"I know that."

"So why were you trying to reach me?" Her question was met with silence. Maura lifted her head and found herself looking straight into Jane's eyes. It was Maura's job to wield a scalpel, but now Jane was the one doing the dissecting, and Maura didn't like being on the receiving end.

"I just came from a death scene," said Jane. "Olmsted Park. A body was found on the bank of the Muddy River, just south of Leverett Pond."

"It's not my case, not today. Why are you telling me about it?"

"Because we have reason to think you might know him."

Maura sat up straight, staring. "Who?"

"That's just it, we don't know. There's no wallet,

no phone on the body. At the moment he's a John Doe."

"Why do you think I know him?"

"Because we found your business card tucked into his breast pocket."

"He could have it for any number of reasons. I give my cards out to anyone who does business with—"

"Your home address was written on the back, Maura."

Maura sat still for a moment, struggling to think through the cloud of confusion that still hung over her. She seldom gave out her personal information to anyone—not her phone number, and certainly not where she lived. She valued her privacy too dearly. "This man," she said softly. "What does he look like?"

"Dark hair. In his forties, well built. I guess you'd call him good looking."

Maura's head lifted. "What was he wearing?"

"Funny you should ask that," said Jane, looking at Maura's evening gown. "He's wearing a very nice tuxedo. At least, it *was* nice, until someone sliced him up with a knife."

Maura lurched to her feet. "Excuse me," she gasped, and made a run for her bathroom. She barely made it in time and dropped her head over the toilet just as she started to retch. Nothing but water came up, every drop of those two full glasses she'd gulped down so quickly. She was left weak and shaking, and she barely heard Jane knocking on the door.

"Maura? You okay, Maura?"

"I'll be—I'll be out in a minute." Maura rose unsteadily to her feet and stared at herself in the mirror. Her usually sculpted hair was in disarray. Her face was sickly pale, with one bright streak of lipstick smeared across her cheek.

*The dead man was wearing a tuxedo.*

She turned on the faucet and washed her face twice, scrubbing away every trace of makeup. Bent over the sink, splashing her cheeks with water, all of a sudden she remembered a face. A man with dark hair, smiling at her. She remembered swirls of color, women in evening dresses standing around them. And a glass of champagne.

She stood up straight, water dripping onto her gown. A gown she never wanted to wear again. She unzipped it and shed the silk. Peeled off her pantyhose and underwear, desperate to get it all away from her because it felt dirty. Contaminated. Even as she threw the clothing into the corner, she knew it was evidence, and she could not wash it. Not yet.

Nor could she take a shower.

In her bedroom, she dressed in jeans and a T-shirt, but as soon as they touched her unwashed skin, the fresh clothes felt soiled, because *she* was. Or might be.

When she walked back into the living room, she found Jane talking on the cell phone. Jane took one look at Maura's face and quickly hung up.

"I want to see the body," said Maura.

"He's probably en route to the morgue right now."

"Do you have a photo?"

"Yeah. I took one because I thought you might need to look at it." Jane found the image on her cell phone, but paused before handing it to Maura. "You sure about this?"

"I need to know if it's him." She took Jane's cell phone and stared at the dead man's face. Remembered how that same face had smiled at her as he'd placed the champagne glass in her hand. And she remembered the name tag with the gold dot. "Eli Kilgour," she said.

"That's his name?"

"Yes. I met him last night, at the Museum of Science reception. He's a donor."

"Okay, so we've got a name." As Jane took back her phone, her eyes were still on Maura. "Now you want to tell me the rest of the story? Because I can see there's more."

"I need to go to the ER, Jane."

"Are you sick?"

"It's possible—I need to be sure . . ." Maura moved to an armchair and sank down. "I don't think it happened. But I need to be examined. For rape."

"You don't know?"

"I don't remember!" Maura dropped her head into her hands. "I don't remember how I got home. I don't remember falling asleep on the sofa."

"What do you remember?"

"The reception. Meeting him. We left the museum and I was feeling dizzy. I remember we were in the parking garage, and then . . ." She shook her head. "After that, I'm not sure."

"Somehow you did manage to get home. Is your car here?"

"I haven't looked."

Jane walked out of the living room; seconds later, she was back. "Your car's not in the garage."

"But my keys are right there." She pointed to the floor.

"Someone drove you here. Someone unlocked your front door and got you to the sofa."

*The same someone who drugged my champagne? Who's now dead from stab wounds?*

Jane placed a comforting hand on Maura's shoulder. "I'll drive you to the ER now, okay? And I'll need your clothes. What you wore last night."

"On the floor, in my bathroom. Everything's there, my underwear, my stockings." Maura sighed. "I know the drill."

"You also know that I've got a problem, Maura. The guy you just happened to meet last night turns up murdered. And you can't remember how the evening ended."

Maura looked up at her. "I guess we've both got a problem."

# TWO

JANE WAS ACCUSTOMED TO SEEING MAURA POISED and in control, the Queen of the Dead unruffled even by the horrors that landed on her autopsy table. So it was a shock to see how vulnerable Maura looked, sitting on the ER exam table, dressed in a hospital paper gown. Maura flinched as a needle pierced her vein and dark blood streamed into the specimen tube.

"That's for the drug screen?" asked Jane.

"Dr. Murata ordered a number of blood and urine tests" was all the nurse would say as she unsnapped the tourniquet, taped gauze to the puncture site. "And that should do it. As soon as you sign the discharge form, you're free to go, Dr. Isles. We'll call you when the lab results come in." She walked out with the blood tubes, sliding the privacy curtain closed.

"Thank you, Jane," Maura whispered. "For staying with me."

"Feel better?"

"Yes. Now that it looks like I wasn't . . ." Maura's voice trailed off before she could say the word. "I just wanted to be certain."

"Nevertheless," said Jane, "we'll need to hang on to your evening clothes, as well as all the collected trace evidence."

Maura frowned. "You're keeping my fingernail scrapings?"

Before Jane could answer, her cell phone rang. "Excuse me," she said, and walked out. Kept walking until she was well down the hall, where Maura couldn't hear her. "Rizzoli," she answered.

"You know that name you gave me, Eli Kilgour?" said her partner, Detective Barry Frost.

"You reach his next of kin?"

"Even better. I reached *him*. Mr. Kilgour's alive and well and living with his male partner on Beacon Street."

"Male partner?"

"You got it. He said he *is* a donor to the Museum of Science, but he couldn't make it to the benefit because he had another engagement. The man Dr. Isles met last night must have picked up a badge from the ones remaining on the table."

"Classic way to crash a party. But in that crowd, it carries risks. You'd think folks in their circle would know each other."

"I called the museum, and they've pulled the security tapes for me. They had four hundred guests last night, so it'd be easy to slip in among so many people. He must be an old hand at this, if he comes dressed in a tuxedo. Hell, I don't even *own* a tuxedo."

"So we're back to square one. Who *is* our dead John Doe?"

"Dr. Isles was with him last night, and she has no idea?"

"She says she can't remember what happened. What about Maura's car? Did you find it?"

"Yeah. It's still in the museum garage, where she says she parked it last night. It was locked, nothing unusual about it."

"If her car was left at the museum, he must have driven her home."

"So where's *his* car? There wasn't any vehicle near the body," Frost pointed out.

She thought about the geography of Boston, and realized that if she drove directly from the Museum of Science to Maura's house in Brookline, the death scene would be right along the way. She didn't like where that line of reasoning took her. It led to the possibility that John Doe was killed and dumped en route to Maura's home. It meant she was *with* the killer when it happened.

Or she *was* the killer.

"Check the cars in Maura's neighborhood," Jane said. "Any vehicle that doesn't belong."

"You're not thinking that . . ."

"We have to, Frost. We have no choice." She glanced up as Maura emerged, now dressed, from the exam room. "Right now, she's our only suspect."

\* \* \*

THE VEHICLE WAS PARKED across the street from Maura's residence, a black Buick LaCrosse with Massachusetts plates, registered to Christopher Scanlon of Braintree. None of the nearby neighbors knew anything about the car, only that it was already parked there when they woke up that morning.

"Unlocked. Keys still in the ignition," said Frost. "And look what's down there." He pointed to the floor beneath the passenger seat, and Jane's heart dropped when she saw the woman's high-heeled shoe. It was the mate to the shoe she'd seen under Maura's coffee table.

"Tow truck's on the way now," said Frost. "Once they get it back to the lab, I'm gonna bet CSU finds her fingerprints in there as well."

"Oh, man. This gets worse and worse."

"If this were anyone else, we'd be reading her her rights."

"But it's not anyone else," said Jane. "This is Maura."

"And we both know a few cops who'd like to see her take a perp walk." Maura's recent testimony against a Boston PD officer had sent him to prison—something plenty of cops viewed as a betrayal of the thin blue line.

"What do we have on this guy, Christopher Scanlon?" she asked.

Frost pulled up the data on his smartphone. "Age forty-one, six foot two, hundred eighty pounds.

Brown hair, blue eyes." He showed her the driver's license photo. "Looks like our victim."

"Who's no longer a John Doe."

"And get this. ME's office sent the victim's fingerprints to AFIS. Scanlon's in their database. Two arrests, both for indecent assault and battery."

"He's a rapist? Any convictions?"

"None. It seems our victim was a very bad boy. Who kept getting away with it."

But not this time, thought Jane as she crossed the street back to Maura's house.

She found Maura still sitting in the kitchen where she'd left her moments ago. Her cup of coffee appeared untouched, and she barely looked up as Jane walked in the room.

"Is the car his?" Maura asked.

"It appears so. His real name is Christopher Scanlon. Lives—lived—in Braintree. That ring any bells?"

"I told you, I never met the man before last night."

Jane couldn't help studying the wooden block of kitchen knives on the countertop. Couldn't help noticing that one slot was empty.

"Was it a Wüsthof blade?" Maura asked softly.

"What?"

"The knife that killed him. That's the brand of knives I own. It's what you're wondering, isn't it?"

"The murder weapon hasn't been found."

"Then you'll want to collect mine for a wound match. Fingerprints, blood. And don't forget the knife in the dishwasher." She raised her head and looked at Jane. "You have a job to do, I understand that."

Jane sat down at the table. "Then you also understand—"

"I'm a suspect." Maura gave an ironic laugh. "Which will please more than a few Boston PD officers. The high-and-mighty ME everyone loves to hate."

"Not true."

"They'll blithely point out that murder runs in my family. Like mother, like daughter."

"Your mother is not *you*."

"My mother is a monster. Do you think we'll be granted the privilege of adjoining prison cells?"

"Stop it, Maura. For God's sake."

"I'm just telling it like it is."

"That's the drug talking. Whatever he gave you, it's kicked you down and out and made you give up." Jane leaned forward and said fiercely: "I *won't* allow it."

They stared at each other for a moment.

Maura leaned back with a smile. "Everyone should have their own Jane Rizzoli."

Jane stood up and slid the chair against the table. "Well, this Jane Rizzoli has a job to do."

CHRISTOPHER SCANLON'S RESIDENCE WAS a rented two-bedroom town house on a leafy street in Braintree. Mr. Siegel, the rental agent who met them at the address, kept shaking his head and murmuring

"Awful, just awful," as they climbed the steps to the front door. "He was a dream tenant. Kept the property in immaculate shape." He waved at the manicured lawn. "You can see how neat the front yard is."

"He never gave you any problems?" Frost asked.

"Never. He moved in about nine, ten months ago. Passed the financial screen with flying colors. Excellent credit rating. Hundred thousand in his bank account. Paid me three months' rent in advance." Siegel unlocked the door. "The kind of tenant every rental agent hopes for."

*Until you find out that perfect tenant is a rapist.*

Jane and Frost stepped into the residence and saw a black leather couch, a big-screen TV, a chrome-and-glass coffee table. A manpad, Jane thought, with no soft touches. If any woman had ever lived here, there was no trace of her in this room with its cold and polished décor.

"See how orderly everything is?" said Mr. Siegel. "Kept it in perfect shape."

"He certainly did," said Jane, focusing on the huge framed photo that dominated one wall. It was a leopard, staring from the grass, eyes agleam, powerful muscles tensed to leap. The consummate predator.

"I guess you folks are looking for leads, huh?" asked Mr. Siegel as Jane and Frost continued their inspection of the residence, moving from kitchen to study to master bedroom, all of it furnished in stark black and white.

"You have any info on next of kin?" asked Frost.

"Never mentioned any. And he was single."

"Friends? Contacts?"

"I'm just the rental agent. Not my job to get chummy with the tenants." He frowned as Jane opened dresser drawers, revealing neatly folded socks and underwear and sweaters. "What's the story with his death, anyway? Was it a mugging or something?"

"It's under investigation," she said.

"Was he shot? Stabbed? What?"

She ignored his questions and focused on the laptop computer on the nightstand. Turning it on, she saw it was password-protected.

"I'm getting the feeling it wasn't just a mugging," Mr. Siegel said. "Is there something I should be worried about here? Like, was he into something illegal?" He frowned at Jane's stony expression and groaned. "Oh, Jesus. I *thought* he was too good to be true! All that rent in advance. Was he a drug dealer or what?"

"Rizzoli!" Frost called out from the bathroom.

She found him kneeling by the under-sink cabinet. He rose to his feet, holding a ziplock bag. "Look what I found. It was hidden way in the back, behind the cleaning stuff."

Through clear plastic, she saw blister packs of white tablets stamped with the pharmaceutical company's name: Roche. She looked at Frost. "Ro-hypnol."

"What? *Roofies?*" Mr. Siegel said. "Why the hell would he have something like that?"

"I can think of one reason," said Jane, turning to the rental agent. "Tell me everything about Christopher Scanlon."

"I did tell you. He was a good tenant."

"Yeah, yeah. Paid his rent, kept the lawn mowed. Did he ever bring women here? Did neighbors complain of any disturbances?"

"No, never. No parties, no loud music. In fact, he was hardly here at night. I thought he was over at some girlfriend's house, but he told me he didn't have a girlfriend."

Frost's cell phone rang, and he stepped out of the bathroom to answer the call.

"What about his job? You said he was a software developer."

"Self-employed, told me he worked from home. I figured I didn't need to see his federal tax return, 'cause he had so much in his bank account. You think that wasn't true? That he worked in software?"

"I can't be sure what's true about Mr. Scanlon." *Except that he was supplied with enough roofies to knock out a few dozen women.*

Frost reappeared in the doorway. "You wanna step outside with me?" he said to her. "We gotta talk."

Seeing the grim expression on his face, she immediately followed him out of the town house.

They stood on the front walk, where Mr. Siegel couldn't overhear their conversation.

"I just got the details on Scanlon's two arrests," said Frost.

"Why was he never convicted?"

"The first case, he was seen on a bar's security camera driving away with the victim, Kitty O'Brien, age twenty-six. Unfortunately, she waited a week to report the crime. The charges were dropped because Kitty couldn't remember what happened. She was also pretty intoxicated that night, which made it a tough case to try. A few months later, she committed suicide. Got hold of her father's gun and shot herself in the head."

"Scanlon fucks up that poor girl's life, and he walks away scot-free?"

"Left her father devastated. Harry O'Brien publicly threatened to kill Scanlon. Which led to poor *O'Brien* getting charged."

"So Harry O'Brien's a definite suspect. If he did it, I'm gonna pat him on the back before I arrest him."

"You and me both."

"What about Scanlon's second arrest? How did he get off that time?"

Frost sighed. "It gets complicated."

"Don't tell me it ends with a second suicide."

"No, the second rape victim's alive. Year and a half ago, Sarah Shapiro, age thirty-two, met a guy at an art gallery reception. She woke up at home the next morning and realized she'd been raped.

Someone at the gallery noticed Sarah wasn't acting right as she got into the man's car, so she wrote down Scanlon's license number. That's how they ID'd him."

"How did that case not end in a conviction?"

"Scanlon claimed he only gave Sarah a lift home and left her there."

"If she was raped, didn't they have his DNA?"

"Here's the part that's weird. There *was* male DNA found inside Sarah. But it wasn't Scanlon's. And she didn't have a boyfriend."

Jane stared at him. "Someone *else* raped her?"

Frost nodded. "We're dealing with a second man. His DNA profile was already in CODIS, for five different attacks in Massachusetts."

"A serial rapist."

"It's worse. His most recent victim, last month, was strangled. This unknown man has now escalated to murder. And it seems like our Christopher Scanlon was delivering the victims to him."

# THREE

**H**ARRY O'BRIEN WAS SIXTY-TWO YEARS OLD, but the man who gazed at them from the doorway appeared far older, his eyes hollow, his shoulders drooping as though under the weight of grief. "I knew the police would want to talk to me someday," he said. "So Scanlon did it again. Didn't he?"

"We believe so," said Jane.

"A monster like that, he doesn't just call it quits one day. He keeps going and going, cutting down lives." Harry stepped aside to let them enter. "Come in, Detectives. Tell me how I can help you take the bastard down."

It was an older home, and Jane could smell its age as she walked into the living room, the accumulated odors of dust and mildew and worn carpets. The first thing that caught her eye was the array of photographs on the wall, images of what looked like the same dark-haired girl through the years. As a child, sitting in a swing. As a teenager in her graduation cap and gown. As a young woman hugging a smiling man. Jane was startled to recognize Harry O'Brien in the face of that man in the photo—a younger, happier version of the bitter man now standing in the room with them.

"Kitty had so much to give to the world," he said, staring at his daughter's photo. "Not just her big heart and her big laugh. She was brilliant, the first in my family to go to college. Worked nights, went to school during the day. She'd just earned her PhD in history. She went out to celebrate that night. Ended up at a bar and drank a little too much. That's when he . . ." O'Brien swallowed and looked out the window. "She couldn't admit what happened to her, until a week later. By the time she reported it, too much evidence was lost. She never stopped blaming herself. Such a smart girl, yet she felt so stupid."

"She was hardly responsible for what happened," said Frost.

"You think I didn't tell her that a thousand times?" O'Brien shot back. His anger suddenly collapsed and he dropped his head. "She used my gun. So I blame myself, too. I could see how depressed she was and I should have gotten rid of it. I just didn't think she'd ever . . ." He shook his head and sighed. "There's plenty of guilt to go around. But Scanlon's the one I blame. The one who destroyed my beautiful girl. My only child."

"Christopher Scanlon is dead," said Jane.

O'Brien's head snapped up. "What?"

"His body was found in Olmsted Park."

"Was it murder?"

"Yes. It was. It happened last night."

O'Brien was silent for a moment, the news sinking in. "Good," he said. "I'm glad someone got him, while I'm still alive." He paused. "That's why you're here, isn't it?"

"You've threatened Mr. Scanlon in the past."

"I sure as hell did. I just wish I'd killed him myself, but I didn't have the guts." He sounded disgusted with himself. "I couldn't go through with it."

"You probably know my next question," said Jane.

"I assume it's *Where were you last night?*"

"You want to answer that?"

"Yeah. I was visiting a woman friend up in Swampscott. Had dinner at her house, watched a few DVDs, drank a little too much. I got home sometime after midnight, I guess."

Jane studied O'Brien's wasted face and sunken eyes, and could not imagine him staying up late, partying with a woman. "What's this friend's name?" she asked.

"Monica Vargas. Her mother was there, too. Monica's in the phone book, so you can call her and confirm it."

"We will."

CHRISTOPHER SCANLON'S SECOND KNOWN victim, Sarah Shapiro, was less willing to speak to them. She peered suspiciously through her barely open door, the chain still in place. "I don't really want to talk about it," she said.

"This is a homicide investigation, Ms. Shapiro," said Jane.

"If Scanlon's dead, then I plan to celebrate. That's all I'm going to say."

"You had every reason to want him dead."

"Damn right."

"Which means we have every reason to be here. I know it's not easy to talk about what he did to you. But you do understand that we have to."

With a sigh, Sarah at last unchained the door and swung it open. "Let's get this over with. Then I can crack open a bottle of champagne."

Her apartment was stunning, with floor-to-ceiling windows that faced Commonwealth Avenue. The furniture and artwork had been chosen with an eye for style, and the ebony shelves were filled with expensive-looking art books.

Noticing Jane's obvious curiosity over her book collection, Sarah asked: "Are you interested in art, Detective?"

"I know what I like."

"That's more than a lot of people can say."

"You own an art gallery, is that right?"

"On Newbury Street. But I'm sure you already knew that." Sarah stared off into space. "That's how he found me," she said softly. "At a friend's gallery reception. Out of all those people, he chose me. Like a lion selecting a lamb."

"We're sorry to bring back such a painful memory," Frost said.

"Bring *back*?" Sarah shook her head. "It's never left me. How charming he seemed. How eager to fetch me a glass of wine. When I woke up the next morning, I *knew* what had happened, even though I couldn't remember it. Oh, I was going to take this all the way to the end. I did everything right, everything a rape victim is supposed to do. I didn't shower, but went straight to the ER and gave a statement to the police. One of the other guests at the reception had seen me wobbling to Scanlon's car, and she had the presence of mind to take down his license number. When I saw his photo, I recognized him at once. I swore to the police that Christopher Scanlon was the man who drugged me."

"But he wasn't the man who raped you," said Jane.

Sarah's face tightened. "I kept telling them there had to be a mistake. The crime lab switched their DNA samples. Or the specimen was contaminated. But no, it was all blamed on *me*. The unreliable witness. The woman who accused the wrong man of assaulting her."

"You don't remember a second man that night?"

"I don't remember a lot of things. Sometimes, there's a spark of a memory. A man's face. I'm not sure it's a real memory, or something I've fabricated." She gave a harsh laugh. "The way I supposedly fabricated my accusation. There was no way any prosecutor would touch the case. Not after the DNA came back."

"Yet you're certain it was Christopher Scanlon you met at the reception."

"Absolutely. I found out later that I wasn't his only victim. There was another woman, Kitty O'Brien. She'd just gotten her PhD, and was out celebrating when he picked her up at a bar. I read about Kitty after she committed suicide, and I realized Scanlon targeted a certain *type* of woman. Confident. Accomplished."

And attractive, thought Jane, looking at Sarah Shapiro. Those were the same words she might use to describe Maura. It sent a chill through her, imagining a predator spotting Maura among the crowd. Circling in on his prey. Somehow, Maura had escaped the fate of Sarah and Kitty: She had not been sexually assaulted.

Instead it was Scanlon who'd ended up a victim.

"So who did it?" asked Sarah. "Who killed him?"

"That's what we're trying to determine," said Jane.

"And I have a motive."

"A perfectly understandable one."

"Fortunately, I also have an alibi. You said he was killed Saturday night."

"That's right."

"On Saturday night, I had a friend visiting. She stayed here, and we ate in. Talked a lot. Went to bed around midnight."

"Your friend's name?" asked Frost, pulling out his notebook.

"Julia Chan." Sarah picked up a personal address book and flipped to the C's. "I'll give you her phone number. Since I'm sure you'll want to talk to her."

"WE'VE CONFIRMED THEIR ALIBIS," said Frost. "Julia Chan said she spent the evening with Sarah Shapiro. And Monica Vargas said Harry O'Brien was at her house in Swampscott. Both these suspects now seem to be off the table."

It was their morning team meeting at Boston PD, and seated in the conference room were Jane and Frost, Detectives Moore and Crowe, and their unit commander, Lieutenant Marquette. More than forty-eight hours had passed since the discovery of Scanlon's body. The murder weapon was still missing; the autopsy confirmed that the cause of death was multiple stab wounds to the back and chest, a frenzied attack indicating uncontrolled rage.

"So we're back to Dr. Isles," said Lieutenant Marquette.

"Where I've always said we should focus," said Crowe. He'd never tried to hide his dislike of Maura; her authority annoyed him. Or was it her intelligence that threatened him? "Her shoe and her fingerprints were in the victim's vehicle. The museum surveillance cameras show them walking out together—"

"Maura wasn't walking," said Jane. "She was staggering."

"And his car ends up parked right outside her house. If you ask me, it looks like they left the reception together, she stabbed him in Olmsted Park, and then she drove home in his car."

"In a semiconscious state?"

"The amnesia story is a little too convenient, don't you think? Plus, there was no evidence of sexual assault, no presence of semen. If Scanlon went to all the trouble of drugging her and getting her home, why didn't he collect his prize?"

It enraged Jane to hear him so casually toss around the intimate details of Maura's ordeal. This was not just a victim they were discussing; this was her friend, and she rocked forward in her chair, planting fists on the table. "Then where's the blood on her dress? Tell me that. You don't stab a guy fifteen times and walk away spotless."

"She changed clothes."

"She was wearing that dress in the museum surveillance video."

"If he was killed by someone else after he brought her home, how did he get to Olmsted Park?" said Crowe. "His car was still parked at her house."

"Obviously there was another vehicle," said Jane. "Someone else was involved. Someone who drove Scanlon to Olmsted Park and killed him there."

"Right. This mysterious second man you keep talking about."

"Unknown male DNA was found inside Sarah Shapiro. There *is* a second man."

"Or Sarah Shapiro's a flake. Lied about when she last had sex with a boyfriend, and then accused the wrong guy."

Frost said, "Sarah didn't strike me as a flake at all. She's a serious professional with a good head on her shoulders."

Crowe looked at Frost and laughed. "So says our resident expert on women."

It was a particularly cruel barb to direct at Frost, whose wife had walked out on him, and who still mourned the breakup of his marriage. Though Frost stiffened, he didn't return the cruelty; he never did.

"You're so fixated on Maura," Jane said to Crowe, "you're trying to make the evidence fit your theory."

"You're the one calling her *Maura*," Crowe pointed out. "Which makes it obvious you've got a problem being objective." He turned to Marquette. "It's hard to conduct an investigation when your friend's the prime suspect."

"*She's* the victim here," said Jane.

"That's exactly what she wants us to believe," said Crowe. "Look, I'm not saying that Scanlon didn't have it coming. Whoever killed him did us all a favor. Maybe he tried to assault her. Dr. Isles flew into a rage and delivered a little justice. After all, she does cut up people for a living. And she's brilliant enough to come up with a good cover story."

Jane looked around the table. "You cannot be seriously considering this."

"We have to consider every possibility, Rizzoli," said Marquette. "What else do we have?" He turned to Detective Moore. "Anything more on Scanlon's vehicle?"

Moore, ever the calm voice of the unit, said: "CSU is still working on the cell phone they found under the front seat. It's a TracFone, password-protected, so we haven't been able to get into it yet. The fact that it was tucked way up under the seat makes me think it's a phone he used only occasionally."

"To call his partner," said Jane.

"We unlock that phone, we may be able to find out the identity of Predator Number Two," said Moore. "I've checked the other cases in the CODIS database. All the rapes where the unknown DNA showed up. They span a period of four years, all within thirty miles of Boston." He typed on his laptop keyboard and swung the screen around to show Marquette the images of three women. "You'll notice the similarities among these victims, as well as with both Sarah Shapiro and Kitty O'Brien. All of them educated, accomplished women. All targeted in upscale venues such as cocktail receptions or business conventions. Most were last seen, before the assaults, with a man matching Scanlon's description."

"But his DNA wasn't found in any of them," said Marquette.

"No," said Moore. "Scanlon may have abducted them. But he didn't rape them."

Marquette frowned. "He was merely the supplier."

"Which may be why he didn't need a job," said Frost. "He claimed to be a software developer, but we can't find any recent employment records to support that. He died with three hundred thousand dollars in various accounts. *That* was his job." Frost pointed to the victims' photos on the screen. "And it looks like he was well paid for it."

"No wonder," said Marquette. "Scanlon takes all the risks. Shows his face in public. Transports the women in his car to their own residences."

"Easy enough to get the addresses off their drivers' licenses," pointed out Frost.

"And that's when the second man shows up. The women are drugged, so they never see the man who's actually assaulting them. The DNA isn't Scanlon's, so even if he is arrested, he can't be convicted of rape. It's a perfect partnership, with Scanlon as the employee."

"Whoever hired him is obviously loaded and pays him well," said Frost. "But maybe Scanlon got greedy. Maybe he tried to blackmail his boss. That would be a motive for murder."

"Then why was Scanlon still working for him?" asked Marquette. "Because it seems that's what he was doing Saturday night. He crashed that reception to look for the next victim."

And he chose just the kind of woman his employer craves, thought Jane. Intelligent. Attractive. Accomplished. All words that described Maura Isles.

"He wants only the best," she said softly, staring at the faces on Moore's computer screen. "Maybe he's afraid of women like this. Or he resents them. And this is how he conquers them, how he cuts them down to size. The question is, Why couldn't he find these women himself? Why take on the risk of a partner?"

"Maybe he's deformed," said Frost. "Unable to get close to them."

"Or he's too prominent," suggested Moore. "Someone who's immediately recognizable."

That second possibility disturbed Jane. Money and power, she thought. Is that what they were up against? A killer who paid someone else to take the risks while awaiting delivery of his next victim?

*It would have been Maura.*

But on Saturday night, something went awry for those partners. It started off well enough at the reception, where Scanlon chose his target and slipped Rohypnol into her drink. He guided his increasingly wobbly victim to his car. In her purse, he found Maura's driver's license and jotted down her address on the back of her business card, which he tucked into his pocket. He drove to her house in

Brookline, used her keys to unlock the door, and carried her inside, where he deposited her on the sofa, unconscious and ready to be taken.

But for some reason, the partner did not claim her. Did he show up at all that night? Or did he decide he would wait for another time?

*He already knows where to find her.*

# FOUR

IT WAS LATE IN THE AFTERNOON WHEN MAURA
walked into the medical examiner's building,
and she saw Dr. Costas freeze beside the coffee-
pot, a cup clutched in his hand. She saw her secretary, Louise, staring at her over her computer screen.
Maura said nothing, but walked straight past
Louise's desk into her own office and closed the
door. No doubt they'd all heard the news; in both
medicine and law enforcement, there were few
secrets. Maura had not been present at Christopher
Scanlon's autopsy, but she knew that Dr. Bristol
had performed it, which meant he knew the circumstances of Scanlon's death. He knew that her
home address was found in the victim's pocket,
that Scanlon's vehicle was parked at her house, and
that her fingerprints and her shoe were in that
vehicle.

But what tormented her most wasn't all the
damning details that made her look like a suspect;
no, it was the details that made her look like a vic-

tim. The gullible woman, charmed and drugged by a predator. Though she had not been raped, she felt as ashamed and exposed as any rape victim, and it had taken all her fortitude to walk into the building today. This is how you fight back, she thought. You start by just showing your face.

Louise knocked and came into the office, closing the door behind her. "How are you?" she asked. "I was so worried. We were all worried."

"I'm fine, Louise." Maura calmly booted up her computer, as if this day were like any other. A day to inspect the wounds of others, not her own.

"Are you, really?" Louise had worked for the ME's office for so long that Maura could not imagine a time when the woman would not be here to greet her every morning, cheerfully fetching her coffee. In an office that dealt every day with tragedy, Louise was always ready with a kind word, a comforting smile. But Maura wanted no sympathy from her today.

"I need Christopher Scanlon's autopsy report," she said.

That request startled Louise. "That's . . . the man . . ."

"I know who he is. Could you get it for me?"

"Yes, of course." Louise opened the door to leave, then glanced back at Maura. "If you need to talk, if you need anything at all, you know I'm here."

No doubt Louise thought Maura needed a hug, a shoulder to cry on. But what Maura needed most

was information. Anything that would help her reconstruct what had happened during the hours she
could not remember. *For all I know, I killed a man
that night*.

She already knew a great deal about Christopher
Scanlon. She knew he'd been arrested twice, accused both times by women who told eerily similar
stories. Scanlon had met them in crowded settings
and offered to refresh their drinks. Both Kitty
O'Brien and Sarah Shapiro woke up hours later
in their own homes, with no memory of what had
happened. In both cases, the charges were dropped.

Kitty O'Brien never recovered from the emotional
trauma. Months later, she committed suicide, a
heartbreaking end to the case.

No, not quite the end.

She found an online news article about Kitty's father, Harry O'Brien, who'd threatened to kill Scanlon. In the photograph, she saw the bottomless
grief in Harry's face, the sunken eyes haunted by
loss. That image so transfixed her that she barely
noticed when Louise laid Scanlon's autopsy report
on her desk and quietly exited again.

*Harry O'Brien. Why does your face seem famil-
iar?*

She opened the report and read the description of
Scanlon's injuries. Dr. Bristol counted fifteen stab
wounds in all, of various depths, in the chest and
back. She turned to the conclusions and was startled by Bristol's statement:

*Based on varying width and depth of wounds, it appears that at least two separate blades were used.*

A frenzied attack. Two different knives.

As far as she knew, the murder weapons had not been found. Her own treasured set of chefs' knives had been confiscated by Boston PD, and was now being analyzed in the crime lab. Could she have done it? Plunged a blade again and again in Scanlon's chest and back? She knew that under the influence of the drug Ambien, patients had been known to drive, to eat, to behave in purposeful ways that made them appear fully conscious, yet awaken with no memory of what they had done. Drugged with Rohypnol, could she have performed similarly automatic tasks? Or had some monster from her id, released from her darkest subconscious, emerged to take control?

*Maybe I am not so different from my mother after all.*

Shaken by the possibility, she closed her eyes, hunting for the flimsiest strand of a memory. Glimpsed lights, heard a voice, distant as an echo. But nothing solid, nothing she could grasp and hold on to.

*If I killed him, would I recognize the place where it happened?*

She barely murmured a goodbye to Louise as she walked out, and once again felt her colleagues watching her, perhaps wondering if she could have done it. Even she didn't know the answer.

It was a warm summer evening, and when she arrived at Olmsted Park, she saw joggers dutifully running along the riverway and couples lolling on the bank of Leverett Pond. She followed the path along the Muddy River, toward the location where the body had been found, according to the autopsy report. It wasn't difficult to spot the place; a bright strand of crime scene tape was still snagged in a tangle of brush. She recognized the riverside bench and the same overarching pair of trees she'd seen in the death scene photos. Parallel gouges in the soil marked the trail of the stretcher that had borne the body up the riverbank, and she stared down at the disturbed earth, which marked the comings and goings of crime scene personnel.

According to the autopsy report, Scanlon had been attacked on the paved path. His body was then rolled down the steep bank and had landed just short of the river's edge, where the stones were stained brown. That's where he bled to death, she thought. But here, on this path where she now stood, was where he had been stabbed.

She closed her eyes and tried to imagine this spot as it would have looked in the dark. Tried to dredge up some memory of being here. Of holding a knife and plunging it, again and again, into flesh.

The snap of a twig made her eyes fly open. She turned and saw, a few dozen yards away, a man standing among the trees. Had he been there all along? In her single-minded pursuit of the death location, had she simply missed seeing him? All at once she noticed how silent it was on this isolated stretch of the riverwalk. No joggers, no strolling couples. Only her and this man, who was now gazing at her through the trees.

He started toward her, and as he passed from shadow into sunlight, she saw that his hair was gray, and he had the gait of someone with a bad hip. No longer fearful, she remained where she was as the man slowly made his way toward her.

"Are you with the police?" he called out.

"No. No, I just came to see . . ."

"You heard about it, then. A man was killed here Saturday night. It's been all over the news." He came to a stop beside her, his gaze on the river below. "To think it happened right down there."

She studied him, and suddenly realized why he looked familiar. "You're Harry O'Brien," she said.

Startled, he looked straight at her, and she thought she saw a similar flash of recognition in *his* eyes. But that was impossible; they had never met.

"How do you know my name?" he asked.

"I know your daughter was one of his victims." She gestured down the riverbank, where Scanlon's body had been found. "I read the article in the *Globe*. How you threatened him, after she . . ." Her voice trailed off.

He finished the painful thought for her. "After she killed herself."

"I'm so sorry, Mr. O'Brien. I can't imagine how horrible it is to lose a child."

"No one can. Until it happens. Then it's *all* you think about, *all* you feel." He stared down at the river. "I came here to spit on his grave. Does that make me evil?"

"It makes you a grieving father."

He nodded, and his thin shoulders slumped. "It doesn't feel as good as I thought it would, knowing he's dead. All I feel is . . . relief." He looked at her, and once again she felt that strange shock of recognition. *Somehow I know this man. And I think he knows me.* "Why are *you* here?" he asked.

"I wanted to see where he died."

"Did you know him?" He paused. Asked, quietly: "Did the bastard hurt you, too?"

She didn't respond, but she felt certain he could see the answer in her face. *Yes, he hurt me. The question is: Did I hurt him?*

"Savor this moment," he said. "The death of monsters should always be celebrated. I was afraid I wouldn't live to see it, but here I am. While he burns in hell."

Those last three words jolted a nerve of recognition. Not just the words, but the voice, deep with rage. She had heard it before.

"Excuse me," she murmured, backing away.

He looked straight at her, his eyes fixed on her face. Seeing too much.

A pair of joggers came around the bend, huffing toward them. That's when Maura made her escape. Swiftly she walked away, heading back to Leverett Pond. Toward other people. Only once did she pause to look back, and she saw he was standing where she'd left him, but his eyes were still on her.

She drove straight home, hands shaking as she clutched the wheel. Only when she was in her garage, the door safely closed, did her breathing begin to steady, her heart to slow.

Inside the house, the first thing she did was call Jane.

"Harry O'Brien," she said. "Did you question him?"

"Of course we did," said Jane. "How do you even know about O'Brien?"

"I know he once threatened Scanlon. It made the newspapers, after Kitty O'Brien's suicide. Jane, I think he's involved. I recognized his voice."

"You *spoke* to him? What the hell are you doing, getting in the middle of an investigation?"

"We met by accident, in Olmsted Park. I went to the death scene, to see if I remembered anything, and O'Brien was there. We had a few words, and I had this—this sudden flash of recognition. I've heard his voice before, Jane. Maybe it was that night."

"Saturday?"

"It's possible, isn't it? Even though there's so much I don't remember, there could be bits and pieces that I did retain. A face, a voice."

"It couldn't have been O'Brien that night. He had an alibi."

"You're absolutely sure it's real?"

"He was visiting a friend in Swampscott. Frost and I interviewed her, and she swears O'Brien was at her house till midnight."

"Is she reliable?"

"She's an architect. Her mother was there that night, too. Apparently the evening was some sort of matchmaking plot to pair Mom off with Harry. It's rock-solid, Maura."

But even as she hung up, Maura could not shake off the certainty that she'd heard Harry O'Brien's voice that night.

She sat on her living room sofa and stretched out on the cushions, trying to call up another memory. Here was where she'd awakened Sunday morning. The night before, someone had laid her on this sofa. Had words been spoken, words that she might still remember? She closed her eyes.

The doorbell rang.

She snapped straight, heart slamming against her chest. She forced herself to rise from the sofa and peeked through the glass panel.

A dark-haired young woman, pretty and petite, stood on the porch.

Maura took a deep breath and felt the tension go out of her. She opened the door. "Yes?"

"I'm sorry to bother you," the woman said, "but I'm trying to find David Chatworth's house. I know he lives around here somewhere, but my cell phone just died. Could I borrow your phone book?"

"Of course. Hold on," said Maura. She turned toward the kitchen, where she kept the phone directory. Made it only halfway up the hall when she heard the front door suddenly slam shut.

Footsteps closed in behind her.

# FIVE

JANE SAT AT HER DESK, TROUBLED BY HER CON-versation with Maura. *Flash of recognition* was how Maura had described her reaction to O'Brien, a certainty that she'd met him. But it couldn't have happened on Saturday night, because O'Brien was at his friend's house in Swampscott.

She pulled out her file on their interview with Monica Vargas, the woman whom O'Brien had been visiting. Thirty-five years old and an architect, she lived alone in an impressive house with a view of the sea. She had been definite about O'Brien's visit, had told Jane and Frost that O'Brien arrived around six pm, dined with Monica and her mother, and the three of them had watched Woody Allen DVDs. Around midnight, O'Brien left her house. Monica had offered the police her mother's phone number, should they need further corroboration.

Yes, a rock-solid alibi.

But now, thinking back to that interview, Jane recalled details about Monica that suddenly seemed significant. Her poise, her beauty. An attractive female professional, confident and accomplished.

Like Sarah Shapiro and Kitty O'Brien. Like Maura Isles.

She spun around to her computer and was just about to do a background check on Monica Vargas when her phone rang.

"We finally got into Scanlon's TracFone," said Frost.

"We have access to his calls?"

"We have everything. And you won't believe what's here."

SHE SAW THE EXCITEMENT on Frost's face when she walked into the crime lab. He sat in front of a computer screen as a printer churned out pages of documents.

"He hardly made any calls on this phone," he said. "But he *did* use it to send text messages." He pointed to the computer screen. "We've got them all here, dating back four years. About a dozen of them. And they were all sent to the same recipient."

Jane frowned at the date of the most recent text. "Scanlon sent one Saturday night. Eight thirty pm."

"Look at what he wrote." Frost clicked on the body of the text, and one sentence appeared. It was an address in Brookline. *Maura's.*

"*This* is how Scanlon told his partner where to find the next catch," she said, and she gave Frost an excited slap on the back. "We've got the second perp!"

"Wait. You need to see something else. The other texts." He scrolled down the list. "See the dates? This one here, eighteen months ago, corresponds to the attack on Sarah Shapiro. And this one, just before it, was Kitty O'Brien."

"So we have a record of every attack. Every victim's address."

"Right. Now look at this one." He clicked on a text from nine months earlier.

Jane stared at the address. Swampscott. "It's Monica Vargas! She was a victim, too?"

"Only she never reported it," said Frost. "And Julia Chan, the woman who gave Sarah Shapiro *her* alibi? Her address is in here as well. Somehow, these women managed to connect. They found each other. We've got a whole nest of victims here, and they're covering for each other. We can't trust *anyone's* alibi."

"Which means Harry O'Brien *could* have killed Scanlon. He *could* have been . . . oh, Jesus." Jane snatched up her cell phone.

"What?"

"Maura spoke to Harry O'Brien this evening. She recognized him."

"Does *he* know that?"

Jane hung up. "She's not answering her phone."

IT WAS DARK WHEN they arrived at Maura's house. There were no lights on inside, and the front door was unlocked. Jane and Frost glanced at each other, a grim acknowledgment of what could very well await them. They both drew their weapons, and Jane gave the door a nudge. She slipped through first, moved into the living room.

Suddenly a lamp came on. Jane froze.

Harry O'Brien stood clutching Maura as a shield in front of him, his gun pressed to her temple.

"Drop it, O'Brien!" Jane ordered, her weapon raised. She heard Frost move beside her, caught a peripheral view of his gun, clutched in both hands.

"We don't want violence, Detective," another voice said, and Jane glanced in surprise at Sarah Shapiro, who rose to her feet from the armchair. "Harry just wants to settle things, once and for all."

"By killing a witness?" said Jane. "The one person who remembers he was here that night?" She looked at O'Brien. "You were stalking Scanlon. Oh, it was in the name of justice, I get that. The scum deserved to die, and any jury will sympathize."

"I don't want to go to jail," he said.

"You should've thought of that before you stabbed him."

"Did I?" He shook his head. "I told you, I was with a friend that night."

"She's covering for you. That alibi will fall apart."

"No, it won't. We built a fortress, Detective. You just haven't realized it yet, because you haven't finished your job."

"I know you're all in this together. And I know this is *not* helping your case." She tightened her grip on the Glock. "Drop the gun."

"Why? I have nothing to lose."

"Your life?"

O'Brien's laugh was bitter. "My life is over. It ended when Kitty died. I'm just tying up loose ends."

"Like Scanlon?"

"And his partner."

*He knows there's a second man.* "We *will* find that partner, Harry. I swear we will. And he'll pay."

"Oh, I know you'll find him."

"Drop the gun and we'll talk. We'll work on finding him together. We'll see justice done."

He seemed to weigh her words, and she saw the struggle in his eyes. The indecision. "It never comes soon enough," he said softly.

"What doesn't?"

"Justice. Sometimes you have to give it a nudge." With that, he pushed Maura so hard that she went sprawling against the sofa. He raised his gun, and the barrel was aimed directly at Jane.

Gunfire exploded as both Jane and Frost opened fire. The bullets punched into O'Brien's chest, sent him slamming backward against the bookcase. He leaned there staring at them for a moment, an odd smile on his lips, the gun already falling from his hand. Slowly he slid down to the floor, and Sarah dropped to her knees beside him, sobbing, screaming.

He had not fired a single shot.

Maura crouched over the body, felt for a pulse, and began CPR. But staring into O'Brien's eyes, Jane saw the light fade away. And she knew there was nothing left to save.

A DAY LATER, THEY found the body.

They tracked down the recipient of Scanlon's text messages, and it led them to the handsome Newton residence of William Heathcote, age forty-two. There they found Mr. Heathcote slumped in the driver's seat of his silver Mercedes, which was parked inside his garage. He had been dead for several days, which meant he could well have died the same night as Scanlon. The cause of death was immediately apparent: a single gunshot to the right temple. A Smith & Wesson nine-millimeter pistol, reportedly stolen in Miami a year before, was in his hand.

In the Mercedes trunk was a plastic bag containing two chefs' knives, both covered in dried blood.

It was almost certainly Scanlon's blood, thought Jane as she watched the CSU team tag the evidence. No case could come more prettily tied up with a bow. The evidence was all there to help the police draw the obvious conclusion: Heathcote stabbed Scanlon to death in Olmsted Park, then drove home and committed suicide. In a single bloody evening, two predators met their end.

Jane didn't believe it for a second; neither did Maura.

They stood together in Heathcote's driveway, watching as the Boston PD tow truck pulled away with the Mercedes, bound for the crime lab. It was late afternoon, dark clouds were moving in, and the air felt prickly with impending thunder.

But for Maura, the storm had already passed. "Harry was a hero, Jane," she said. "He never meant to hurt me. He came to my house without a single bullet in that gun."

"We didn't know that. We had no choice."

"Of course you had no choice. It was *supposed* to happen this way. He wanted to go out with a blaze of publicity, so his daughter would be remembered. And he wouldn't have to face any questions." Maura paused. "He had cancer."

"Harry told you that?"

"No. Dr. Bristol did the autopsy this morning. Harry's body was riddled with tumors. I think he knew he was dying, and he chose this way to end it."

Leaving me with the nightmares, thought Jane, looking up at the darkening sky. Taking a man's life leaves a stain on your soul, even if you're forced to do it. Even if the man you kill wants you to pull that trigger.

"We both know it was a conspiracy," said Jane. "Harry and those victims, they planned this together. They covered for each other. For all I know, they each took their turn stabbing Christopher Scanlon. Fifteen stab wounds, two different knives? And not a single fingerprint." Jane sighed in frustration. "I *know* what happened, I just can't prove it."

"Do you really want to?"

"*You're* the one who's always hung up on the facts, the truth. But you're willing to ignore the truth of this case?"

"I could have been a victim, too. I was like a staked goat, drugged and laid out on my sofa, where anything could have been done to me. But it never happened because *they* stopped it. I don't know which of them was there in my house, or how many. All I know is that this time, the victims fought back. They caught and killed two monsters." Maura looked straight at her. "And they saved me."

Maybe that's worth more than any truth, thought Jane as she watched Maura climb into her Lexus and drive away. And she remembered what Harry O'Brien had said: *Justice. Sometimes you have to give it a nudge.*

*That you did, Mr. O'Brien. That you did.*

Read on for an exciting peek at

# GIRL MISSING

By Tess Gerritsen

# ONE

**A**N HOUR BEFORE HER SHIFT STARTED, AN HOUR before she was even supposed to be there, they rolled the first corpse through the door.

Up until that moment, Kat Novak's day had been going better than usual. Her car had started on the first turn of the key. Traffic had been sparse on Telegraph, and she'd hit all the green lights. She'd managed to slip into her office at five to seven, and for the next hour she could lounge guiltlessly at her desk with a jelly doughnut and the morning edition of the *Albion Herald*. She made a point of skipping the obituaries. Chances were she already knew all about them.

Then a gurney with a black body bag rolled past her doorway. *Oh Lord,* she thought. In about thirty seconds, Clark was going to knock at her door and ask for favors. With a sense of dread, Kat listened to the gurney wheels grind down the hall. She heard the autopsy room doors whisk open and shut, heard the distant rumble of male voices. She counted ten seconds, fifteen. And there it was, just as she'd anticipated: the sound of Clark's Reeboks squeaking across the linoleum floor.

He appeared in her doorway. "Morning, Kat," he said.

She sighed. "Good morning, Clark."

"Can you believe it? They just wheeled one in."

"Yeah, the *nerve* of them."

"It's already seven ten," he said. A note of pleading crept into his voice. "If you could just do me this favor . . ."

"But I'm not here." She licked a dollop of raspberry jelly from her fingers. "Until eight o'clock, I'm nothing more than a figment of your imagination."

"I don't have time to process this one. Beth's got the kids packed and ready to take off, and here I am, stuck with another Jane Doe. Have a heart."

"This is the third time this month."

"But I've got a family. They expect me to spend time with them. You're a free agent."

"Right. I'm a divorcée, not a temp."

Clark shuffled into her office and leaned his ample behind against her desk. "Just this once. Beth and I, we're having problems, you know, and I want this vacation to start off right. I'll return the favor sometime. I promise."

Sighing, Kat folded up the *Herald*. "Okay," she said. "What've you got?"

Clark was already pulling off his white coat, visibly shifting to vacation mode. "Jane Doe. No obvious trauma. Another body-fluid special. Sykes and Ratchet are in there with her."

"They bring her in?"

"Yeah. So you'll have a decent police report to work with."

Kat rose to her feet and brushed powdered sugar off her scrub pants. "You owe me," she said, as they headed into the hall.

"I know, I know." He stopped at his office and grabbed his jacket—a fly-fisherman's version, complete with a zillion pockets, some with little feathers poking out.

"Leave a few trout for the rest of us."

He grinned and gave her a salute. "Into the wilds of Maine I go," he said, heading for the elevator. "See you next week."

Feeling resigned, Kat pushed open the door to the autopsy room and went in.

The body, still sealed in its black bag, lay on the slab. Lieutenant Lou Sykes and Sergeant Vince Ratchet, veterans of the local knife and gun club, were waiting for her. Sykes—a black homicide detective who always insisted on mixing corpses with Versace—looked slim and dapper as usual in a suit and tie. His partner, Vince Ratchet, was, in contrast, a perpetual candidate for Slim-Fast. Ratchet was peering in fascination at a specimen jar on the shelf.

"What the hell is that?" he asked, pointing to the jar. Good old Vince. He was never afraid to sound stupid.

"That's the right middle lobe of a lung," Kat said.

"I would've guessed it was a brain."

Sykes laughed. "That's why she's the doc and you're just a dumb cop." He straightened his tie and looked at her. "Isn't Clark doing this one?"

Kat snapped on a pair of gloves. "Afraid I am."

"Thought your shift started at eight."

"Tell me about it." She went to the slab and gazed down at the bag, feeling her usual reluctance to open the zipper, to reveal what lay beneath the black plastic. *How many of these bags have I opened?* she wondered. A hundred? Two hundred? Each one contained its own private horror story. This was the hardest part—sliding down the zipper and unveiling the contents. Once a body was revealed, and once she'd weathered the initial shock of its appearance, she could set to work with a scientist's dispassion. But the first glimpse, the first reaction—that was always pure emotion, something over which she had no control.

"So, guys," she said. "What's the story here?"

Ratchet came forward and flipped open his notebook. It was like an extension of his arm, that notebook; she'd never seen him without it. "Caucasian female, no ID, age twenty to thirty. Body found four a.m. this morning, off South Lexington. No apparent trauma, no witnesses, no nothing."

"South Lexington," said Kat, and images of that neighborhood flashed through her mind. She knew the area too well—the streets, the back alleys, the playgrounds rimmed with barbed wire. And, looming above it all, the seven buildings, as grim as twenty-story concrete headstones. "The Projects?" she asked.

"Where else?"

"Who found her?"

"City trash pickup," said Sykes. "She was in an alley between two of the Project buildings, sort of wedged against a Dumpster."

"As if she was placed there? Or died there?"

Sykes glanced at Ratchet. "You were at the scene first. What do you say, Vince?"

"Looked to me like she died there. Just lay down, sort of curled up against the Dumpster, and called it quits."

It was time. Steeling herself for that first glimpse, Kat reached for the zipper and opened the bag. Sykes and Ratchet both took a step backward, an instinctive reaction she herself had to quell. The zipper parted and the plastic fell away to reveal the corpse.

It wasn't bad; at least it appeared intact. Compared to some of the corpses she'd seen, this one was actually in excellent shape. The woman was a bleached blonde, about thirty, perhaps younger. Her face looked like marble, pale and cold. She was dressed in a long-sleeved purple pullover of some sort of polyester blend, a short black skirt with a patent leather belt, black tights, and brand-new Nikes. Her only jewelry was a dime-store friendship ring and a Timex watch—still ticking.

Rigor mortis had frozen her limbs into a vague semblance of a fetal position. Both fists were clenched tight, as though in her last moment of life they'd been caught in spasm.

Kat took a few photos, then picked up a cassette recorder and began to dictate. "Subject is a white female, blonde, found in alley off South Lexington around oh four hundred . . ." Sykes and Ratchet, already knowing what would follow, took off their jackets and reached into a linen cart for some gowns—medium for Sykes, extra large for Ratchet. The gloves came next. They both knew the drill; they'd been cops for years, and partners for four months. It was an odd pairing, Kat thought, like Abbott and Costello. So far, though, it seemed to work.

She put down the cassette recorder. "Okay, guys," she said. "On to the next step."

The undressing. The three of them worked together to strip the corpse. Rigor mortis made it difficult; Kat had to cut away the skirt. The outer clothing was set aside. The tights and underwear were to be examined later for evidence of recent sexual contact. When at last the corpse lay naked, Kat once again reached for the camera and clicked off a few more photos for the evidence file.

It was time for the hands-on part of the job—the part one never saw on *Bones*. Occasionally, the answers fell right into place with a first look. Time of death, cause of death, mechanism and manner of death—these were the blanks that had to be filled in. A verdict of suicide or natural causes would make Sykes and Ratchet happy; a verdict of homicide would not.

This time, unfortunately, Kat could give them no quick answers.

She could make an educated guess about time of death. Livor mortis, the body's mottling after death, was unfixed, suggesting that death was less than eight hours old, and the body temperature, using Moritz's formula, suggested a time of death of around midnight. But the cause of death?

"Nothing definitive, guys," she said. "Sorry."

Sykes and Ratchet looked disappointed, but not at all surprised.

"We'll have to wait for body fluids," she said.

"How long?"

"I'll collect it, get it to the state lab today. But they've been running a few weeks behind."

"Can't you run a few tests here?" asked Sykes.

"I'll screen it through gas and TL chromatography, but it won't be specific. Definitive drug ID will have to go through the state lab."

"All we want to know," said Ratchet, "is whether it's possible."

"Homicide's always possible." She continued her external exam, starting with the head. No signs of trauma here; the skull felt intact, the scalp unbroken. The blond hair was tangled and dirty; obviously the woman had not washed it in days. Except for postmortem changes, she saw no marks on the torso either. The left arm, however, drew her attention. It had a long ridge of scar tissue snaking down it toward the wrist.

"Needle tracks," said Kat. "And a fresh puncture mark."

"Another junkie," sighed Sykes. "There's our cause of death. Probable OD."

"We could run a fast analysis on her needle," said Kat. "Where's her kit?"

Ratchet shook his head. "Didn't find one."

"She must've had a needle. A syringe."

"I looked," said Ratchet. "I didn't see any."

"Did you find anything near the body?"

"Nothing," said Ratchet. "No purse, no ID, nothing."

"Who was first on the scene?"

"Patrolman. Then me."

"So we've got a junkie with fresh needle marks, but no needle."

Sykes said, "Maybe she shot up somewhere else. Wandered into the alley and died."

"Possible."

Ratchet was peering at the woman's hand. "What's this?" he said.

"What's what?"

"She's got something in her hand."

Kat looked. Sure enough, there was a tiny fleck of pink cardboard visible under the edge of her clenched fingers. It took two of them to pry the fist open. Out slid a matchbook, small and pink with raised gold lettering: "L'Etoile, fine nouvelle cuisine. Two-twenty-one Hilton Avenue."

"Kind of out of her neighborhood," Sykes remarked.

"Hey, I hear that's a nice place," said Ratchet. "Not that I could ever afford to eat there myself."

Kat opened the matchbook. Inside were three unused matches, and a phone number, scrawled in fountain pen ink on the inside cover.

"Think it's a local number?" she asked.

"Prefix would put it in Surry Heights," said Sykes. "That's still out of her neighborhood."

"Well," said Kat. "Let's try it out and see what happens." As Sykes and Ratchet stood by, she went to the wall phone and dialed the number. It rang three times, four. An answering machine came on, the message spoken by a deep male voice:

"I'm not available at the moment. Please leave your name and number."

That was all. No cute music, no witty remarks, just that terse request, and then the beep.

Kat said, "This is Dr. Novak at the Albion medical examiner's office. Please call me back, in regards to a . . ." She paused, unwilling to reveal that she had a corpse whom he might know. Instead she said, "Please call me. It's important," and left her number. She hung up and looked at the two cops. "We'll just have to wait and see who calls back. In the meantime, do you both want to stick around for the autopsy?"

It was probably the last thing the men wanted to do, but they remained stoically by the table, wincing as she stabbed various needles into the corpse.

She collected blood from the femoral vein, vitreous fluid from the eye, and urine from a puncture through the lower abdominal wall. After they watched a needle pierce an eyeball, a blade did not hold nearly as many horrors for them. Kat picked up the Henckel knife and this time neither man flinched, even as her blade sliced into the torso. Even as she snapped apart ribs and lifted off the sternum, releasing the odor of blood and offal.

Inside the chest, organs glistened.

Kat put down her knife and picked up the far more delicate scalpel. Reaching into the chest cavity, her gloved hands registered the neutral temperature of those organs. Neither warm like the living, nor chilled like a refrigerated corpse. As Goldilocks would have said, Not too hot, not too cold, but just right—this description suitable for a corpse that had been lying exposed on a spring night. She sliced through the great vessels, freeing the heart and lungs, which she lifted out of the cavity.

"These lungs feel pretty heavy," she noted. She set them on the scale and watched as the dial confirmed her judgment.

"What would cause them to be heavy?" asked Ratchet.

She noticed the fleck of froth that had leaked from the bronchi. "There's foamy edema. The lungs are filled with fluid."

"Meaning what? She drowned in an alley?"

"In a sense, she did drown. But the fluid came

from her own lungs. Foamy edema can be caused by any number of things."

"Like a drug OD?" asked Sykes.

"Absolutely. This could certainly happen after an overdose of narcotics."

She sliced open the heart, examined the chambers. Except for the soggy lungs, the organs appeared grossly normal. The coronary vessels were healthy, the liver and pancreas and intestines undiseased. Cutting open the stomach, she found no food remnants, only 20cc of bilious fluid.

"Died with an empty stomach," said Kat.

"Look at how skinny she is," said Sykes. "When you're shooting crap into your veins, I'd guess eating takes second priority."

Kat moved on to the vagina and rectum. It was the one aspect of the postmortem that made her uncomfortable, but only because two men were in the room. As she inspected the external genitalia and inserted swabs to collect body fluids, they watched intently, and she felt more than just Jane Doe's privacy was violated. "I don't see any evidence of sexual assault," she said.

She turned her attention to the head. Of all the parts of a corpse, the face is the most personal, and the most disturbing to contemplate. Until that moment, Kat had avoided looking at it too closely, but now she was forced to. In life, the young woman might have been pretty. Shampoo her hair, animate those facial muscles into a smile, and she would probably have caught the eye of more than a few men. But death had made her jaw droop and her mouth gape open, revealing coffee-stained teeth and a tongue dried out from exposure. It was a blank face, revealing no secrets.

Her cranium didn't provide any answers either. Kat sawed open the skull and the brain within showed no signs of hemorrhage or stroke or trauma. It was a healthy-looking brain, a young brain, and it should have given its owner many more years of service. Instead that brain, with its lifetime of memories, was now dropped into a bucket of formalin. And the body—what was left of it—would go into a refrigerated drawer, dubbed with the name shared by far too many other un-identified women who had come before her.

Jane Doe.

KAT WAS SITTING AT her desk later that morning when her phone rang. She picked it up and an-swered: "Dr. Novak, Assistant ME."

"You left a message," said a man. She recognized at once the voice from the answering machine. Its deep timbre was now edged with anxiety. "What's this all about?" he demanded.

Kat at once reached for pen and paper. "Who am I speaking to?" she asked.

"You should know. You called *me*."

"I just had your telephone number, not a name—"

"And how did you get my number?"

"It was written on a matchbook. The police

brought a woman into the morgue this morning, and she—"

He cut in: "I'll be right there."

"Mister, I didn't catch your—"

She heard the click of the receiver, then a dial tone. *Jackass,* she thought. What if he didn't show up? What if he didn't call back?

She dialed Homicide and left a message for Sykes and Ratchet: "Get yourselves back to the morgue." Then she waited.

At noon, she got a buzz on the intercom from the front desk. "There's a Mr. Quantrell here," said the secretary. "He says you're expecting him. Want me to send him down?"

"I'll meet him up there," said Kat. "I'm on my way."

She knew better than to just drag a civilian in off the street and take him straight down to the morgue. He would need a chance to prepare for the shock. She pulled a white lab coat over her scrub suit. The lapel had coffee stains, but it would have to do.

By the time she'd ridden the basement elevator up to the ground floor, she'd rearranged her hair into a semblance of presentability and straightened her name tag. She stepped out into the hallway. Through the glass door at the end of the corridor she could see the reception area with its couch and upholstered chairs, all in generic gray. She could also see a man pacing back and forth in front of the couch, oblivious to her approach. He was nicely dressed, and didn't seem like the sort of man who'd be acquainted with a Jane Doe from South Lexington. His camel-hair jacket was perfectly tailored to his wide shoulders. He had a tan raincoat slung over his arm, and he was tugging at his tie as though it were strangling him.

Kat pushed the glass door open and walked in. "Mr. Quantrell?"

At once the man turned and faced her. He had wheat-colored hair, perfectly groomed, and eyes a shade she'd never seen before. Not quite blue, not quite gray, they seemed as changeable as a spring sky. He was old enough—in his early forties perhaps—to have amassed a few character lines around those eyes, a few gray hairs around his temples. His jaw was set with tension.

"I'm Dr. Novak," she said, holding out her hand. He shook it automatically, quickly, as though to get the formalities over and done with.

"Adam Quantrell," he said. "You left that message on my answering machine."

"Why don't we go down to my office? You can wait there until the police—"

"You said something about a woman," he cut in rudely. "That the police brought in a woman." No, it wasn't rudeness, Kat decided. He was afraid.

"It might be better to wait for Lieutenant Sykes," she said. "He can explain the situation."

"Why don't *you* explain it to me?"

"I'm just the medical examiner, Mr. Quantrell. I can't give out information."

The look he shot her was withering. All at once she wished she stood a little straighter, a little taller. That she didn't feel so threatened by that gaze of his. "This Lieutenant Sykes," he said. "He's from Homicide, right?"

"Yes."

"So there's a question of murder."

"I don't want to speculate."

"Who is she?"

"We don't have an ID yet."

"Then you don't know."

"No."

He paused. "Let me see the body." It wasn't a request but a command, and a desperate one at that.

Kat glanced at the door and wondered when the hell Sykes would arrive. She looked back at the man and realized that he was barely holding it together. *He's terrified. Terrified that the body lying in my refrigerated drawer is someone he knows and loves.*

"That's why you called me, isn't it?" he said. "To find out if I can identify her?"

She nodded. "The morgue is downstairs, Mr. Quantrell. Come with me."

He strode beside her in silence, his tanned face looking pale under the fluorescent lights. He was silent as well on the elevator ride down to the basement. She glanced up once and saw that he was staring straight ahead, as though afraid to look anywhere else, as though afraid he'd lose what control he still had.

When they stepped off the elevator, he paused, glancing around at the scuffed walls, the tired linoleum floor. Overhead was another bank of flickering fluorescent lights. The building was old, and down in the basement one could see the decay in the chipped paint, the cracked walls, could smell it in the very air. When the whole city was in the process of decay, when every agency from Social Services to trash pickup was clamoring for a dwindling share of tax dollars, the ME's office was always the last to be funded. Dead citizens, after all, do not vote.

But if Adam Quantrell took note of his surroundings, he did not comment.

"It's down this hall," said Kat.

Wordlessly he followed her to the cold storage room.

She paused at the door. "The body's in here," she said. "Are you . . . feeling up to it?"

He nodded.

She led him inside. The room was brightly lit, almost painfully so. Refrigerated drawers lined the far wall, some of them labeled with names and numbers. It was the time of year when the occupancy rate was running on the high side. The spring thaw and warmer weather brought the guns and knives out onto the street again, and these were the latest crop of victims. There were three Jane Does. Kat reached for the drawer labeled 373-4-3-A.

Pausing, she glanced at Adam. "It's not going to be pleasant."

He swallowed. "Go ahead."

She pulled open the drawer. It slid out noiselessly, releasing a waft of cold vapor. The body was almost formless under the shroud. Kat looked up at Adam to see how he was holding up. It was the men who usually fainted, and the bigger they were, the harder they were to pull up off the linoleum. So far, this guy was doing okay. Grim and silent, but okay. Slowly she lifted off the shroud. Jane Doe's alabaster-white face lay exposed.

Again, Kat looked at Adam.

He had paled slightly, but he hadn't moved. Neither did his gaze waver from the corpse. For a solid ten seconds he stared at Jane Doe, as though trying to reconstruct her frozen features into something alive, something familiar.

At last he let out a deep breath. Only then did Kat realize the man had been holding it. He looked across at her. In an utterly calm voice he said, "I've never seen this woman before in my life."

Then he turned and walked out of the room.